There ... **of fly...**

The Executioner popped up, triggered a burst as the gunners kept charging. Bolan knew he was fast running out of time to call the shots in there, and he needed Broadwater to hold back the cavalry, now more than ever.

Bolan palmed his radio. "I'm still in the picture, Broadwater."

"I just tagged one coming out of the store!"

"Call your boss, do whatever it takes, but don't let SWAT storm this place. I've got women and children, unscathed...."

"I read you, loud and clear. I'll do what I can."

"Make it happen."

Bolan was up and searching for more targets.

MACK BOLAN ®
The Executioner

DON PENDLETON'S

THE EXECUTIONER®
DEVIL'S ARMY

THE
DOOMSDAY
TRILOGY
—————
BOOK I

A GOLD EAGLE BOOK FROM

W♦RLDWIDE®

TORONTO • NEW YORK • LONDON
AMSTERDAM • PARIS • SYDNEY • HAMBURG
STOCKHOLM • ATHENS • TOKYO • MILAN
MADRID • WARSAW • BUDAPEST • AUCKLAND

First edition July 2002
ISBN 0-373-64284-9

Special thanks and acknowledgment to
Dan Schmidt for his contribution to this work.

DEVIL'S ARMY

Copyright © 2002 by Worldwide Library.

Printed in U.S.A.

There and then our best men were killed.
—Homer, *Odyssey*

Men must be judged by their words and deeds.
They pass sentence on themselves with their
actions. I provide justice.
—Mack Bolan

THE
MACK BOLAN®
LEGEND

Nothing less than a war could have fashioned the destiny of the man called Mack Bolan. Bolan earned the Executioner title in the jungle hell of Vietnam.

But this soldier also wore another name—Sergeant Mercy. He was so tagged because of the compassion he showed to wounded comrades-in-arms and Vietnamese civilians.

Mack Bolan's second tour of duty ended prematurely when he was given emergency leave to return home and bury his family, victims of the Mob. Then he declared a one-man war against the Mafia.

He confronted the Families head-on from coast to coast, and soon a hope of victory began to appear. But Bolan had broken society's every rule. That same society started gunning for this elusive warrior—to no avail.

So Bolan was offered amnesty to work within the system against terrorism. This time, as an employee of Uncle Sam, Bolan became Colonel John Phoenix. With a command center at Stony Man Farm in Virginia, he and his new allies—Able Team and Phoenix Force—waged relentless war on a new adversary: the KGB.

But when his one true love, April Rose, died at the hands of the Soviet terror machine, Bolan severed all ties with Establishment authority.

Now, after a lengthy lone-wolf struggle and much soul-searching, the Executioner has agreed to enter an "arm's-length" alliance with his government once more, reserving the right to pursue personal missions in his Everlasting War.

1

It was his guaranteed ticket to Paradise. Assured of divine approval in the eyes of the God of his Koran, Hasab Shabak was to call the moment of truth on his own terms. The way God would want it. The coming onslaught would be not only for himself, but also to right a few of many atrocities inflicted on clan and country by the Great Satan.

There was no turning back from where he stood, packed in among the infidel cattle. Once he began sending as many of these godless savages to the fires of eternal damnation as possible, it wouldn't be long, perhaps the next stop, before he was forced to go out in a martyr's glory. Truth was, this decision was long overdue. The plan—details of which he wasn't privy to—was some dark conspiracy engineered by a North Korean.

Soon, within moments, the tool of the wrath of God was about to go to work, he thought, on this mass of devils entering Manhattan from their outer boroughs.

Just another day at the office, people? he thought, fighting back the laughter. Looking forward to that lunch at one of those gilded palaces, where the average American feasted like royalty? Oh, he'd seen that much, every day, in fact, while bussing plates off their tables, strangling down the rage over the sinful waste of food left for the garbage, baffled and seething still more by the injustice of how a single gluttonous American could spend more on a meal or a bottle of wine than the average Iraqi, who earned no more than three dollars a month.

Well, one car on the F train, at best, would soon prove a rolling coffin. Revenge was the day's special, and Shabak intended to serve it up cold. Indeed, it would be a day, he knew, long after his martyrdom and ascent to heaven, where the children and the grandchildren of the dead would remember what happened. Of course, the survivors would wail and gnash their teeth, never understand, much less seek out redemption on behalf of the sins of their fathers and their mothers.

No matter. No mercy, no exemptions.

To the smallest child on board, they were little more than fattened calves in his eyes, long since ready for slaughter. He could be sure, given what he'd seen in America so far, that down to lowliest infidel they all wallowed, smug and certain, from cradle to grave inside the honey-lined cocoons of money, food and pleasure. They looked oblivious, soft from wealth and privilege, no doubt, as he searched their faces for signs of life or even passing interest in his presence. Why was he surprised? Before stepping into the car, he had expected to find no less than human leeches who bloated themselves on the blood, sweat and suffering of peoples around the world they would never meet, much less care existed, as long as they were out of sight, out of mind, the poverty and misery of others little more than a sound bite from their nightly newscasts. Bearing in mind he had heard somewhere that most Americans couldn't even pick out their own state on a map, he decided their ignorance would become his bliss.

Deeper than contempt burned a feeling of superiority, of divine righteousness, as he continued scouring the faces buried in newspapers or paperbacks or pretending to stare at nothing while avoiding eye contact with their fellow passengers.

Unaware they were marked for extinction.

It was a shame, he concluded, he was only one warrior, two weapons, with an equal number of grenades. So many devils to slay, so few bullets.

It would have to do.

A part of him had another regret, as he ran a roving eye up and down the car, looking for any threat in the form of a policeman. They were known to frequent the subway, since America, the Korean had told him during one of many briefings, was a land of criminals.

Yes, he knew he was jumping the gun, so to speak, in danger of perhaps bringing an abrupt and violent end to the plans of his benefactors. Not to mention striking out on his own would bring a certain death sentence down on his head, as well as on his brother's transplanted family in Brooklyn. The innocent blood of Saddam Shabak's clan would be on his hands, but in the end, he decided life would be far better for the children in the next world. They ran the risk, after all, of forgetting their Islamic roots, forsaking their holy commitment to God and the Koran, as they grew up in this land where they only worshiped at the altar of money and sex. Yes, he thought, this was a subhuman culture, godless and without redemption, able to reach out any and everywhere to corrupt even the most innocent and purest of souls. Surely those people were an abomination in the eyes of God, soulless beasts who would corrupt and consume unless they were stopped.

He glanced at the woman in the short skirt, the whore baring long legs, crossed and sheathed in white hose, her perfume filling the air. The heated tug he felt in his crotch warned him she would have to be one of the first. Their women, he wondered, were they like that all over the land, showing off bodies in public, seeking to entice any man who came along? He suddenly recalled his amazement and confusion the first time he had seen one of the American talk shows. American women were allowed to voice opinions on their television, would even bully and shout down the men if they were disagreed with. Unheard of, he knew, in the Koran, where woman was created from the rib of Adam, meant by God to be a faithful, obedient and loving mate. What sort of men were these Americans? Sitting by, allowing brazen and shameless daughters and wives to flaunt their immorality in public forums. They had laws that even allowed for the legal killing of the unborn or permitted men to marry men. Indeed, he decided, being the indirect hand, responsible for the executions of his brother's children...well, death would spare their souls, save them from damnation.

And Shabak didn't think he could wait much longer to free himself of this cursed land. Surely Satan was alive and well in America. His own charade had gone on long enough.

As a former officer in the Iraqi army, a tank commander, no less, it had been a daily insult—despite the elaborate smoke screen to infiltrate him and the others into America—to bus tables, wash dishes while waiting for the phone to ring to call him to glory. Nearly a year now, he had endured masquerading as little more than an underpaid, overworked slave, held in thinly veiled contempt by the very people he intended to eventually kill.

No more.

Instead of allowing their mysterious Korean benefactor to determine his fate, Shabak, as a holy Islamic warrior, believed it was his right, his sacred duty to God, to chart his own path, choose the time and place where he would slay his enemies before pulling the pin and riding the big blast straight to heaven.

Actually, he thought, his fate had been carved in stone many years ago, before he'd even set foot in this land of fat bellies and fat wallets. The cowardly bombing of Baghdad by the western vultures, with their smart bombs, their laser-guided death delivered from a great distance assuring them of safety.

Well, they had no one but themselves to thank for the coming slaughter.

Shabak was surprised at how calm he felt. This was no dry run, no walk-through of some target on the horizon to blow up. Surprised next, yes, that the raw hatred he had come to accept like a second skin had receded behind the cold armor of vengeance when he made this final choice.

Besides, other than revenge, he had nothing left to live for. His two sons and his daughter were in Paradise, having been crushed beneath the rubble of the hospital where they had sought shelter from the American vultures during the war. Somehow his wife had survived, only life after the bombing had left her damaged worse than if she'd simply lost a leg or an arm. The shell of the woman who remained could not have been God's will, as Shabak briefly recalled the catatonic creature he'd come home to after the Americans had released him from one of their POW camps. For hours on end, he would watch the lifeless woman, praying as she stared at nothing. Sometimes she would mutter words he couldn't understand, or rock herself, rolling her head from side to side. Unable or unwilling to speak—much less rebuild their lives or bear him another child—she would erupt on occasion in hysterical outbursts that bordered on demonic whenever he attempted to reach out and hold her. In time, seeing that the woman he once knew and loved was dead and gone from him forever, he considered killing her, if nothing else than to put her out of her misery, send her to heaven where she could rejoin their children. But that had seemed too cruel, a sin against his own he didn't think he could live with, so he clung to hope that someday she would—

"Sir, are you all right?"

The American was staring at him, his cologne overpowering in Shabak's nose. He couldn't be certain if he'd cursed, but knew he needed to pull it back together before someone became suspicious. He muttered something at the American, looked away, feeling the train slowing for its next stop.

Shabak kept his hands buried deep in the pockets of his trench coat, his arm shielding the bulk of the compact M-12 Italian submachine gun, hand wrapped around the Heckler & Koch USP .45-caliber pistol. He was weighted down with four spare clips each for the instruments of his judgment. He twisted his body away from any passing contact as they disgorged onto the platform. He was ready, but wondered why he was hesitating. Was he afraid he was about to lose the desire to go through with it, believing instead his benefactors had something far bigger and more glorious in store?

No.

Despite himself, he started remembering the North Korean's words about the odd assemblage of weaponry. The benefactor—known only to him and his brothers-in-jihad during the briefings as the colonel—always appeared to be smiling. He never shared his private joke, but kept it to himself, as if mere Iraqi cannon fodder were too lowly or too stupid to understand whatever words of wisdom were on the tip of his tongue. Even still, the smiling Korean could never resist doling out the personal insights or schooling on how to proceed.

"You have been trained in the use of many weapons," the Korean had told them. "Do not come to prefer any one weapon. You see, once you have finished your mission and are on your way to your Paradise, the American authorities will be confused about the mix of weapons. Some Russian, some European, some Chinese, even some American. Confusion as to the origin of the supplier, you understand. Their American commando murderers do the same when they invade foreign countries, not wishing to leave behind evidence as to their true identities. They, like you, know their own deaths are simply part of the scheme.

"Now, once you begin the deed, you must spare no

one. Not even a child or a mother. No mercy, but I can see you understand this much. However, perhaps you will encounter one of their men who has seen one too many Jackie Chan movies. What I am telling you is do not underestimate the sudden impulse by one of their men to prove himself a hero."

"Excuse me," a man said, interrupting his memories.

There were two men. Shabak had moved a step or so toward the door, anticipating blocking off at least one exit, grateful there was some elbow room to get it jump-started. There were fairly unobstructed fields of fire for both ends of the aisle. The men were shouldering their way past him, bumping their way on through other passengers, men in suits clearing a path, heads bowed, eyes averted. For a moment, he found their hostility and rudeness most curious. He watched them glaring back, the coldness inside revived now, his grip tightening around the new American law-enforcement pistol. They had some sort of colored rags on their heads, with pant legs dragging the floor, the seats hanging down their rears to a near obscene point. Gangsters, or so they were called in America, he believed.

The Korean's voice came back. "You will see them in America, mostly in the cities. They call themselves disenfranchised, claim they are the voiceless under-privileged, forever crying that the majority rule has forced them to turn to crime. You will wonder about the sanity of this country, where their young carry weapons and sell poison to their own while casting the blame on someone else, where these young animals will shoot someone dead over the smallest insult or a simple look or for a pair of tennis shoes. Do not speak to them, do not stare at them and, by all means," the Korean had added with a chuckle, "do not wear expensive tennis shoes.

"Now, you may become confused by the mindless rage, the gratuitous vulgarity of their criminal class—contact with them will be unavoidable in the city—where you can plainly see no rhyme or reason for such atrocious behavior in a land that has more wealth, privilege and opportunity for all than any other nation on the planet, or in the whole of mankind's history for that matter. Except for my own country—and, of course, your nation, which, we all know, is rich in culture and things of honor. You may find yourself wishing to retaliate on the spot, strike them down for their impertinence and lack of manners. Resist the urge to kill needlessly and wait for your appointed hour."

"What you lookin' at?"

Shabak knew he was staring at the first two dead infidels. He only wished he could see himself in a mirror, as he felt an enigmatic smile shape his mouth that would have made the Korean proud. Several suits buried their faces deeper in newspapers, one or two of them slinking deeper into the car. Clearly, he thought, no heroes were going to be found here.

They were throwing each other looks, he saw, deciding what to do next, but shuffling toward him, just the same, as if the one was bolstered by the other's anger and hostility.

"I have many problems," Shabak told them. "Two of which I can see are to be solved right about now."

They pulled up short, uncertain, glancing at each other, grumbling curses.

Shabak was momentarily amazed at what Americans would tolerate, as he sensed he was one hundred percent on his own with these two, no one even glancing their way. "As for what I am looking at—I am looking at nothing. Absolutely nothing."

Shabak believed he could almost see their minds working, confusion gone next as the insult got them launched ahead, all rage and streaming curses. Shabak let the smile go, his limbs suddenly feeling lighter than air as he hauled out the pistol and shot them both high in the face, exit holes scalping the bandanas off their heads. One of them had appeared to be reaching inside his jacket, perhaps going for a knife, maybe a gun.

Shabak would never know, nor did he care, not giving them another thought as they dropped.

It was just the beginning.

The anticipated screaming hit the air next, figures bouncing off each other near the end of the car, diving beneath their seats or scrambling, shoving their way down the aisle for an exit. Maybe a dozen passengers closest to him remained seated, looking to him like frozen puppets waiting only for him to jerk the strings. He suspected they were glued to their seats out of both fear and a hope that maybe the gangsters had simply pushed their luck with the wrong New Yorker, wrong place, wrong time when some city-dwelling vigilante decided enough was enough.

Shabak dispelled any notions they were safe when he dumped the handgun into his pocket and swung the compact subgun out in full view on its swivel rig.

Now with the adrenaline kicked in all the way, the moment seemed to carry him forward all by itself. He couldn't recall a time when he'd ever felt this alive, whole, in charge. He savored the moment of their terror, the car rolling on, all of them knowing full well they were trapped and destined now to be slaughtered. They were fuzzy shapes in his sight, their shouts of panic coming to him from some great distance beyond the roar in his ears. He was vaguely aware of the sound of his own voice, bellowing out insults and cursing them in Arabic as he held back on the subgun's trigger. Number-three victim was a suit dropping his paper, streaked with blood and dribbling brain matter from one of the gangsters. The man held up pinkish hands and begged for his life, something about how he had a wife and sons.

So did I, Shabak thought, once upon a time.

Firing on, Shabak laughed as the paper vanished in a cloud of shreds and red mist. Swinging his aim, Shabak spotted the whore next, rushing to join the stampede surging for the back of the car, as if she could save herself in a crowd. He chopped her down with a burst up the back, flinging her into the rolling mass, deadweight bowling down a few screamers in flight.

It was reflex and a sort of angry, giddy will from there on, wheeling around, aiming the muzzle at anything that sat or tried to hunch for cover or run. He found no heroes daring to make some suicide charge, so two full clips later he was walking over mounds of bodies, silencing the pleas from a few hiders under the seats with short bursts on the slow roll. A whimpering noise, and he turned, found a woman huddling two small boys to her bosom. They didn't look American, and he thought she was pleading for the lives of her sons in Farsi.

He stepped up and told the woman, "It is Allah's

will. They—and you—will be better off in the next world."

Six or seven rounds later, he finished sending them on to Paradise, mother sliding off the seat to drape crimson ruins over her children. Then he spotted the cop, the uniformed figure throwing open the rear door to the car, pistol in hand.

Shabak palmed a fragmentation grenade. The policeman was nearly through the doorway and barking for the passengers to get down when the Iraqi armed the steel bomb and let it fly. The subgun chattering next, he drove the policeman to cover behind the door with a flurry of 9 mm rounds that rattled off the frame, the survivors crying out, huddled on top of each other when ricochets rounds snapped the air, scored flesh from the tangled pile.

As the grenade blew, the air filled with shrieking and howls of pain for a moment, lost quickly to the stammering of his subgun. He marched on, the smells of cordite, emptied bowels and blood swelling his senses, a heady intoxicant, it seemed, that fueled him to new heights of fury and determination. He was pleased the subgun had little recoil, didn't tend to rise up as most SMGs did, allowing him four to five quick kills with not much effort or aim. The third 40-round clip home and bolt racked, he surveyed the carnage, homed in on moaners. There were a few still clinging to hope, calling out for mercy, help, whatever.

And Shabak singled them out and gave perhaps seven or eight more devils a quick burst to the face, relishing the taste of their blood on his lips as gory juices struck him in the face, their screams for mercy ringing in his ears. Briefly he found himself both amazed and appalled at how terrified these Americans were of dying, unwilling to leave behind, he guessed, their worlds of money and pleasure. He had heard how they had watched the bombing of Baghdad on their televisions, twenty-four-hour coverage, in fact, as Iraqi bridges, buildings and hospitals were pounded to rubble, crushing to death scores of women and children. Perhaps a few of them in that very car, he suspected, had even viewed the destruction of his country while gorging themselves on food and drink, chortling to each other that the Iraqis were simply getting what they deserved.

Fair enough, he decided, the tables, as he believed they would say, were now turned.

At the far end of the car, he noted the door, smoking and warped, bodies and body parts strewed in front of the roiling cloud. No more of New York's finest. In the other direction he found more mass panic, as passengers in the next car were bumping and grinding their way to gain distance from the slaughter. Shabak was walking on top of bodies now, the subgun's muzzle sweeping around as he searched between the seats for live ones, when he noticed the train had stopped. It was difficult to see through the windows, where long smears of blood or brain matter ran in jagged streams like obscene graffiti, all but obscuring any decent surveillance of the tunnel.

He heard them crying out in the next cars. He wondered if they were fleeing the train, but that wasn't possible unless the driver also opened the doors on his car. Or was it? How long had it been since he'd begun the massacre? He thought he saw shadows passing beneath the running curtains of blood. He moved to the middle of the car, swiveling his search from one door to the other. The police, he knew, or SWAT or some rapid-response team would be on the way. Or were they already boarding the train, running at the car of death from both directions?

It was impossible to take an accurate body count, but Shabak had to figure he had tallied something in the neighborhood of fifty to sixty kills. Not great, but good enough to see him soaring past the gates and into Paradise. The last decision was made next. Waiting for the American authorities to storm the car, Shabak knelt in a puddle of his enemies' blood, believed he was facing toward Mecca. He tried to tune his ears into the sounds of feet stomping his direction, ready for them to show up, but he focused on one last round of prayers. He prayed for the souls of his late family. He prayed for his brother and for the souls of his brother's family, soon to be slain by their benefactors for his personal jihad. He prayed that when he saw them in Paradise they would understand what he had done and why, and forgive him this impulsive transgression against them.

He heard them coming now, surprised for a moment how quickly they had responded. Slipping his hand into his coat pocket, he fumbled with the grenade, finally got the pin pulled, felt the spoon drop. They were barreling through both doors now, shouting for him to get his hands up. Shabak rose and bulled ahead into the wall of bullets fired from the policemen unfortunate enough to be the first into the car.

IT WAS THE WORST and the last day of his life. The grief was wound tight, dammed up in Saddam Shabak's chest, holding back for the moment, but it was set to blow, come gushing out of his mouth in a wailing that, once begun, would never end...until he took his own life or was shot dead by the visitors he knew were on the way.

"This reporter cannot even begin to describe the horror..."

He'd heard the initial reports already, the phone call not more than twenty minutes after the first special broadcast. He hit the mute button on the remote, no longer requiring the loud volume to mask their cries, the sound of dead bodies crashing to the kitchen floor. It was done, and he didn't care if some neighbor called in a domestic disturbance to the police or not.

His own brother had already bulled ahead, striking out for his own personal jihad before the appointed time. So what did it matter if he was left behind now to go to Paradise in some shoot-out with the authorities in his own apartment? Still, how could Hasab have been so willful and reckless, knowing before he fired the first bullet that his actions would have consequences beyond his own death? It was extremely selfish.

He felt so numb, stained by what he'd done, he believed even a prayer to God for mercy and understanding seemed like a grievous blasphemy that might only reserve for him a special place of fire and agony in the bowels of Hell if he uttered aloud the first plea for forgiveness. He dropped onto the couch, buried his face in a hand, sucking down his grief. He didn't need the voice of the Korean over the phone, the newscast about the subway massacre or the missing weapons in the cache hidden beneath the floorboard in the hall closet to tell him what had happened, who was responsible or what was coming. His life was numbered in minutes.

He looked at the pistol, still clutched and smoking in his hand, wondered what life would have been like if only he had stayed in Iraq. But, no, he was Saddam—which meant "the Stubborn One." And he had made the choice, freely and with righteous anger to burn following the war, intending to find a way to strike back against the enemies of all Iraqi peoples, whatever it took, whoever could help. Even though his own immediate family had somehow been spared the horror of the war, either by an act of God or some fluke of fate, he still carried his hatred, a badge of honor in his eyes, for the Americans ever since. He moved chemical and biological ordnance around the country, whisking it from under the very noses of the CIA and their inspectors, in fact. He also did strong-arm work, killing Kurds, too. Then he was called upon to go and fulfill a destiny that had only once seemed an impossible dream.

Now his quest for vengeance, so close at hand, would never see its holy fruition.

It had been quick, for the most part, beyond Jahih's begging for him not to do it, a moment's hesitation before he put one bullet each in the heads of his wife and three sons. He would never have thought this moment would come to pass in his worst nightmare. But hadn't he, his brother and the others been warned during the briefings this was exactly the sort of horror they could expect?

The North Korean colonel's voice seemed to intrude into his thoughts as he sat, staring at nothing, hating himself for what he had done—what his brother had done. "Should there be any breach in security for any reason, should any one of you be found out, far worse still, should one of you be captured by the Americans, then a phone call will be placed to your residence. If there is no man present, should he be in the custody of the Americans, then two men assigned by myself for this unfortunate task will come to visit your families. I do not think I have to spell out what will happen to your families in that event."

Having already gone ahead and spared himself the shame of watching a stranger execute his family, Shabak rose to follow through with the next step of covering up any trail that would point toward his country of birth or raise suspicions on the part of the American FBI. Perhaps the plan, whatever it was, would succeed without him. At least he could hope the blood on his hands would be avenged in due course.

He went and removed the passports from the top desk drawer, the most painful act coming next when he gathered any photographs he'd kept of his family. He dumped it all into a metal wastebasket, lit a cigarette then doused any evidence in the apartment of their existence, real or false, with lighter fluid. He removed the batteries from the smoke alarm, then torched his own passport, the face and assumed identity of Ali Hassham of Lebanon melting before his eyes.

He was back on the couch when the expected knock on the door came. He had left it open, as per the instructions from the voice on the phone. Two short, slender Korean men in dark suit jackets stepped into the living room. One of them toted a large duffel bag, while the other shut the door. Shabak turned away from them, detecting the look of disapproval, even judgment in their eyes. The first man went to the hall closet where he began stuffing the bag with the few pistols, grenades and the single remaining subgun. They knew where to go, of course, since Shabak was aware this apartment was set up by their North Korean sponsors specifically as his waiting place, the weapons already hidden away before he even set foot on American soil.

Shabak drew on his cigarette, found his hand shaking. He wondered if he was trembling with shame or outrage that the North Korean was already threading the sound suppressor on his pistol, moving into the kitchen as if checking to make certain he hadn't left any of his family alive by accident. Shabak felt his anger rising at the mental picture of the man toeing his family with his shoes or feeling for heartbeats that weren't there.

He finished his cigarette, grinding it out by foot on the floor. He could feel the North Korean moving up behind him.

"It would be better if you did it yourself."

Shabak chuckled. It wasn't difficult to interpret the point between the lines. Family man goes berserk, slays wife and children, shoots himself. No motive, no reason, happens all the time. America. A stressful, dangerous place to live, where most murders occur between family members. Not even the police would be baffled or pursue an investigation. At least that was how the colonel had explained it.

"May I have a moment to pray?"

"There is no time for such nonsense."

Perhaps it was his overpowering guilt and shame.

Perhaps it was being denied his last request or perhaps it was his potential executioner's choice of words and tone. Maybe it was a combination that made Saddam Shabak snap inside, grabbing up the pistol, lurching to his feet, turning the weapon on the insolent bastard.

But he never got the chance to fire.

2

It was something of a rare occasion when Mack Bolan found Hal Brognola out for an apparent stroll. A workaholic, the big Fed usually earned his room and board in the name of national security in one of two places—either in his office at the Justice Department or at Stony Man Farm out in the Shenandoah Valley of Virginia, where America's number-one ultracovert operation was housed. Bolan, who was also known as the Executioner, was at the Farm when he got the call from Brognola to saddle up—weapons and gear ready—and chopper in to Reagan National where his longtime friend had a driver standing by.

The soldier now read the worried expression on Brognola's face as he strode deeper across the manicured expanse of lawn. It was the time of day where the happy-hour bunch was winding it down from the Hill to Georgetown, waiting for the herds of nine-to-five commuters to thin out. As for Bolan's friend, there was rarely the time or privilege in his world for a few quickies at the local pub to rub elbows, schmooze over the day's doings. The big Fed's rank and classified job description also saw him pulling double duty as Stony Man liaison to the President of the United States, who sanctioned missions for the Farm's warriors. The Justice Man's time clock was never punched, but it was real simple—twenty-four hours, seven days a week. Thus, it was no stretch for the soldier to conclude this was no walk in the park for Brognola, or rather the Mall in this case.

Duty beckoned, he suspected, and Bolan was there to get the particulars before moving on for a new campaign. The Executioner put on his game face.

The soldier angled toward the big Fed, who saw him coming, strode next for an unoccupied bench and parked himself. Despite a nip to the air, Bolan found the joggers, cyclists and scattered gaggles of meandering tourists still out en force. Normally the director of the Sensitive Operations Group didn't conduct business out in the open, where passing ears might pick up matters pertaining to national security.

Closing on Brognola, Bolan read his friend's own game face. On second study, Bolan detected some wistful but weary observing of the various historic landmarks staggered from east to west. The Capitol Building. The white granite monolith of the National Air and Space Museum. The red castle marking the Smithsonian. The Washington Monument. Bolan sensed his friend's mood of solemn reverie and took in the sights himself. He could well appreciate the need to get out once in a while, stretch the legs or sit idle, even when duty beckoned. It wasn't so much the need to grab some fresh air, but maybe the warrior psyche simply had to review, assess and digest somehow all the hard miles logged in defense of what the landmarks stood for.

Freedom.

It was something neither man ever took for granted. And sometimes, Bolan knew, what was taken for granted could be gone tomorrow, snatched away, or trampled by the savages, unless a man understood in the core of his being what it was he had. And was likewise willing to go the extra mile to insure truth, justice and liberty for one and for all.

Bolan took a seat next to his friend. "So, what's up?"

Brognola smiled. "I gave it a few hours, fielding the usual calls, picking the brains of reliable sources before I sounded any alarms your way."

"Referring to the situation in New York."

"Right. Feelers out, called in a few markers to get the scuttlebutt."

"You're going to tell me what happened wasn't just the random act of some disgruntled New Yorker who was mugged one too many times."

Brognola gnawed on his unlit cigar. "If what I suspect pans out in even the slimmest, most remote way, shape or form, this is way beyond one lunatic who thinks death-wish-type vigilantism should be the eleventh commandment. Okay, first a little background, straight from my sources, with more than a fair share of digging and detective work from my own people at Justice and the FBI. Bear with me on some of the obvious.

"We both know the last two Administrations tried and failed to bomb Iraq back into the Stone Age. Not necessarily through any fault on their behalf, it's just that their leader is that one mosquito in the room you can never catch with a swatter. We know the CIA failed— miserably—to try and take him down using his own people, all of whom were wasted during any one of a dozen attempted coups against the great mustache since the end of the Gulf War."

"Right, as usual. So far, so bad."

"You know about the genocide campaign against the Kurds in the north and, of course, the CIA-UN weapons inspectors were long since sent packing. In the prover- bial nutshell, it's all left him with plenty of elbow room to carry on putting together the mother of all bombs, keep on gassing Kurds, execute relatives, rattle his saber over the coffee, muffins and the head of whatever son- in-law or ranking officer fell out of his graces that day."

"On goes the party."

Brognola grunted. "We still fly sorties, of course, drop a few dozen tons of ordnance on his head some days when he's in an especially pissy mood."

"Business as usual over in Mesopotamia."

"Or it's business in the unusual. Okay, so the leader is still up there, head of the class of Uncle Sam's Bad Boys Club, and our side would like nothing more than to take him out. But between his multiple palaces, his four-hundred-foot yacht, where he uses a human shield of foreign dignitaries while tooling around the Tigris, tack on God only knows how many underground labyrinths where he buries himself when he hears what he calls 'the hostile crows' coming to say hello...well, it's little wonder he's still Mr. Fun of the Islamic fun- damentalist party."

Brognola paused as an elderly lady with a small dog

walked past. Riding out the wait, Bolan knew the big
Fed was leading up to the clincher. Brognola was not
one to waste time on frivolous sound bites. "Ma'am,"
Brognola said, shooting her something of a patronizing
smile, then nodding at the lady, who steered the dog well
clear of the bench.

"At any rate, Iraq has recently become open to air
traffic from all points. Baghdad's not exactly up there
on my choice spot for a vacation, but you've got Jordan
and Egypt, allegedly allies to Uncle Sam, leading the parade for the rest of the Arab world who wants their
leader and Iraq brought back into the cozy bosom of civ-
ilization. Lift sanctions, no strings, let the oil flow, the
war's over, what's the problem."

"Let it be, in other words."

"Yeah. No hard feelings, we should adopt a kinder,
gentler approach to him and his butchers. They've suffered enough. So lately, instead of trying to shove a
thousand-pound bomb up his nose, and risk blowing
some Egyptian delegation back across the Sinai, our
side has taken to parking satellites over ancient Babylon. Monitoring the air traffic, sifting through the cast
of characters turning up on satellite imagery, stuff like
that."

"Telling me we've picked up a rogue's gallery, doing
more than just sharing the champagne with him on his
yacht."

"Try North Koreans on for size. Try an esteemed en-
tourage of officers and what we believe are special-
forces goons from above the thirty-eighth parallel, there
in what the CIA and the NSA believe is a military ad-
visory capacity."

"Nice to know our intelligence folks still know how to sugarcoat and spin."

"Well, I defy them to sugarcoat one Kim Jong Il, son of the late Kim Il Sung, seen yukking it up with Iraq's leader and some lady friends. You've heard of Dr. Germ?"

"She's the leading lady in chemical death, the brains behind his chemical-weapons program. Earned her Ph.D. in plant toxins at the University of East Anglia, her education funded, I believe, by the British government."

"I'll never accuse you of idling away your free time catching up on soaps," Brognola cracked. "Back to the good doctor. The Britons are still wiping the omelette off their faces over where and how she acquired her higher learning and to what end. The CIA is also ducking the occasional hand grenade lobbed their way by politicos in the know on that score. For years they knew her talents were being tested on Iraqi prisoners, Kurds, any and all Iranian POWs unfortunate enough to get scooped up on the wrong side of the border during their leader's eight-year attempt to become the Iraqi version of Patton. Part of the problem now is we no longer have eyes and ears in the country."

"Courtesy of Langley."

"You got it. Not only did they fumble the ball on more than one occasion, but the CIA bailed out on their operatives in Iraq when UNSCOM packed it in."

"Left them twisting in the noose."

"Literally. Any ops they want to tell the numbers crunchers on the Hill they still have under contract over there to watch him have long since been digested by the buzzards. Now we discover, just for one thing, Kim and Dr. Germ aren't bashful about the photo ops for our eyes in the sky."

"I hear exchange program."

"No tea leaves, crystal balls or Tim Russert with his board to tell both of us what the future holds if two of the most dangerous and volatile countries in the world decide to go further than singing 'Kumbaya' together."

"No secret where Iraq stands."

"Missile technology. They still have plenty of missiles lying around. Their leader even has a couple of nukes ready to fly, but they lack the fissile core."

"We hope."

"Plus he's in desperate shape as far as getting the required and all-divine guidance systems—we hope."

"Enter North Korea."

"Smart money says we're looking at some end game in the brewing stages."

"But no bottom line?"

"Not yet."

"How does the subway massacre play into all this?"

"I'm almost there. Okay, we've got North Korean 'advisers' apparently arming and training Iraqis. We've got Kim and Dr. Germ exchanging goo-goo eyes. Now, say what you will about Kim Jong—despot, psychopath, pathological liar with delusions of grandeur—"

"You mean he didn't discover all those scientific theories? Or create the car and the toaster—and the Internet—like the Democratic People's Republic of Korea claims he did?"

Brognola returned Bolan's wry grin. "Nor has he walked on the moon, written a thousand epic novels in one year or invented the wheel like the good old DPRK tell the starving masses north of the thirty-eighth parallel. Hey, you still wear the jaded wit pretty well for a guy who's been sitting on the sidelines for a couple days."

"You know what they say about idle hands." Bolan lost the look, his eyes turning hard. "Kim Jong's a butcher, no more, no less."

"I hear that loud and clear. This guy sits around all day, according to our intel, spends a million bucks a year on Hennessy, watches *Rambo* and *Star Trek* reruns...it's hard to believe this buffoon, a fat, alcoholic scam artist who—besides thinking our own State Department can somehow land him his own talk show on cable—is the mastermind behind a number of terrorist attacks. The same guy who tried to whack the South Korean president in Burma, excuse me, Myanmar."

"The very same lunatic who plotted and brought down that Korean Air jetliner back in '87. Sometimes it's the clowns who can fool even the discerning eye the most. By the time you see past the smile or the tears, it's usually too late in the game."

"If he's trying to smile and bullshit his way down the Tigris with Iraq's leader, it looks like the Iraqi has bitten."

"And beyond this latest gathering of a psycho circus?"

"Two items. One—our martyr on the F train. Took himself out with a grenade as he charged the guns of the first New York cops on the scene."

"I heard."

Rage danced through Brognola's eyes. "This asshole

murdered fifty-plus commuters, Striker, most of them where they sat. I'm talking mothers with kids, too. The body count is still going up as they try to figure out which arms and legs belong to which torsos and so on. And five cops dead, two on the critical list."

Bolan felt his own fury rising.

And then Brognola dropped the bomb. "The FBI believes they tracked down where the bastard lived. Brooklyn apartment, Atlantic Avenue, heavy with the Mideast crowd. Seems a concerned citizen called in a domestic disturbance. The police responded to the apartment in question. They found what at first appeared a murder-suicide, a family man who went berserk, recent immigrant, executed his wife and children, then took his own life. That was the running scenario until the FBI took over. The gentlemen in question might have had a hard time shooting himself right between the eyes, then putting another round through his heart, then making the weapon vanish with him on his way to the great beyond. And the waters grow murkier next when I tell you the concerned citizen was questioned, just happened to see two gentlemen of Asian origin coming from the apartment."

"Of course, no weapons found, no ID."

"The Feds found a wastebasket full of what they believe were documents, passports, the works, burned to crisp."

"And we're thinking our lunatic on the F train got ahead of the program."

"And that just maybe he was shipped here from Iraq. And the mysterious Asian gents—North Koreans, I'd wager—were marched in by the sponsors to tie up a loose end before the Feds came knocking."

"Could be the start of an elimination game."

"My thinking exactly. A whole cell of Iraqi lunatics, ready to shoot and blow up half of New York. Only now one of their own has mucked up the play and the sponsors are sending in the cleanup boys."

"We're still reaching."

"Could be, but I don't think so. Here's something of a clincher. After they questioned the neighbors of the apartment, I'm hearing the description of the bastard on the F train by the police who survived the final blast matches that of an individual who shared the abattoir in question."

"So, you want me to go to New York."

"The Man," Brognola said, referring to the President, "wants you in New York, ASAP."

"What are the particulars on my end?"

"Attached, as commander and chief, to a special task force out of my office that specializes in hunting terrorists on U.S. soil. I'll have the blanks filled in on that score by the time I get back to the office."

And the soldier knew his friend would. By the time Brognola wrapped it up, the Executioner knew he was a short flight away from getting cut loose, carte blanche to do what must be done to uncover any loose Iraqi cannons about to run amok and slaughter any more innocent American citizens. As he thought about those slain commuters, he caught the look in Brognola's eyes. It told him the big Fed damn near pitied anybody who had helped that particular savage get safe and free passage to American soil. Almost, but actually far from it. Sometimes, they both knew, vengeance was simply part and parcel of a warrior's duty.

His heart beating a little faster, the Executioner felt his game face harden up a little more. He was good to go.

"DAD, DON'T YOU ever quit trying to save us from nuclear war?" Sara Shaw asked.

"A defensive shield over the earth, my dear, specifically the continental U.S., would prevent the other side's missiles from landing and turning our country into a radioactive wasteland that only the cockroach would inherit."

"Thermonuclear bombs lighting up the heavens, you mean. What about the fallout? What if one of a dozen or so ICBMs somehow gets through your magic laser net? One would be more than enough to start World War III."

"I'm working on that particular problem now," Thomas Shaw answered.

"It's not too often you get both your daughters in the same place at the same time. Can you give it a rest?"

"I'll consider shutting it down, at least in the interests of quality family time, the day you quit smoking."

"And bring home Mr. Right, too?"

"Trust me, I'll decide if he's right or not. I'm reserving that one and only privilege I'm asking as a father to his twenty-something daughter."

"Four. Twenty-four, Dad."

"Yes. My big girl, all grown up."

Sara took a seat at her father's workstation. He was smiling when he said that, but she often wondered if she had somehow let him down, searching the eyes behind his glasses for a moment before he turned his full attention back to the computer's monitor. She couldn't think how she might have disappointed him, other than not putting her journalism degree to work for her as soon as she graduated college, maybe land that steady job at the *Washington Post,* giving her the advice, hinting the future was now. Cub reporter on the climb up the ladder of success, indeed, the present stable and secure, future nothing but roses, dad proud.

Instead, she postponed the future, whatever might lie ahead, opting to bartend to make ends meet, a trip once a year to Europe or Miami Beach when her Annandale apartment started feeling too small and she grew too restless. Well, at least she hadn't gotten pregnant, didn't do drugs and she'd never fallen into a promiscuous lifestyle during her college years or since, as a number of her girlfriends had. She smoked cigarettes, her only vice, liked to go out with her friends once in a while, maintaining her right to independence, Cosmo girl.

On the other hand her father, she knew, was old school, fashioned decades ago by Catholic tradition to believe in a world where there was no gray. Perhaps that was the problem, she thought. The world had changed, but Thomas Shaw still believed it was the fifties, when birth control meant the rhythm method. She suspected he didn't much care for the attitudes of modern American females, although he was a perfect gentleman, married to her mother for something close to forty years. He didn't curse, drink or smoke. He was moderate in everything he did, beyond, of course, his work. She often wondered what it was he did to unwind, or if there was some secret eccentricity he reserved for himself.

Oh, well, part of growing up, she believed, was sim-

ply accepting what couldn't be changed. Twice a year
she might make the trip out to Middleburg to see her
family when her younger sister was on break from college. Maybe it was enough that they were all gathered
under the same roof. If she'd been younger, still getting
whisked from school to school and state to state because
of her father's position with the military branch of
NASA or the NSA—and she was never certain whom
he pledged allegiance to—she might have squawked
some when old dad was too busy to pay her more than
a passing interest.

His life was his work.

She watched as his fingers flew over the keyboard,
computerized graphics of satellites, what she believed
were grid maps, missiles in flight over the North Pole,
and numbers in the corner scrolling through at light
speed. She might find him remiss when it came to what
he might see as mundane matters pertaining to simple
hearth and home, but her father was an important man,
his work top secret, or rather classified, she knew, in the
jargon of his world. Had his work been "Eyes only,"
meaning the official badge of the Strategic Defense Initiative with Department of Defense at the bottom would
be plastered at the top of the monitor...in that case she
knew the grim bodyguard assigned to the house, Mr.
Congeniality, as she referred to him, wouldn't have allowed her to set on foot into this sanctuary.

Over the years she had tried to understand what it
was her father did. Sometimes she tried to engage him
in conversation about Star Wars, but it was something
of a rare solar eclipse when he discussed his work,
which, of course, could leave her that much more curi-

ous. Space warfare, in layman terms, she thought, was pretty much the stuff of science fiction. He called what he was attempting to create—missiles that would knock enemy missiles out of the sky or hundreds of miles above the earth—like hitting a bullet with a bullet. It was all beyond her, but still she admired him, despite her ignorance on the subject. For one thing he was part of a group called the Titan Four, missile geniuses, two of which—her father included—had been interviewed on various cable talk shows. His world might be alien to her, but she still knew a celebrity when she saw one. She had taped the episodes for posterity, and to show him off for her friends if the mood struck her. So it was her father's task to develop both theoretical scenarios and create advanced blinding systems. She'd heard him talk briefly about laser-guided warheads on space stations, space sensors, a web of orbiting mirrors needed to tangle up any missiles launched out of the earth's atmosphere, to be shot down before they had a chance to reenter and vaporize American cities. Long-wavelength infrared probes, DEWs—or Directed Energy Weapons—exo- and endoatmospheric interceptors...it boggled her mind to even attempt to fathom how her father could keep it all straight in his head. But to her, despite what might be a strained relationship at times, he was brilliant.

"Mom's been slaving away on your favorite dish."

"Linguine and clams?"

"With red sauce."

"Slaving, you say?"

She frowned. "Bad choice of words."

"You're asking, then, how much longer?"

She was about to do just that when the intercom buzzed, the bodyguard's voice cutting through the study, all business and concern.

"It's all right, Rodgers. What I have up is not classified."

"Sir, but..."

"We can bend the rules this one time. Thank you for your concern."

"I guess he'll report you now to the principal?"

"Merely doing his job."

"Is it even necessary for him to be around?"

"Yes, it is, my dear. Unfortunately, there have been...some breaches, I understand, in security at two different installations, some rumors I have heard... threats."

"Threats? Against who? How come I don't like the sound of any of this, Dad?"

"Nothing for you to be alarmed about."

"You're not saying you or the rest of us are in any danger?"

"The world has changed, Sara."

If it wasn't for the seriousness of the talk, she would have smiled at this admission.

"You needn't look so surprised," he said, smiling. "Yes, even staid old dad can admit times have changed."

"So the guard stays, gun and all."

"For now."

"Until these security breaches are plugged up? Should I plan on buying him something for next Christmas? Cleaning oil, or whatever it is he uses to polish his gun?"

He was smiling now, but his silence told her she

wasn't going to get much more out of him on the subject of security, or his thoughts on any perceived or real threat to himself and the rest of the family. If she stopped and thought about it, she knew his work alone placed him in some shadow world where classified documents were stolen or sold all the time. The danger might be way out there on the fringes for her father, Rodgers with his gun always there to watch his back, but what was to stop foreign agents from putting an offer to him that he couldn't refuse? Her father's work was on the cutting edge, jealously guarded, but what if...?

She stopped herself before the train of paranoia could sour a mood that was on the verge of lapsing into full-blown annoyance anyway. This was Middleburg, after all. Horse country, big Thoroughbred money. Each home pretty much sat on pristine acres of wooded land, fortified enclaves where folks spent more on security than most Washingtonians made in one year. This was far removed from any spy central where armed guards patrolled and searched every nook and cranny for saboteurs, shadow assassins.

"I'm going see if Mom and Patti need any help," she said, but knew she'd cave to the urge for a smoke as soon as she was out of the room.

"Leave the window in the bathroom open. By the way, cigarettes are not biodegradeable when you flush them down the toilet."

"Thanks, Dad, I'll remember that."

She was grateful when she found Rodgers wasn't hovering around when she made her exit, veered next on a beeline for the guest room. It was on the bottom floor, close to the patio, so she had quick access for a late-night smoke if she wanted a change of scenery from the adjoining bathroom. She heard her mother clanging about in the kitchen, found her sister setting up the dinner table. She decided against some lame excuse for not assisting them, vanishing into the bathroom before someone noticed she was making herself scarce for a smoke break.

Closing the door, she lit up, then opened the window. She was blowing out the first stream of smoke, when she thought she heard the bleating of helicopter blades, coming from some point but growing closer from beyond the dark mass of rolling hills to the west. She was about to turn away from the window when the chopper landed on their property. There were no lights on the helicopter, but enough glow shone from the lampposts near the gazebo for her to make out—

She nearly dropped the cigarette on the carpet. They were shadows, running hard across the patio, moving like some well-oiled machine, but she made out the distinct shapes of machine guns in their hands.

She felt the panic and terror rise up in her throat, her mind racing for answers that eluded her. Or did they, the answer simply a shout away from her father's work study? Did this have something to do with the mysterious breach of security her father alluded to?

She heard the shouting beyond the closed door, the chaos of several voices rolling her way in various degrees of anger and confusion, fear and demands. Oh, God, she thought, what was happening? She thought she was going to be sick. Why hadn't the security alarm sounded, alerting them that invaders, armed to the teeth, had stormed their house? Realization of what was hap-

pening and why began to take shape in her mind as she
searched for her voice. She was trapped, but she
wouldn't allow herself to be at the mercy of strangers
with guns, not if she intended to help her family. But
how? She dumped the cigarette in the toilet to a splash
and a sizzle, glanced out the window in time to see
more shadows with guns barreling through the kitchen
door, her mother and sister shrieking in panic. A voice
was drifting her way, as someone bellowed for her to
be found. Her father was out there, demanding to know
what was happening, who they were.

Think quick. She knew what was happening, even as
she tried to lie to herself that everything was going to
be fine.

This was a kidnapping. And these men, whoever they
were, were there to snatch her father. His work, through
no fault of his own, was about to see them abducted,
maybe worse. Taken where? For how long?

A part of her demanded she charge out into the living room, but she believed if she hid she could better
serve her family. If she could somehow escape the coming search. And do what? The logical course of action,
naturally, would be to phone the police, the FBI, whoever would come there.

She ran for the guest room, crawling under the bed
when she caught the babble of voices speaking in some
rapid-fire Asian language. Okay, the window was open,
and when they hit the bathroom she could only hope and
pray they believed she was outside, fleeing into the
woods, running to get help. She could feel their men-
acing presence, scurrying about in the bathroom now,
so close she feared they'd smell the smoke clinging to

her body. Again they were talking in Asian until another
voice barked, "Speak English!"

"She is gone!"

"She's not gone. She's outside somewhere. Get out
there and find her! You have two minutes!"

Sara Shaw held her breath as she heard the bathroom
door leading to the bedroom bang open. She could see the
man's legs, some sort of combat boots, just feet away from
her face. She hugged the floor, not trusting that her ploy
had worked, the air locked in her chest, waiting him out.

Leave, she silently urged.

He left, after what felt like an hour. For a moment she
detested her own relief and wondered if she was simply being a coward. Hiding, like some little child from
the bogeyman, hoping she wasn't found. But what was
she going to do against men with guns anyway? She
heard one of them cursing from the bathroom, and knew
she was safe from discovery as the sound of boots
tromping over tile faded.

Knowing she was helpless, defenseless against this
unknown menace, Sara offered up a silent prayer for the
safety of her family. It was the only thing she could do
until the invaders left and she could call the police.

THOMAS SHAW KNEW what was happening and why,
even before he burst into the living room. The only
questions left hanging were the identities of the invaders, and how they'd slipped past the security system.
This was just the sort of moment he had dreaded for
years, aware his work jeopardized the lives of his family. He never believed the day would come, but there he
was, now witnessing his worst nightmare.

They were there for the work he had stored on disk, no question, all the classified data he had on the building and refinement of the guidance systems for the Medusa satellite. He would gladly give it to them, everything, if only they would leave his family unharmed. If he simply handed over his classified work on SDI, his superiors would eventually question his motives under their microscope. It would cost him more than just his security clearances, perhaps even his job.

He was forging ahead into what felt like an invisible wall of fear, when he spotted Rodgers pulling away from a group of four Asians who had his wife and daughter corralled on the couch and under the muzzles of automatic weapons. Now he knew, as he stared at Rodgers, how they had slipped the security net.

"Why?"

It was the only thing he could think of to ask a man he had trusted with his life and the lives of his family. The answer galled him, but he wasn't surprised.

"For the money. What else?"

He was calling out to his wife and daughter, worried why Sara wasn't in the living room, when a figure in black detached himself from a mix of Asians and Americans streaming out of the hallway that led to Sara's room. They hadn't found her, or if they had...

Before he could begin to try to comprehend the insanity of the moment, shout out a barrage of questions, a man with gray eyes, matching skin and white buzz cut strode up to Rodgers. The man fixed a sound suppressor to his pistol, then, without warning, shot Rodgers in the back of the head. Shaw froze at the sight of blood taking to the air, less than two feet away, his wife screaming now, loud enough, he feared, to send the neighbors running.

"And we appreciate the help. Now, Mr. Shaw..."

Cold-blooded murder, and this man acted as if it were nothing worse than simply flushing a toilet.

"Don't hurt my family. I'll give you anything you want."

"And so you shall. As for your family, sir, whether or not they stay breathing is up to you and to them."

Shaw was about to brush past the man when the pistol seem to frame itself in his face. "Stay put. Do as you're told and everything will work out."

"We can't find the other one."

Shaw felt the hope flickering back, aware Sara had escaped as one of the Asians gave the man in gray the report. It was dashed next by the realization this might simply enrage the leader into another impulse killing.

"It doesn't matter. We're out of here. We'll tie them up and blindfold them on the way."

"Where are you taking us?" Shaw heard his wife demand, the exchange nearly muted as his own roar of silent anger and terror filled his ears. "Thomas, give them what they want!"

"Oh, he will, ma'am, don't you worry. It just may take a little longer than you like. Could even take some persuasion that might get a little rough—or unsavory," the leader said, smiling at the women. "Sorry, folks, there's no time to pack your toothbrushes."

And Shaw knew this was only the beginning of being held captive. He read the cold look in the man's eyes for what it was. Doom, plain and simple—tomorrow, the day after or next week, but it would come.

Shaw well suspected what it was he was supposed to do, give up, create. And when he was finished, his purpose served, he knew they were all dead.

The last thing he remembered hearing, as he was grabbed and shoved ahead, was the leader ordering his study packed up for the ride.

Colonel Bok Chongjin of the North Korean special forces believed he understood Americans better than they understood themselves. It was the mentality, an appetite whetted by generations of greed, he thought, where the average American barbarian could easily be manipulated to his advantage, do his bidding, if the price was right. If, Chongjin decided, he played his cards correctly from there on—balancing the scales somewhere between threats and necessary dispensing of actual physical force—all he had to do was move the appropriate human chess pieces around until he was at the threshold of proclaiming checkmate. What little time he had spent in this land of plenty, he understood one basic factor that motivated these barbarians. From the lowest slug of a petty criminal all the way to the privileged elite, they all bowed before two gods.

Money and power.

Which equaled freedom, which translated into absolute power in their primitive minds. As they would say the more, the merrier.

It was a definite plus in his own power column, concerning his endgame to be exact, that the men he dealt with and controlled would never bite the hand that fed them, as long as that hand kept their bellies full and their numbered overseas accounts bulging. It also aided his cause to see their beds were warmed on certain nights by imported Asian beauties to keep carnal desires sated, while the agenda rolled ahead, smoothly and on target. With their needs met, he knew there was little room for whining, doubt, whatever negative energy might dump a wrench into the cogs of the coming juggernaut. Of course, the trump card, if all else failed, was a subtle reminder, now and again, of certain evidence he was armed with, involving everything from those ladies of questionable morals to high treason. Blackmail was always fair game, the last resort to keep the sun shining on his dreams.

But there was trouble and it was something he needed to address before it all unraveled and three years of laying the groundwork blew up in his face. The current problems in question might be many states away, but the backlash could well find him and his barbarian counterparts unless he started plugging up the holes before the whole dam cracked apart. Personal safety in a world of sabotage and subterfuge was always about as guaranteed, he thought, as the professed love of one of his call girls. Yes, he might be parked on a dark, empty prairie, somewhere between Tulsa and Oklahoma City, but he could sense some unknown danger headed his way.

Well, the right dose of paranoia could find him still breathing beyond any figurative or actual grenades lobbed his way.

He heard the man pulling up in his Land Rover, door

slamming, gruff voice barking out the indignation a moment later. "Hey, what the hell! Easy on the sheepskin, Kim. The gun stays...why, you little..."

Chongjin smiled. The man was all bent out of shape as he was patted down for hidden minimikes, tape recorders and relieved of his holstered side arm. The American was threatening to kick ass all the way back to the thirty-eighth parallel, and so on.

Strange, he thought, how they still believed they could hold on to even a vestige of respect and dignity when they had sold out their own in the worst of treasonous acts.

The colonel checked his Rolex—the man late again for their third meeting in as many months. He ran his hands down the length of his cashmere coat. He smiled, enjoying both the feel of the fine Tibetan wool and the operative's foul mood and empty threats. He reached up and snapped on the low-wattage bulb. He wanted to view the face of his pawn—or potential nemesis, depending on the future— while reading the eyes for any hidden meaning behind the words. Likewise he was braced for some arrogant tirade, ready to verbally shoot down the man before he fired off a barrage of needless questions, designed simply to assuage his own guilt, lay his own worries to rest.

No time for small talk.

The side door was opened by one of his soldiers, the man from the Defense Intelligence Agency bounding his considerable bulk inside, plopping down in the seat directly opposite Chongjin. He scowled around the interior, as if he couldn't believe a foreigner was allowed the one simple perk of decent transportation by his own people. The van itself was customized, in fact, built by the DIA man's black-ops comrades on the sly. It was armor plated, meant to double as a rolling command center, complete with fax and computer modem, radio console with secured lines and police scanner, the whole superspy works hidden in the side paneling. With valid Oklahoma plates, all the necessary paperwork stashed in the glove box, even a lengthy background check by some suspicious redneck out there in the boondocks with gun and badge would find the vehicle traced back to a legitimate car dealership in Tulsa.

Perks.

When the door slid shut, the DIA man growled, "First, I don't like being ordered to clean up other people's messes, especially not after I warn the other guy about such a particular mess happening. And the next time one of your boys gives me a frisking like I'm some rat bastard flunkie, he'll be getting his next sushi fix through an IV. We clear?"

"Yes. We understand each other."

"I hope to hell so."

Even as his senses were pummeled by the winds of whiskey, Chongjin kept the smile in place, studied the DIA man he knew as Adam Turner. For some unclear, even borderline absurd reason the man insisted on dressing up as one of their cowboys of Western lore. From black Stetson, sheepskin coat, cowboy boots, down to the holster on his hip now empty of his pistol, he was something of a caricature of what he really was, which was a superoperative with access to all manner of classified intelligence and top-level clearance. Hardly the spit-and-polished picture of the many blacksuited covert operatives who were part of their organization. He was also a traitor to his own country. But the man seemed determined to play out the role of some rugged gun-slinger, as if he wished his life were simply shrouded in myth and eccentricity. This was, indeed, Chongjin thought, a strange land, full of paradox and contradiction, an obscure subculture that mingled fact with fantasy, desire with reality. Like Turner, they were restless, never satisfied, always wishing to be something other than what they were, or to have more money and material things than they were already blessed with.

"Understand, my nerves aren't in the best of shape, Colonel."

"Yes. I can plainly smell that the pressure is getting to you."

The wide jaw clenched, the man grabbing the cowboy hat off his head, running an agitated hand through silver hair. "Is that supposed to be funny, Colonel?"

"I can assure you, nothing is amusing at the present."

"To understate the whole situation. Damn straight."

"Shall we get down to business? You know already I require a report from you on the progress I expected regarding the potential crisis."

"I guess you're talking about your sudden decision to use my man for something we didn't agree on in the beginning?"

Chongjin almost lost the smile, his patience thinning. "I don't like word games. You know what it is I want to hear. Let me explain this very simply. Your man is my man."

"Whom I brought out of a closet, one that is rattling full of his skeletons, and who has fulfilled already the one obligation he signed on for."

"Yes. And he did a superb job, if I understand correctly from our phone conversation, which my own people confirmed."

"Checking now to verify my sit-reps? Where's all the trust between us gone, Colonel? What happened to your 'we are the world' mantra?"

Chongjin ignored the barb. "Am I mistaken now or does he want an additional fee for his new services?"

"It's not the money, but depending on how the situation develops..."

Chongjin held up a hand. "Please. The detail about additional payment can be worked out. I assure him, through you, as I have assured you before. When we leave this country, all of you will have enough money to live out your lives in a style befitting royalty, better even than your Hollywood movie stars Americans seem so enthralled with. In a country, I might add, of your choosing. With new identities."

"As I was saying, it's not necessarily the money."

"What, then? Out with it."

"Part of the problem is, since it looks like a kidnapping, the FBI has already been called in."

"The way it was designed to appear."

"Not this soon. The risk factor, in other words, seems to be taking quantum leaps by the hour, Colonel. For one thing, your people, and my—our—man left behind the missile genius's little darling. In the interests of time, they bailed before they could find her."

Chongjin kept smiling, noted the scowl on Turner's face. His expression, he sensed, was both mystifying and infuriating to the American. "I see no problem in that regard. So she talks to the FBI. There will be no ran-

som demand. Their FBI will sit around, staring at a
phone that will never ring. And since the human cargo,
as we and our organization outlined, will be delivered
here by truck in no more than twenty-four hours, it
would appear that all systems are go."

"Not so fast. My—our—man hasn't exactly en-
deared himself to certain folks in the intelligence community. If they think he's loose on American soil, he
might find himself getting bagged before he nails down
the big scores you ordered. Songbird. Witness Protection Program. Fingers aimed our way."

"So, you have told me all of this before. Refresh my
memory. You have called this wonder assassin what?"

"The Reaper."

"Yes. As in the Grim Reaper." Chongjin felt his smile
widen. Perhaps his first assessment of Turner wasn't entirely accurate. Propaganda and myth didn't contain
themselves within the boundaries of any one country,
restrict the lies and half truths of bravado to any single
culture. Like America, his own country reveled in
shrouding itself in myth, even spun out bald-faced lies,
glorifying men of rank and power when and where it
suited those in charge of the masses. That was particularly true, he thought, of the present leader, an obese
drunkard and lecher who required a steady diet of Via-
gra just to feed the myth of his so-called sexual prowess.
In Chongjin's personal but silent estimation, Kim Jong
Il was far from anything glorious or even worthy of the
first scintilla of respect. Sad but true, even his country,
he had admit to himself, had serious problems, due in
large part to who held the reins of power at the very top.

The current son and the deceased father had both

made the masses believe they were gods to be revered. The starving peasants in the desolate countryside actually believing stories of how they had come down from the heavens on chariots of fire to rule and to lead the Korean people to glory and greatness. It was a known fact that the peasants believed Kim Il and now Kim Jong were actually responsible for the sun rising and setting. He often wondered about the sanity of his own countrymen, swallowing such childish nonsense. It was also aimed at brainwashing those who were too miserable and wretched to know, or to want any better. In time, he would change all of that. In time, he planned to drink a bottle of Kim Jong's imported cognac, over his dead body.

For a brief moment, aware of how highly regarded this Reaper had come to him, he tried to conjure up an image of this superassassin he had never seen. He pictured some gaunt, steely-eyed killer who probably, in all reality, had shot more unarmed or unsuspecting men in the back than anything else. The fabled Grim Reaper, that skeletal figure cloaked in black, but wielding a pistol instead of a scythe, coming in the dead of night to take lives at the appointed hour.

Chongjin dropped the smile. "Kindly and with brevity explain what you think the problem is."

"Okay, you want succinct. One of your recruits out of Baghdad went crazy this morning, slaughtered fifty-something New Yorkers on a subway train, including cops, before he blew himself up for the glory of Allah. That kind of body count tends to draw attention. Not to mention cops get kind of pissed off when other cops get killed. They get this vendetta thing in their heads."

"I ordered the removal of his next of kin, which was successful."

"And you informed me a while ago you already ordered your own people to hand any remaining cleanup over to *our* man. Meaning you've still got a full cell of Iraqis, probably already have word the Iraqi and family were waxed, and now have a full head of steam. Wondering who they can trust. Wondering if they just shouldn't go ahead and act out their wildest jihad fantasies. Let me further spell out the problem. One of your recruits bulls ahead of the program meant to secure our own bailing out as a ruse, or a trump card to hold back a potential armada of F-15s, stealths, whatever. Maybe, as we speak, not only the New York cell, but the other two cells, are locked and loaded, ready to hit the streets and take out as many infidels as they can. All this, worst case, well before I've secured our ride out of the country. Problem two. Our man is now putting himself on the front line to clean up the garbage before it gets any messier."

"So, he is already in New York?"

"Yes, Colonel, he's there. He has the scent and he's moving in, as we speak, to start the bloodbath. Another item—he's not going in solo. Meaning he's brought his own handpicked crew. What I'm saying, Colonel, New York is set to go hot. War."

"I'm still not seeing the problem."

"Goddamit. Reaper's face has been around the block. He's a freelancer, bouncing around from every alphabet-soup agency from here to Tombouctou. I'm talking wet work that would make anything you could produce in your neck of the woods—"

"Enough. You are concerned this Reaper or one of his operatives will be picked up by the FBI."

"And he knows about our organization, through both of our cutouts, since some of the recruitment came from my end. The man's not stupid. He wants to know who's buttering his bread and why. I believe he knows at least some of the score, since he's already versed in some of the finer points of the drill."

"Meaning he knows more than he should."

"Meaning he has his own ways of accessing information. Not even I have a full scorecard of who's on the team or who has said what exactly to who. Or maybe he and a few other guys are running around now, thinking they, too, could be expendables like the Iraqis they're marched in to eliminate. No payday for them? Well, maybe they have something on disk, copies of what they think they know about our own gig stashed all over God only knows where."

"Is he or any of his operatives aware of our immediate end game in this country?"

"Not that I'm aware of. The bottom line here, Colonel, is I've marched in my loose cannons to knock your loose cannons from Baghdad off the deck."

Chongjin kept his anger in check at the American's impertinence. "I understand the predicament. It was an unfortunate miscalculation on my part, regarding the depth of rage and hatred of my chosen cannon fodder. I didn't anticipate one of them becoming so impatient."

"You agree we could have a serious situation ready to blow up all to hell in our faces?"

"I'm telling you to stick to the original plan. No war was ever won, Mr. Turner, by not overcoming some adversity. Crisis breeds character, if a man has any character to begin with."

"Speaking of adversity, there's something else we need to discuss. Such as getting coordinated on the final leg of the logistics."

"Twenty-four hours, the major flies. It is very simple."

"Whoa..."

"Make it happen. I won't tolerate excuses or failure."

"So, when it hits the fan, you think we all just go skipping off into the sunset, no chance of a Sidewinder or Sparrow or even a Tomahawk come streaking up our collective ass. You know something else, I don't like being kept in the dark like this at the eleventh hour. Like I said, I don't even know the faces of all the players on the team."

"You will know them when the time comes."

"Yeah? How?"

Chongjin let the smile come back. "They will be the ones who are not shooting at you."

"Colonel, do you hear me laughing?"

Chongjin kept the smile. "Do your job. That's what you're paid for."

"You know, I almost bailed, skipped out on this madness."

"Really? You must reconsider your moments of sobriety. When you begin thinking too much, I suggest another shot of whiskey."

"Ha-ha. Too late for all of that, Colonel. I'm smart enough, or too scared of dying, I'm not sure which. I took your money. You have the pictures. I'm in to the finish line, for better or worse."

"I have more than a few dirty pictures of you in various unsavory scenarios. When you drink yourself to stupidity and carelessness, then fornicate, you should be careful how much classified information you are willing to divulge to a mere whore. Whores are likewise notorious thieves."

"I'll keep that in mind, Colonel, the next time you send Jun or Su Kim or whatever her name is to ply me with drinks."

Chongjin could feel his face flush with anger. "When this is finished and we are on our way with the other human cargo, you will have all the whores and whiskey you desire." He watched the American for any sudden moves as he slowly slipped a hand into his coat, withdrew a fat white envelope and dumped it in the man's lap. "There. That should put some steel into your backbone." Chongjin saw something dangerous flicker in the American's eyes as he hefted the envelope, tucked it away inside his coat. "You're welcome."

"You know, because of the coming program's finale, we're both aware I know a couple of the men in the so-called council. Contact with them has been unavoidable. I'm telling you they're fanatics, Colonel, bad if not worse than your Iraqi recruits. They're in this for more than just money or a good time or securing some tropical paradise where they can live out their golden years, scratching their bikini briefs."

"I am aware of the motivations of the men in the Phoenix Council. Their goals coincide with my own. If, however, in the future they begin to conflict..." He paused. "Again. Do your job. You'll have the necessary assistance inside the compound."

"The way you say that, I hear a threat between the lines."

"I don't threaten. I deliver. I produce results. I will contact you at some point within the next twelve hours. I'll want another situation report. My people and members of the council will soon be gathering at this cowboy farm—"

"Ranch house," Turner interrupted.

"Whatever. I, for one, am tired of living in cheap motels."

"That's your choice, considering all the cash you've thrown around."

"That money does not necessarily come from me."

"You're telling me the Iraqi leader has financed this operation from his pilfered oil billions."

"I'm telling you as much as you need to know. I'm telling you to make happen what you have been paid an outrageous sum for."

"Oh, I'll make it happen. Just ask yourself what if a squad of American fighter jets wants to blow us out of the sky?"

"Mr. Turner, this operation has not been put together, at considerable expense and risk to my own life, for me to come to your country and commit suicide." Chongjin's face turned to stone. He looked away, finished with this American who came to him practically bursting apart with doubt and anxiety. He didn't know it yet, of course, but Chongjin had no intention of keeping his promise of delivering a paradise of whores, booze and cash to this man. He looked forward to killing this American himself.

"That will be all for now. My men will see to it your

gun and your flask are returned to you on the way out."
He could feel that look again, boring into him through
the shaft of light. He pinned Turner with a cold measuring gaze of his own, then the American was up and
opening the door.

It was good to be alone at last, the colonel thought,
free from the face of weakness, the stink of whiskey and
fear. He needed time to think, puzzle through the logistics, work it out in his mind before he addressed the
council and the soldiers who would perform the real
dirty work.

There was much to do in the coming hours before he
initiated the first act of the plan. If every man who was
bought and paid for did his job, they would all succeed.
If someone squawked, bailed, ran to the military authorities in some weak attempt to save himself...

To fail was unthinkable. If he failed at this late stage,
it would simply mean he would die in this land of barbarians. That abhorrent notion alone, he hoped, should
be enough to see him pull off the first of many grim
chores to come.

The endgame was only just beginning.

THE FBI CREDENTIALS were every bit as phony as the
good senator's public charade. "Special Agent" Armand
Geller knew so much about the boy wonder's double
life, this ballyhooed Democrat's poster phenom as the
Mr. Family Man-Captain America of the new century,
it was all he could to keep from puking.

The man's life was a whopping fat sham. Welcome,
he thought, to politics.

Well, the scam was gaining momentum on two

fronts, both crucibles heating up, in fact, for the men
who doled out the lion's share of campaign contributions to the fine senator from Oklahoma. And the coming scorching heat the men of the Phoenix Council were
about to unleash was why he had come to the man's
gilded cowboy palace on the prairie.

After having zapped the entire security system, he
was now sitting in the senator's study, marveling at the
wonders of inheritance. From his seated post in the
leather-bound swivel chair behind a teakwood desk the
size of most offices, he took in the sprawling opulence,
all of it handed down to the only son, courtesy of the
old man, who had been the last of the cattle barons out
there. Some hefty petro bucks had likewise assisted
nicely in paving the boy wonder's golden road, Old
Man Winston having finagled his way into the state's oil
boom when the good times were rolling. Before the last
gusher had sputtered out, the Sterling fortune was reckoned in the neighborhood of ten billion and change,
climbing every day, of course, on interest alone.

That was then.

When the old man kicked off from liver failure, notorious for his love of Jack Daniel's, their fortune could
have fed Somalia and Ethiopia combined for a decade
to come. The main vacuum for the bucks was the kid,
who, incredible as it sounded, had squandered vast sums
on bad investments and a closet playboy Shambala until
he was down to a paltry twelve million. Then there was
the first marriage, shot to hell, because the only son
couldn't keep his pants zipped up. Then the always
helpful and concerned tribe of lawyers marched in, making sure the fair offended damsel was generously mol-

lified, lest she go public with a scandal. Then there was a private Lear, a Rolls-Royce, his own political meteor ride to the top, which required more siphoning of dough....

And the good folks of Oklahoma seemed to have forgiven him every bit of his foolishness and indulgence, chalking it up to "boys will be boys." Not only that, the Democrats were parading him around now to be their man of the hour for the next presidential election.

Only in America.

The kid still had plenty of toys left, and Geller felt a tad of envy flaming up as he scanned the room. Video games were spread around the massive study. Pool table in the adjoining game room, indoor pool, hot tub. And then there were the trophies—stuffed elk, black bear, musk ox, bighorn, all bagged, of course, by Pops Sterling.

Geller swiveled around, grinning up at the regal figure looming on the wall. The oil painting, he guessed, was fifteen by six, if it was an inch. Old Winston Sterling, looking majestic in a surly sort of way, long black frock coat, frilly cowboy shirt, with an old Springfield rifle clutched at port arms in big, raw-boned hands. The picture of rugged individualism, Mr. Wild West himself.

He heard the senator scuffling beyond double doors. Geller had already found the stainless-steel .45-caliber Colt in Sterling's top drawer. It made him wonder just how nervous Darren Sterling had become, or if the piece was being reserved, a .45-caliber round his last meal if all his present woes came crawling like vipers out of the hole to bite him on the ass.

He was leaning back, chucking the cannon up and down a few times, when he called out, "In here, Senator."

Geller was smiling, eyeing the pistol when he felt the man moving in, his wife calling out from somewhere, wondering what was going on. He heard him inform her he had been expecting a late-night guest, the silky voice smoothing it over, kindly asking her to return to bed.

The doors were closing, the lawmaker demanding, "Who—? How did you...?"

He went silent, noting a stranger was in possession of his gun, a man in black sitting in his chair, half-smiling but solemn, looking as if he was the harbinger of bad news and very bad news.

Which, Geller knew, was to a large extent true.

Geller looked up, measuring the man. The robe was bulging some in the midriff, indicating the senator liked his calories as much as he did his Korean prostitutes. Sterling, he noted, was doing some sizing up of his own, and plainly nervous about the view. Understandable, since Geller knew the senator was looking at quite the contrast. Where Sterling was soft, with a mane of white hair neatly coiffed from hundred-dollar styling jobs, Geller was a lean, mean SOB. He saw the senator balking at the sight of a skeletal face that looked carved by an ax, military-issue buzz cut, a high forehead that was mottled with purple splotches from some adversary's near miss with flying lead. Where Geller knew he was a killer, a warrior, the senator was little more than a walking pile of bullshit he'd just as soon step around.

But duty called, and the council had appointed the man to tighten the noose, iron out a few matters that needed to be brought to the senator's attention.

The guy was checking the alarm box on the wall, when Geller called out, "You're going to need another system."

"What did you do to it?"

Geller produced a small black box from inside his leather jacket. He smiled at the instrument, about the size of a cell phone. "Amazing what some of those guys at NSA can do."

"Is that what you are? An intelligence operative from the National Security Agency?"

"This thing emits a laser beam," Geller said, "a transference of heat, invisible to the naked eye. You don't want to get in front of this thing when it's turned on, I understand. Heat something like two thousand degrees Fahrenheit, light a guy up like a Roman candle, or so they say. Right before I called and woke you and the little lady up—extend my apologies to her, will you—to let you know we needed to chat, all I had to do was aim it at your surveillance camera out front, and the heat actually ripples through the whole system. Probably melted the guts of your whole main box to jelly. Oh, and you're also going to need a new pane of glass on the door leading out to the gazebo."

"What the—? My wife thought there was an intruder on the grounds. How am I going to explain any of this?"

Geller shrugged. "Just do what you do best, Senator. Lie."

The politician was stepping toward his desk, flacid features hardening best they could. "If you're here to try to intimidate me—"

Geller stopped the guy in midstride when he slowly trained the muzzle crotchward. "That's exactly what

I'm here to do." Geller took the sheaf of papers from another pocket, flung them on the desk. When the senator grabbed them, and before he could start squawking, Geller went on, "You can keep those. I helped myself to your laser printer on the way in. Amazing. You went from riches to rags, and now you're back to riches again. Look at those whopping offshore account numbers. Dummy companies, assumed identities." He whistled, the chuckle all rolling bass. "Made in the shade, son. Does the little missus know how much cash you have lying around?"

"What is it you want?"

"I also have some rather interesting pictures of you and a lady friend—I believe her name is Su Lin?" He saw the flash of anger wrestling against the shame in his eyes.

The guy was shaking now, but seemed unable to move, take his eyes off the gun aimed at his family jewels. "Do you mind? You're making me..."

"Nervous? Sorry. That is kind of rude of me." He chuckled, smiled, lost the look and put an edge to his voice as he set the pistol in front of him. "Here's the short and the bitter. I was sent here by some very powerful men to remind you that your soul has already been bought and paid for. You are going to return to the Hill. There is a certain bill your colleagues have been trying to grease up and slide through."

"Concerning normalizing relations with North Korea? The exchange program of technology if the North Koreans agree to go less militant?"

"You are going to fight it, make the stand, charm the pants off them, whatever you have to do or say to make folks think you've lost your marbles."

The lawmaker was a scripted act, Geller comparing him to a used-car salesman, always on the con, looking to schmooze it out until he had the upper hand. Sterling fell into the contrived role he was famous for in front of the cameras or the Sunday-morning talking-head shows. "Let me speak quite frankly here. There are a few points on that matter that never fit, which I strongly urge you to reconsider. I suggest we take a look at the whole picture first before I attempt to sell..."

"I understand your dilemma."

"How can I be expected to take some hawkish stand that's completely out of character with my party's position on North Korea?"

"Senator," Geller said, rising and sidling a few feet to the side. "You are on our need-to-know leash. Period. The beauty of it is that in a matter of days, perhaps even less, your contradictory position is going to make you a hero. You are going to be leading the pack, a genius, no less, who gets to shout out loud, 'I told you so.'"

"It still doesn't make sense."

"Where you're concerned, it doesn't need to. The Senate is split nearly in half on this package. You are part of the Committee on Foreign Intelligence, head of a subcommittee that deals with relations between the U.S. and both Koreas. This much I will tell you. Several of your esteemed colleagues have become fallen angels like yourself, their own wings so badly soiled, a few are worse off than what we have on you, if you can believe such a thing. They are playing ball with the people I represent or else certain embarrassing matters go before the public forum. No names at this time, but let's just say the real power I represent has proof of various improprieties involving interns, page boys, like that. We even have the dirt on one of your colleagues who enjoys huffing up a little cocaine now and then."

"Preposterous!"

"It's fact. By the way, I suggest you pack up, Darren. You're going to want to be out of this neighborhood anyway. Send the little lady on a long trip while you're at it."

"What does that mean?"

"Once you're back in Washington, you will be contacted with further instructions." Geller walked out from behind the desk, the lawmaker glancing from the gun to his course. He almost hoped the guy went for it, give him an excuse to put his Glock .45ACP to work. "Oh, and Su Lin? She'll be at the Ramada at Tysons, just in case you get the itch. Under the name Jane Fonda." Sterling didn't get the humor, the guy all but locked up in the misery of his own creation. "I'll show myself out."

"And that's it?"

"For now."

4

The third sighting of the black van kicked the Executioner into high alert. It was lights-out this time around, as the vehicle swung off Atlantic Avenue and eased into an alley between the Lebanese taverna on the FBI's hot list and a chain of apartment buildings gone to seed.

"No drive-by this time. And that's not one of ours. What do you think?"

"Not sure," Bolan said.

"Third time's the charm? Those windows, by the way, are illegally tinted. The more I watch this place, the bigger knot I get in my gut. Guys coming and going. Same guys, like they're out for a stroll, wanting to check the sights, see who's watching the store. Stroll back in, report to the boss."

Bolan had plenty of thoughts on the subject, but kept quiet in the shotgun seat of the Crown Victoria. A heightened sense of combat readiness always put the soldier in a mode to let actions do the talking for him. On the other hand, Special Agent Marcus Broadwater seemed to feel the need to hear his own voice, whether from bottled adrenaline, too much coffee or muscles stiff from hours of being cramped behind the wheel on both roving and sitting surveillance, Bolan couldn't say. He went on to inform Bolan a number of items the soldier already knew. Such as the late hour, a full house of Arabs still inside the restaurant. Such as the day's rousting of the occupants inside, meant to sweat any guilty ones into showing a dirty hand or head for the nearest subway for slaughter act two.

So far no takers for an absolute revelation that there was a terrorist congregation holed up in the block's favorite Mideast eatery.

Up to that point too many hours had hung floating in limbo, but the soldier had a gut churning over with a familiar grim anticipation it was about to hit the fan. Without fail, waiting was always something of a grueling test before the action kicked in to separate the givers from the takers in the ultimate of exams. He was armed with his trusty Beretta 93-R in shoulder rigging for starters, if and when the terror dragons starting breathing fire his way. The .44 Magnum Desert Eagle, tied down on his hip, was visible enough beneath the tail of his loose-fitting windbreaker to have drawn more than a passing curious eye from Broadwater. And what was stashed away in the nylon war bag in the Crown Vic's trunk definitely bucked the standards for field hardware outlined in the Justice manual. Uzi submachine gun, enough extra clips to field a full squad of commandos charging an enemy's door, and that was just for warm-ups. Throw in a pouch stuffed with an assortment of frag, flash-stun and incendiary grenades, a SPAS-12 autoshotgun to boot, twenty pounds of C-4 just in case. Any reasonable homegrown G-man would wonder if

Special Agent Belasko hadn't come to New York to start full-scale urban war.

Then there was a combat harness and blacksuit, the Marine Ka-bar knife in a sheath around his lower leg, if he needed a silent, up-close takedown or two on the way in to the real room-clearing butcher's work. Aside from the killing goodies, Brognola had handed Bolan the keys to his own safehouse, a brownstone in trendy Brooklyn Heights. There, the soldier had access to spare weapons, a sat-link with fax modem, all the high-tech toys to keep him tied to the big Fed and Stony Man Farm.

Many hours ago all the details were ironed out to get the soldier there, ready and waiting as dawn crept around the corner. After a military shuttle to JFK, the soldier had been whisked by a Justice courier to a joint special task force in a Brooklyn office. No one on the home team had much to go on. Standard briefings had earlier struck Bolan as next to window dressing over the real problem, as far as any decent leads that would land them on the doorstep of whatever terrorists in hiding remained in the cell. If there was a cell.

Call it bureaucratic wrangling. Tag it as the wheels of promotion turning faster than a lower-ranking agent's pay raise, or simply folks at the top of the hierarchy a little gun-shy as they had hot flashes of careers getting flushed down the old toilet if they bulled ahead and made the tough call, afraid of stepping on toes connected to ass they might have kiss the next day. Whatever, some doubt, incredible as it sounded, echoed down the rank and file about the existence of a terror machine getting itself gassed up to go on high-octane hate.

Bolan decided to stick with the grunts, the kind of men who usually had their noses chasing the scent on the street, running on a hunch provided him by a few special agents he handpicked to assist him in combing the perimeters of any hives swarming with possible lunatics poised to burn down half of New York. The gist of it from his chosen foot soldiers, he recalled, was that the Lebanese taverna was where one of the day's two mystery Arab casualties had worked as a waiter. The FBI had marched in the local health inspectors, the INS going to bat next, all of it designed to rattle cages or get the fishing expedition started with a few choice pieces of chum tossed into a suspected pool of human sharks. Then, while the nerves were still jangling from top to bottom, the Feds weighed in behind the whole mass of officialdom to grill and drill the owner and various and sundry employees and their families. It was borderline unconstitutional, letting the insinuations the Arab-Americans knew more than they were telling hang like a radioactive cloud. But given the day's horrific slaughter on a commuter train, with NYPD blue howling for justified vengeance and the families of the victims demanding answers, the FBI had taken off the gloves. According to his ride, every single Arab male they questioned at the Lebanese taverna was nervous, evasive as hell on many of the finer points during Q and A. That alone didn't mean much, but then every single passport checked them out as either Jordanian or Lebanese nationals. And in Bolan's hard experience, if there was nothing to hide, why all the irradiated nerves and talking out of both sides of the mouth? He hadn't been on hand for the FBI's session on attitude readjustment, but Broadwater's synopsis and personal gut feeling led him to strongly suspect they were right now where the action was.

Or about to go down.

The husky black agent kept his sights trained on the darkened restaurant facade. "Notice you don't say much. Can't be the company you keep, since you asked for me yourself."

Bolan said nothing.

"I get the impression, Special Agent Belasko," he said, using Bolan's alias, "you're not real big on this partner thing. Something telling me we're not destined to be a Glover and Gibson act."

"Nothing personal."

Broadwater sounded off a grunt that could have meant anything or nothing. Whatever the man's sentiment, Bolan had nothing but the highest regard for any law-enforcement official, federal or otherwise. Unless he missed his guess, an elimination game was on the table. The stakes were about to go off the chart, with unknown killers moving in to storm the taverna. He could be sure Broadwater, the FBI and Justice agents on stakeout detail had wives and families to think about beyond the job. Risk, of course, and the possibility of the ultimate sacrifice were always inherent when it came down to lawmen performing their duty, tracking and corraling the bad guys, even in the line of fire. Bolan wasn't looking to cowboy the play. But he didn't intend to see any personal assistance provided him by the FBI and Justice, courtesy of Brognola's standing order, thrown into a firefight that would see them leaving behind grieving widows and fatherless children. Plain and simple, Bolan wanted his team there for field intelligence and support. The Executioner knew he was the one best suited to do any shooting, if a gunfight erupted. He figured Broadwater wouldn't especially cater to what he might see as a patronizing or arrogant point of view, so Bolan kept the line of thought to himself.

The soldier began thinking he might have to crash through the front door, bulldoze in to take care of business the old-fashioned way. "When you were there earlier, what was the layout?"

Broadwater's brow creased, hinting at a frown, the man obviously not caring to be the one doing all the giving. "Dining room, wall-to-wall bar on the west side. Posh and spacious spread all around. No expert, but I caught a view of some of the Mideast trimmings, down to a hanging scimitar, some kind of golden bull smack in the middle of main dining, like something maybe the ancient Babylonians would pray to. Ambiance, who knows. Kitchen was your standard stainless steel, walk-ins, freezer, like that. Back room, though, made me think we had something a little more than your usual mom-and-pop dining establishment feeding the regular Arab American clientele."

"How so?"

"They had the backgammon boards out in plain sight, but they have a long table in there, couple dozen chairs scattered around, everything looking too neat and clean for appearance's sake. I'm thinking the back room is for war council."

Likewise that was Bolan's take. "You said there were families upstairs?"

"Right."

"How many women and children?"

"Didn't take a head count, but it looked like they could have packed half of Beirut upstairs just over the dining room. Place was renovated about two years ago. I found out Lebanese contractors did all the additions. From the outside itself, it looks like half an apartment complex fanning out from the restaurant. Inside...who knows? The way it feels to me, I'm thinking maybe somebody had in mind all along to bring over half their country."

"What else?"

"Like what?"

"Did you go upstairs? Go inside any storerooms? Maybe a room that didn't look like it quite belonged there in what you called a war council?"

Bolan was thinking weapons cache, some hidden chamber that housed a communications layout.

"We weren't exactly armed with a search warrant."

"Gotcha."

"The judge did sign off for a phone tap."

"That call to Chicago, you mentioned."

"Right. Traced it to a pay phone on Fifty-ninth near Midway Airport. Another call, two hours ago from here. Again a pay phone, this one on the other side of town near the University of Chicago. You know this already. Mind me asking what you're thinking?"

"I'm thinking somebody needs to alert the Chicago field office. I'm thinking problems."

"This whole town's already under the military equivalent of ThreatCon Delta. Silent alarm, that is, security beefed up from the Statue of Liberty, clear out to Plum Island Animal Disease Center, I'm told. Chicago's al-

ready gotten the bad vibes we're feeling about those two
calls. Right now I'm more worried about my home-
town. If this thing is about some terrorist cells reaching
from here to Chicago...that is what you're implying?"

"Something tells me we're about to find out, Agent
Broadwater. Pop the trunk for me, will you?"

"Where you off to?"

"Taking a walk."

"By yourself?"

"Right."

"And leave me to keep the meter running?"

"I'll stay in touch."

"What the hell am I, Belasko, just overpaid taxi service?"

Bolan kept his look neutral. "Stay put unless you
hear otherwise. Have the other units fan out, make it
about two blocks apart, and sit tight. All units on Tac
One. You and me on Tac Two."

Broadwater muttered something to himself, but knew
better than to push it, since the field director had handed
down orders that came straight from the Justice Department.

Bolan was out the door, the trunk popping up. He decided to skip the harness, but made himself ready to go
full tactical just the same. The Uzi came out of the war
bag first, a small nylon pouch up and slung next over
the soldier's shoulder, stuffed with spare 40-round clips
in 9 mm Parabellum. One frag, one flash-stun grenade
dumped into the pocket of his windbreaker. He checked
the narrow maw of an alley that would allow him to approach the taverna from the east side at the back. The
Executioner chambered the first round in the Uzi, ig-

nored Broadwater's scowl and headed across the street. It was little more than the usual gut feeling, but it was a rare solar eclipse when combat instinct let Bolan down.

Stoked for this slice of predawn Brooklyn to blow into a noisy crucible of hell on earth, the Executioner gathered momentum and melted into the momentarily friendly cloak of the deep shadows.

HUSAT AL-MAHLID HEARD the voice of the North Korean colonel invading his own angry thoughts as he listened to the squawking around him.

"I thought they were supposed to protect us! Not slaughter our friends and their families if they believed they would be exposed to American authorities!"

And the voice floated in, taking him back in time.

"Take heed. The waiting for word from my end may fray your nerves, perhaps turn some of you against the others. One of you may even decide his life and the lives of his very family are more important than the mission...."

His memories was interrupted by his colleagues.

"I agree with Mushadah. Our alleged benefactors have become more of a threat to our lives than those FBI crows who descended on us today."

"And what is to become of all of us now that the North Koreans see us as liabilities? Will they march in their ninja assassins in the middle of the night to execute us in turn?"

"Many of us have families. I, for one, do not care if I martyr myself, but if I wanted to see my family butchered, I could have remained in Iraq, wandering about, risking a laser-guided bomb from the American buzzards!"

Dangerous talk. Even though they squabbled among themselves in Arabic, Mahlid was aware the FBI jack- als were clever enough to have wired the room when they had strolled around earlier, wearing their collective mask of indifference, grunting out some cool appraisal of the area, but he knew better. They couldn't hide their suspicion. It rang through, the clang of a death knell, in every question they had put to them.

"That Hasab did what he did is no fault of his own."

"He was tired of waiting. Wondering. Worrying."

"Each of us is committed to jihad, but I won't sit still while the Koreans who have proclaimed allegiance to our own cause circle in like buzzards for the feast."

"Then what are we to do?"

"We take up arms and march out into the streets."

"I agree. But what if, like Hasab, we are martyred be- fore our time in the eyes of the Koreans! These dogs have proved treacherous. Our families shouldn't be marked for execution, murdered in a foreign land like Saddam's family."

"It is a blasphemous thing indeed for these foreign- ers to slay our families."

"Allah will not forgive us if we allow our families to be killed by vipers who view us as nothing but an alba- tross to their plans."

"And what, may I ask, is this great plan of theirs?"

Mahlid closed his eyes, drawing on his cigarette. As was his right and duty, he claimed the seat at the head of the table. This was a war council, a gathering of holy warriors, all of them sworn to a sacred duty, prepared long ago to sacrifice their own lives, committed solely to taking fifty or more infidel eyes for every eye plucked by American vultures during the Gulf War. Only now it was all beginning to sound more to him like one of those wretched American talk shows where infidel families screeched and cursed each other over sins of the flesh. Perhaps, he thought, America had contaminated their souls, the tough hide of the warriors he once knew sloughed off like so much shedding of a snake, baring now some underlying weakness due to exposure of this land's many cursed temptations and contradictions.

As their chosen leader, he could indulge the squawking up to a point. At the moment he viewed himself much like a father would quietly referee bickering between sons, hoping they could resolve their differences or put aside their fear and anger on their own before he stepped up and started the serious backhanding. For one, he knew far more details on the mission than the others, but he had been warned to keep many secrets to himself. Loose talk and backbiting would serve no purpose now but to guarantee some reckless course of action.

He was one of the first to be funneled through Lebanon, a country, he knew, that had become a factory for phony passports, visas and the exporting of freedom fighters through certain prearranged filter channels designed by various intelligence agencies. Getting in wasn't the problem, nor was building the false fronts of lives as humble immigrants seeking only a slice of the pie that was the so-called American dream. When they arrived here, yes, their role was to play out the honest and diligent pursuit of a better way of life. It was all, of course, simply a ruse leading to judgment day. Had he known then what he knew now, though, he would have demanded up front from their sponsors a guaranteed concession that if one of their own did something to jeopardize the mission, they would handle it on their own.

Twenty-nine men, including himself, were Tikritis, hailing from Iraq's desert soil. He wondered what the great leader would think now if he could hear them clucking about like so many old hens. It was disgraceful. There was more blood on the hands of these men than perhaps the entire Republican Guard or the special-forces brigades had shed during the rape of Kuwait. He opened his eyes, peering into the hanging clouds of cigarette smoke, hoping his extended bout of silence would calm the anxious talk.

"We have been abandoned. Our enemies are now anyone who is outside this room."

So much for patience.

He knew them all by name, deed and prior life. Abdullah and Jabal were in the cleansing business after the war against the infidels, gassing countless sprawling Kurdish villages so thoroughly that it was believed every living thing, down to plant life, or a scorpion in its hole, had been wiped off the face of the desert. Muhmad and Mohammed were the personal executioners in the service. They shot generals dead in cabinet meetings, or pumped a wayward son-in-law full of bullets on the whim of their leader himself. So Mahlid understood, then, how execution could become the order of the day, when treachery and backstabbing walked the shadows, hand in hand. A part of him understood the thinking of the North Koreans, how certain messes, once made, could only be cleaned up with one degree of finality. Still, he wasn't about to sit by and watch the foreigners butcher his own people in this filthy land.

A moment of silence was on the verge of dropping over the room as Mahlid found several of the elders looking his way, as if noticing him for the first time, waiting now on words of wisdom. A few of the younger Tikritis babbled on, but their voices trailed off as heads swiveled about, nervous hands toyed with cigarettes, lifted coffee cups. Granted, he was feeling the heat of his own paranoia, having sounded the alarm himself, but keeping up appearances while so doing. In calm and orderly fashion, he removed every pistol, subgun or rocket launcher, every brick of plastic explosive from different hiding spots around the restaurant. Some had chosen to keep pistols and subguns within easy grasp on the table, as if fearing the vaunted FBI would come crashing through the door any moment, while the bulk of the mother lode was heaped at the base of the wall. The fact that the duffel bags that would carry the weapons and explosives through the city were now gathered in the room should have told them he had already made his decision. Perhaps they simply needed a reminder of who and what they were, reassurance beefing up faltering nerve from the voice of authority.

"I am disappointed in what I am hearing." He wandered a disapproving eye down the table as the younger ones fidgeted with cups and cigarettes, glancing about as if believing their self-appointed Mahdi must be referring to someone else. "We are of the Tikriti clan. It is believed we are related to the very blood of our great leader. We are men, we are warriors, not a bunch of old hags fretting about matters which cannot be changed. Not even Allah, it has been said, can change the past. Hasab did what he did, and he has gone already to his reward. Now..." He paused, the elder lion about to rise up among the pride, the passion for the hunt building a storm in his eyes. "It has always been my call to make and I have made the decision. Our actions will affect our families, but I pray and I believe in my heart Allah will protect and provide for them. What we are going to do will also see grave consequences for the other cells beyond this city. I can only pray for them, that they, too, see that we must not become puppets of fate dictated by the whims of the Koreans. No more. I believe the other cells will take initiative, knowing in their hearts that we didn't come to this country to die for whatever is the cause of the Koreans. We didn't come to this accursed land of jackals and vipers to see our jihad fail. The time has come. In a few short minutes we will leave here and go meet our holy destiny. You will be allowed to pray one last time. You won't be allowed to say goodbye to your families lest they wail and gnash their teeth and attempt to change your hearts."

He stabbed out the cigarette, his wide nostrils flaring, the great bull riled up. "We will leave here in twos and threes. We will look at the map of this city, and I will grant each of you a target of your choosing. Remember, after what Hasab did, the police will be out everywhere. They wear body armor. They may attempt to shoot you on sight, since this country seems to think," he said, and smiled, "all of us are crazed terrorists. I suggest," he said, recalling vaguely what the Korean colonel had told them, "when you see a policeman you shoot first. Shoot for the head. If that is unsuccessful, I don't believe their body armor covers the groin area or the legs. Let us rise, let us pray to Allah for success and for glory in his name. And then we will prepare to leave. Our war against the Great Satan has only just begun."

5

His real name was Robert Bowen, and normally he loved New York. It was a big, mean, dirty mother of a town.

New York had attitude.

In terms of sprawl, population density and the total sweet ambiance of rampant desperate criminal intent in all five boroughs, he had to rank it up there with, say, Mexico City, Calcutta, Bangkok. The nice thing about urban jungles, he knew, there was always work for the freelancing disposal artist with his degree of talent, not to mention plenty of places to hide the bodies. Another plus about concrete battlefields was general civilian apathy, that see-no-evil act after the violence and mayhem, so muddied or doctored up by conflicting eyewitness accounts that homicide detectives were usually left shaking their heads.

Despite the call now over the secured line, forced to soothe tweaked nerves at the worst possible time, he briefly hashed over the good old days, wishing to hell and back it could all be what it once was.

Clean and simple.

When the Five Families owned the town, lock, stock and barrel, he thought. When graft and corruption was the accepted routine from city hall down to a beat cop with alimony and six kids. Back then, when cash got tight, or the CIA brass was feeling its knees buckle before some Senate Committee on Intelligence and black ops went under a political microscope, he'd struck out on his own, used his considerable skills in the disposal business to help those New Yorkers who could help him.

Of course, that was the past. The present New York wasn't offering too many attractive propositions. He needed to get refocused, or his final view of the town would be from behind bars, if he even got that lucky. No amount of wistful yearning and recollection of past bloodshed, bodies dumped in the East River and numbered accounts swimming in six figures would steer them to the other side of the job ahead.

The voice on the cell phone was a reminder of where the line began to blur when it came down to national security, every shade in between black ops and standard military operations. Spookdom always wanted instant results, no delays, no excuses, especially when the heat was cranked up on their rear ends. A hit like this took time, planning and an exit strategy, none of which he had. It was straight bulldoze work, and he was thinking his original asking price of a cool million was next to minimum wage. Naturally he'd siphoned off the lion's share for this outing, handing a quarter of it off to be split eleven ways. On the upshot, and to their credit, there'd been little squawking about the division of funds from his crew. But this crew had been on around-the-clock call, weeks before the snatch of the rocket genius, Thomas Shaw. They were grateful, it seemed, just to have work, to get back in the game, overwhelming risk, poor pay and all.

Beyond the Turner's fever pitch for a rush job, there was a second problem, he thought, which was the FBI convention in the neighborhood.

Bowen, aka the Reaper, told his wheelman, Zervic, to park, then barked back into the cellular. "I'll call you when it's done. I understand." He heard he might be needed in Chicago for much the same disposal routine, so he was to stick close to the phone. The heat was on. If he could have reached through to the other side and throttled the guy...

Despite every scanner, radio and surveillance gadget available to black ops in scaled-down package in back of the van, he feared a ten-year-old kid with a fax modem and access to the Internet could plug in and triangulate their location. It would take a little more than that, he knew, but those exaggerated thoughts were urging him to end this conversation.

"I'll be in touch. We'll talk about it," he growled. "Let me take care of one fucking mess for you at a time." Hanging up, he said to no one in particular, "Guy probably still believes in Santa Claus and the tooth fairy."

"And Elvis is still alive," Cutler added.

"And the mother ship really did take Mulder," Stillwell said.

Some chuckles from behind his seat, but he knew they were all business. Dressed in black and completely harnessed, they were settling com-links in place, threading sound suppressors on HK MP-5 submachine guns.

A love tap or two on the slides of Glock .45ACPs, and the first round was chambered in side arms.

Down to business, good to go, he thought. The Reaper's Wild Bunch.

He checked the closed steel door to the target area. According to his local intel source who had already done the recon work, that would be the back service entrance. The problem now was he had virtually no idea how the interior unfolded. Another problem was the number of both combatants and noncombatants. In that regard, if it could walk, it was fair game. Scratch one headache then, since he had plenty of lead aspirin to spare.

It was seat of the pants, just the same, but it wouldn't be the first time he had to wing it when called upon by the shadow lords who wrapped themselves up in the holy shroud of national security. On the upside he knew some of the particulars on the DIA man's end of things, since he never went into any gig shooting deaf, dumb and blind. Since knowledge was power, he had spread a few items about the big play out in Oklahoma to a few of his men he could trust with absolute certainty. Guys who been down the black-ops road with him in some Third World hellhole and lived to chuckle out the war stories over beer and broads. He never went into a gig without a few juicy details to back him up, some extortion ace in the hole, just in case he was deemed expendable after cleaning up the other guy's mess.

Bowen took up his own HK subgun, fixed the sound suppressor. "One baseball each, gentlemen. Give me a flash-bang on top of mine. If we need more than that for this job, we won't be coming out." A sheet of inky black seemed to hang over the alley in both directions, nothing but shabby apartment complexes locked together or separated by service alleys for the garbagemen. They were all alone. Still, it was looking and feeling too easy.

Once the frags, plus one flash-stun, were handed out and clipped to webbing, Bowen addressed his crew, Zervic first. "We've seen the federal Ringling Brothers have come to town. Eyes wide open, Zervic. Battering Ram Two is in the vicinity. First glimpse we're going to have badges up our six, call them in and have them unload everything they've got."

"Aye, aye, skipper."

Bowen turned to the four men he would go through the door with. "Cutler. That golf ball ready?"

Cutler held up the glob of plastique, primed with detonator and cord. "Your razor's good to cut, boss."

"I go through first, standard high and low. Cutler, you're with me. I'm told these boys brought the harem, gentlemen, kids, too. All of it goes down. Let's rock."

And the Reaper was out the door, leading his black-clad wraithes across the alley. Time, he thought, to deliver a lesson in attitude readjustment. Just maybe, he hoped, as he closed on the door, this would go down, little fuss and muss. He hadn't gone over the details for his bonus fee on this job, but a clean sweep would go a long way toward brightening the rainbow of retirement he envisioned.

A river of blood first, a sea of cash later.

THE HARDMEN GOT it started with a bang. A swift shadow, advancing double time, and Bolan had the gap shaved to easy striking distance when the plastic explosive blew in the door on a clap of thunder. They were official-looking enough, com-links and HK MP-5 sub-guns fixed with sound suppressors, the whole unit moving as one with precision military bearing as they broke for the charge, two high, two low, one lagger to watch their six. Could have nearly passed themselves off as a legit SWAT unit, but Bolan suspected otherwise. Despite interagency rivalry with matching rhino-sized egos forever striving for the brass ring of the big collar, Bolan knew any official raid would have been brought to the attention of Broadwater's superiors.

In this case, silence on the official end was not golden.

This was a killing crew, and they were through the smoke and inside just as Bolan was bringing the Uzi to bear on the ghost assassins who had the drill down. The three *W*s—who, what and why—were shelved as the soldier marched ahead, scoping the van. He was thinking that with any luck at all he could bag a gunner or any mark fortunate to make it through the coming massacre when the van with all of the antennae appeared.

With the engine running, Bolan knew the crew had left behind the wheelman, maybe another gun or two in back to help hold down the fort in the alley. Smart money told the soldier their eyes and ears were on the horn, alerting the hitters that a threat of unknown origin had made the scene. The van was practically rocking now, the watcher agitated, no doubt, Bolan imagining the guy was a human pinball shooting around on his seat, one hand on the blower, another one grabbing up hardware to make a stand.

Combat radar blipping off the screen, Bolan anticipated what happened next. He was veering across the

alley, going for temporary shelter from any storm behind the van, Uzi up and aimed at the doorway, when
the trailing gunner popped up. The hardman was already
in Bolan's full view, going for the easy tag, his muffled
subgun slicing lines through the drifting smoke.

Bolan shot from the hip on the fly, the Uzi rising as
held back on the trigger, and washed the fusillade
around the doorway. Puffs of dark vapor took to the air,
the shooter twitching in the doorway, absorbing hot
lead. No Kevlar, then. The hardman was still fighting
off the inevitable, grunting and flinging wild rounds
that went skidding off the wall beyond Bolan. A few
more 9 mm flesh shredders stuttered on, and the Executioner had the shooter waxed, limbs folding as the figure dropped in a crunch.

The wheelman jumped into the act next. Bolan
glimpsed the van lurching as the driver dropped it into
Reverse, going for instant roadkill. The soldier was out
and running, angling up the side of the van for the killshot. Any slower on the break and Bolan knew he would
have been bowled down, squashed. The Uzi chattered
out long, angry volumes as Bolan's lead swarm im-
ploded the window on the driver's face. He couldn't tell
if he'd scored, but a dark cloud was ballooning up the
hole he'd blown in, and the soldier kept grim hope alive.
The van was swerving to starboard, then the aft slammed
into the wall on a screech of metal and shattered glass.

The Executioner stepped up, Uzi spraying the windshield, right to left and back. The whole sheet came
apart and blew lethal glass bits through the interior at
gale force. He burned up the clip, hosing the interior,
then stole a second to view the shattered ruins of the

wheelman's skull, gray matter dribbling across the dashboard. Some sparks were jumping around in back, the snapping fireworks from behind the dead man telling the soldier he'd fairly gutted their communication and surveillance system.

Inside they were rocking and rolling beyond the battered doorway. It was a hellish racket of shouting, autofire and a thundering crunch of someone bent on bringing down the roof with a grenade.

The Lebanese taverna had just turned hotter than hell.

The first real danger, Bolan knew, slapping home a fresh 40-round clip into his Uzi, would be the charge in, running up on the rear of the blacksuited shooters without getting cut to ribbons before he fired the next round. Soon enough there would be more Feds, more blue and more SWAT barreling onto the battle zone. Throw in choppers, urban tanks, various departmental and precinct captains and commanders firing off their two cents over bullhorns....

This one, the Executioner suspected, was poised to rocket right off the ugly meter.

The tide of bellicosity rose in rock-concert decibels next when Broadwater's voice came booming over the soldier's tac radio.

"Belasko! Goddammit, Belasko, talk to me. Tell me that's not the sound of gunfire I hear. Tell me those aren't grenades I'm hearing."

Bolan threw himself against the wall, hugging close to his point of penetration. The bedlam was rising to new levels of fury, a babble of voices swelling the doorway, competing for the ceaseless roar of automatic weapons. The soldier knew he'd have to deal with

Broadwater sooner or later. Now was the worst of times, but Bolan unclipped the handheld.

"Stay put, Broadwater!"

"What?"

"Have our units seal off a perimeter. When the locals show up, flash your badge, grab someone by the scruff of his neck, whatever it takes. No one on our side is to crash this building."

"Are you nuts? I'm hearing World War III less than fifty feet from where I sit!"

"That's an order, Broadwater. I'm a little busy right now. Later."

"Whoa, wait a goddamn—"

It was a definite stretch to assume Broadwater could hold back the cavalry, much less sit on the sidelines while half the neighborhood threatened to get shot up to hell. In the heat of the moment, Bolan had neglected to mention that one of the home team was going inside. Should SWAT and whoever else came barging into the firefight...

Well, Bolan could only hope for the best as far as not ending up a friendly casualty.

No time to ponder what might happen.

The soldier went low, scoping out the way in. Muzzle-flashes were winking like Christmas lights, shadows wanting to come into view but the corridor angled to the right. The way in was wide enough, and Bolan heard the new round of howling, bodies thudding next, the dead, no doubt, already stacking up somewhere ahead.

The Executioner drew a deep breath, let it go, then surged around the corner, charging full bore into the slaughterhouse.

6

They were in and moving hard, a thundering juggernaut, and Bowen was itching to get the good times rolling. There was no such thing as overkill in the Reaper's unwritten tactical manual. The sight of blood, and lots of it, always got the juices running. The length of his body, scalp to toes, was feeling like one giant overheated radiator set to blow when the killing started.

The usual high.

They went for the gusto right off, not missing a beat, rounding the corner and hitting the first five Iraqis with extended raking bursts of autofire as soon as the jihad troops started barging out the doors to what Bowen guessed was their version of a war room. The first wave was ventilated to human sieves, lead dropping them hard, when the Reaper saw they were quickly getting their act together, grabbing up an international hodgepodge of weapons, swarthy guys streaming for the stockpile in the corner, howling in their native tongue. Everything from Uzis to AK-47s, Glocks to Makarovs, Spectre subguns and Ingrams were coming into play.

"Frag 'em!"

Three grenades aided the Reaper and his Wild
Bunch. The bodies of their first victims had been
pounded to the floor where the swing doors led to the
kitchen, blood running like burst faucets thanks to the
slice-and-dice treatment. It was mighty kind of them,
Bowen thought, to fall so they could keep the doors
wedged open, allowing him an easy toss. Frag one was
armed and sailing into the kitchen as a group of five
came streaming into view near a long stainless-steel
counter used for food prepping. They were ducking
autofire when the blast went off in their faces.

They were hell-bent on going down with the house,
jihad troops bouncing off each other, holding back on
triggers, bellowing out the rage, spraying and praying.
They came close. Bowen was flinching as scorching
lead went stinging over his scalp. Two more frag explosions tore through the war room, the shrieking of
men getting shredded by countless lethal steel bits like
classic rock to his ears.

An arm, sheared off at the shoulder, came whirling
out of the smoke, skidding past Bowen's position at the
corner. There was pounding of feet from some point
above. That would be the families of some of the jihad
boys, women and kids, crying out in panic, stampeding
around the second floor, wondering what was happening. At best, they would provide human armor on the
way out. Either way, he knew they were marked for permanent deportation.

Then it turned even dicier, the world about to fall
apart, his instincts having already warned him it had
been too easy, too quiet on the way in. And Bowen
heard Zervic alerting them to an intruder coming for

their rear. A big dark guy with an Uzi subgun. It didn't quite sound like standard FBI hardware to him, but it was another headache to deal with, just the same. He kept hugging the corner, catching sight of more Iraqis breaking through the kitchen, triggering weapons on the fly. It cost him a critical second, bullets whizzing all around, drumming the wall, but Bowen got his bearings, saw that the hallway they'd secured as a firepoint led out to the dining room. If they gained access to the dining area, and now with an unknown hostile—or even a platoon of Feds storming the place—they'd be hemmed in, soon to be chopped up into dog meat.

Bowen barked out the order for Stillwell to fall back and take care of their mystery guest. Bullets were snapping the air around Reaper and crew like a buzzing swarm of wasps, rounds gouging furrows through the wood paneling, missing their scalps by millimeters. He signaled for Cutler and Simmons to move out for the dining room, gave the order for another round of frags. That left him and Tyler to nail it down in the war room.

Cutler and Simmons hauled it for the short run leading to the dining area, firing in unison as they made the far corner, one high, one low.

Teamwork.

Bowen went back to work, hit the kitchen with a long stream of 9 mm lead, scored another jihad flunky, sent him crashing through pots and pans while the storm chased the runners toward the dining room to get a lead greeting by his troops down there. A fresh magazine slapped home, cocked and locked, he was rolling for the smoke cloud when he suddenly discovered he was alone. Glancing over his shoulder he saw Tyler pitching to the floor, the back of his skull blown off. The direction of the killshot told Bowen he was in all likelihood down two more men beyond Tyler.

Mr. Uzi was on the march, he knew, coming to join the fun and games.

IT WOULD PROVE a colossal waste, a sorry and unseemly death of the jihad dream, if they all went down under the FBI guns. Mahlid wasn't about to see all the blood, sweat and toil go down the toilet simply because he'd neglected to post a few lookouts. Part of the failure was certainly his to bear, but there was no time for regret, any degree of mental self-flagellation that might cost him more than a place of business. Either way, the restaurant was finished, and they were bailing.

Which looked a definite reach for the stars at the moment, considering the amount of ass getting kicked by their mystery invaders.

Whatever was happening, it was all the sound and fury of hell unleashed, and none of it was good. The enemy had blown the back door, sounding the alarm to get them jumping to their feet and grabbing up the hardware. Four, maybe five of his men had bulled out the door of the war room, perhaps pumped by his steely words of wisdom moments earlier, only to go down in the opening rounds. These killing sweeps were so long and overextended, the Iraqi leader knew something was wrong with the black-garbed invaders. It was almost as if they were killing his men with glee. For some reason, the sound suppressors on their subguns didn't swell him with much confidence, either. Then the grenades, something of a flagrant contradiction against sound-suppressed subguns, started flying, and he knew these blacksuited marauders were not there to issue search warrants, raid the store for a clean lockdown, Miranda getting recited, chapter and verse.

This was an execution squad, plain and simple.

Quick feet saved his skin for the moment, as Mahlid saw the steel eggs flying into the room. It was foresight, more than anything else, when he had gone over the architectural layout with the Lebanese contractor. Plenty of offshooting hallways, antechambers, four doorway exits altogether, with a fire escape up top, near the end of the second floor. That didn't include windows in each of the four apartments, nor a stairwell that led to the roof. Tragic but true, his own family of six was the last concern on his plate of woes, since he didn't figure to see the next sunrise. Everybody was on their own. And if and when these executioners finished with the men, the women and children were sure to be next in line, a killing encore that would show them just as much mercy as the first casualties.

None.

The closet that had housed a fair bulk of weapons and explosives was in his sights. He went in, tumbling deeper into the hole when the pealing wrath of twin thunderballs rocked his world. Smoke came billowing into the cubbyhole like some cloud of doom, choking his senses, stinging his eyes with tears. There was plenty of screaming now, meaning whoever had survived the scything whirlwind of flying steel bits out there was reeling about, firing deaf and blind. Somehow, he needed a riposte, but he couldn't think of much else to do but stand, square his shoulders and weigh back into the bloody mix.

On the stagger, he got lucky, finding a discarded AK-47 near the edge of the stockroom. The stock and barrel were dinged and scarred by the blasts but otherwise it appeared in working order. He grabbed it up and began flaying the doorway where a blacksuited figure was crouched, hosing down his bloodied and blinded brothers-in-jihad. He was pitching them all over the room, blowing them back into the smoke. It was an unholy sight, nothing more than a glimpse of bodies and torn limbs strewed about, and Mahlid knew if he didn't turn the tide quickly he would be on his way, sans any chance of success for even a mini-jihad on the streets beyond. He hadn't come this far, risked so much, put his very family on the edge to not go all-out and try to save whatever he could to keep the dream alive.

He was moving to the side, firing on the run, and came up behind four of his men who were piling into a doorway that led past the kitchen to a hall, which in turn fanned out toward an exit. As luck, fate or the simple need to stay alive would have it, the foursome had snapped up subguns and assault rifles, pouches and duffel bags stuffed with ordnance. He took this as a sign from God that there was still hope not all of them would go down in senseless slaughter.

That the jihad could stay alive and well.

He barked out the orders, telling them to leave the building. "If there are police out there, kill them on sight. Shoot for their heads. Grenades, whatever it takes. Run! Hide awhile if you must, but I command you to take to the streets. It is Allah's will you are still alive. Take as many infidels with you where you find them. Go!"

And they went, Mahlid pivoting, spotting a body slumped against the wall. He plucked three spare clips from the waistband and sprayed the war room as the invader swung his subgun around the corner.

He held his ground, willing the shooter to show himself. If necessary, he owed it to the dream to sacrifice his own life, if only to see a few of his men made it out of there to turn Brooklyn into something that would make Beirut look like a walk in the park by comparison.

THREE ENEMY KILLS. The Executioner was in and surging down the hall, another couple of frag blasts having just thrown more sense-cleaving racket into the fray, when he nailed the third blacksuit with a burst to the back of the skull, nearly taking the shooter's head off at the neck. That left three marauders. But how many terrorists under the roof? And then there were families upstairs, no doubt moments away from getting burned down in the cross fire, either shot for the hell of it or as part of the standing order....

Or snapped up as human shields.

Bolan was low, Uzi leading his advance, eyes wide open for any sudden grenades bounding his way. If the killing crew had called in backup, how many more shooters could he expect to come crashing in?

The soldier knew he had his hands full, whatever form of cavalry broke the perimeter and wanted to join the slaughter circus. They were shooting up the house from all points, it seemed, a din of reverberating autofire and the sharp cries of combatants getting gutted by hot lead. Two opposite firepoints sounded off. Long, angry bursts told him the frag bombs hadn't cleared any rooms of standing opposition altogether.

The Executioner took up position at the end of the hall, glimpsed a skeletal figure with a complexion gray as smoke, and lurched back. The guy was good. Bullets were flaying the edges of the corner, chasing the soldier for cover. Bolan considered a frag bomb, but checked his hand as he started to reach up. Staying penned down was the worst of possible worlds. Second worst might be using up a frag grenade on one hardman, just to get him closer to both warring parties, navigating some course of action where he could secure an unimpeded firepoint to create his own shooting gallery.

A few jihad troopers, snarling off to his side in Arabic, made the call for him. Coming low around the corner, Bolan was holding back on the Uzi's trigger, his tracking line nearly catching the first gunner in midflight before the man had flown over the stack of dead men and vanished into the kitchen. The gray marauder must have done all the damage he figured he could for the time being, Bolan glimpsing three, then four bloodied stick figures stumbling out of the smoke where the frag detonations had wiped out at least a dozen men in there for good, hard to tell since a few severed legs and arms were scattered here and there.

The Executioner saw they were focused on the blacksuit, unaware at the moment he had joined the party. They were cursing in Arabic, directing autofire into the kitchen, hoping to catch him with a lucky burst, when Bolan pulled the pin on a steel egg and chucked it their way. In the process, he nearly got his arm blown off as some alert shooter from the other end poured it on, rounds slicing a hot slipstream over his forearm, tattooing the wall above Bolan and driving him back to cover.

HE DAMN NEAR BOUGHT it, sailing over the prep table headfirst, gun extended, as the bullets started. Bowen did a belly slide off the other side, tumbled to the floor, jumped up and got his bearings on the run for cover at the end of the raised stainless-steel window that separated the stoves from where the wait staff picked up the food. Jihad fanatics now turned to wounded rabid animals, a couple faces half-eaten off by shrapnel, had almost charged into the kitchen, going for broke, when the roaring fireball shredded them out of play.

Mr. Uzi.

Who the hell was that guy? Bowen wondered. That was no standard G-man issue or even a garden-variety SWAT shooter. Unless they changed their method of taking down the bad guys, he hadn't heard where lawmen came crashing through the door these days—not in a PC age where the lawyers and the ACLU were still looking to coddle thugs, out there displaying all manner of sympathy for even the devil. Unless the thrower was a tried and true pro.

And Bowen had caught sight enough of the big guy to know a seasoned war dog when he saw one. He didn't have to walk back outside for eyeball confirmation Stillwell and Zervic had been eighty-sixed. He didn't need to get bogged down, trading fire with their mystery guest, either, to know it wouldn't last all but a few seconds. That guy was a hitter, just wading right into the damn shooting gallery, as if he belonged there. Something about the eyes, the way he moved. Bowen found it hard to believe, having ranked himself and his crew right up there, but he was looking at a serious heavy hitter.

There looked and sounded to be plenty of jihad goons left to hold down the fort, shoot it out to the last man, as he saw at least eight swarthy ones had somehow secured a firepoint at what looked to be a server's station beyond the far end of the cook area. Bowen also knew a few runners were beating a hasty exit down some adjacent corridor attached to the war room. One guy was still somewhere beyond the wall now, Bowen having already traded fire with the guy before he sensed Mr. Uzi about to boil up on his six. He stole a few moments to call in the cavalry, patching through to Battering Ram Two.

"We've got some problems here, gentlemen. Move in, but keep our wheels parked precisely three blocks north. Barnes and Crafton, stick with the wheels. The rest of you move in and give us a hand. Bring the heavy equipment and don't hesitate to light up a squad car or two. It's our asses or theirs. No exceptions."

They copied, and he was signing off when the lead starting hammering the counter above, a pan the size of a basketball falling and banging off his head. Reaper was cursing, the very notion some chef's frying pan nearly cost him his life, getting him in gear. It was the guy from the war room, coming through another entrance, firing his AK-47 as if there were no tomorrow.

There was little doubt in Bowen's mind that for a lot of guys under the roof, and maybe even outside, tomorrow would never arrive.

But Bowen wasn't ready to leave. He found himself itching for another stab at Mr. Uzi.

7

The Executioner rode out the blast, senses spiked by shock waves. The roaring detonation swelled the air with agonizing pressure to his eardrums, the ground and wall shimmying as he held on, counting on the grenade to make short work of more enemy numbers. The smoke and cordite blew past his cover. In no way, shape or form was Bolan looking to aid and assist the leader and his men of the killing crew—they were right up there on his list of guys to wax—but any gunman under the roof now was fair game, and any shaving down of prowling shooters was a fat plus, no matter how the soldier achieved a quick body count for the win column.

It was only a matter of seconds, half a minute or so, tops, since storming in behind the unknown marauders, laying waste to whatever lurched up in his face right off, but Bolan knew he was on the clock. The last thing he wanted or needed was for a bunch of SWAT heroes and NYPD's finest to come barreling into this apocalyptic cross fire. They didn't know the score, maybe wouldn't even care that a heavily armed bulldog on the home team was also inside, helping make Brooklyn a kinder, gentler place for its law-abiding citizens.

The Executioner was up, over and braced against the opposite wall, senses stung by all the blood, guts and other leaking body matter, going low around the corner when the shooting took on new dimensions of sound and fury. And the hardmen at the other end were gone—then he spotted the enemy blacksuits, leapfrogging over tables, vaulting boothes out in the main dining room, tossing around weapons fire to cover some new angle of attack.

The soldier gave his other flank a search. All clear but for the dead. Hearing became a definite problem all by itself, the din of autofire diminished by the ringing in his ears. Near deafness leveled the playing field on all sides, but Bolan knew his own burning sights for targets and raw combat instinct would take over next.

The Executioner spotted a feral face, swathed in beard, framed by a nest of curly black hair, shooting up the kitchen with an assault rifle. The terrorist—and Bolan could well assume this slaughterhouse was nothing other than a once swarming hive of jihad fanatics planning some doomsday for the citizens of New York—was hosing down the kitchen with long bursts from his AK-47. He was going for the blacksuit leader, most likely, when Bolan decided to clean up any malingering threat on his rear, whether it was one or ten shooters. The Uzi up and locked on, he hit the trigger, stitching a quick burst across the shooter's chest, flinging him from sight.

Another one down, but how many left?

The Executioner charged on, the waves of autofire breaking through the ringing in his ears, urging him on as he hit the end of the corridor. They were going at it, nearly toe-to-toe, he found, flinging dozens of indiscriminate rounds all over the dining room. It was nothing short of a storm of flying glass and wood chips scything the air, all of it just another lethal rain from hell. Bolan saw the marauders firing again on the fly, threading quick, short dashes from table to table, pillar to pillar.

At the west wall a group of fanatics was pumping out the autofire from an assortment of subguns and assault rifles. Bolan knew he had secured dicey cover at best, his rear exposed to anything that might pop up from the smoke and ashes. The marauders appeared intent on cutting off the terrorists from making some charge for the front doors and gaining the street to flee the scene. Bolan took in the foyer, the running plate-glass window, the massive golden bull right where Broadwater claimed, looming up in the middle of the room like some pagan god from ancient Babylon.

Bolan noted several hopping points to gain a closer killing edge were staggered all over the joint. The other side of that double-edged sword was any shooter could hunker down, take this one way past any reasonable wrap-up point if he had enough clips.

The soldier knew he needed this nailed down quickly before the good guys bulled in, throwing still more gasoline onto an uncertain fire that was rapidly spreading out of control.

Bolan scoped out two, then three runners breaking from a pack near some expanded service station, computers and glass racks taking a hell of a pounding over there, gunners howling out the pain and surprise. Beyond that circle of sadistic thrashing, there was general pandemonium. The soldier made out the wailing of women from some point above the shooting mob, a couple heads turning, shouting something up the steps in Arabic.

Staying put was tantamount to a sure death sentence, so Bolan began firing on the marauders, drilling a few errant rounds up a pillar, chasing them to cover but alerting the blacksuit duo he was back in the game.

Breaking cover, the Executioner shifted his aim to the lunatic pack, holding back on the Uzi's trigger on the fly. He was bounding up a short flight of steps to a landing when two runners burst from the far end of the bar, racks of liquor bottles going off like minefields. If they were looking for some fighting withdrawal, one of the mystery blacksuits helped them achieve their goal. It was most certainly not quite what the terrorists had in mind, as they were shot on the dash, lifted off their feet and pitched through a plate-glass window.

"THANKS, GUY."

Whoever he was, Bowen knew the lone dinosaur wasn't thinking about saving anybody's skin but his own, while torquing up the killing heat on his end. The Reaper was now back in play. The jihad nut with the AK-47 had nearly bagged him, driving him into some narrow alcove between the end of the waiters' window and a small office cubicle. The line of Uzi autofire had followed up almost on the heels of the frag bomb, which had blown the swing doors to smoking matchsticks, bits and pieces now floating through another pall of smoke, fluttering to rest on more Iraqi bodies.

The Reaper scoured the kitchen, the smoking mouth where Mr. Uzi had decimated his batch of Iraqis, then focused on the shooting gallery just ahead.

All systems go, locked on again. He hit the trigger on his HK MP-5, catching one jihad trooper up the spine downrange before he sprayed the whole station, added more bedlam and terror to the whole churning bloody mix. They were shouting all around, whirling this way and that, shuffling away from his swarm of lead, when Bowen forged deeper across the kitchen.

This one, he knew, was a long way from getting wrapped, with the outcome every bit a fat mystery as his guest. He'd keep his eyes peeled, just the same, since every bit of battle instinct he owned told him the loner could rise out of nowhere, anytime. No more surprises, Bowen told himself, feeding his SMG a fresh clip as the magazine burned out.

It was time to go for the gusto once again.

MARCUS BROADWATER wasn't the sort to stand around, while the mother of all urban wars hit the fan, and right in his face. Inside the target building it was nothing short of full-scale war. The windows were lighting up with muzzle-flashes like some illegal indoors Fourth of July show. Fire hazard was the least of it, but some raging out-of-control blaze was sure to start soon enough. Beyond all the racket of autofire, he heard grenades thundering off, crunching blasts resounding every few moments or so. It was close-quarters slaughter in there, no doubt, since he made out the lancing cries of men getting cut to ribbons by bullets and bombs, a lucky— or unlucky—few carved up by all the flying steel whipping around after the frag blasts. Hell, this was something out of Bosnia, he had to imagine, or Beirut, even the West Bank these days. Not Brooklyn. There wasn't a cop or SWAT bunch in this town, he feared, who had the weaponary on hand to nip this kind of action in the bud.

Not a chance in hell.

But there it was, the world—or this pocket of it, at any rate—going up in raging warfare. If he hadn't seen it himself...

He was wondering how to proceed, since Belasko's standing order made it sound as if he was supposed to take five, grab a doughnut and some coffee, when the front window blasted out and two bodies slammed off the sidewalk. Broadwater hadn't spent fifteen years kicking down some doors along the way and being the first one to lead the charge himself to spectate now. He refused to relegate himself to some flunky role to simply file a boatload of after-action reports in triplicate when this storm finally blew over.

If it ever died down, much less sorted itself out. And sort out what? Beyond zipping the rubber up over a bunch of bodies...and then there were the women and kids upstairs...

Before he could give the mess any further speculation, Broadwater was out the Crown Vic's door. The agents under his and Belasko's command were squawking over the tac net, having heard all the commotion, wondering how the hell they were supposed to proceed. They had their orders, and he could almost sympathize with their stay-put-and-watch-the-store dilemma while the whole damn sky was falling around them. Almost, but his own problems, he was sure, were moments away from multiplying.

It was a faint noise at first, given all the hellfire threatening to bring down the roof of the taverna, but Broadwater made out the distant cry of sirens. He was moving for the trunk, watching the bodies heaped on the sidewalk, when another figure came flying out the gaping hole in the window. Broadwater had a good memory for detail, faces, and he recognized one of the waiters he'd questioned earlier. There was a big ugly assault rifle in his hands, a look in his eyes that warned Broadwater he was whacked out of his gourd on fear, adrenaline, the smell of blood or whatever. The M-16 was in the trunk, and Broadwater was marching hard, bent on arming himself for this special hellish occasion, when the gunman came bounding off the sidewalk, bringing the assault rifle up and aimed his direction, as if the bastard was looking for the first available body to mow down.

Broadwater had the moment pegged before the guy even wheeled his way, was already hauling out the .45-caliber Glock when the first few rounds chattered from the weapon. He felt the heat, flinching some as the lead shaved past his scalp, then reflex took over, his finger squeezing the trigger over and over. He didn't quite see the hits open the shooter's chest, the target jerking all over the place in some weird jig step.

The gunner was down, flopping around for a long moment, then went utterly still, the life leaking out of him in great red spurts, pooling in the gutter. He hadn't counted the shots, but Broadwater figured he'd pumped five or six big .45ACP rounds into the guy.

Now he was the one jacked up, eager to get in there

and kick some butt. Not only that, but Belasko was only one guy, and Broadwater knew he could use the help. He cursed next, however, holding his ground as he heard the sirens closing from what sounded like the north, Fulton or Bedford Avenue. Belasko needed him out there now, waving his arms around, holding back the cavalry. But why? A strong hunch told Broadwater this Belasko character was a lot more than just a federal badge. Unless he missed his guess, Broadwater was reading military, covert-issue even. Washington had sent up a one-man wrecking crew to lop off some bad-guy heads, no questions supposedly getting asked on his end of things. The FBI, he believed, were meant to serve as little more than garbagemen.

Broadwater keyed open the trunk and grabbed the M-16. Just in case it came spilling out into the street.

Okay, he figured, he'd play Belasko's game, flexing official weight, reining back the army of blue, the SWAT guys, whoever else wanted to crash this particular Devils party. When this was finished, he was thinking, if nothing else, he'd covered his end, and watched Belasko's back in the process. The guy owed him a few straight answers.

That was assuming, of course, Belasko even came back outside in one piece.

"GET UPSTAIRS! Stay in the rooms!"

Jamil Tabrak was forced to bellow out the demand again as Mahlid's family piled at the top of the back steps, his view taking in still more shadows heaping up near the group. Women and children, he saw, and his heart nearly shattered.

Something about this was so wrong, and what he was telling them to do...

They had been in flight, going for the same back exit to the northwest service alley he and the three other appointed jihad brothers were looking to flee through to take their war to the streets of New York. The terror was stark in their eyes, and for a brief moment Tabrak felt a boil of heated pity for them. They had been brought here from Iraq, smuggled in, part of the whole charade, but their role was quite different than that of being front-line martyrs. He supposed now, with the amount of shooting and explosions, all the dead bodies he'd left behind, that their fate would be much the same as the combatants.

Death would spare no one there, not even the smallest child.

"Jamil, we must go!"

He heard the sirens somewhere in the blocks beyond the service alley, but he knew the American police would soon circle the entire building. And they would storm inside, join the pitched battle. And what if they were captured? Their leader's order was clear, and it was divine. Capture was unthinkable. Flee the building and take the jihad to the streets. Find the infidels wherever they walked, rode on subways or buses or sat in restaurants. Kill them all, and let the Devil sort them out.

Tabrak lifted the AK-74, prepared to trigger a few rounds over their heads to get them unglued, send them on their way to hide and to hope. Tahira gave him a look, contempt, if he wasn't mistaken, then began tugging her children away, shoving them back down the hall.

Death sentence.

A part of him wanted to believe there was another way, that he could lead them out of there to safety. There was a degree of hope, even still. If the police came and managed to gain control of the building, then the families upstairs would perhaps simply be taken into custody.

Jabal, Ali and Mohammed were yelling at him, urging him to go. A wave of sorrow and—God help him, he thought—self-pity held him rooted for a moment. He had no family himself, his own wife and children murdered by one of the many bombs the Americans had dropped on Baghdad. He had all too willingly, gladly accepted to join the plan the North Koreans had engineered with Iraq. He had nothing left to lose, and even his own life had not meant much to him after the deaths of his family, beyond doing the bidding of their leader, killing Kurds, executing officers and whoever else the great leader believed was a threat to his rule. Soon enough, he believed he would join his family in heaven.

Now was not quite the time or place. There was a war left to drop, the wrath of God himself, on the infidels. Should he die there, then living for as long as he had after the horror of what had happened to his family...

It would be for nothing. It would mean nothing.

He hefted the large nylon bag, slipped an arm through the loop. "Listen to me," he said as he shouldered his way past them and threw open the exit door. "We split up. Ali and Mohammed, up this fire escape. Go roof to roof over the next apartments. Find a way somehow. We are the only four who will survive here. We must carry out the jihad. I suggest perhaps one of you remain in Brooklyn, while another makes his way to Manhattan."

"How?" Ali asked, nearly shouting as the roar of

weapons fire kept swelling the air around them. "There will be police everywhere!"

"Find a cabdriver, I don't know. Put a gun to his head and force him to take you to Manhattan. There will be more targets there."

He heard the sirens, so close now.

The AK-74 up, he burst out the door, feeling his brothers-in-jihad on his heels. Sure enough, a blue-and-white NYPD squad car was barreling down the service alley, going into a long slide now as the driver stood on the brakes. Two faces behind the windshield, he saw, lit up with anger and uncertainty at the sight of four guns, no doubt, aimed their way. Only one unit, as far as Tabrak could tell.

Jamil Tabrak stepped forward, bellowing, "Death to America!"

And cut loose with his assault rifle, blowing in the windshield on the startled faces of the policemen.

"BELASKO! Talk to me, dammit! I just need to know if you're still breathing. I got an all-points. I'm getting set to stare down a whole army of SWAT. Give me something to believe in."

The Executioner was under a renewed storm of flying lead, bullets eating up the banister of the partition separating his latest roost from the main dining area. He popped up, triggered a burst as the blacksuits kept charging, vectoring, it looked like, for the bar. Bolan knew he was fast running out of time to call the shots, and he needed Broadwater to hold back the cavalry, now more than ever.

Bolan palmed his tac radio. "I'm still in the picture, Broadwater."

"I just tagged one of them coming out the store."

Bolan had briefly caught sight of a third runner, the terrorist having just made his dash to freedom. Only the faintest crack of a pistol had carved its way from out on the sidewalk through the racket piercing the soldier's ears. He didn't see the body fall, but had heard the familiar stammer of an assault rifle, fearing the worst for a moment. No time to feel relief that Broadwater or one of his men hadn't been shot down. The shooting war had maybe only hit the fifty-yard line.

"Call your boss, whatever it takes, Broadwater, but do not let SWAT storm this place. I've got women and children, unscathed, I think."

"Understatement! I read you loud and clear. I'll do what I can."

"Make it happen. Later."

Bolan was up and searching for targets when the hiatus nearly cost him. Two more seconds on the blower and Bolan knew he would have never known what hit him.

The hardman was in the process of going for it, wheeling around a pillar, a grenade in hand. The soldier had to risk it, rising up a few inches over the railing to draw a bead, his Uzi stuttering. Downrange the red minigeysers were spurting from the gunner's chest, but the frag grenade was already in flight.

Bolan was up and racing from the point of impact when it seemed half the restaurant vanished in fire and thunder. He was launched off his feet, hurtled toward some distant black hole that was quickly swallowing him up.

8

It was time to bail. Little more than a keen grasp of the obvious, Bowen knew, but if he judged the wailing sirens right, the light show was moments away from turning into a cop convention, with SWAT and federal troops ready to bombard the joint from all points.

End game.

The skies were likewise about to swarm with NYPD choppers, as Glenndennon patched through, telling Bowen they had one set of hawkeyes vectoring in. Bowen needed to clean up the rear before he cleared out or even passed off the next round of orders. Backup was on the way, and that was enough. He could talk when he was able to walk without the opposition trying to drill him up into human Swiss cheese. If he heard Glenndennon right, they had just parked Ram Two in a weed-choked industrial lot at the far northwest end of the alley. His men were coming out of the lot now, lining up the chopper, waiting on the flyboys in blue to get within range for an easy dusting with M-203s. He copied, just to let Glenndennon and the troops know he was still in the picture. He'd get back to them with further orders.

The Reaper had some ideas how he was going to vanish into thin air, but it would require a fair amount of finagling his own guys, maneuvering them into position, words of encouragement most likely needed to keep their resolve steeled. Maybe the promise of a bonus for a job well done, cash dividends, of course, keeping hope alive. Quick feet and loads more of deadly precision shooting were called for from there on, not to mention a little good fortune to help pave the golden road out.

Still under fire by Iraqi opposition, the Reaper moved out deeper across the kitchen, away from the cook's cubbyhole, gained a better angle of fire on their back side. He sprayed the service station, advancing, zipping them with a hellstorm of 9 mm manglers. The SMG stuttered on, Bowen sweeping it back and forth, the overkill chopping them up to dancing sieves. The final three jihad goons went down, limbs flailing and grunts sounding more like the angry barking of attack dogs. It was how the doomed final opposition struck him anyway, enraged to the last bitter breath—God, these bastards were hard to kill. He noted the last of them had been chewed to bloody tatters by shrapnel already, having somehow managed to survive their initial fragging to get it this far, only to get smashed for good by his lead hammer. One of them was minus an eye, and another jihad shooter was missing half his face, bone exposed from scalp to jaw. Another was an amputee, nothing below the elbow of his left arm.

Their pain was over, bodies crashing through glass, bringing down racks and computers, and Bowen was left wondering if his own horror show was next.

It was over, or so it appeared, just him and Cutler, a

pack of noncombatants above on the second floor. He wasn't about to assume anything on the way out. There seemed to be hallways and offshoots all over, meaning a few jihad shooters could have secured the second floor for a suicide finale. He didn't think so...or maybe some enraged wife and mother would be up there and waiting with a meat cleaver.

What a sorry way to go that would be, he thought. Time to blow the joint, no matter what was up top. Simmons, he'd glimpsed, had dropped for the count a few heartbeats ago, sacrificing himself to pitch an explosive where their mystery guest had apparently accessed a firepoint on some sectioned-off raised area of the dining room to the far east. Another thunderclap threatened to bring down the roof over there. Probably the smoking section, and it was, indeed, he saw, smoking up there now. He wanted to mentally tab up the number of frags they'd used, figured they were empty now, save for his flash-stun. He was grateful the late Simmons had hung on to one bomb, just the same. The guy had probably missed the earlier command to blow the war room to hell due to all the weapons racket, or maybe he'd snagged another grenade for himself before....

Ancient history.

Bowen rolled out into the dining room, glancing up the stairs off to the side of the bar. "Cutler, close it up to me, but cover my play. I'm going up top to grab some body armor."

The Reaper was feeding his SMG a fresh clip when he sighted the figure rising from the smoke and ashes. One eyeful was all he got, Mr. Uzi maybe a little worse for wear, cut and dinged, but the mystery shooter was vaulting over a section of banister still intact, like some Olympic hurdle champ. He hit the floor standing, bulling ahead, firing away with his Israeli SMG.

Just who the hell was this runaway human freight train anyway? Bowen was starting to think he was looking at Mr. Eveready Battery Commando and the Terminator in one unstoppable, rampaging package.

Cutler was returning fire, not missing a beat, barely grabbing some cover of a pillar closest to the steps. The mystery shooter's bullets were pounding wood and glass around the service station as Bowen hit the steps. He took them two at a time, several rounds tattooing wood from somewhere to his side, focused next on all the commotion as he topped out, kids crying, voices of women hidden behind doors bleating out the terror, hoping the storm would pass them by.

Tough, and damn unlikely.

Bowen kicked open the first door he came to, barging inside, shouting curses. Two steps in, and he was forced to slash his SMG across the face of a dark damsel who rushed him with clawed hands like some lioness protecting her cubs. Not a second to spare, so Bowen snatched the nearest available kid—a good-sized teenage boy—manhandled him out into the hall.

"Cutler! Heads up!"

He saw Cutler's head poking up, midway down the stairs, his guy pouring out a blanket of autofire, and flung the kid over the edge of the steps. Cutler nearly missed his human shield, the kid flopping up at his feet on the topple, but checked his firing long enough to snap up the body armor.

Cutler didn't waste a second letting their mystery

shooter know the score. "I've got a hostage! Drop your weapon, big guy! It's all over but the crying, hero! We've got a whole floor of live ones!"

While Cutler bellowed out the riot act in between bouts of threats and cursing, Bowen charged back into the room. Maybe it was pride, but out of a dozen quaking selections, he chose the lioness for his own shield, fisting a chunk of hair and lifting her to her feet.

"Come to Papa, Mama!"

Arm locked around her throat, Bowen dragged her out into the hall.

"We're walking out of here, asshole. We see one SWAT goon or Fed, we start wasting the women and children. It's your call. It's their blood on your hands if we don't walk."

Cutler was now shimmying into view, snarling out the play, working his way in an awkward backpedal up the steps, the kid locked to his chest. Bowen was halfway down the hall, looking over his shoulder, spying what looked like a set of steps leading to the roof, when his shield came alive in his grasp, the wildcat thrashing around, nails like spikes swiping for his face. She came close, nearly taking out an eye, but Bowen flinched back, felt the swish of air from the near miss cross his nose. Enough. Wrong choice for armor. Cutler would have to hold on, buy him a few seconds, he decided. Bowen shoved the wildcat away, brought the SMG on-line, and hit her in the back with a short burst of subgun fire.

HE LANDED ON TOP of a table, his crashing weight bringing it down on top of him, offering protection from both

ground zero and flying steel bits. No time to thank Lady
Luck, Bolan kept on ticking. He was up and over the
railing, landing with catlike grace and firing the Uzi on
the charge, when a worst-case scenario went down on
the second floor. They were taking hostages now, as
Bolan saw the gunner grab a boy who had been tossed
like a ball over the edge of the steps. While the guy
stayed jacked up on the curse-and-threat routine, Bolan
secured cover behind the golden bull. The sirens were
piercing the interior now, Bolan glimpsing the light
show strobing against the jagged teeth of shattered glass
over his shoulder.

He let the Uzi hang low by his side, unleathered the
Beretta and slowly stepped out from behind the bull. It
was a risk he had to take, and one shot would be all he
got. He watched the woman on the second floor struggle with her captor. The familiar release of a sound-suppressed SMG made the other gunner falter, look over
his shoulder, his eyes going wide as if he expected the
rounds to come tearing into him.

Bolan didn't let him down for the surprise.

The Executioner seized the opening, caressed the
Beretta's trigger. The 9 mm round cored the hardman
between the eyes, a red hole blossoming, framing
stunned features just as the hardman had returned focus
back to his immediate problem.

They were wailing like the damned from above now,
feet stampeding the hall, voices shooting down the stairs
in Arabic. There was hysterical crying and gnashing of
teeth up top, but Bolan had to wade through it if he
wanted to track down the leader. The soldier was giving the boy a safety check on the move, the kid up and

stumbling back up the stairs, when an armed and bloody figure came staggering from the kitchen.

The hideous wheezing of a punctured lung was followed by a brief stutter of autofire. Bolan darted to the side as the 7.62 mm rounds sliced off the golden bull. The Beretta was up in a heartbeat, tracking on, and Bolan squeezed the trigger repeatedly on raw adrenaline. The terrorist he thought he'd nailed in the kitchen went down for good this time, his face obliterated in a crimson wash. The falling shooter held back on the trigger, unwilling to give it up, pitching, wild rounds slamming into the ceiling, shattering a bank of lights. Glass rained down on top of his twitching form.

Running, the Executioner stowed the Beretta, then bounded up the stairs. Uzi up and leading the way, he was braced for the leader to be on hand, even firing away as he topped out, maybe another human shield in tow. One look beyond the teeming mass of terrified women and children, and he knew the hardman had stolen enough time to make a run out of there. Up or down? Bolan wondered. He then saw he would be forced to deal with the mob, uncertain of what he read in their faces. Fear, for sure, but a few of the women looked set to tear into him with bared hands like talons. Understandable to some extent, since they had just been left widows, but on the other hand they most likely knew why their men had been slaughtered. Beyond the children, Bolan wouldn't count anyone under the roof as innocent.

Bolan told them, "Police! Get in your rooms and stay there. It's over. You'll be safe."

The Executioner was waving the Uzi around, repeating the order, shouldering his way through the mob. He spotted a dark-haired woman, on her knees beside a bloody figure, halfway down the hall. She was weeping, shaking the body as if that would somehow raise the woman from the dead. A wave of hot rage boiled up in Bolan. For whatever reason, the leader had mowed her down, the line of ragged holes telling Bolan he'd shot her in the back. The woman was letting him know about it, too. It was pointless asking her exactly where the gray butcher had gone, to the roof or out a ground-floor exit, since she was hysterical, her ranting indicating she held Bolan every bit as responsible for the woman's murder as the killer himself. He was past her, leaving her to it, a good portion of the mob melting back for the safety of their rooms.

The leader was the only thing on Bolan's mind. The blue squad was outside, standing on the brakes, rubber squealing, doors opening and slamming, with cop voices snarling over each other.

Bolan skidded at the end of the hall, the Uzi fanning both directions. Yet another set of steps to his left, going for the roof. The opposite direction, more stairs, descended for some point beyond the kitchen, leading, he guessed, to a service alley. He was in the process of deciding up or down, when he made out the rotor wash, closing down on the slaughterhouse.

Scratch the roof. The leader probably had it figured a ground run was his best option.

The Executioner, senses buzzing on combat overdrive, descended the stairs.

"LIGHT 'EM UP! Take the shot!"

In record time, Bowen was across the service alley, up two flights of fire escape when he heard the rotor wash, damn near falling on top of him. He was at the window now, keying his com-link and barking out the orders in between searching the alley for flying blue-and-whites and the mystery guest. The glass was wire reinforced, meant to keep out burglars, crack heads and other neighborhood persona non grata. One-handed, he triggered the HK subgun, punching in the window in chunks while keeping the line open to Glenndennon.

"I'm under fire in the service alley!" Bowen used the weapon as a battering ram, slapping out the jagged edges that didn't want to give after the blast. "Take out that bird and get your asses down here to give me a hand! Can't miss it! I've got one unit shot up!"

"Aye, aye!"

"If we clear the field here, gentlemen, there's a fat bonus in it for you. If I have to, it'll come out of my cut."

"On the way."

Incentive was tossed into the hopper, or so he hoped. Bowen heard them laying on the tread along Atlantic Avenue, the cop floor show about to snatch center stage. He was squeezing through the window when he saw the citizens creating a maze down the hall, bleating out the confusion and fear. At first look, they were immigrants of various nationalities, but this stretch of road was awash with foreigners, he knew. That could spell trouble if any of them were linked to the dead Iraqis he'd put behind.

"Police!" Bowen shouted, subgun out and ready to start shooting if they didn't clear a path. "Inside! Now! You have terrorists in your building!"

That got them moving, doors slamming, a few malingering civilians needing some barking to on the way
before Bowen found his flight for the fire escape at the
far end coming into sight. The ploy itself, he knew, was
a long shot, but escape alone was right then nothing
more than a roll of the dice. He needed only a few
choice moves while his foursome took out the eyes in
the sky, clear sailing back to the van. While they un-
wittingly blew by him and charged the service alley,
he'd be on his way. Already he was putting together a
story for Barnes and Crafton....

Which reminded him. He keyed his com-link and
told his ride to stay put until they heard further.

Now, if Glenndennon and the others followed up,
threw themselves into the mix, going for broke against
cops—

Then the sky blew up, the force of the blast shaking
the floor beneath him.

Home run. Sweet.

It galled him to some degree, sacrificing his own
troops so he could live to fight or spend the cash reward
another day. But what could he do? Escape was hardly
guaranteed, even if those four served him like some
winning jackpot lotto ticket. Once he hit the ground, he
could well leap out of the frying pan, into the fire, forced
into suicide by the cops. Beyond New York, there was
still a job in Chicago, and the council needed him to
keep breathing so he could kill again. But he had a few
demands on that score before he headed out for the
Windy City. One mess was mopped up—well, almost
at any rate—but personal survival came first, last and
only.

Looking out for number one.

At the end of the long run, he threw open the window. Subgun poised, he gave the narrow alley below a search, the light show on Atlantic Avenue now shining like high noon, thanks to all brilliant fireworks of the mother ship blown out of the sky, down for the crash landing. All clear.

He caught four shadows, hauling M-16/M-203 combos, flying past the corner's edge.

Outstanding.

His luck was holding.

"FBI! I'VE GOT a man inside!"

Broadwater was marching down the middle of the avenue, official credentials out, waving the works around. He couldn't even begin to count the blue-and-white units screaming onto the scene, rubber smoking as squad cars fanned out, lurching to a halt. A look the other way, same thing. Barricade, as he found more cops, more guns, more snarling faces popping into view, edged out. Weapons were aimed toward the restaurant, then he spotted a few guns pointed at him.

"FBI, goddammit! Hold your fire!"

Suddenly he was thinking they'd shoot him down, for one reason or another, some of it having to do with the battle zone they found, maybe a few of them wanting to believe he was on the wrong team, wrong color.

It happened.

In fact, someone was barking at him, "Drop the rifle! Put the weapon down!"

Not good. He realized he'd hauled out the M-16 next, glanced at it as if were some radioactive hot potato. If he read those looks right, they were a breath away from mowing him down.

Broadwater wasn't sure which way it would fall, but the boys in blue were holding their turf and their fire. He heard the chopper coming in next, filtering through the roaring in his ears. Broadwater was looking up, thinking a sniper was maybe perched in the doorway, homed in on him when—

The sky lit up, a flash of fire consuming the chopper, stem to stern.

A roiling mushroom cloud towered for the sky, signaled all the way, he imagined, to Jersey. What the hell? They—whoever they were—had just added another dimension to this holocaust, telling all of them—the law—they might as well spit into the wind if they even thought they stood a chance at turning the tide there.

And Broadwater stood frozen in disbelief, his eyeballs feeling as if they were swelling at the sight of the flaming skeleton, wreckage now raining down or ricocheting off the roof, cops ducking for cover. Then the whole ball of conflagration that was once an NYPD chopper seemed to float for the ground. The boys in blue saw it coming, and even Broadwater was wheeling, sprinting back for any cover the Crown Vic could offer. He was in the air, skidding on haunches over the engine hood, looking back when he saw the flaming shell bang into the roof's edge of an apartment complex, carom next off the building, winging down, sheared rotors going for decapitation. They were little more than darting stick figures down the street as cops hauled ass a moment before the wreckage squashed a few units to scrap.

TABRAK GRABBED the barrel as Jabal lifted the AK-74. They had come this far, and he believed they had been blessed by divine fate. Whoever the four men in black were—and he was certain they were a backup execution squad moving in to aid the other vipers in killing their brethren—Tabrak had spotted them at the end of the alley. They had been too busy lining up the launchers fixed to their assault rifles, holding their position outside a fence that sectioned off an industrial park. So intent on blowing the police helicopter out of the sky, they missed two shadows running their way. Or so he clung to hope.

It was a snap decision, based solely on the need to clear the area unmolested, and follow through with the sacred duty appointed them by Mahlid. The stairwell housing, leading to a steel door, beyond which he suspected was a boiler or maintenance room, was yet another gift from God, he thought. They were burrowed deep now, hugging the wall. They had nearly cleared the end of the next apartment complex, when Tabrak had seized Jabal by the shoulder and practically slung him down the steps. They waited, the explosions and shouts of men in panic seeming to hover over their hiding hole. Boots pounded, Tabrak holding his breath, not releasing his hold on the AK-74 until he spied the four shadows running past the stairwell.

Jabal had fire in his eyes as he put his face close to Tabrak. "There will be police on the way. One of us must make it out of here. I will take care of the police, but you must survive, keep running."

That Jabal, whom he'd known since a boy in Tikrit,

would sacrifice his life, so he could carry the holy war to the streets of Brooklyn...

Tabrak felt the lump in his throat, then fought off the moment of weakness and nodded. "Go with Allah, then."

"Go with Allah."

And they were climbing out of the hole, the butchers none the wiser as they ran on down the alley. They were going to do whatever they wanted to, and Tabrak wished them the worst. He stole a second to pray for their deaths.

9

Four more hell hounds of urban Armageddon were unleashed and on the way. Murderous contact was unavoidable, unless they bolted on, down the main alley, passing the cross-running service corridor between buildings, and charged into the slaughterhouse. Bolan had made the visual seconds after bursting out the service door next to kitchen when he'd gone hunting for the leader. Rounding the corner, he halted at the sight of them. He was sure the blacksuited foursome had likewise spotted him before he lurched back, taking up cover behind a Dumpster. The numbers, types of weapons and the gap between them on first sighting called for a change in tactics.

A fresh clip already fed to the Uzi, the Executioner was betting they were the reinforcements, summoned in by the leader, and they would pursue him as the odd man out before they moved on to do whatever it was they were told to do. Which was most likely burn down lawmen, secure some sort of fighting evacuation for their lord and master. The downed chopper, the noise of the tremendous explosion fresh in his ears, was confirmation enough to the soldier that they had been ordered in, backup with the heavy ordnance to help the leader and crew blast their way off the block. Bolan had their selection of hardware filed away, and it was a safe bet they were going after uniforms with badges. Four M-16s with attached M-203 combos, the rocket launchers with their 40 mm payloads that had blown the chopper out of the sky. Two of them also had LAW rocket launchers slung around their shoulders, armor-piercing HEAT rounds that would cut through a SWAT urban APC and decimate the troops before they knew what hit them. The nylon pouches bouncing around their chests were stuffed with grenades, he'd bet. Plenty of killing tools to keep Brooklyn rocking for some time to come.

Not after he'd taken it this far, Bolan determined. He was way overdue to wrap this up.

The Executioner mentally ticked off the meter on the next set of doomsday numbers, opting for a flash-stun grenade to greet them when he made out their approach. With the sense smasher armed, Bolan kept his back pressed to the Dumpster. He could almost reach out and touch the metal hearse that was the final resting place for two New York policemen, the windshield obliterated, blown in on their shocked faces.

He couldn't recall having heard any gunfire outside when he'd hit the second floor but he'd been tied up in a shooting war himself. Which left him wondering—if not the leader, then who? Now cops were dead, just the sort of tragic disaster he had wanted to avoid happening.

"Where did he go?"

"Move out!"

Bolan released the spoon, mentally gauged the distance to targets by memory and voice, and whipped his arm around the Dumpster's edge. It was a low toss, a miniature steel ball skimming the surface, as it bounced along. One look was all he snagged, Uzi up and ready to flame. But the Executioner glimpsed the stunner roll up right between the legs of the leading gunner who had skidded to a halt, the horror bulging in his eyes. It was way too late to save the family jewels. Flash-stuns, the soldier knew, were most effective in tight quarters where the punch and blinding light was trapped to carve the opposition's senses out of their bodies, render them deaf, dumb and blind, virtual walking dead. The space between the buildings was a tight fit, just the same, and Bolan squeezed his eyes shut, hands over his ears as he anticipated a crippling blow, close to maximum lethal. Light and thunder burst in sound and fury, a scream echoing out from the eye of the supernova.

The Executioner rose, wheeled around the Dumpster's edge and went to work, chopping them up where they reeled in the smoke.

Two of them started shooting blind, spraying the air, the 5.56 mm rounds ricocheting off the metal of the fire escape beyond Bolan. But it didn't matter. They were already getting nailed, the Executioner's extended burst marching across them, left to right. Two men were tumbling when numbers three and four caught the last of the 9 mm rounds tearing into their flesh. When they were stretched out, Bolan took a step forward, thinking one of them was still breathing. Closing, he was sure of it, as the third gunman choked on blood, limbs thrashing.

"Bowen...bastard..."

The Executioner's senses felt pummeled by all the sirens and shouts of confusion and panic hitting his back from the street. He focused on the dying hardman, his fading gaze searching him out. Bolan thought the man was clinging to life, eager to tell him something.

"Bailed...sent us...right to you..."

With his eyes roving for any sign of danger, Uzi cradled, Bolan filed away the name. He could imagine what had gone down. The leader, aka Bowen, had called out the SOS, duped the troops into thinking he needed help for his fighting withdrawal. Too late, they realized they were nothing more than pawns.

"Rocket men...missile brains...they have one...."

A part of Bolan wanted to believe the man was delirious, lapsing into shock from loss of blood. Something in the eyes, though, the voice had just enough ring of sincerity to it, as if the dying gunner was trying to tell him something that might open an avenue for his own revenge beyond the grave.

"Three more...rocket men."

BOWEN WAS TREATED to the evil eye when he hopped into the van's shotgun seat. He was wound tight enough, having made it back. And that was a harrowing chore, listening on the run as what sounded like an all-units call from all five boroughs came screaming onto Atlantic, the whole siren show making it next to impossible to think. The last thing he needed was the looks now, but he was braced and armed with answers, just the same, for the obligatory round of questions, fired off in anger and more than a little suspicion.

"Where are the others?" Crafton, the wheelman, demanded.

"What the hell happened back there, Captain?" Barnes nearly barked in his ear from behind the seat.

"Cops, that's what happened. They're dead, all of them."

He caught them exchanging a look. Unconvinced.

"You want to drive us out of here, Crafton? Or maybe you want to go back and hope New York's finest is in a listening mood?"

Crafton looked set to pound the wheel, the storm building in his eyes. "Where to?"

"Take us to Queens." Bowen checked the street beyond the lot. Clear. There were enough side streets and residential neighborhoods but part of the problem was the city was just about to come awake, and the neighborhoods were sure to be up and watching now. "We'll take the Queensboro into Manhattan. Easy," he growled, as Crafton gave the engine some gas, looking set to give any NASCAR driver a run for his money just to put quick distance between them and the cop circus. "Nice and easy. We'll cut through Manhattan. Hey, I think the UN Building will be on the way. If one of you guys has to take a leak we'll stop and hang the lizards right there on the steps," he said, trying to lighten their mood, but the stony looks he received warned him they were short on more than just humor.

"Okay. We'll take the Lincoln Tunnel into Jersey. We need to hole up, a motel in Hoboken, Union City, something like that. Cool our heels. I need to make a call to our employer anyway, figure out the next move."

It was a good time to build a smoke screen, the end

of the line already mapped out in his head. "The short and the bitter—it hit the fan, gentlemen. The people who sent us neglected to mention a couple of items. Number of marks for starters. We must have left behind thirty dead Iraqis. We did our part, and I never like losing even one man. But somebody's math on the other end isn't computing. That also goes for the chump change they shelled out for us to nearly eat the worm there."

He couldn't be sure if they were buying it, since these guys were former black ops for the Company and NSA at one time or another. They could smell con job a mile off, keep it to themselves with a straight face until they decided to even the score. They weren't squawking, bombarding him with any more questions, so he wanted to take that as a sign he had put out the fire of suspicion for the moment. "Okay. Crafton, when we get in Jersey, stop at the first convenience store you see. I don't know about you guys, but I could sure use a cold beer."

ANOTHER TASTE of hell was waiting for Bolan as he cautiously moved out of the alley and onto the street. Uzi grasped in one hand, hung low by his leg in what he hoped was a nonthreatening gesture, the soldier was all fire and iron just the same. He was steeled for anything, but what he found—and feared next—was that whatever happened there was only a small dose of something far more monstrous lurking in the wings.

First thing after tagging the four hell hounds, Bolan had raised Agent Broadwater to tell him he was coming out, pass the word to NYPD. As anticipated, the Executioner now found more cops, more squad cars choking the avenue in both directions, their lights strobing the immediate sky above to form an illuminated halo. The air itself was a chokehold of burning fuel, roasting flesh and stinging cordite.

And the way out the alley was on fire.

The chopper's flaming carcass had crushed a couple blue-and-whites at the end of its plunge, the firestorm raging to his two o'clock. Fuel tanks were ignited in the blaze, and twisted metal went winging around, banging off residential or commercial abodes, glass shattering as storefront windows took a beating, burglar alarms touched off to add to the next round of hellish racket. By now, civilians were out in force everywhere, it seemed, mostly on the fringes or hanging out windows. Spectators, for the most part. Whatever cops could be spared were holding back the curious and frightened throngs. More distant sirens were screaming from somewhere, everywhere.

And the war wasn't quite finished.

The soldier found a small army of blue locked in a firefight with enemy unknown, a block or so west. Small-arms fire rattled the air, muted to some extent by a solitary voice of booming rage and the assault rifle barking from some distant point at the edge of an apartment complex. Bolan could have rushed down there, hurled himself into the mix, but the danger of getting dropped by understandable itchy trigger fingers by the home team became a grim reality if he made any sudden moves. Voices were already barking at Bolan, the expected bombardment of confused and angry questions hammering at him from several points, but the soldier clearly heard Broadwater.

"Hold your fire! Don't shoot! He's a Justice Department agent!" The FBI man was forced to grab a cop's arm as he made a sudden swing with a pistol toward Bolan. "He's with us, goddammit!"

A thunderclap sounded down the street, and all focus turned back to the shooting in that direction. A squad car was flipping on its side, two uniformed figures sailing out of the fireball. It was a suicide stand. The fanatic showed himself next, charging out of the shadows after dumping his grenade, the AK-47 sweeping the iron wall of blue. Lights and windows blew in storms of glass under the shooter's barrage, but it was over in the next few heartbeats. It was hard to tell, with all the shouting and cacophony of weapons fire blistering the air, but Bolan thought he heard a short burst of Arabic curses, divvied up with "Death to America!"

It took an extended salvo by the men in blue to drop him, the suicide charger doing his damnedest to try to bulldoze his way into the line of squad cars, jerking as the pistols cracked on, gutting him open, swelling him with hot lead. The fanatic got his death wish, finally toppling under the hail of bullets.

Broadwater started relaying orders to his other FBI agents, sent them on their way to follow through, then stole a few moments to discuss procedure, house-to-house searches and roadblocks and such with police.

And Bolan kept his long deliberate march toward Broadwater, who continued calming and reassuring the blue force that the soldier was one of them. The Executioner felt dozens of pairs of eyes drilling into him, watching him in some curious mix of awe, confusion and anger. If he read the faces right, the blue force was peering at him as if he was an abductee who had been whisked off into thin air, only to be plunged straight into the very bowels of hell, now reappearing out of the void itself to live to tell about it.

Bolan, of course, hardly saw himself as any hero of the hour, not by a long shot. And he could be sure, given the fact there were a few dead cops scattered about, no one was about to hand him the keys to the city. It was never about heroic antics anyway, he knew, grabbing the spotlight, stealing the thunder, whatever. It was duty, pure and simple, and he'd been there with tried and true skills to back him up, bulling into the fray to tackle a ferocious enemy who might have slaughtered scores of innocents had Bolan been somewhere else.

Fate, then? Right place, right time?

Whatever it was, Bolan was hardly about to break out the champagne and cigars. Cops were dead. Bad guys were on the run. He knew from experience to trust his gut. And the soldier felt his instincts just short of a wild-fire burning up his gut. The leader was somewhere, beating an exit as fast and brazen as he could. Worse, what if more terrorists had slipped off into the dawn hour, using the one-man suicide stand to cover a vanishing act?

At the moment there was little Bolan could do, but he had some ideas on how to proceed. It might require pulling rank or getting Brognola to throw his weight around, but the soldier wasn't about to sit on the sidelines, getting his ear burned about what he'd done or what he had to do. All manner of threats from the field director would be hurled his way if he hung around

with debriefings and irate grilling by desk jockeys and
paper pushers on the next horizon for weeks to come.

No chance.

Judging by the swirl of official voices barking out orders to get units fanning out and seal a perimeter, he
knew NYPD was in high gear to chase down any fanatic
runners. Already cops were charging into adjoining
apartment buildings, marching into alleys, hunting for
gunmen. After—if and when any more fanatics were
taken down in the immediate vicinity—there would be
long rounds of calming citizen nerves and hours of questioning. Armored and subgun-wielding SWAT commandos, the Executioner noted, were right then
disgorging from any number of urban APCs. Bolan left
them to it, angling deeper across the street as Broadwater headed to intercept him, then pulled up short.
There was a far-off look in the FBI agent's eyes, as if
he were seeing a ghost or something. Clearly he
couldn't believe Special Agent Belasko had walked
away from this with little more than a few nicks and
cuts. The official soldiers went on doing what they had
to do, but all they'd find, Bolan knew, as they barged
into the slaughterhouse, SMGs leading the charge,
would be hysterical survivors and enough bodies to load
up more meat wagons than the borough probably had
budget allotment for this sort of gruesome haul.

The M-16 in Broadwater's hands lowered, then the
thousand-yard-stare wandered to all the SWAT guys
pouring into the charnel house. "How many meat wagons should our guys call in?"

"A bunch. Let's take a drive. We're through here."

To his credit, Broadwater pulled it together, didn't

read Bolan the riot act. They were splitting up at the rear of the Crown Vic, Bolan feeling the big FBI agent treating him to a long measuring from the other side. "A second, if you don't mind."

Bolan stood by the passenger door, waiting for Broadwater to vent or whatever he was going to do, as the frenzy of the official mop-up buzzed all around them. He'd already gathered a read on the situation unfolding. Cops and SWAT were scurrying around on all points, too busy for the moment to pay much attention to anything other than diving sifting through the madness and the wreckage as uniforms waved in the meat wagons, emergency medical vehicles and firetrucks, or holding back civilian throngs spilling out from other buildings. Bolan knew this was the best chance—or the worst time, depending on the point of view—to make a quick and quiet exit.

"You know, my career's probably going to get hung over the toilet bowl after this. I'm seeing the Director, hell, the mayor and I'm poised to flush it all, pension, benefits, the works. But you know something, Special Agent Belasko? For some strange reason, beyond taking care of my wife and kids, I don't care if they hang me out for the wolves. I'm looking at dead cops, guys with families like me, something that's not supposed to happen here. I'm looking at you, and I'm thinking but for the grace of God this could have been worse, only don't ask me how. My gut's talking to me, Belasko. It's telling me you're not some standard issue out of Wonderland. I figure you owe me, at best, a half-assed answer, since I kept the boys in blue from storming your rear or cutting you to ribbons on your walk out. So, what are you really?"

Bolan held the man's look across the way for a moment. "I'm a soldier."

Broadwater nodded. "And this is some kind of dirty war against terrorists bringing jihad to America?"

"Close enough."

"Suppose that's as much as I'm going to get for my trouble."

"It's the best I can do."

"Need-to-know, and all that?"

"Agent Broadwater, if you catch any flak about what happened here, the man who sent me will make a call to the right people on your behalf."

"Telling me you've got that kind of clout?"

Bolan didn't answer. He gave the slaughter zone one last scoping, felt the rage knotting a cold ball in his gut that a few good men had gone down for good. "Take a look around."

Broadwater did.

"I'm thinking there are a few murderous snakes that somehow slithered away. Pure murder and mayhem in their hearts. All it would take is one or two like the butcher on the F train. One pistol or subgun, a couple grenades..."

"This is just a preview? Of what? The coming attraction?"

Bolan couldn't be sure what the next hour would bring to the city. Beyond their own two-man roving sweep of the surrounding blocks—hunting for armed wanna-be martyrs, or the leader himself, while Broadwater tried to plug up the coming dam burst of rage from his superiors—the soldier needed to touch base with Brognola. And beyond dumping the bad news on the big

Fed's doorstep, the soldier would keep moving, searching, waiting for madmen to blow. Again he couldn't be positive there were a few human time bombs set to go off, but Bolan wasn't ready to close shop yet.

Bolan opened his door. "The main event, something like that, I'm afraid. I hope I'm wrong...but I'll spell it out for you best I can while we ride," the Executioner said, and climbed in with Uzi in hand.

The soldier was closing the door, but caught Broadwater falling back into jaded grumbling form. "Yeah, let's get the hell out of here before these guys start calling you Callahan, or Cobra, or something."

Broadwater was inside, took the wheel, dropped it into drive, and not a moment too soon. He was pulling away as Bolan spotted two uniforms rolling up, one of them calling out, "Hey! Where the hell you two going?"

10

Mohammed Khuban viewed the crack smoker and his fate as simply another door opened by God. He felt his heart hammering in his chest, pulse racing as he hugged the edge of the dirty brick wall. Ali was behind him, spying on the junkie sitting at the wheel of their ride to Paradise. They were close, but so far away from seizing a vehicle that would take them into the heart of Manhattan to fulfill their dream of jihad. Roughly fifteen feet to be exact before they were on the way.

Their AK-47s had been shoved in the nylon bags after the roof-to-roof flight from the embattled restaurant. They had climbed down the fire escape of the last building, farthest from the fighting, while police shot it out with unknown gunmen on Atlantic—presumably the same snakes who had blown the police helicopter out of the sky—but God had seen fit to bless the two of them with safe passage.

Beyond Atlantic Avenue, they made good speed and time, sticking to the deep shadows of alleyways, keeping off the main streets as he had them recorded to memory. Khuban believed they had moved on a northeasterly course, closing on either the Brooklyn or Manhattan Bridge. They searched for a cab to commandeer, along the way, as the sirens and the shooting faded behind them and the immediate danger of confronting police passed them by. No luck spotting a cab on duty.

The city was now coming alive, horns tooting around the neighborhood, the sun beginning to shed light over the jumble of redbrick tenements and empty lots. Driving would present a nerve-racking chore if the police had thrown up checkpoints, barricades, whatever else, short of citywide martial law with tanks and troops choking bridges and main streets. If they took it that far, they would have to deal with the possibility of unleashing jihad on the police. Neither one of them had bothered to count the number of banana clips, bound together in twos by duct tape, or the number of grenades in their respective bags. Judging by the weight alone, he knew they had enough to kill a slew of infidels on the streets before they themselves were martyred at the hands of the American police.

After searching the windows and fire escapes, he found they were alone with the crack smoker. In Khuban's heart and soul, the fire burned for jihad, the swelling heat from its core in his belly telling him it wasn't enough they'd made it this far. The blood of their slain brothers cried out for vengeance. Nothing short of wholesale slaughter in the teeming crowds of Manhattan was acceptable.

A search behind, the cross-joining intersecting alley clear, and Khuban told Ali, "Stay here. Bring the bags when it is done."

He took a 9 mm Makarov pistol from his bag, chambered a round, then stepped into the alley, stare fixed on the black Oldsmobile. The junkie, he saw, was too consumed keeping the flame from his lighter to the stem, inducing his own artificial Paradise, a smoke cloud thick enough to gag a mere passerby roiling out the window. Something inflamed a righteous fury inside Khuban at the sight of this American, sitting there, openly defying the law with such brazenness and contempt. He realized how much he despised the country, its people. They were so rich and privileged in a land with its legions of unclean souls, he thought, they could afford to squander vast sums of money on poison, ruining their minds, condemning their souls in the process, even shredding apart their own families without so much as a care to the consequence on others with such sinful behavior. How much they threw away on drugs in this country he couldn't say in a precise dollar figure, but he suspected it had to be enough to feed the starving the world over. All the hope for a better tomorrow so many took for granted. The money they wasted on such foolishness, he decided, was the same as stealing from those who truly needed and deserved it most.

Had not the Korean colonel warned all of them they would bear witness at some point to such despicable weakness, such abominable lusts for demonic pleasures?

At around ten feet and closing he broke into a sprint as the junkie cried out in alarm. Khuban was bringing the Makarov up as the junkie tossed away the stem and lighter and keyed the ignition. His habit cost him his life, but Khuban saw this as something of an act of revenge, cleansing the earth of more sin, eradicating any future misery the man's behavior might wreak on the lives of people connected to him. He pumped two 9 mm rounds through the open window, into his skull. Blood and bits of flesh speckled the windshield, enraging Khuban for a moment over the mess as he threw open the door. Ali was already running with the bags, giving their surroundings a wild-eyed search. Whether the killing was seen or not, Khuban didn't care. He would be content to end it there, if necessary, shooting it out with the police.

He reached in, hauled up the corpse and dumped the body on the alley floor. The junkie, he saw, had three cans of beer left in a six pack. Khuban took a can, shook it, popped it open and directed a foamy geyser to wash some of the muck and gore off the windshield. He jumped in, took the wheel as Ali claimed the passenger seat.

"Where?"

Khuban eased the transmission into Drive. "If Allah wills it, I believe I can find the Rockefeller Center."

THE ACT, from start to finish, was rehearsed, down to individual pat moves and abbreviated dialogue, with the right dosage of heat and determination scripted and hashed over in his mind during the drive to Hoboken. First Bowen had the living to take care of, then act two, the call to Mr. DIA in Oklahoma.

As the first one into the motel room, Bowen claimed a bottle of Miller Lite from the twelve pack, then bummed a cigarette from Barnes, lit up, popped open his beer. "Help yourselves, gentlemen. Hour, two tops, then we're on the road. Turn on the tube, see if we made the news." Actually he knew it would only take ten or fifteen minutes to do the deed. They had the end unit, the walls were built of cinder block, good to muffle noise. Beyond the door, chained and bolted by Crafton, with the man giving the lot and the industrial park the obligatory paranoid sweep by cracking the curtain, Bowen was thinking ahead. Since his description had probably been passed around, meaning APBs from there to Shanghai, he'd ordered Crafton to take care of the cash transaction with the desk clerk. Bowen managed his own bellhop duties, handling the duffel bag, with a cell phone with secured line and a sound suppressor inside, setting it now on the floor on the blind side of the second twin bed closest to the bathroom. They were near enough to Kennedy Boulevard, with bailing options from there to either Newark International or I-78. A flight to O'Hare sounded like the wise choice.

Moves first, then the big play.

The television came alive instantly with a female reporter on the scene of the urban battle zone. Bowen smoked, listened for a moment, unzipping the duffel while Barnes and Crafton worked on their beers. The reporter stated she didn't know much at the present, fulfilling her own role as the shocked and horrified messenger of tragedy, speculating next it had something to do with the massacre on the F train and terrorists. FBI was on the scene, as was SWAT, and so on, but nobody official was talking to her.

Bowen drained his beer in one gulp, flipped the empty on the bed. Cigarette perched on his lip, he reached down in the duffel, looking over his shoulder. Crafton was taking a seat in a chair near the radiator, with Barnes doing a slow step back toward the other bed.

"Not too loud, gentlemen, I'm making the call of our lives. Securing the future, you understand. Further orders from the top, but I'm going to make sure our friends understand they need to open the bank first. Way I see it, we've earned a bonus."

Neutral looks aimed his way, and he sensed their suspicion reaching critical mass, narrow gazes telling him they were chewing over the Brooklyn scenario, wondering. They were armed with Glocks, like himself, the weapons tucked in away in shoulder rigging beneath windbreakers.

Again something dark and smoldering in their eyes as they looked at him.

"You know, I've been thinking," Barnes said, reclaiming his perch on the edge of the bed.

"Yeah. What's that?" A quick delve, hunched, hands out of view, and he slipped the sound suppressor in the left pocket of the windbreaker, watching them out of the corner of his eye. He took the cell phone next, making sure they saw it as he stood, body angled to keep the bulge of the suppressor hidden.

"The time frame."

"Yeah? What about it? Keep talking," Bowen said, moving into the bathroom, easing the door three-quarters shut and setting the cell phone on the toilet's tank.

"The minute the hawkeyes went down, the others were headed your way. On your strict order. You were under fire, you said."

"Then you called us. 'Stay put,' you said."

"And?"

He kept his ears tuned in, envisioned them still on the other side of the room, looking at each other, working up the courage to get to the punch line. An extended silence he didn't trust followed, as if they were listening to make sure he was taking care of his business.

He let the cigarette fall from his mouth. "You've got something to say, say it," Bowen called out, the smoke sizzling out as it hit water. "We're all *compadres* here." He flushed, stepped back, eyes on the mirror. He couldn't see their reflection—which meant they couldn't see him—but he could feel them, holding turf on the other side of the room.

"It all happened too quickly, Captain."

"What happened? I'm listening." He was all empathy now, just enough sincerity, not too aggressive in his concern, he thought. Nice. Holding them back, but he could feel the snow job melting. Quickly and noiselessly he retrieved the sound suppressor and Glock, threaded in two shakes.

Ready.

"Hey, one of you pop me another beer, if we're gonna sit around and commiserate and draft eulogies for our fallen comrades?"

Grabbing the door's edge, he heard the hiss as one of them unscrewed the cap on a brew. Seeing the gun in Bowen's hand they froze, aware way too late there was no chance to jump clear from getting clobbered. He begrudged them credit for trying, just the same, hands digging inside jackets, but Bowen was already out the door and squeezing the trigger.

He nailed Barnes first, drilling one .45 ACP round between his eyes. Crafton was up now, clearing his weapon when Bowen beat him to it, tapping the trigger to give the man a third eye matching Barnes's. They fell hard, Bowen wincing at the noise, the blood and gobs of brain matter splashing the door and wall as hollow-point rounds cored out the exit.

He listened to the silence for a moment, any hint the occupant in the adjoining room might be roused and scuffling about, wondering. Nothing. He checked the parking lot, watched the traffic sweeping past, then went and retrieved the cell phone. He punched in a series of numbers. Two rings, and the familiar gruff voice barked on.

"Yes?"

"It's me."

A pause, the man's mind no doubt scrambling for one of his patented mantras. "You got some pair on you calling me like this."

"Thanks. I appreciate the flattery."

"Yeah. I'm watching the results of your work now on CNN. What the hell happened out there? You want to tell me why it looks like you created just the sort of mess I wanted to avoid? You want to tell me why I—and our people—am deeply concerned you might become a TV star?"

The Reaper glanced at the bodies as he walked out of the bathroom. "Let's just say I had a few problems, but everything's under control."

"Is it?"

"You're watching too much TV. I suggest something light for your nerves. A soap or a game show. I like the one where the babes parade around in bikinis while the contestants bid on prizes."

"CNN's got all it wrong, is that it?"

"You're giving me way too much credit, Turner. I had

more than a little help from an unknown source with the urban renewal."

"I hear the needle on my bullshit meter making these funny little whining noises all of a sudden."

"Speaking of whining, anybody ever tell you that you worry too much?"

"I get paid to worry. Part of the unwritten job description."

Bowen chuckled, hoping he came across every bit as mean and insolent as he felt. "In my experience guys who go thrashing around, claiming the sky is falling, worrying all the time have this peculiar way of creating their own self-fulfilling prophecy of doom."

"Now you're a philosopher."

"No. Now I'm the man of the hour who's set to name his own price. That is if you still want Chicago cleaned up. If you do, here's my nonnegotiable fee, cowboy, so get your wallet out...."

HE WAS WEDGED between them, felt the heat emanate off the bodies of his wife and daughter, out of pure terror or something else—rage and shame—he couldn't be sure.

Hours ago—and how could Thomas Shaw accurately judge time?—his wife had spoken briefly to him, asking questions he couldn't answer before the voice with the Asian accent barked at her to shut up. Shaw knew his wife as well as he knew anyone, had endured on more than one justifiable occasion a tongue lashing, and he anticipated her flaring up with righteous indignation and fury, ready to fight. She had growled a few questions at their captor, demanding to know where they were being taken and why before he'd heard him scuffling a few steps toward them, the voice raising in clear threatening decibels, the man perhaps poised even to lash out with fists or worse.

Shaw had a good idea why this was happening, and he knew the danger was very real, and imminent. He might have lived on the cloistered fringes of the violence and subterfuge that came with the turf of classified work, but he'd heard more than a few stories of what the black operatives, those jealous guardians of high-tech Pandora's boxes, were capable of. Quietly he had implored his wife to do as she was asked, offering what sounded now like lame words of encouragement to stay strong, the promise that everything would be all right.

Just what could he do anyway, other than offer words of hope, meant to soothe nerves more than anything else? He was a scientist, pursuing what he believed was a course of peace his entire life, searching for that one giant leap across the Rubicon where his own hands would effectively neutralize the threat of nuclear war. He was a thinker, an idea man, not some warrior who could fearlessly charge into danger and spit on the face of death. Violence to him was an affront to human dignity. Yet there he was, searching, hoping for some way to strike back, justifying imagined scenes of harm befalling their captor, believing if he didn't do something...

He pushed extreme images of any number of possible dire fates to the darkest nooks of his mind.

Wherever they were going, whatever was going to happen, he felt a growing and shameful sense of utter helplessness he'd never known. He knew it would be too easy right then, with nothing but time and mounting anxiety on his hands, to sit there and wallow in self-pity, doubt, loathing that he wasn't up to physically fighting back. Assuming he even found the opportunity for an attack that would prove suicidal in the end, maybe even fatal for his wife and daughter.

Since the past night minutes had dragged by like hours, time suspended, all but irrelevant other than getting to their unknown destination. It was mind games now, a way to keep his thoughts occupied, off the fear. He tried to piece together events, but after the three of them were herded into the chopper, the hoods were tugged over their faces, their hands bound before them with plastic cuffs. It struck him as some ghoulish act of arrogance on the part of their captors, the hangman's hoods instead of mere blindfolds. They were morbid trophy pieces now, if only for their captors's amusement and gloating. Their blind degradation was something he had always only believed happened in Beirut or Baghdad or Bosnia, where shot-down fighter pilots or American diplomats or CIA agents were abducted off the street, paraded before the cameras, black hoods hiding their faces as if they were moments away from execution.

The tight cuffs began biting into his wrists not long after they were fastened, but fear of interrupted blood circulation became the least of his worries. He tried to measure time, just the same, thinking he could mentally gauge direction. A left here, right there, listening for identifiable sounds, church bells or airplanes taking off, like he'd seen kidnap victims do in the movies. As if he could somehow slip away at some point, unseen, call the police or the FBI from a pay phone, direct them to the spot for a daring rescue. Grim reality was far different than the trappings of fantasy. So he gave up dwelling on direction and time, dreams of lawmen crashing down to free them.

Now they were sitting in the back of what he suspected was a truck. He was seated on the hard floor, cold on his rear, metal most likely. The bed was covered, with just a brisk shaft of cold air seeping through some crack, but enough to drive a shiver through his bones. The way muffled sound from the road below echoed around them, he imagined they were in a U-Haul, maybe a horse trailer, though he didn't breathe the usual smells of hay or the lingering taint of removed animal waste. The constant vibrating of the wall against his back told him they were traveling fast, on open highway. All these details, he concluded, meant nothing. They were prisoners.

Despite himself, he began feeling a wave of regret building inside. If not for him, his family wouldn't be there, kidnap victims, hauled off by men of violence. It was his work, his life, that might cost him his wife and daughter. It was some consolation, at best, that Sara was missing. And what had become of her? Was she...even still alive? He could only pray that she was safe, and free. If it was him, his brain they wanted, which he suspected, then killing any member of his family would only incite him to rebel. Or would they execute his wife or daughter simply as a warning? Say Sara had contacted the police? What could she tell them? Not much. Some of them were foreigners, he had seen at the house, but all of them, he strongly suspected, were links in a running network of connections and contacts to the violent shadow world that had always existed just beyond his ivory tower.

He could feel himself spiraling down into depression every bit as black as the inside of the hood. The waiting. The fear of the unknown. The hoping. His mind wandered, searching for reason out of this horror. He had heard once, unable to recall the occasion, that at the moment of death the entire panorama of a human being's life flashed before his or her eyes. From cradle to grave, every moment, good, bad or neutral, came together in an instant, the blinding wink of a supernova of truth and mercy, the sum total of events during his or her life for the individual to behold and to judge on its merits. There, then gone, or so he'd heard, but branding in its wake the revelation of truth and meaning of one's existence, with all the sorrow and joy, love and hate, regret, failure and triumph, every thought and feeling and experience of that particular life...

Well, he certainly wasn't dead yet, but he saw—or maybe conjured up—entire passages of his own life in his mind's eye. It came next without warning, an intense desire to curse himself as he suddenly loathed the selfish pursuit of his dream, with ultimate achievement as the only worthy goal in his life.

He could see it all, or the parts most worth remembering, or least painful perhaps. The wedding day. The honeymoon in Hawaii, the joy of their love that was fresh and new and exciting as they charted the course for their future together. The birth of his daughters. Every Christmas. Every Thanksgiving. His father's funeral. He saw them next, clear as day in his mind—Rebecca, Patti and Sara—the perfect family unit, happy on the surface, the husband and father doing and saying all the right things at the right time. Everything in order, no fuss, no frills, no interruptions.

But the picture he formed came to him full of holes, and he now suspected why.

Oh, God, he heard his mind cry suddenly, a tortured, lonely voice echoing out from the darkest corner of his heart. They had been more like window dressing for the world at large than real, feeling human beings.

They said truth always set a man free, but he wasn't so sure. Truth was, they had loved him, without condition, accepting him for what he was—driven, ambitious and aloof from their own needs, dreams and hopes and aspirations—while he forged ahead, leaving each of them behind, trapped in their own islands of silent suffering just to be loved.

Even then he wasn't sure how to react to these feelings, but a small voice in the back of his mind was growing, stronger by the minute, the more he saw the loneliness of their lives, the frustration he had created through his own neglect. The voice told him if he had the will, there was a way to change it. But when? And how exactly? And would he ever get the chance to try to make it right? And how did a man make up for years of stubborn living one way, then suddenly turn around and tell the world he'd seen the light? It wasn't that Rebecca had felt unloved all these years, or hardly abandoned while he chased his dream of saving the world from Armageddon. Or had she? And his daughters? How did they see him? Did they, too, feel adrift, disconnected from the human race somehow because he'd never shown much more than a passing interest in their lives? Or was simply on hand when necessary to pass down a bit of stern fatherly advice? He couldn't help but wonder now if he had gone ahead and taken his work to the base, as the DOD had tried to persuade him, if this would have never happened.

It hit him then, the air leaving his lungs in a sudden rush, as if he'd been punched in the stomach. His colleagues. Oklahoma. It was inconceivable, but he had already been betrayed by Rodgers, an assumed name, he was sure, an operative ostensibly with the NSA who was supposed to guard the castle. What if one of his colleagues had likewise turned traitor? Was this some dark conspiracy, envelopes of cash changing hands in some back alley? Were the four of them, who were on the verge of creating the prototype missile laser net for a bona fide SDI satellite, been sold like some commodity to a foreign government? Had one of them turned on the rest?

"Dad?"

Beyond the obvious fear, he heard something else in Patti's voice. Something, he thought, he'd not given her over the years. It was awkward to move, but he reached over and folded his hands over hers, gave them a gentle squeeze. An anger he'd never before felt coursed through him at the touch of her cold, trembling flesh. The very notion she was being forced to endure this shame, ride out whatever the danger to its conclusion, filled him with the closest he'd ever come to rage, and a primal desire to strike back.

"I'm here, Patti. I'm right here." He wasn't sure quite what he heard in his voice, but it sounded new, and foreign to the way he normally spoke to her. New, and leaving him to wonder if he was on the verge of turning some corner he never saw until now. Even some crossing over to a point of no return, becoming what he hated most in his captors.

11

Bolan knew the clock was winding down in New York. The Executioner also knew Broadwater couldn't run interference with FBI brass much longer.

Enter Brognola.

The soldier led the FBI man into the safehouse. Broadwater checked out the Spartan accommodations, the shell-shock still hanging on his expression.

"I need to make a call. There's coffee in the kitchen."

"I'd ask you got something a little stronger, but I'm in deep enough as it stands," Broadwater said, moving for the couch, tac radio in hand.

Bolan felt empathy for the man's predicament. He was a soldier in his own right, and duty had called him into the fray, the man laying it on the line for Bolan, and beyond his own career considerations. Broadwater had children to feed and a wife who worried about him coming home every time he stepped out the door. And now the FBI hierarchy would want to pull the AWOL Broadwater up on the military equivalent of dereliction of duty, just for starters. It would take some heavy Brognola muscle to put things back on track, everything short of a presidential directive probably, but Bolan knew the storm would pass as far as Broadwater was concerned. The Justice man's wonder touch was equal to raising the dead.

Beyond any concern over his personal future, the soldier could sense Broadwater was disappointed their sweep of Brooklyn neighborhoods on the way to the safehouse was uneventful. Other than threading their way past other units arriving on the scene, no terrorists, no murderous blacksuits turned up. It was possible the last one had gone down in a hail of bullets right there on Atlantic Avenue, but unlikely. In all the chaos and confusion of battle, with the Brooklyn borough offering every nook and cranny by way of alleys, parks, sewers, and with bridges leading into Manhattan, with Queens just up the way...

The Stony Man warrior's gut told him they were out there, human sharks circling, the smell of blood in their noses.

The enemy wasn't finished.

He walked into the bedroom, closed the door and found the specific section of floorboard in the middle of the room. He bent and fingered the edge, pulled up the large cut-away piece. He dialed the first series of numbers on the lock, clicked in, then went through another set to disengage the acid tank meant for felonious or curious hands if they got that far.

The backup war bag came out first. He didn't know what waited in the early-morning hours, but Bolan would be prepared with the works either way. The aluminum briefcase with sat-link was out, settled on the dresser. He worked the combination from memory, opened up and punched in a long series of numbers, opt-

ing for speakercom instead of the headphones and throat
mike.

It wasn't unusual to find Brognola in his office
around the clock when a mission was on the burner. The
big Fed came on right away, and Bolan cut to the chase,
updating the Justice man on all fronts. As usual, Brognola always expected nightmare news and didn't bela-
bor the headache of having to chainsaw through the red
tape. He'd deal with the FBI, and Broadwater could
count on getting nothing but a commendation.

That said, it was Brognola's turn.

Bolan was pacing, wondering exactly where to take
it from there, when the big Fed dropped the bomb and
froze him in his tracks.

HE WAS BREATHING way too hard, hyperventilating,
Tabrak believed, his heart like a jackhammer, ready to
blow a hole through his chest. Adrenaline? he wondered. Fear? What? Some voice he should have recognized as his own, but couldn't make out clearly, was
shooting all manner of tortured questions through his
head. Tabrak growled out loud, shook his head, trying
to quiet the voice. What was wrong with him? This was
his moment to shine, something he'd lived for most of
his life.

He had a sacred duty to carry through, for Muslims
everywhere, for himself, for God. And it didn't really
matter that he was unfamiliar with Brooklyn beyond his
own block. He figured he'd put enough distance from
the battlefront.

Tabrak had moved hard and fast, using the shadows
of alleys for concealment. The din of sirens had faded

long ago, and when he nearly stumbled across a police car rounding a corner, he'd hidden in a Dumpster. So why was he so afraid? He was still alive and on the move. Was he scared of dying? Was he questioning the mercy and the wisdom of God? Surely what he was about to do was right in the eyes of God?

He was on Seventh Avenue, breathing hard, catching strange looks now from passing infidels. He looked from the street sign to what appeared a commercial area coming awake in the early-morning hour as commuters and pedestrians began swelling the sidewalks.

Numbers. Targets. Plenty of potential, right there, he decided. What little he knew from war plans about this area of Brooklyn, mapped out by Mahlid, there were subway stops somewhere in the vicinity of Grand Army Plaza. Scratch the subway, he decided, shouldering his way through a couple, ignoring the brief outburst behind, forging down the walk. After yesterday, police were sure to be stationed on every subway platform, every car maybe. He told himself someplace where they gathered in decent-sized groups at this hour, somewhere with walls, few exits. A diner, then. Go straight through the door, the AK-74 coming out of the bag, grenades shoved in his pants pocket before he went to give them a final wake-up. Two clips were wound together, to be reversed with next to no lost precious time. Figure sixty rounds to get it started, more wrapped twin clips in the bag.

He was searching the street when the decision was made. He wasn't sure why the two policemen were boring dark stares through him, but the North Korean had warned them all their lawmen operated on something called profiling. Essentially, he recalled from one of the many briefings, they only needed to believe someone looked suspicious, fell into a stereotyped outline that gave them a right to stop, question, even search "the type." Mostly, he remembered the North Korean tell him, they were members of an ethnic minority, deemed shady looking on the spot, not belonging where the police thought they should belong.

Tabrak figured he must have fit the profile of what a bad guy looked like to them. He fit the whole bill.

Tabrak couldn't stand the struggle for air any longer, thinking his brain was about to shut down from lack of oxygen. The bag was already open, allowing him an easy draw of the AK-74. He laughed at the shock etching their faces. His breathing slowed, natural now for some reason, the voice of torment vanishing from his thoughts, as the patrol car lurched into a sliding halt near the curb. Tabrak swung the assault rifle up, held back on the trigger and blasted in the windshield.

"ROCKET MEN. That's what he said," Bolan stated.

"Became Judas on his deathbed," Brognola responded.

"It can happen."

"Dump on me, will you? I'll get the last laugh. Okay. I've got my own people, Striker, already at the Shaw residence."

"Don't expect the phone to ring."

"I'm not holding my breath for any ransom demand on this. My guys are staying put in Middleburg, both for the daughter's protection and to try to keep her calm. No media, so far, but I can almost see them licking their chops."

"She's sure they were Asian?"

"Positive. Bright girl, lucky, too, or somebody was watching over her, who can say. She's hanging in there, worried as hell naturally, I understand, but she's showing guts, considering her parents and sister were abducted at gunpoint right under their roof. The body left behind belongs to a branch of DOD black-ops security. My people found the whole security system, alarm, cameras, the works, shut down when they got there. According to Sara Shaw, only two people there had the access code to do that particular trick. And I don't think her father would have turned it off. The daughter says he was as security conscious as they get."

"Inside job. And they're cleaning up as they go."

"I know that voice all too well. I'm way ahead of you, Striker."

Bolan had no doubt they were on the same page. Questions hanging still, but the Executioner could be sure both Brognola and the cyber team at the Farm, led by Aaron Kurtzman, had done the usual digging, getting answers as fast and best they could to start piecing together the shrapnel on this puzzle.

"Here's where it stands," Brognola said. "Initial satellite imagery is showing me what looks like a spook convention in this little slice of Oklahoma prairie we touched on. U.S. government property, something like four to five square miles recently snapped up by DOD. The Army Corps of Engineers built this particular spook central.

"The rocket men are called the Titan Four. DOD, or whoever is actually running the show out there, has the civilian workforce, whatever spook or military personnel likewise housed on the base. There's a ranch house the Farm has put under the microscope. It sits all by its lonesome, a mile and change north of the compound, with plenty of vehicles, some with government tags, some luxury wheels, like they've got high-profile out-of-town guests. It has satellite dishes and armed sentries—I'm thinking black-ops central. Where the real shadows dwell. This is a classified project, involving SDI technology. Not quite a black project, meaning it would be buried so deep or floating out there in cyber limbo that not even our people would find the first glimmer of dark light.

"Striker, I don't know how they plan to pull it if off, but I know you're with me thinking this is a well-planned and well-financed conspiracy. I'm thinking it's going to hit the fan out there, a straight snatch of missile geniuses, I understand from Kurtzman, who can calibrate a guidance system on anything armed and built to fly."

"They're that good?"

"Number one. Gold-medal talent."

"It's going to happen, Hal. I hope I'm wrong, but I don't think I am. It's wanting to come together, has been since yesterday. Hell of a thing to point out, but we might have never gotten it this far, still in the dark, if the opposition didn't start eating their own."

"Because of the F train they had liabilities. One of their jihad recruits jumped the gun on the master plan, which was a massive terrorist strike. I'm thinking they covered their exit, or used it as a threat to unload on American citizens while they hauled the Titan Four out of the country."

"That would be my guess." The Executioner relayed his suspicions about Chicago, while Brognola stated he'd put the FBI and Justice on alert across the nation. "We've been down this classified road to hell before, Hal. Guys on our side selling out. Money, blackmail, warped ideology. It's all the same dirty laundry."

"A traitor is a traitor. The upshot is, the Man agrees. You've got carte blanche to go out there, knock on doors. Or kick them down. Your call."

"How soon?"

"Give me two, three hours maximum to work out travel arrangements, put together the whole intel package for you, what players we can manage to put on your scorecard on our end. And I'll deal with the FBI, the mayor, whoever else is on the warpath, looking to squeeze you and Agent Broadwater. In other words, you're free to go."

"Never a doubt."

"Call me back. It sounds like you've done enough. I'm thinking the cell up there has to be burned down." Brognola paused, waiting for a response. "I hear silence, Striker. I'm thinking my next suggestion to lay low until I get you to JFK is not an option."

"The hit team. It's just a hunch, but one, maybe more of the gunmen got away."

"There has to be a hundred thousand ways to get out of the Big Apple."

"I can't let it go."

"I'm not asking you to. But we're familiar with the drill. There will be no ID, nothing, zip, not the first computer file or document telling us who these guys are. They're black ops, ghosts, like you said. They were created by our side to stay faceless and nameless to do the kind of dirty work that would have the politicians screaming for complete control over the CIA, NSA and every other alphabet-soup agency. These guys are just part of the spook machinery."

"Now a murdering juggernaut gone amok."

"I have to run. Fires to put out and at least one to start."

"I'll be in touch."

"Hopefully from a cab on your way to the airport."

Bolan let that go. No point in causing his friend any more unnecessary stress, as Brognola punched off from his end. The soldier wasn't about to hang around the fort while he suspected a few savages were still on the hunt for innocent blood. With the sat-link back in its hole and locked down, Bolan took the second war bag. The Executioner read the look of more bad news on Broadwater's face as he entered the living room, the FBI man lowering the tac radio.

"One of them just turned up on Seventh Avenue." Broadwater stood, his eyes smoldering with anger. "Two more officers down. Another citizen body count in double digits before the bastard shot his way into a diner and blew himself up."

IN THE TWISTED MIND of the terrorist, Bolan knew he saw no shortage of murderous opportunities, with so many choice targets in a city like New York.

Well, covering all of them was next to impossible, he knew. At roughly the start of rush hour, the mayor had sounded the alert over radio and television, urging New Yorkers—nonessential personnel, he called them—to remain home. That wasn't about to happen, Bolan knew, short of a nuke dropping out of the sky. Tough and determined, attitude to spare was the rule in that town, not the exception. Most New Yorkers, Bolan knew, would march out there, middle-finger salute and all to defy whatever the odds a few maniacs might rear up in their face to snatch it all away.

Which meant teeming streets, normal rush-hour madness, streets jammed with vehicles, sidewalks swollen with foot traffic, restaurants and businesses packed. Just as he found it as they came to a dead stop in snarled traffic in the glass-and-concrete canyon of Midtown.

Broadwater had informed Bolan during the drive across the Brooklyn Bridge that everything short of martial law, meaning troops and tanks and gunships, was descending on all five boroughs. He didn't elaborate, but a tally of all the blue-and-whites and his discerning eye picking out the unmarked units, Bolan found the police hunkered down, scouring their surroundings with an unflinching grim eye, ready to take care of business. And poised, Bolan could be sure, to return a lethal favor or two to any armed wanderers they even suspected were linked to the killers of cops and civilians alike.

Part of the problem the way Bolan saw it was it might prove too little too late. For instance, only now, as rush hour was in full gear, were police setting up checkpoints on both sides of the East River and the Hudson. Uniformed cops were stacking up on subway platforms, Grand Central station, and so on. Security was beefed up on full alert from the Statue of Liberty all the way out to La Guardia, JFK and back to Newark International. Overtime for every beat cop and detective, with the National Guard right then rolling in to set up camp in Queens and Brooklyn.

Broadwater was scowling at the stalled traffic, glancing around, searching for something, anything out of the ordinary. "Has to be a police checkpoint, maybe down Forty-fourth or over on the Avenue of the Americas holding everything up. Only nobody in their right mind drives into Midtown this time of the morning. I guess that's what you're counting on? Somebody not being in their right mind, that is."

"I'm counting on the last of them already dead."

"Yeah, well, just in case...you've got eight million, maybe more like ten million faces in this city, what with the immigrant flow, most of them illegals these days. It's still your show until I drive you out to JFK."

Bolan glanced at the big agent. Broadwater was tugging at the sleeves of his oversize windbreaker with FBI on the back. "Sounds like you're not going to miss me."

Broadwater grunted, gave Bolan what he assumed passed for a friendly smile. "I appreciate your man going to bat for me like you said he would. The brass had a different tone when I checked in last, damn near respectful. Like somebody down your way made them believe their careers and pensions were on the line. Thanks."

"It wasn't your mess. And I couldn't see the point in you catching the heat, acting on my orders, while I fly off into the sunset."

"Decent of you, just the same."

"I would have done it for anybody who backed my play."

"Well, clout or not backing you up from Wonderland, I don't think you want to come back here anytime soon. A few of the guys over me might be the lost spawn of J. Edgar himself, if you get my drift."

"I've seen the type."

"Okay. Beyond sitting in traffic, hoping a crazed shooter or two turns up, any ideas?"

Bolan caught the gist of the man's point. Granted, it was a long shot, plodding around Midtown, searching, hoping for a lucky break, but this was the guts of Manhattan. Like any detective hunting a killer, Bolan tried to put himself in the opposition's head. The rough triangular outline of the Theater, Diamond and Garment Districts between Fifth and Ninth, with Rockefeller Center, various and sundry museums and galleries and Wall Street north, St. Patrick's Cathedral, with the churches of St. Thomas, St. Peter in the vicinity if Muslim fanatics wanted to make a statement...

All of it was way too ripe with easy pickings for any terrorist worth his murderous impulses to pass up. Still, Bolan was starting to think he might just call it off and head for JFK early.

Then the shooting and the screaming hit the air.

A lightning burst of bedlam came from the direction of Forty-fourth where the famed Algonquin Hotel stood, and he believed the Tradesmen Building towered on the same block.

Bolan grabbed up the Uzi, shouldered out the door. A stampede had already begun in the kind of grim earnest that would see victims falling under the mad rush alone, bones breaking or worse. The whole mass of howling pedestrian overflow was a rolling wave of countless bodies surging around the corner, pedestrians already toppling, left or trampled where they fell. Beyond the shouting and wailing, the Executioner clearly heard twin stutters of autofire.

By now stranded commuters were in panic, laying on the horns up and down Fifth Avenue, metal rending next as vehicles attempted to bulldoze any path of escape they could create. A few of the more daring or curious came out of their cars in various states of confusion and fear, then began running in all directions to clear the battle zone. The whole bottleneck of man and machine was about to cost even more lives.

Bolan bounded up on the trunk of a cab, charging ahead, leaping roof to hood, pounding ahead over the vehicular bridge, veering for the stampede. He was flying off the roof of a Mercedes, landing and bulling his own charge through the crazed pedestrian traffic when the autofire and the wailing of wounded or dying victims multiplied in his ears. He knew he was nearly on top of the shooters, and was gathering speed as the rushing mob took him for another mass murderer and leaped out of his path by taking cover in doorways, between parked or stalled vehicles or wherever they thought they could hide and hold on.

There were two of them, as the Executioner gave the pandemonium a search on the run, charging off the sidewalk, weaving between the logjam of vehicles. He was locked in on the shooters, tunnel vision obscuring racing figures and looming structures as nothing but a blur. The reasons why the fanatics had chosen this stop to make their murderous stand Bolan didn't know or care. It was way too much bad luck for too many innocents already that they'd made it this far.

They were splitting up, AK-47s sweeping the dispersing crowds on both sides of the street, then extended bursts of autofire raked immobilized or abandoned vehicles, the lunatics blowing apart glass, stitching a few motorists who were attempting to outrun the tracking storms of lead.

The Executioner hung the Uzi around his shoulder. With innocents scrambling to clear the area or with a noncombatant suddenly popping up at the worst of times, the soldier opted for the steadier and more certain high-velocity punch of the Desert Eagle.

The hand cannon was out and tracking as the warrior dashed up the narrow space between sitting vehicles, heads of noncombatants sliding past his gun sights, whipping into view, there then gone. One heartbeat for a clear shot, the shooter sliding back into the street, and Bolan tapped the trigger. The thunder from the Desert Eagle cut through the brick wall of autofire, horns and screams.

Downrange the shooter took the .44 Magnum round through the sternum, heart blown to mush before a misty burst hit the air on the round's pulverizing exit from between the shoulder blades.

One down.

The soldier was wheeling, Desert Eagle tracking toward the other source of slaughter when he saw the fanatic jerking around in a crazed dance step. Whether mindless rage, adrenaline or both kept him going, the fanatic was holding back on the AK-47's trigger, somehow held it blazing on-line even as crimson spurted from the holes marching over his chest. Bolan squeezed the trigger, dropped him for good with a headshot.

The fury of the howling mob was deafening, as Bolan whipped around, searching for the initial source of gun-fire that had riddled the second terrorist. He had a good hunch who had provided the help, but Bolan wasn't prepared for the angry surge, the sick feeling that slammed his gut next.

Broadwater was sliding down the side of a FedEx truck, toppling out of sight.

Bolan jostled and shouldered a charge through a smattering of runners. Rage over this senseless slaughter seemed to obscure his sight with a red film. He was stowing the Desert Eagle, flying around the front end of a vehicle and moving up on the fallen FBI man when a guttural choking drifted through the ringing in Bolan's ears. He was crouching beside Broadwater when a pained smile stretched the FBI man's lips, and he shuddered up on an elbow.

Broadwater touched the holes in his sweater, grimacing, the bottom of the ill-fitting parachute that passed for a jacket touching the street. "Kevlar." He looked up at Bolan. "The wife...she never lets me leave home without it."

12

Wahbat Mazad was on the edge of the couch, rapt but anxious, listening to the gray-haired anchorman.

"As most of you now know this morning in Midtown, Manhattan, the very epicenter of New York itself, was turned into a scene that can only be described as an urban war zone. What we know is that an undetermined number of gunmen opened fire with automatic weapons on crowds of commuters and pedestrians near Fifth Avenue. We believe most of the shooting was right in front of the Tradesmen Building, the, uh, carnage spilling also in front of the famous, long-standing landmark that is the Algonquin Hotel. How many are dead and wounded we do not yet have any confirmed reports, any indication...just a minute. We are receiving confirmed reports now that there were two gunmen. Both of them are dead, whether they were shot by police, or took their own lives, we cannot confirm. This, as you know, comes only one day after the massacre on the F train..."

"It has started. But why have we not received our own call? What is happening, that we would be kept in the dark like this?" asked Yulat.

Mazad didn't have any answers, but he had some clues, vague as they were. The only thing he was sure of right then was the power of his own AKM assault rifle. Yesterday he had received two phone calls from his personal contact in Brooklyn, arranged with Mahlid before they left Iraq, eighteen months ago. According to the leader of the New York cell, one of their own was responsible for what the famous American news anchor was describing as a massacre on the F train.

There was trouble, yes, but Mazad couldn't be positive who was in the most dire straits. Was it his own cell? Or was it their enemy, whom he could only hope and pray was still being hunted in the streets of New York? The special report, which had interrupted their normal afternoon round of soap operas, didn't seem to have much more to offer, at least in terms of rising body counts. Then there was a report about a massive shootout at a Brooklyn restaurant, complete with explosions and dead police officers. The media had run film footage of a burning police helicopter in the middle of Atlantic Avenue, painting the war zone in their usual colorful language and analogies, expressing their shock and outrage, speculating—unconfirmed reports, of course—that an army of international terrorists had invaded the United States.

If they really only knew, he thought.

New York was only the beginning.

But something had gone terribly wrong with the Brooklyn cell, and Mahlid, wording it all very carefully over the phone, had hinted their sponsors may want to pull the plug on their end in New York. Which left a slew of questions tumbling through his mind. Had their brothers-in-jihad in that city been in danger of being eliminated because of the actions of one man since yesterday? Would their sponsors, the Koreans, abandon them there in Chicago? Why hadn't they called, if word had gone out to launch the jihad? Worse, if New York had fallen from grace with the sponsors, then would they come to pay them a personal visit, as in shooting first?

The knock on the door jolted him off the couch. He hissed at Yulat to turn down the TV, then padded for the door. He stared into the peephole, the assault rifle clutched in hands suddenly moist with sweat. His heart was already racing uncontrollably, terrified as he was of finding the hall swarming with police or SWAT, but he felt the pounding in his chest become even more furious now at the sight of the man standing on the other side. He had never seen the face, but why should he recognize the man? Still, there was something in the eyes that warned him.

That was no policeman, which was the good news. But it was the coldness, the lifelessness in the eyes, the way a lizard might view an insect it was about to pounce on for a meal, which made Mazad almost throw open the door and start blasting away. Something, too, about the man in black, standing there, at ease, skin so gray it looked like cigarette ash. And a face with features so sharp, or blunted, he couldn't decide if it was more suited to be on one of those statues he believed was called a gargoyle.

He almost didn't look human. "Who is it?"

No response, then the man bared his teeth in a smile, stepped back and held his arms out by his side, palms shown, as if to say, "What's the problem?"

Mazad drew back from the peephole, waved his assault rifle in an angry gesture for Yulat to hide in the bedroom, the implication clear that he was to come out shooting if this was a raiding party. He unbolted, unclicked and unlatched the series of locks he had installed himself the first week they had rented the apartment. Backing up, he raised the AKM, said, "It's open. Come in."

And he came in, taller and even more whip lean than he'd looked on the other side of the door. More like a reptile in the face and eyes, now that the tiny bubbled peephole wasn't exaggerating the features like the distortion of carnival mirrors.

The man shut the door, reset the locks and bolts when Mazad told him to do so. Mazad had been in the Republican Guard, and he had smelled plenty of death on men, women and children, during the war with the infidels. This man reeked of blood on his hands. He wasn't awash in blood, of course, but Mazad smelled something he could only imagine was akin to a rotting of the soul, evil ingrained into his flesh, past deeds of murder in the eyes, a haunting reminder of a similar future to come. A gray serpent, then, Mazad thought, not to be trusted. He stepped deeper back into the living room, the man actually grinning at the AKM.

"Relax, Wahbat. I come in peace."

The voice was slightly raspy, deep but soft. Controlled, Mazad thought, in a low-key manner—meant to deceive—with an intensity just beneath the surface tone. He found himself both mesmerized and afraid. He couldn't decide if it sounded as if the man mocked the world around him or was prepared to destroy it.

"How do you know my name? Who are you?"

"Just a messenger. Good news or bad news, that's up to you."

"What? Who sent you?"

"Hey, easy with that thing. Guns make me nervous. I'm reaching for a cigarette, okay?"

The slight hump beneath the black leather bomber jacket didn't escape his eye. The man was armed with a pistol. Slowly he took a pack of cigarettes from a pocket, lighting up as he turned that damnable smile on the television.

"I see you've heard the bad news already about your buddies in New York."

"What happened to them?"

Instead of answering, the man looked around the drab apartment with its cracked walls and peeling paint, grunted at the cockroach skittering over the bare wood floor near the couch. "What a dump. I didn't think they'd put you up in a suite at the Hilton, but they could have done a little better than this."

"You are making me very angry!"

"Look at this guy, Wahbat. I've seen that clown before." The man chuckled, again ignoring the question as he shook his head at the television. "Now we've got the expert, the right hand of God himself, coming on to sort it all out for us, the great unwashed. Everybody's an expert these days, like they chat with the Almighty every night or something. Ever notice that, Wahbat? Constitutional law, the stock market, prostate cancer, terrorism. This is a country filled with experts. How do you get a job like that anyway, get paid good money to be a smug know-it-all? Huh?"

Mazad took a threatening step toward the man, then stopped when those dead eyes bored into him. "You talk too much. Answer my question."

"Tell your buddy he can come out of hiding. Both of you need to listen real carefully to what I've been sent to tell you, then somehow pass it on to the others. But watch what you say over the phone. These days, the air itself seems to have ears." He was moving away from the TV, angling for the kitchen.

The rage seemed to roar like a crashing wave in Mazad's ears as the insolent bastard actually went to the refrigerator and opened it. "Feel free to make yourself at home."

"No beer? Oh, I almost forgot. You're Muslim."

He glimpsed Yulat moving into the living room, his own assault rifle aimed toward the kitchen. When the man turned, he dropped the smug comedy act, the eyes turning even colder, if that was possible, Mazad thought.

"We can go for it right here, gentlemen, or you can get those pieces off me and hear me out. Your call."

Mazad snapped at Yulat to lower his weapon.

"By the way, I know Arabic."

Mazad balked, felt the brief quiver in his hands as he let the AKM fall by his side. "What is your message?"

"It's real simple. You are to stay here. You will receive the call you've been waiting for."

"When?"

"Rough time frame? They told me to tell you twelve to eighteen hours."

"And you will sit on us, baby-sit us?"

"I'm leaving—hey, unless one of you goes out for some beer, calls up some whores, I'll throw you a nice going-away party before the jihad starts. No? Well, South Side is not my style. But I'll be close, so will a few others. Watching. Make sure we don't have any more F train situations before the time."

"The Koreans? They are spying on us?"

"Nobody's spying. Just stick to the plan. Do that, then you'll be free to go out there and burn down half this city."

Mazad didn't know what to believe, but he felt the full probing weight of the man's stare, then the stranger smiled, and added, "Jihad, brothers, it's all about jihad. You hang tight, and it's going to be a wonderful day in the neighborhood."

"WHAT THE HELL is this?"

"It's a chopper. A Kiowa JetRanger OH-58, used by both the Army and the Navy, to be exact. Also armed, both minigun and TOW missiles."

"A gunship?"

"A gunship."

Armand Geller was on the verge of adding "you silly bastard," but the DIA man was clearly out of sorts, flailing around, scowling and huffing at the bank of monitors as if a show of antics alone would make the chopper go away. Not the time to antagonize the guy, he decided. Whatever was happening, Geller knew it smacked of trouble.

Turner aimed the dark expression at Geller. "I know what it is. I want to know why it's there."

"One way to find out."

"How's that? We start winging away with the surface-to-air missiles at an Army helicopter?"

Geller stepped up to the control bank, ignoring both the DIA man and the command center assistants—two of his own people, black ops—and stared at the chopper. Flying in from the north, which could mean anything, about two hundred feet up. Slowing now as the pilot cut back on speed, coming in for a closer look at the whole compound. Recon. But why?

"Not quite anything so dramatic," Geller told the DIA man.

Compton, he saw, was working dials and punching buttons on the radio console, looking to cut in on their mystery guest's frequency, ordering the pilot to respond. Their own frequency, so classified not even the Pentagon knew it existed, was courtesy of a FEMA black magic touch. It worked one-way, supposedly, he thought, meaning they could cut into all airwaves, civilian or military, while essentially a firewall was built around their own command channel.

"Then, what?"

Geller waited to hear something from the other side, but his gut told him their company was ignoring the call, making some statement. Not good. Considering the New York situation, he suspected the worst. Somebody had smelled them out. They weren't the only covert act on the block.

The sit-rep Turner had passed on to him earlier, after Bowen had landed in Chicago, was fraught with any number of gloom-and-doom scenarios. Cell Two was on edge, ready to blast out of the gate on its own, until Bowen apparently calmed the troops with a few choice words. Cell Three, he understood, also required a visit by North Korean referees, who reported they strongly suspected that jihad bunch was under an FBI magnifying glass.

"Let's take a ride up there," Geller told Turner. "Polite gesture, get them down on the ground where we can take a closer look."

Geller read the agitation in the DIA man's eyes. Turner might have been stamped by the Department of Defense to officially run the base, the man instrumental in blowing smoke at the right people in Washington, but Geller had long since been sought out by the colonel himself to watch and monitor the whole operation. He caught the flicker of regret in Turner's eyes as he turned back to the monitors, the man probably sinking back in time to the day he bit the hook and was reeled in. Then Geller watched the screens, found the chopper hovering now at the north edge of the compound. Turner would do as he was told. Like the senator, Geller viewed the DIA man as nothing but a trapped rat, in every sense, with his own hand always poised to drown them both if the colonel gave the order. Turner was stuck, all right, the usual vices nailing him to his own cross, the whores, the gambling, trading off a little classified intel here and there for a few dollars more. One of the team, but barely.

Geller moved and took the HK MP-5 subgun off a table. He could almost read Turner's thoughts, the man working his nervous look over the weapon. "Just in case they aren't the reasonable sort, Mr. Turner."

THE PLAN, WAS to go to work immediately on their nerves, start smoking them out using the Justice Department heat at his disposal. In short, the Executioner wanted them to know he was in the neighborhood, while implying when they met he was adding up the score.

Keep it simple. Light a fire.

He was squeezed into the cockpit hatch, looking over Jack Grimaldi's shoulders, the Farm's pilot having just called him in from the troop hold in the belly of the Kiowa. They were hovering now, the soldier confirming, "I see it. Stay afloat, right here."

Bolan watched as the rough equivalent of the Blackhawk SOF MH-60 was lifting off from the helipad in the distance. Coming in for a closer inspection of their visitors or something more heavy-handed? he wondered. He spied three more such gunships grounded near the string of hangars to the distant southwest, a jumble of twin-engine aircraft, two sleek Gulfstreams parked on the tarmac. A control tower rose from the prairie floor, but there was a squat concrete structure that made Bolan wonder what was behind the door. The Farm had antiaircraft batteries concealed in housing similar to what he found there. A reasonable guess, and the spooks on this prairie stretch were likewise capable of taking out any aircraft deemed hostile or suspicious—or whose pilot wouldn't respond to their radio signal. On his order, Grimaldi had shut down the Single-Channel Ground and Airborne Radio System, SINCGARS. Any warning to clear out went unheard and thus unheeded, if that was the message being relayed to them. They weren't quite in the hot zone yet, with missiles streaking to blow them out of the sky, or the chopper wouldn't be on its way. Bolan was also betting they were smart or wily enough, or had plenty to hide, to realize that downing an Army helicopter would only put them under official microscopic examination.

He watched the gunship gaining altitude, nose swinging around, vectoring now, hard and fast their way. He'd seen this particular spook gunship special before. Brognola had stated this wasn't quite a black project, but it was near enough to warrant the classified prototype black gunship, which was basically a cross between an Apache and a Blackhawk, with pylons housing missiles, a minigun in the turret nose.

The compound itself could have the Area 51 conspiracy crowd, Bolan thought, nodding in righteous confirmation they weren't the lunatic fringe fantasizing out loud just to grab their fifteen minutes of fame. Coming in, the soldier had stood in the hatch and found the Farm's satellite imagery on the money. Of course, up close it was larger, more sprawling than pictures snapped from outer space. Under the late-afternoon sun, the main buildings of the complex glittered now, their silver skin made of aluminum or some other alloy, Bolan guessed. West he'd noted the two silver rows of mobile homes, where the workforce was quartered. Then a massive dome just beyond Silver Row, the fenced-in outdoor tennis and basketball courts and Olympic-size pool telling the soldier they weren't strictly all work. A vast motor pool, official government vehicles, mostly SUVs and vans, was situated in a gravel lot that fanned away from what the Farm believed was the main work area. The assumption was that particular mammoth abode doubled as command central, the sweeping stretch of rooftop, prickling with antennae, satellite and radar dishes of various size, a good indicator Aaron Kurtzman had pegged it right.

It had taken a fair amount of time and sweat on Brognola's end, not to mention an exchange of heated dialogue with the FBI to get him to Oklahoma, in the

backyard now of what he suspected was a brewing conspiracy. Both the Kiowa and some blacksuits had been
waiting for Bolan at the end of his military jaunt from
JFK to Tulsa, the gunship requisitioned by Barbara
Price, the Farm's mission controller, from an Army am-
munition depot south, near McAlester.

Logistical pieces in place, it was once again Bolan's
show.

Then there was the ranch house in question. A swift
pass over the compound, and Bolan had taken in more
government vehicles, a smattering of armed guards outside to keep watch, radar and satellite dishes on the
roof.

The whole picture flared up a nagging suspicion in
Bolan's gut.

Hinky. All of it.

The blackbird was suspended now, dead ahead,
swinging around, the fuselage door thrown open. Two
figures wedged themselves in the opening, a big, beefy
guy in a cowboy hat gesturing toward the ground. He
was clearly bent out of shape. There was a man beside
the cowboy, holding an HK MP-5 subgun, and he didn't
strike Bolan as the type to restrain himself if the itch to
shoot first and ask questions later struck a mood. The
soldier had his proved side arms holstered beneath his
windbreaker, considered opting for the M-16/M-203
combo in a bin in the fuselage, then decided against tip-
ping any hand where he might need to deliver the
knockout blow later.

"Drop us down," the Executioner said as he moved
back into the fuselage, waiting in the open hatch. As
soon as they touched down, he bounded onto the

ground, marched into the rotor wash and found the two men already moving to intercept his course. They pulled up between the choppers.

"Who the hell are you? You have any idea this is private U.S. government property? Do you realize we are authorized to use deadly force against trespassers?"

Bolan slowed his advance, the Justice credentials out and open. He closed the gap to roughly two feet, intent on invading more than just their personal space. "I must have missed the sign on the way in." The gunner, he saw, was dividing the suspicion and anger between the Kiowa and the cowboy. The designated mouthpiece was an odd match, Bolan observed, against both the blacksuit and the space-age dwellings. Cowboy boots, sheepskin coat, with a hip holstered revolver displayed, the cowboy, Bolan saw, held the Stetson on his head as the rotor gust threatened to send it sailing. The smirk was forming on the cowboy's lips when Bolan told him, "Take a good look. This didn't come out of a bubblegum machine." The man peered, grunted, bobbed his head. The other gunner, Bolan glimpsed, was boring the evil eye into him, measuring, thinking dark thoughts, no doubt, and looking twitchy to use the subgun.

Even with the rotor wash it wasn't necessary, as close as they were, but the cowboy was still nearly shouting in Bolan's face. "Okay. So? Special Agent Belasko. That still doesn't give you the authority to trespass on classified U.S. military property."

Bolan put the credentials in his pocket, cut to the meat of it. "I'm part of an ongoing investigation. Kidnapping. So that gives me some latitude."

"Really? All my personnel are present and accounted

for. You took a long flight out here for nothing. Good-bye."

"Thomas Shaw," Bolan said, and that froze them just as they were spinning on their heels. "His wife and daughter were abducted from their home in Middle-burg, Virginia. The man's under contract with the DOD as part of a project here. You people, the way I hear it, are on the cutting edge of Star Wars technology. The Titan Four—ring a bell? The other three of this rocket-brains circle, I'm told, are on this compound. I'm think-ing they might have some ideas. But you can start this mutual cooperation by telling me about Shaw yourself."

The cowboy was dancing now from boot to boot, clearing his throat, glancing at his partner as if he needed help. "Nothing, that's what I'm going to tell you. Whatever happened to Shaw and his family is a matter under investigation by people with a lot more au-thority than the Justice Department."

"Telling me to go home, is that it? It's all under con-trol?" And Bolan tossed it out next, ready to gauge their reaction. "Just like New York."

He thought the cowboy was going to faint, teetering for a dangerous moment, jaw slack, then righting him-self as if it were only the rotor wash threatening to suck him out of his boots. "I think it is best if you go quietly on your way...."

The other guard stepped in, as if to cut off his part-ner before he shot his mouth too much. "Justice De-partment or not, we are authorized to use deadly force."

"So use it."

The hardman chuckled, playing it off, but Bolan could see the dark look passing through his eyes, considering the option. "I trust you'll be on your way and leave this matter to us." He looked at his partner, jerked a nod toward the blackbird, started to turn, then added, "Oh, and if you decide to come back? Make sure you have a little more than some pissant warrant from Washington."

Bingo. Ill will to spare. The challenge was issued, the gunner unable to contain himself from striking the killer pose. It wasn't exactly absolute confirmation of his worst suspicions, but it was close enough, and the Executioner knew human snakes when he saw them.

Bolan stood his ground, watching the rats scurry back for their gunship hole, then turned and retraced his path back into the Kiowa. He told the Grimaldi, "Tulsa. But give me one more look at the ranch house on the way."

"Aye, aye, Striker. You know, those two," Grimaldi called over his shoulder, working them into liftoff, "I've seen more pleasant looks on dead men."

Bolan nodded. "They're dirty. That's why they look dead."

At least, he thought, as far as their souls went. Unless he was way off the mark, and he couldn't remember the last time instinct had let him down, the Executioner had arrived in a viper's nest of traitors.

Soon, very soon, he intended to go out, one with the night, and let the trampling begin.

13

In his experience it was dangerous, bordering on reckless and foolish, to stray too close to the fire of other
men's ambition, especially where they sought to con-
quer and divide those they believed existed only to serve
and obey. The obvious question in Armand Geller's
mind, then, was who would rule and who serve?

Some of the details for the final conflagration—the
Phoenix scenario—were sketchy. However, he knew
enough about the running schematics, and he believed
he could surely read into the methods and motivations
behind the madness of the council's founding fathers to
catch a glimpse of the future. When the smoke from
their ultimate war finally cleared, he knew whoever was
left to rise from the ashes would have grown obscenely
rich, with numbered accounts that could buy and sell entire Third World armies. And thus, he believed, enter
men's true colors to begin separating wheat from chaff.
Human nature being what it was—untrustworthy on a
good day—he suspected excessive disposable cash
alone would present a series of future dilemmas, po-

tential embarrassments, since at least two among the central core had proved track records of self-indulgence.

What went around, Geller mentally weighed, was a lesson that could prove fatal.

Beyond any glaring peccadilloes among their group, he understood the ultimate goal of seizing absolute power was an extreme hazard by itself. Where they might soon determine who lived and who died—and by the droves, mass murder to them easy as flicking a light switch—it was wise to be wary he wasn't some sacred idol above getting crushed and trampled in the fray if it served their purpose. Hell, they'd even claim his head just for chuckles, he suspected, stroking their monumental egos while mounting one more trophy on their mantel of duplicity and backstabbing. It was a cold reality, holding hands with the devil. And he had seen many men, professionals like himself, who had thrown their lot too close to this particular brand of fire, only to be consumed when it finally burned out of control. And why was it, he wondered, the warriors who did all the dirty work were always the first casualties, deemed expendable when the tide turned or the first whiff of crisis hung in the air?

So there he was, Armand Geller thought, sitting among the gods. Playing the game of life and death right beside them, helping, no less, to pave their rapture to the heavens while the rest of the world would bow, pay homage and beg to be spared from the coming Armageddon of their end game.

There were six of them at the table, seven if he chose to include himself. Something personal, pride, he decided, kept him feeling apart, as different from the rest as heaven was to hell. Not that these six came up short in the ambition and tenacity department; he simply lived on another cosmic plane, a deified mortal in his own right. Beyond the job he'd signed on for, he simply wouldn't count himself among their ranks. Not that he felt unworthy, unclean to be in the presence of men who made much of the intelligence world go-round, eyes to the near future where they planned to send far more than just political and military infrastructures flying off their axis. Far from the bashful sort, the first hint that Geller was being viewed as little more than a monkey to the organ grinders he wouldn't hesitate to speak his mind, or worse if they caught him on an especially bad day. They could dream and scheme all they wanted, even successfully execute unfurling the end game of the Phoenix Council all the way to unleashing the fires of the Apocalypse. But at the first sign their own *Titanic* had sprung a leak, he was guessing—looking ahead himself—that one, maybe two of them would consider abandoning ship, leaving the others to drown. Oh, no mistake, in the event of disaster he would fight to save their mighty ship, professional pride getting the better of him, he reckoned. But if it appeared they would leave him chained to a bag of rocks to go down with the wreckage, he wasn't beyond killing the gift horse.

A full-blown crisis hadn't yet arisen, but an iceberg, he suspected, was right then looming in their path, ready to slice through the hull as the ship tried to stay its course. So far, they'd danced around the one obstacle he was most concerned with, but he sensed a couple of them were building up the courage to broach the subject.

The big guy in black. This Belasko from the Justice

Department. The man who had the stones to fly in unannounced and start asking questions.

Geller leaned back in the barrel swivel chair, peering into the smoke, checking them out one by one through the shroud of white light filtering into the haze, which was contained like choking smog within the walls of the war room. Faces were obscured, but he knew five of the six by voice, shadow and stature. The two men from FEMA, for instance, that murky but almighty Agency that had the power to declare martial law in the event of a national emergency. One of them was retired, but had maintained his old network of contacts, black-ops netherworld connections that were critical to keeping an eye on potential troublemakers in Washington. The other FEMA demigod, still active and so high up the feeding chain it would only take one more "accident" for him to grab the reins of power, was designated as the right hand of the council when the coming storm landed. Then the Chief of counterintelligence from the DIA, Turner's superior, sitting directly across from his counterpart in the NSA, which was counterterrorism. The fifth man he wasn't so sure about, but he had the look of a bruiser, a covert mangler of expendable flesh who knew his way around the wet-work block.

The rumor mill in spookdom, he knew, could churn out any number of wild fabrications, spinning out all manner of doublespeak meant to hide the skeletons, keep friend and foe alike guessing, when more often than not the line between the two was blurred. DOD? CIA? NSA? None of the above? All the above? he wondered. A freelancer, selling his services to the highest bidder? Not even Geller knew who and what the man really was, despite all his cyberspace wizards, the black-ops freelancers at his beck and call. The shady truth was the man was classified, buried so deep from the light of day that even his own mother would deny he'd ever been born.

Whoever the man was, the others, the colonel included, appeared to sit in quiet deference when he'd first called the meeting to order. If Geller wasn't mistaken, one or two of them looked as close to being intimidated by his presence alone—fidgeting some or lighting another cigarette off the butt of a smoke they'd only half-finished—as he'd ever expect to find in the eyes of these carnivores. He could be reading it wrong altogether, but the big man had staked his claim at the head of the table first, then the others took their place. The ceremony, unwritten or performed solely on instinct and respect, struck Geller as equal to lesser Dons waiting on the Godfather's next breath. Even Colonel Chongjin, seated at the other end, watching all of them in his inscrutable way, appeared unusually subdued. Hard to tell, since the only time the man showed any sign of life for as long as Geller had known him was when he bared that smile, which was meant, he supposed, to keep the other guy off balance.

A cloud of cigar smoke hung in front of the bruiser's face as he cleared his throat. When he spoke, everyone listened, Geller finding a couple of them edging forward in their chairs, the voice of God about to come through the cloud. "Gentlemen, I would like to commend you for getting it all this far."

If they took that as a compliment, Geller didn't see

them looking set to raise a toast. The Retired FEMA man worked on his whiskey glass in the silence, while the NSA man was clacking a Zippo, an act that seemed to encourage the DIA man and the active FEMA man to pursue the next round of chain-smoking and whiskey sipping.

Say what he would about a few of them, looking down his nose at perhaps their lack of battlefield experience, but Geller still saw them as old school. It was a no-shit look in their eyes, coupled with what he'd heard them say among themselves in past such gatherings. They were determined to a fault, unyielding in principle to stay their chosen course, unwilling to bow to the changing winds of a world that was passing them by, in all ways. They would stick to their guns, voice their radical opinions in time, some of them sounding extreme to the point of lunacy. But this wasn't some board meeting or congressional hearing, Geller thought, where whatever few dinosaurs left were allowed to waddle around the fort, and only then if they went with the flow.

The silence hung, and the smoke thickened. A particularly mean edge of sarcasm knifed through Geller as he watched them, gathering their thoughts, most likely feeling out the dark edges in each other. He was thinking this was where one of them was supposed to stand and applaud, or bow to the Godfather as a group. There was nothing commendable, admirable or remotely clever about how they had arrived at this juncture. Conspiracies, extortion, the buying and selling of leverage and such were the routine and not the aberration in spookdom. They kept gaining steam and momentum on their rise to the top, winning smiles all around, similar to the defense attorney handing off the weekly envelope bulging with cash in the judge's chambers to get the next verdict in his favor. They kept mounting their own shadow army.

Geller caught the man's narrowed gaze at the end of the table, aimed at him like two pieces of sharp flint inside the smoke cloud.

He went on between puffs of his stogie. "We are down to the wire, gentlemen. But before we proceed, there are a few matters we need to address. As we all know, New York did not fall according to plan. I trust the necessary steps have been taken to correct any such future snags. We are open for discussion."

They had already touched on the night's logistics, but brief reports of the day's events all around seemed to Geller to get glossed over by a sense of urgency building in the room by the minute.

"I have been assured the Chicago cell is contained," the DIA man said. "Regrettably I didn't exercise more control with subordinates."

Geller fought to keep the grin off his face. The buck was being passed to Turner. He could almost see Turner now, ears burning over in command and control, keeping his nerves and paranoia in check as he slipped off to the can for a deep slug from his flask.

"As for the third cell," the man went on, "in brief discussion with the colonel and Turner, I'd say it's fifty-fifty they get blown out of the water."

Chongjin didn't wish to address the matter. Geller glimpsed the colonel as a stone portrait of silent musing.

"Which is why we are moving ahead immediately to initiate," Geller heard the Big Man state. "I agree with the colonel. Unforeseen events have forced us to accelerate the whole process."

The man from NSA spoke up. "Our specialists have warned me there is no absolute undetectable corridor we—or several of us—will take on our way out. Virtually impossible, with satellite passovers, NORAD so close, in fact, although our experts believe there might be a narrow window of opportunity further out for us to pull off our vanishing act. Considering our detail out west isn't scheduled to leave until 2400 hours their time...but given the day's events, I concur that we move immediately on this."

The retired FEMA man killed his drink. He rattled the ice around some, seemed poised to search the room as if a butler would materialize out of the smog, then asked, "How about the schematics?"

The question was directed at the DIA man, who answered, "Blueprints, essential ballistic date, telemetry mathematics and other classified technical data, including X-ray laser systems and the Medusa's web shield layout—all logged on disc."

"Under lock and key, we take it?"

"Good to go on the way out with Turner. I have the access codes to all files."

"I hope they're committed to more than just memory." the big man said.

"Right here in my briefcase, sir."

"And our catch from back east?" the retired FEMA man wanted to know.

The man from DIA checked his watch. "Any time

now. Within the hour, but I will double-check on progress before we leave."

"Colonel?" the big man said.

Geller felt the heat rise a notch as he saw Chongjin stiffen in his seat, glance his way before he took center stage. "I feel it imperative I refresh memories at this late hour, so that we have a full grasp of the immediate future and a clear understanding of all of its meaning to each of us. This is not and has never been simply about one aim, one goal, one man. On either side. The time has come for us to put aside personal philosophies which shape our various end plans. I have heard plenty already about how the face of America is changing for the worse, how in the next generation you dread who might land in your White House."

Geller felt the grunt rolling around in his chest, decided it was time for a cigarette himself, if only to keep his face free of an easy read.

"You have your political puppets, with more appointees guaranteed to join them as our campaign contributions filter their way to Washington. Part of the package of our mutual cooperation," Chongjin stated. "However, Geller can confirm the senator's state of mind, if you choose to ask him."

Geller played it cool, fired up, drew easy on his smoke while waiting out the next round of silence. No one seemed so inclined to inquire about the senator's mental and emotional health, taking it for granted it was under control.

Then Chongjin took him off the hot seat and went on to other matters. "This is about SDI technology, but that is only one item. Our own exchange program, devised by all of us gathered here. Yes, you are giving me this Titan Four, lending me their brains, if you will. With schematics on Medusa, I—we—will soon be in a position to become our own power, dictating world affairs. On our end we already have the basic materials, alloys, rocket fuel, uranium, plutonium, processors and so forth. We also have some of the technical expertise, but nothing close to the four men we will take out of this country.

"Further, the goal, or one of them, will be not only seeking to neutralize and render useless any future so-called Star Wars technology, but we will be build our own SDI net in outer space with satellites we hope to likewise arm with thermonuclear laser-guided warheads. During the entire process, those of us in this room, along with my country, will become a nuclear superpower. A conquering elite. With the army we have recruited and assembled outside the United States, with the various ordnance at their disposal, Washington can and will become nothing short of a slave to our demands. Especially after they get a taste of the anarchy to be unleashed, a look into their future if they do not bend to our will. I will tell you now, in no uncertain terms, this is the hour we are to be at our most resolute, our most determined, our most brave.

"Now, there has been a slight alteration in our immediate plans to initiate."

Geller saw the colonel look down to the far end of the table. The big man picked up the ball, said, "The bulk of nonessential personnel will be left behind, of course. Fortunately there are only two families with children. Once initiation is under way, the ones who will be going will be rounded up."

"The story they will be told is that the base is under attack," the colonel said.

"Attack?" the NSA man inquired. "By whom?"

The colonel showed the smile. "Terrorists." He lifted a hand before inquiring minds started bleating out the confusion. "I am sure they all watch the news. These are not stupid people. It shouldn't be too far beyond the realm of possibility that such a thing is possible. Mind you, resistance will not be tolerated. Turner and two of our operatives have the list of nonessential personnel who won't be making the trip. They will commence initiation once we are finished here."

A bloodbath in the wings, Geller knew, mass execution. A mental scan of civilian numbers, among them engineers, labor and maintenance, cooks, and he guessed a ballpark figure of a hundred bodies, one-fifty tops. Women and children? Roughly a quarter of that.

"We will be flying," the colonel said, "all available aircraft to a designated area inside New Mexico. Recent events, as stated, have forced us to move swiftly, and likewise we have formed a contingency strategy due to circumstances beyond our immediate control. Plan B is for us to fly several of our operatives to a private airfield. From there we will be transported by vehicle to wait for our detail from Nellis."

That was all news to Geller, and judging the NSA man's furrowed brow and the DIA man's quizzical frown, they'd been likewise left in the dark on this tidbit. On top of a sudden shift to this mysterious Plan B, Geller knew all about the recruitment angle, having had a hand in the original hunt for suitable cannon fodder. He briefly considered just how much could now go badly wrong. In the beginning he had voiced several objections when the recruitment was launched, with candidates chosen, for the most part it seemed, solely on the merits of sociopathic tendencies. Well, his input had been ignored, the council bulling ahead, snatching them out of dead-end lives for one last shot at the elusive brass ring, shipping them off to the wild Pacific yonder to become what he could only think of as the council's doomsday soldiers. Killers. Marauders. The recruitment, the whole retraining program alone, bordered on insanity since most of their army had been drummed out of the military. Now mass slaughter of civilians. Jetting off to hole up in New Mexico while Nellis did or didn't make it to the scene. Changing the plan, in short, just as the game was about to start. Why did he feel the sudden urge, he wondered, to interrupt and recite to them Murphy's Law?

The colonel had either said enough on the matter, or handed the ball off again to the big man for further explanation. "It's an underground, abandoned, little-known fallout shelter once used by the Army from the old litmus days of atomic testing."

"A bunker," the man from NSA said.

"More or less," the big man said. "It's where we will wait it out until our ride from Nellis shows up. It's remote enough we're hoping no one will think to give it a thorough search, either from ground, air or outer space. Upshot—it makes for a shorter haul on both ends."

"Which brings me back to the original reason for this change," Chongjin said, and seemed to direct his words to Geller. "New York, it would appear, has nearly thrust us to the very edge of exposure. Does anyone find it remarkable that this superassassin, this Reaper, was the only one who managed to make it out of New York? More, he stated it wasn't the police or SWAT commandos who, in his words, 'mucked his play.' He claims it was one man who sent him running. A nameless adversary who now has a face that appears to match this superassassin's vague description of the individual who flew in to the main compound today. Mr. Geller?"

Geller smoked, took his time, feeling the knife coming his way. "Exactly what are you asking, Colonel?"

"Your opinion. Is this man a special agent from the Justice Department?"

"In my opinion, no."

"Then, what?"

"Covert. Black ops."

"Someone, some agency or covert arm of the military, knows of our existence. And where we are," Chongjin told the group.

Geller felt the chill ripple through the room, the insinuation being someone had talked, jumped to the other side of the tracks.

The NSA man spoke up. "He was checked through by my people when I first got word from you," he said, glancing at DIA. "All the i's are dotted, the t's crossed on this Belasko individual. Ask me, it's too neat a package."

"A front?"

"That would be my guess," the man from NSA told Chongjin.

Geller could feel Chongjin building steam to pursue some line of interrogation, but Geller's pager beeped.

He could almost hear them drawing a collective breath as he felt their stares boring into him. His ops were calling him out to the command and control room, which, Geller knew, signaled an emergency. Excusing himself, he ignored the questioning eyes inside the smog, stabbed out his cigarette and beelined for the double doors. His gut was churning, suspecting what he already knew awaited. Grillo was already moving away from the banks of monitors, but Geller found the problem on the first set of screens. Their equipment was state-of-the-art surveillance and countersurveillance, everything from simple camera detection down to laser beams and infrared scanning that would light up an intruder's face in the dark in living color.

And the guy was filling up the screen. Belasko. Geller bit down the curse, no time for a show of nerves to the troops. He needed to get control of the situation.

"He just rode up," Grillo reported. "Sitting there. Watching us."

Geller glimpsed the shadows, illuminated in white-and-green glows. There was scuffing behind him, and one of Chongjin's five commandos said, "I need to tell the colonel."

"Wait a second. We'll handle this." Geller picked five volunteers on the American team, then told Grillo, "Two vehicles. Go out there and take care of this problem. I don't want to hear another word about this," he added.

Grillo agreed, and Geller watched as they grabbed up assault rifles and subguns, moving out for the motor pool to claim vehicles. "At ease," he told Chongjin's hired guns as they danced a little, exchanging looks.

"What do you have?" he snapped at his radar man, who shook his head. The screens were clear of air traffic. The normal flow of air traffic in and out of Tulsa, of course, but the FAA people were under strict federal guidelines issued them from DOD. Since this was restricted military airspace, routine flights were diverted from this area.

Geller looked back to the screen. The guy sat in his SUV, checking them out. Surely he knew he was being watched. Surely he knew someone would be sent out. Well, it didn't matter now, Geller thought, he could be armed with a presidential directive but that wouldn't help him.

But why was he alone? No gunship in the vicinity now. And why did that bother him? Geller wondered. Who the hell was this guy really?

He could feel the Koreans getting more antsy with each passing second. He told them, "We're ready to pack it up." He wanted to add, "The show must go on." But every shred of instinct earned on the killing fields warned him Belasko was there to crash the party.

THE EXECUTIONER WATCHED the two SUVs pull around the far west edge of the building, headlights flaring on as they angled his way. The structure itself was dark, top to bottom, end to end, leading him to wonder on the drive in across the prairie if they had packed the up place until a scan through his infrared binos turned up a wandering sentry. The armed guard vanished quickly inside the building once Bolan braked the Jeep Chero-kee rental, some two hundred yards north of the ranch house, nose and headlights aimed dead ahead at the compound.

The alert had been sounded.

Recalling the gunner's earlier words, Bolan had returned, armed with a lot more than warrants to back his suspicion. The M-16/M-203 combo was ready for action, muzzle up as it was canted against the shotgun seat. The soldier was now weighted down in full combat harness and webbing, ammo pouches stuffed with spare clips, grenades. Both side arms were resting beneath the baggy windbreaker meant to shield the battle works from the eyes of passing motorists or curious highway patrolmen on the ride in from Tulsa. The nylon satchel dumped on the passenger seat was nearly bursting with the mixed party favors of frag, incendiary, flash-stun and buckshot rounds. Both the hand-tossed variety and missiles for the M-203.

Bolan had waited with the Farm's blacksuits at their own restricted area at the airport. Final planning, touching back with Brognola, and Bolan made his decision to come back hard, ready to open the cage door for the savages to come snarling out, show their hand. Night fell, and he left the Farm blacksuits with the Kiowa, a radio call and fifteen minutes, give or take, away, due east on the prairie. Backup in the wings, but Bolan didn't want Grimaldi showing up on radar screens, warning the troops he was moving in before Bolan was close enough to reach out and touch them.

Bolan checked the darkness beyond the coming vehicles, his surroundings, in case the ride out was a diversion to sneak in lethal shadows on foot. Clear all around, it looked, present company excluded. He watched as they pulled up, SUVs, side by side, trailing spools of dust, forty, fifty yards at the most. They tipped their hand, hitting high beams as they braked the vehicles, but Bolan anticipated the blinding lights, squinting away from the harsh beams lancing his face.

Show time.

The Executioner lifted the assault rifle by the muzzle, slipped his hand down to the stock but held it horizontal, out of view, as he opened the door, stepped out. Just in case, on the far reach of suspicion he was wrong, the Executioner intended to give them the last benefit of the doubt. Beyond the hum of his vehicle's engine, he heard doors open, hard-soled feet crunching packed earth. He figured four to a vehicle, eight tops, but his eyes were adjusting to the white shroud now, peering, making out four, then five distinct shadows.

"Belasko," he called out, "Justice Depart—"

He saw it coming, assault rifles and subguns swinging around, muzzles lighting up. The first rounds were drilling his door, punching out the window in a spray of shards when Bolan dived back onto his seat.

War had been declared, and Bolan figured he hadn't come this far to put it in Reverse and race a retreat out of there. He wasn't about to stay put, either, as rounds slammed the windshield, slivers raining down on his face next as the storm of autofire started pounding fist-sized holes in glass.

He was under fire, with a nest of traitors hunkered down and watching what they hoped was a quick execution of a snooping G-man.

Not this night, the soldier thought, and decided to seize back the advantage.

He reached up, dropped the transmission into Drive. It was awkward, but adrenaline settled him into place quickly, as the Executioner squeezed around, low beneath the rounds snapping overhead and slicing off the interior. Bolan took the wheel. To the furious beat of bullets drumming the hull, Bolan floored the gas. When the needle shot up to twenty and climbing, Bolan took the satchel. Hunched low, the M-16 was grasped, ready to go out the door beside him as he maintained an awkward loose hold on the steering wheel to keep the battering ram on course. As slugs kept thudding glass and metal, the startled war cries of armed shadows sounded uncertain in the next heartbeat. It was clear, just the same, they were either holding their ground, firing on, or piling in to get their SUVs out of the onrushing missile's collision course.

Bolan bailed out the door, certain the SUV's momentum would carry it through to create the diversion he sought to get him started. The Executioner took the jarring impact on his shoulder, rolled up and let the M-16 rip free on full-auto to begin trampling the black-ops vipers.

14

Duplicity, of course, cut both ways.

Beyond the usual charades, the lurking hands of treachery simply came with the turf. Colonel Chongjin wasn't sure what to believe, much less what to expect next. Naturally, long before the orchestration of current events was even on the drawing board to abduct the Titan Four and fly them out of America, his mind had been firmly set to not trust his counterparts; he barely trusted his own people to follow this through to its conclusion.

Chongjin begrudged it was a new age, especially with the coming future of supertechnology looming just over the horizon. The kind of power that, if he didn't obtain it now, would leave his country lagging far behind the competition. His countrymen would keep starving, denied any economic opportunity that came with production and flourishing of cutting-edge technology, would remain mired in what he could only best describe as Stone Age. Not that he especially cared, one way or another, if entire herds of simple-minded rice farmers lived or died, but there was his own bottom line to consider—the dream of ousting Kim Jong Il, and he would require as much peasant backing and approval as he could tolerate. In time, he told himself, it would happen, but only if all went well in the present, people carried out their duties and responsibilities, lived up to their end of the bargain.

A coup d'état to seize the reins of power had joined him with old rivals. It was a strange coalition, indeed, he thought. Chongjin knew these men by rank, stature, deeds. Basically they had willingly turned their backs on their country and their constitutional duty out of primal hunger for absolute power, to create a new America as they saw it. The bottom line, or so they claimed, was to disrupt and shatter the infrastructure of American society so the eventual endgame was a nightmare beyond imagination. These men envisioned anarchy, spoke openly of how terrified masses of armed citizens would take to the streets when the frenzied civilian populace realized a military regime from hell had landed among them. That what most Americans cherished—money and jobs, surrounding themselves with all the creature comforts and toys of privilege, the future bright with promise for the children—was about to be no more. Enter FEMA. Exit law and order as the final flaming vestige of democracy. The American dream dead. Next the other members of the council would restore order—their order—and their martial law implemented by ruthless legions of former U.S. military men, with a smattering of felons tossed into the savage mix, recruited over the past two years or so. There was much more to the bigger picture, he knew, including the terms of peace they'd put to their government, the method of extortion, or the vow of punishment for resistance and disobedience as they took down the palace—the White House and the Pentagon for starters.

A number of dark thoughts kept boiling to mind as he half listened to the council hashing over the situation in New York, debating the merits of what their superassassin had passed on to them about his encounter with the unknown, as if mere speculation would help them solve the riddle. Geller came as close as he would dare to trusting any of them. The colonel had met Geller while both of them were counterintelligence operatives in South Korea, rumor having it Geller was perhaps for sale if the price was right. The abduction scheme had its humble origins in a simple cash transaction, where Chongjin had reached a conclusion—after Geller eliminated a few of his own operatives—that both their sides had mutual goals, ending primarily in a search for power. Geller knew of like-minded men, introductions eventually made, details and dreams...

Ancient history, he decided.

What was the ruckus? Shooting out back? Had a small army of American covert operatives come to storm the place? Chongjin knew his own men wouldn't hesitate to barge through the door, armed and prepared to die to make sure he found safe passage from there.

At the sound of the first shots, a sense of urgency, even an air of panic, seemed to find its way into the smog. The colonel was rising, thinking it best to end the meeting and begin the initiation when the explosion occurred.

Chongjin nearly jumped out of his seat. The explosion was coming from somewhere out back, but close enough, it seemed, to shake the walls. He knew any heavy ordnance, grenades, rocket launchers and such were stored back at the main complex. If not their people, then who?

The stampede outside the doors, the sound of boots pounding wood, men scrambling all over the place, deepened his anxiety. They were shouting now, voices competing to try to fathom what was happening. Chongjin was out of his seat, wheeling toward the commotion, when the doors flew open and he found Yuk Kim, wild-eyed and rattling on about an intruder on the way. One man? Nonsense! Impossible!

Chongjin whirled as the other council members prepared for flight, chair legs scraping, breathing heavy. The DIA man stood, nearly pitched in sudden haste, his foot catching the chair, when Chongjin barked at him, "The briefcase!"

The colonel was leading the exodus for the doors, the sound of weapons stuttering on as their people ran down the hall leading out back, hope coming alive in his heart that whoever was attacking them was soon to be extinct when the explosion ripped through the heart of the ops center. The blast was so close, fire and smoke in his face, some wet object slashing off his skull, the wrecking ball of shock waves bowled him down.

THE EXECUTIONER'S SUV missile was a home run, a head-on collision that bought him precious heartbeats. His enemies were torn between scrambling to get out of path of the runaway bulldozer or searching him out to resume firing. The Executioner expected at least two or three gunners to come into sight from the other side as his metallic rhino rumbled past them.

Anticipation paid off.

Bolan was already on his feet, M-16 up and shooting from the hip, the soldier milking short precision bursts across their chests. Two shadows spun, dropping in their tracks.

They had called the killing play, so the Executioner decided not to disappoint the opposition, much less waste one second that could find him out in the open, exposed to return fire. The SUV's impact had shot glass through the air. One of men howled briefly as glass slashed his face.

Bolan tapped the M-203's trigger, and blew the three survivors into flying broken mannequins, sent them sailing from the fireball shredding apart their SUV, screams trailing away into the night.

With the grenade satchel around his shoulder, Bolan parted the Velcro straps and opened it for quick delves, the 40 mm rounds already marked according to their particular wallop. The Executioner marched ahead, spotted a mangled form, right leg missing below the knee, crawling beneath the umbrella of firelight, and treated the moaning snake to a mercy burst of autofire.

All done there, he found, and the Executioner jogged past the hungry flames, his sights laser-focused on the command center. Bolan was beyond anger, forging on, cold to the core. Still, someone inside had marched the first round of hitters out to take him down, all hands thinking they had little more than a lamb waiting to be slaughtered. A hundred yards and bearing down, the soldier was on the way in to shoot and blast out the very heart of the rat's nest. The Executioner stole a moment to load the M-203 with an HE round, then drew target acquisition on what he guessed was a large bay or observation window beside the double doors.

A few shadows came running now, just as the soldier triggered the launcher, pumped the missile through the targeted window. The ensuing thunderclap pealed from the other side of the building. The round must have flown unimpeded until the impact fuse slammed into resistance. If there was any lingering doubt left he sent another HE hellbomb on its way for the shadows venturing a few ungainly steps into the unknown. They were professionals, though, he was sure, backed by training, experience and maybe the blood of past victories on their hands. Flight or even retreat was clearly not an option in their minds. They were on the verge of splitting up to make themselves less available targets.

Too late.

And more casualties were snapped up by oblivion as the HE round was dumped into the heart of the shadows.

Bolan reloaded the M-203's chute again with another HE pulverizer, and sent it streaking through a narrow doorway. A thunderclap was followed by a brilliant saffron flash from inside the belly of the nest. It was clear he had their undivided attention now, as the din of voices raised in panic reached his ears.

Bolan figured he had a few seconds to burn while they reeled about in the smoke, survivors scraping themselves up off the floor, he imagined, digging themselves out of wreckage. And opting, most likely, for an exodus out the front for the motor pool.

Not so fast.

The Executioner slipped an incendiary missile down the M-203's snout. A brief scouting of the building's corners, clear of blacksuit traffic, and Bolan decided it was time to burn the down whole viper's nest.

The Executioner slowed his jaunt, raised the assault rifle and sent the fire starter winging for a second-story window.

THE CALL TO ARMS, an instinctive urge to retaliate, to save the night, had spared Geller from the first explosion in the command center. He was halfway up the stairs, HK MP-5 subgun leading the ascent, when several of his people bolted down the hall, charging past him to assist their comrades outside. One of Chongjin's henchmen thrust himself into the war room's doorway, bellowing the alarm in his native tongue when Geller had caught sight of the flaming tail streaking past in the corner of his eye. Whatever it was, he knew it was the worst of more bad news on the way, so he hugged the wall, covering his head as the world blew up below him.

Being a little smarter, tougher than the rest, his worst suspicions were all but confirmed. The guy—whoever he was—was no G-man, far from it, but he'd already guessed as much. Geller wanted to kick himself for marching five good ops to their doom. One man, no less. How could this be? How hard a killing task to nail one man, no matter how good, how big or titanium hard the professional stones?

He should have known better. He'd seen the guy earlier, looked into eyes—mirrors of the soul—that wanted to warn him this Belasko was every bit the stone-cold killer he was. Pride, he guessed, had gotten the better of judgment.

One more step up, he glanced back, unable to pry his

eyes off the destruction he was rising above for a long, dangerous moment, hacking out the grit that swirled up, choking his senses. Unbelievable, he thought. Seven figures worth of cutting-edge countersurveillance equipment up in smoke and flames, the very guts of the command center ripped out in the blink of an eye, ruins now laced with dancing sparks like the fading encore of a fireworks show. Beyond that, he figured at least three more of his own were down, somewhere below in the hall. Hard to tell with all the smoke, a severed limb turning up, here and there, in the whole mass of devastation. One of Chongjin's gunmen, he spotted, had taken the rocket ride across the room with the blast, kicked into the bay window where he now sprawled over the sill, wedged in the jagged shards. They were staggering from the war room next, frantic voices he recognized calling out for assistance. Incredible, but Geller then found four of the Koreans and a matching number of his men had somehow cleared ground zero, figures rising from the deepest corners to begin a slow march through the smoke. It wasn't hard for Geller to figure where the council was going next. Chongjin and company were bailing.

Geller left them to their flight.

Go! he urged himself.

Something burned deep inside Geller, and it went way beyond pride. Even though it bucked traditional cold professional logic, this had just turned personal. The sleeping quarters, he knew, were upstairs, windows that looked out to the north. From there, he could take up a sniper's roost, assuming of course, the bastard was still an available target.

Another blast, more screams, then gone, spiked his senses. He felt his teeth grinding together, a red film squeezing into sight as hot rage shot the blood pressure up to where his brain started pulsing against his skull. He was nearly topping out when the next thunderball seemed to roar up directly below. A scorching heat shot up to envelop him before the stairs were yanked away by the explosion, vanishing behind groaning wood and billows of smoke. He was falling when a storm of debris flew up, slamming off his head to douse the lights.

THE EXECUTIONER, tuned to every sound and sight, waded into the rubble and the slaughter. The M-16 already fed a fresh clip, another HE round dropped into the launcher's tube and ready to fly, Bolan had the scent of enemy blood in his nose.

He was close now, moving up on their rear, and ready to clobber any survivors with the knockout punch.

Finish it.

The Executioner heard the frenetic shouts of men in flight, well beyond the piled wreckage, shrouded by gray walls of smoke and cordite. He peered at the sprawled forms, checking for signs of life, poised for some blacksuited Lazarus to rise from the carnage.

Not a groan, not a twitch.

It was treacherous, slow going, just the same, threading his advance between mounds of wreckage, stooping to clear the gnawed edges of hanging beams. The incendiary blaze was already hard at work upstairs, eating it up room by room, moments from bringing down the roof.

The Executioner gathered steam, spying the last of

them charging out the hole in front where his HE round had done a fair amount of renovation. Senses, instinct reaching out beyond the crackle of fire, and the soldier had to believe any live ones were on the way out.

Time to help them.

The Executioner fanned the destruction with his assault rifle, scoping out the few strewed bodies for signs of clinging life.

Nothing.

Bolan caught the shouting out front, a babble of English and an Asian tongue that wanted to strike a memory chord....

Korean.

So be it. Hardly any comfort, that prior suspicion now became dark truth.

The heat from up top reached down suddenly, an angry wave pounding the soldier in the back, drawing sweat, urging him on as Bolan rolled through the vandalized hole. He got his bearings a heartbeat later. A van, sprouting antennae similar to what he'd seen in New York, was pulling out, leaving on behind a cloud of dust. How many were left to bail it was near impossible to say, but it didn't matter now.

Walking wounded or not, they were going down for the count.

Doors were slamming, tires spinning, maybe a half-dozen gunmen trailing two suits, a couple of the lords and masters of the conspiracy, he reckoned, the hard-force protecting their rear. Just as Bolan slid past a support column, sights settling on the van, one of the hardmen took that moment to claim the spotlight.

The Korean shooter whipped around, as if sensing or

anticipating the next avalanche of doom set to drop on
his back. He was hitting the trigger on his subgun, two
or three rounds slicing off the column, but the Executioner beat him to it with a pinpoint stitching up the
torso.

Again the soldier had their undivided attention, hardmen whirling, jerking away from their falling comrade
as if his death was some contaminating omen. Bolan had
no time to spare trading fire. He caressed the M-203's
trigger. The round took its wobbling flight for the sitting SUV just behind the hardforce. Two of them
stopped firing, eyes going wide as they saw doomsday
streaking for them, and bolted a heartbeat before the
40 mm grenade hammered home in a deafening peal.
Bodies were sailing, runners toppling from the shock
waves reaching out from the motor pool. A quick search
in the distance, and Bolan found the van and another
SUV swallowed up by darkness.

Three bloodied moaners could wait a moment, their
senses pulverized as they crawled from the flaming
wreckage. The engine of another SUV was gunning to
life on the far left edge of the motor pool when Bolan
filled the M-203 with another HE round. It had the usual
dark-tinted glass, hiding the numbers inside, but the
Executioner knew any crushing of the smallest force,
even down to the loneliest number, was no wasted effort.

Bolan sent the HE bomb flying, then the Executioner
moved on, hunting the vipers who had wriggled out of
the net.

THE SHADOW OF DEATH, Geller found, had passed him
by. He wanted to believe this was his lucky night, but

he was gagging, sucking air into starved lungs getting seared by all the heat and grit swelling his chest. As the fog cleared in his sight, tasting the bittersweet flow of blood in his mouth, he made out the next round of shooting, and yet another explosion. It was out front, he knew, as the sound and fury filtered into his ringing ears. He kicked out at the shards that had buried him. It took a full second, but he realized he had somehow kept a grip on the subgun. Miracle of miracles, but there was no sense in questioning any good fortune on this night.

Belasko, he knew, was out front. Another explosion—how many grenades had the bastard dumped on them already?—thundered from the direction of the motor pool.

Enough.

One way or another, Geller was bent on ending it. Besides, pride had him by the short hairs, and he knew he couldn't stomach living one more minute in this world, tasting the gall of this savage drubbing.

It took every ounce of angry will at his command, but he choked down the fit of coughing, kept the noise of his stagger through the litter of glass and shards to the barest minimum. The bastard seemed to have that second sight, eyes in the back of his head, the closest thing to a psychic gift Geller knew experienced killers and soldiers with ten lifetimes of combat behind them were bestowed with.

He focused on the next round of shooting, which seemed to spill out in a direction farther from the front of the house. Cautiously he squeezed through the gaping maw, across the porch, then heard the sharp grunts coming from the motor pool.

Belasko.

His heart raced, but this wasn't the moment to smile. Not yet. His adversary's back was turned to him. Geller watched, unable to comprehend his own moment of triumph was right there, thirty feet away. Victory dumped by fate in his lap. Belasko was rolling on, the shadow of death itself, over the fallen wounded, triggering mercy bursts into their chests, acting oblivious to the firestorm sweeping out over the other vehicles.

A wave of noxious smells swelled his nose, everything from blood and emptied bowels to burning fuel, but Geller crept an inch or so forward, the bitter stench merely fuel for his determination. This was it. The shadow of death, back to him still, might as well draw a bull's-eye between the shoulder blades, the man even in the act of changing magazines, searching the firestorm for live ones. Geller lifted the SMG, locked his sights for a burst up the spine and took up slack on the trigger.

MACK BOLAN FELT the ice creep up his spine. Then the hair stood on the back of his neck, danger registered, the double whammy alerting the Executioner something was wrong.

In a flash the HK MP-5 subgun sliced its sound and fury through the fire devouring more of the motor pool when Bolan shoved himself ahead, his M-16 sweeping around as the 9 mm rounds scalded the exposed flesh of his neck.

The Executioner was clearing the fire when a ruptured fuel tank was sparked off, an SUV bursting apart and spewing gas, with winged debris impaling into an engine hood, the roiling black clouds enveloping the vehicle. Bolan absorbed bites of shrapnel on the shoulders and back, blistering heat in his face, but the whole commotion of shooting wreckage and his bolt ahead allowed him to clear the tracking autofire by an eye blink, as he likewise propelled himself a few paces from the incinerating touch of the blast.

The hardman made the adjustment next, lining him up with the SMG, when the Executioner held back on the trigger of his assault rifle, shooting from the hip. Even with features plastered in blood painting, Bolan knew those eyes, matched them to the blacksuit who made the threatening noise when his Kiowa JetRanger had touched down earlier at the main compound. The Executioner ducked from the hail of bullets, the gunner's SMG jumping around next as Bolan hit him with a rising burst of autofire. Starting low, not leaving anything to chance, Bolan opened him up, crotch to throat, a straight chopping line, pinning the shooter to a support column, a lurching crucifixion in progress. The guy held on, still firing the subgun in a one-handed pose. Another burst of 5.56 mm rounds to the head, and the Executioner sent him toppling.

The Executioner gave the killing grounds a thorough scouting. The same fire that had saved him was well on its way to consuming any savages who might stir for a break out of the blaze. The walls caved in, the roof was coming down in a jettison of sparks, smoke balloons rising for the sky.

No live ones within or beyond the ring of fire around the motor pool.

Check.

No point in belaboring the oversight now, having

missed a shooter on the way out the front door. It was
a rare moment, even under combat stress, when Bolan
didn't drop and put down for good his target or left his
back exposed. Perfection in any arena was a common
human goal, unattainable, to be sure, usually driven,
consciously or otherwise, by ego and ambition. But
anything short of perfect in Bolan's world meant no
second chances to get it right.

The Executioner discovered just how imperfect a
world it was when he grabbed at empty space where his
tac radio used to hang. He must have lost it on his dive
out the door of the SUV rental during the bull charge
against the first group of gunners. Possibly shot off his hip,
or simply left it behind in the SUV when he'd come under
fire. Moot point, no time to spare, backtracking, combing the area. Scratch air support or any form of backup.

Alone again.

And the war was just beginning.

* * * * *

*The heartstopping action continues
in The Executioner 285,*

FINAL STRIKE
Book II of
THE DOOMSDAY TRILOGY

available July 2002

James Axler
Outlanders®

DRAGONEYE

Deep inside the moon two ancient beings live on—the sole
survivors of two mighty races whose battle to rule earth and
mankind is poised to end after millennia of struggle and subterfuge.
Now, in a final conflict, they are prepared to unleash a blood
sacrifice of truly monstrous proportions, a heaven-shaking
Armageddon that will obliterate earth and its solar system. At last
Kane, Grant and Brigid Baptiste will confront the true architects
of mankind: their creators…and now, ultimately, their destroyers.

In the Outlands, the shocking truth is humanity's last hope.

Take
2 explosive books
plus a
mystery bonus
FREE

DEATH LANDS®

Amazon Gate

Available in
September 2002
at your favorite retail outlet.

In the radiation-blasted heart of the Northwest, Ryan and his companions form a tenuous alliance with a society of women warriors in what may be the stunning culmination of their quest. After years of searching, they have found the gateway belonging to the pre-dark cabal known as the Illuminated Ones—and perhaps their one chance to reclaim the future from the jaws of madness. But they must confront its deadly guardians: what is left of the constitutional government of the United States of America.

"Sometimes it's good to be impulsive."

Hunter smiled at Bryony as he said this.

"Don't you believe in impulse as a rule?" she inquired, her heart singing irrationally.

"Not as a general rule," he said. "I've got my life very carefully mapped out. But you're the impulsive type. You probably let life take you over. Not me. I'm an orderly man. I like to be in charge of mine." His eyes were teasing, but she knew it wasn't entirely a joke.

"Don't you ever get knocked sideways by life?" she asked.

He regarded her thoughtfully. "Not if I can avoid it. It tends to be painful."

She said, "I know." And she had a sudden premonition of the pain he could cause her.. . .

Celia Scott, originally from England, came to Canada for a vacation and began an "instant love affair" with the country. She started out in acting but liked romance fiction and was encouraged to make writing her career when her husband gave her a typewriter as a wedding present. She now finds writing infinitely more creative than acting since she gets to act out all her characters' roles, and direct, too.

Books by Celia Scott

Don't miss any of our special offers. Write to us at the following address for information on our newest releases.

Harlequin Reader Service
901 Fuhrmann Blvd., P.O. Box 1397, Buffalo, NY 14240
Canadian address: P.O. Box 603,
Fort Erie, Ont. L2A 5X3

Love on
a String
Celia Scott

Harlequin Books

TORONTO • NEW YORK • LONDON
AMSTERDAM • PARIS • SYDNEY • HAMBURG
STOCKHOLM • ATHENS • TOKYO • MILAN

Original hardcover edition published in 1988
by Mills & Boon Limited

ISBN 0-373-02998-5

Harlequin Romance first edition August 1989

With gratitude to Skye Morrison
because she spoke so eloquently
about kites.

CHAPTER ONE

IT WAS a perfect day for flying a kite. The wind brisk but not too strong, the air fresh but not too cold, and no trace of the fog that so often covered the island of Newfoundland.

Bryony Porter let out some more kite line and dug her heels into the scrub of Knucklerock Field. An onlooker might have been excused for mistaking this petite slip of a girl for a young boy. Dressed as she was in faded blue jeans and loose windbreaker, a cotton hat pulled down on her head, she could have been of either sex—and about twelve years old.

She listened happily to the sound of her Delta kite singing in the wind. Strictly speaking, she should have been working back in her studio in St John's, packing the dozen stunt kites she had just finished making for a store in Toronto, but after a week of almost constant rain this afternoon had been too glorious to resist, for Bryony not only designed and manufactured kites, she was mad about flying them too. She had been ever since she'd been given a paper one for her tenth birthday, fifteen years before. She had flown that particular kite when there had been even the *suggestion* of a breeze, rescuing it from trees, and painstakingly patching the rents and tears until, at last, it had grown too tattered to mend, and then she'd made another out of newspaper which had infuriated her soldier father—they had been stationed in Germany at the time—when it turned out that Bryony's kite had been made from his Canadian *Globe and Mail*, which he had not yet had a chance to read. But even her beloved father's indignation had not dimmed her passion, and the newspaper kite had been followed by a succession of others.

7

When she was eighteen and the family had returned to Canada, she had taken a course at a school of Crafts and Design in Toronto, graduated with honours, and started designing kites to sell wholesale. It had been a struggle at first, but Bryony had inherited her father's dogged persistence—she was as stubborn as old Nick, her brother Bruce said—and now she had orders from shops across Canada and the United States. She was becoming known in her field, and her bank balance was slowly growing.

She felt a steady surge of energy on the line as her Delta started to ride a thermal, and her wide, unpainted mouth curved into a smile as the kite spiralled lazily upwards. She loved the multi-coloured, swooping feel of it; loved the glitter of sunshine on the green-black sea and the wrinkled granite face of the cliff which fell sheer into the water. On the point she could see the roof of Santu House, deserted for more than twenty years, standing sentinel over the Atlantic Ocean that stretched below.

One day, thought Bryony, I'd like to live in Santu House, or a house like it. As close to the sea as I can get. And then, even though it was a warm afternoon, she felt a shiver of apprehension, for the sea in these parts did not always lie lazily under a blue sky. It was often whipped into violent storms that battered and pounded the rocky coast. A storm viewed from the tall windows of Santu House would be an awesome sight.

She pulled her hat down firmly over her ears, for it was still cool on the cliff-top meadow, and then she became conscious of a sound like an irritable buzz-saw rasping in the sky behind her. Turning, she saw a gyrocopter heading towards the ocean. Gyrocopters! Inventions of the devil, thought Bryony, who hated them. Ugly triangular tubes of metal with some idiot sitting in the middle, a propeller over his silly pointed head, and an engine droning away noisily at his back. She considered them little better than airborne lawnmowers! She could see the pilot quite plainly now, and she glared up at him, her green eyes narrow with disgust.

The machine came doggedly towards her. She could see its three wheels, like giant currants stuck on the points of the frame, and she heartily wished it would keep on going until it arrived on the coast of Ireland three thousand miles away, never to return.

The figure above her waved and she stuck out her tongue. It was a childish thing to do, but the racket of that flimsy piece of machinery had shattered the calm of the peaceful afternoon and brought her unpleasantly back to reality. She knew the pilot could not see her, although she did catch a glimpse of white teeth for a moment, as if he were laughing.

She muttered a word she'd picked up during her years as an 'army brat', a word that would have earned her a spanking when she was a child, when suddenly her kite line gave a violent jerk, nearly pulling her on to her face. The sensible thing would have been to let go, but Bryony didn't always do the sensible thing, and now she clung on to the line for grim death while it dragged her rapidly towards the edge of the cliff.

'Idiot!' she yelled impotently at the gyrocopter. 'Noisy, polluting idiot!' But, of course, the pilot couldn't hear her. Anyway, he seemed to be too busy clawing at his head, which must have somehow become entangled in her kite string. Oh, God! What would she do if he lost control of his gyrocopter? He might crash on top of her! She was spared this macabre fate, however, since at that moment the strong line snapped and she fell backwards with a crash. There was a muffled thump nearby and she saw a pair of goggles roll into the scrub. Swearing heartily, she got to her feet and shook her fist at the departing craft that had stabilised and was again flying out to sea, trailing Bryony's rainbow-striped kite behind it.

Still muttering, she started to wind the broken string round the control handles. This kite had been a particular favourite of hers, and although she had lost kites in the past, she had never before lost one so dramatically. This felt more like armed robbery!

She remembered the thump of the goggles and started to look around for them, and after a few moments she saw a glint in the short grass and picked them up. She examined them carefully, but there was nothing to identify their owner. Turning them around, she noticed that they were quite well worn, but once they had clearly cost a lot of money. Well, she thought grimly, it figured that people who owned gyrocopters had more money than sense. She would hang on to them, although what on earth she could do with a pair of goggles was beyond her. Perhaps young Teddy would like them. With a bit of fiddling, she might get them to fit his child-sized head. She gave a final glare at the offending machine, that was now just a dot on the horizon, and headed for the road. No point hanging around Knucklerock Field any more, not now that she had lost her kite.

Before driving off in her station-wagon, she yanked off her hat and pulled her fingers through her thick, short hair. Bryony's hair was red, but not by any stretch of the imagination could it be described as chestnut. It was a vivid, unrepentant copper, and it sprang off her head in a riot of tight curls, a brilliant nimbus that the sun now turned to orange fire.

She shifted uncomfortably in her seat. She'd bruised her bottom when she'd fallen. This seemed to make the loss of her kite more annoying, and she growled, 'Damned gyro...*scooter*!' as she turned the key in the ignition and headed home to St John's.

Bryony lived with her brother and his wife in a narrow house that stood on a hill overlooking the harbour. It was painted brick-red with a white trim, and was poky and inconvenient, but Bruce and his wife Janice loved it. Bryony had originally come to visit them three years before, and when Bruce and his wife had suggested she move permanently to St John's she had agreed readily, for she had fallen in love with Newfoundland the moment she had stepped off the plane. Her business was not yet established in Toronto, and whether she made kites there or in Timbuctoo couldn't matter less. She had been delighted that they had wanted her to stay. She had always

been close to her elder brother, and she got along well
with her sister-in-law. As for the children, she adored
them! Three-year-old Teddy was the apple of her eye,
and now there was Jane, six months old, adorable, and
a glutton for affection. But the brick-red house was a
bit cramped for three adults, two children and a dog,
and Bryony had tentatively suggested that it was time
she looked for a place of her own, but Bruce and Janice
would not hear of it. She was part of their family, it was
senseless to talk of moving out, particularly since
reasonable accommodation in St John's was not easy to
come by. For a while she had toyed with the idea of
moving into the converted loft of an old store on the
main street which served as her studio, but she had
abandoned the idea. There was hardly enough space for
the organised clutter of her work, without adding more.
Besides, the Canada Goose Kite was taking up more and
more of her precious space.

The Canada Goose was a kite Bryony had been
working on for some time now. She was making it for
herself, not one of her clients, and one day she hoped
to fly it at one of the international kite shows in Europe,
if she could ever save enough money for the fare. Or,
better yet, if she could only get the town council
interested enough to back her in organising a kite festival in Newfoundland, she would fly it first from
Knucklerock Field. So far she had not managed to get
anyone in the local government even to give her a
hearing, but, being Bryony, she intended to keep on
trying. In the meanwhile, she worked on the Goose every
spare moment she could.

It was an ambitious kite, based on the famous Chinese
Centipede kites, a series of fifteen white paper discs, each
painted with the bold motif of a Canada goose, with
feathered spars to represent wings, which when eventually assembled and in the air would resemble a line of
flying geese. She had completed ten discs so far, but it
was a slow job, requiring meticulous precision.

She parked the station wagon in front of the house
and went into the small front hall. A black, animated

dust-mop hurled itself at her, barking a welcome. 'Oh, Bunty—you *fool*! Get down,' she said, laughing as the small dog ran in circles, yapping happily and doing its best to trip her up.

The door to the kitchen opened and Janice poked her sleek, dark head around it. 'You're back early,' she said. 'I was just about to make a cup of tea. Want one?'

'Do I ever!' Bryony shrugged off her windbreaker and hung it on a peg. 'My kite was hijacked and I'm madder than a hornet.'

Janice, who was used to Bryony's sense of drama, smiled tolerantly. 'What do you mean—"hijacked"?'

But before the girl had a chance to reply a small boy, with hair almost as red as her own, burst out of the kitchen, demanding in a loud voice, 'Where you been, Bry? I woked up an' you wasn't *there*!'

'You *weren't* there,' Janice corrected, 'and stop shouting, the baby's still asleep.'

Bryony picked up the child, hugging him close. 'I'm sorry, sweetheart. You were still taking your nap when I left.' She kissed the top of his head and set him back on his feet. 'But you can help me with my seniors on Sunday...OK?'

'I always *do*!' he replied scornfully, and then, grabbing at her hands, started jumping up and down, shouting, 'Mommy's made choklit-chip cookies an' I've had *two*.'

'You've had three,' his mother said, 'and if you'll go back into the kitchen and practise whispering, you can have another.' She smiled ruefully at Bryony. 'I know bribery's not the ideal way to bring up a child, but I had a terrible time getting Jane to sleep—I'll *kill* him if he wakes her up now.'

The kitchen was warm and fragrant with the scent of baking. Janice took a cookie from a plate on the kitchen counter and handed it to her son. 'Here you are, Teddy. Try not to get it all over your face, and play quietly for a bit, I want to talk to your aunt.' She poured boiling water from the kettle into a teapot and asked again, 'What's all this about hijacking?'

'It's a fact,' insisted Bryony. 'Some idiot on a gyro-copter flew right over my head and broke my kite line.' She reached for a cookie and bit into it with her even white teeth. 'Those things should be banned by law. They're a menace.'

'I wonder who around here would have a gyro-copter?' mused Janice, 'I shouldn't have thought this was the climate for them.'

Bryony said, 'Maybe he'll get lost in the fog and ditch over the Grand Banks. That would teach him!' Then she grinned, a warm, wide smile that lit her face like an arc lamp.

'Malicious, aren't you?' teased Janice. 'Which kite was it?'

'My old rainbow Delta. Lucky for him it wasn't one of my newer ones, or I'd be out now trying to borrow a shot-gun.' She held up an imaginary gun and aimed at the corner of the room. 'Pow!' And Teddy echoed, 'Pow, pow, pow!' hopping from one leg to the other, enthusiastically spraying cookie crumbs. Bunty joined in, jumping up and barking excitedly.

There was a wail from upstairs. 'Now look what you've done!' scolded Janice. 'You've woken Jane. Honestly, Bryony, you're just as bad as Teddy.'

'Sorry, love—just getting rid of my temper!' She went to the kitchen door. 'I'll get her, you stay there.'

'She may need changing,' said Janice.

'I've done *that* before,' smiled Bryony. 'Come on, Teddy! You can give me a hand.'

In the children's room she lifted her niece, who hic-cuped between sobs. 'There, there, buttercup! Did we wake you, then?' she murmured into the baby's silky neck.

'She's real dumb, she cries a lot,' Teddy, who still suffered from occasional pangs of sibling rivalry, told her.

'You cried a lot too when you were a baby. All babies cry,' Bryony told him. 'Now, make yourself useful and get me a fresh nappy.'

'*Yuk!*' the little boy said disdainfully, but he did as he was told, and beamed with pride when Bryony allowed him to sit in the nursing chair and hold his dry sister while she tidied up.

When the trio returned to the kitchen, Janice was standing before a large map of North America that was pinned to one wall. 'Do you remember where your parents had got to?' she asked when Bryony came to stand beside her.

'In their last letter they'd just reached Virginia.' Bryony's eyes narrowed as she gazed at the map. 'Look at that thing! It's like a *war*! You'd think they'd want to settle down now that Dad's retired.'

Major Porter had left the army two years ago, and within a week of civilian life he and his wife had bought a mobile home, and now they spent their time driving around Canada and the United States. At present they were on their way to Newfoundland to visit their family.

'Your folks go mad with boredom after only two weeks in the same place,' laughed Janice, moving the pin that bore a tiny Canadian flag from Tennessee to Virginia.

Bryony shook her orange curls. 'I don't understand it. After all those years of being sent from pillar to post, you'd think they would want to put down roots.'

'Well, you and Bruce certainly don't seem to have inherited your parents' wanderlust,' Janice agreed. 'I've never met a more home-loving pair. Don't let your tea get cold.'

'All those countries,' mused Bryony, shifting the baby to her other shoulder and picking up the mug of tea. 'It was fun—but how I *longed* for a permanent home. After living abroad for most of my childhood, I almost forgot that I was a Canadian.' She sipped thoughtfully.

'And look where you wound up,' chortled Janice. 'In the middle of the Atlantic on a big rock, constantly covered in fog!'

'Not true,' Bryony retorted hotly. 'That's just a rumour started by the rest of Canada because they're jealous.'

'There's nothing like a convert,' observed Janice, who had been born on the island.

'Convert or not, Newfoundland is my home now.' Bryony thrust out her determined little chin. 'And I don't intend to move away from it . . . not *ever*.'

'Don't say things like that,' Janice warned her. 'You can't predict as far ahead as "ever".' Jane started to whine and she took the child, shushing her gently. 'You never know what's around the corner, Bryony. Why, you might meet some man and go off to live in . . . in Arabia. You never know.'

'If someone wants to spirit me off to Arabia, he'll have to drug me first,' the red-headed girl declared. 'I'd *never* go willingly. Never!'

Janice started to waltz and sing, ' "I'll nev-ah say nev-ah ag-hen ag-hen," ' but stopped when Jane started to cry in earnest. 'I think she must be hungry. Are you hungry, my pet?' she said to her screaming daughter.

'Maybe she's commenting on your singing,' suggested Bryony, and Janice made a face.

'*I'm* hungry,' Teddy said loudly from the table where he'd been playing with a toy car. 'I'm so hungry, I might *die*.' He looked accusingly at his mother.

'It's not time for your supper yet, Teddy,' she told him. 'I'll get you something when I've seen to the baby.' She made for the door. 'I'll feed her upstairs, Bryony,' she said. 'It's more peaceful up there.'

Teddy stuck out his lower lip belligerently. 'I'm *hungry*!' he repeated.

'Jealous is more like it,' said his mother. Then Bryony remembered the goggles and, in order to divert a temper tantrum, told him she had a present for him.

He brightened considerably. 'What is it?'

'It's in my pocket. Stay there and I'll get it for you.'

In the hall Janice turned to her. 'Not only a successful businesswoman, but a child psychiatrist as well.' She started up the stairs. 'Bless you, I love Teddy, but sometimes he drives me to the brink of murder.'

Bryony pulled the goggles from the pocket of her windbreaker. 'Understandable. You've got your hands full. Do you want me to start on supper?'

Grinning, Janice leant over the landing. 'My hands aren't *that* full,' she said. 'You can feed the dog, if you like, but let's play safe and leave it at that.'

Bryony's cooking was a family joke. When she had first arrived she had prepared breakfast for the family, but after a few days of fried eggs which were crisp as burnt lace on the bottom and glutinous jelly on the top it was agreed that peeling potatoes and opening cans was the extent of her culinary skills.

The goggles were a great success, even if they didn't fit very well. Bryony did what she could by making extra holes in the strap with the potato-peeler, and Teddy was delighted. He zoomed around the kitchen, arms spread, shouting, 'I'm a plane! I'm a jet-plane,' looking like a red-headed insect with huge goggle eyes.

She fed the dog and was about to peel some potatoes when the phone rang. 'It's Bruce for you,' Janice called from upstairs, and Bryony picked up the kitchen extension.

'Good! You're home,' said her brother. 'I rang your studio, and when you didn't answer I was afraid I'd missed you.'

'Why afraid?' asked Bryony. 'Oh, do pipe down a minute, Teddy, I'm talking to Daddy.'

Teddy stopped zooming, and started to bounce up and down shouting, 'Daddy, Daddy!'

'Hold on a minute,' said Bryony, and went over to the excited child. She held him by the shoulders. '*Stop* that, Teddy,' she said firmly, and he stopped in mid-word. 'That's better. Now, you stay quiet till I've finished on the phone.' Meek as a lamb, Teddy returned to his toy car. She picked up the receiver again. 'Sorry about that ... you were saying?'

'I'm in a jam,' said Bruce. 'My second guest has let me down at the last minute and I have to find a replacement.'

'And I'm it?'

'You got it!'

Bruce worked in the newsroom of the local television station producing a daily television interview show. The

guests ranged from local politicians and union officials,
to ladies who organised bazaars, as long as they were
interesting and articulate. Bryony had been a guest
before, talking about her kites and trying to drum up
interest in an annual kite festival.

'I take it this has nothing to do with my dazzling television personality?' she asked, but Bruce was under
pressure and not in the mood for banter.

'Will you do it or not?' he barked.

His sister crooned, 'Temper, temper! Of course I'll do
it. Who else is going to be on?'

'A guy named Grant who is just back from Africa.
Look, I don't have time to chat. Be here in an hour, will
you?'

She went upstairs to tell Janice what was going on.
'And what I'm going to wear, I don't know,' she
grumbled. 'Not that your husband gives a hoot. As long
as he gets his show on the air, it wouldn't matter if I
turned up stark naked.'

'That should boost the ratings, but perhaps you'd
better settle for your yellow jumpsuit,' suggested Janice.
'It's a little more conservative.'

'You have no sense of adventure at all!' mocked
Bryony as she climbed up to her third-floor bedroom,
pulling her shirt over her head as she went.

The jumpsuit was new. She liked to wear jumpsuits
when she went kiting, for they were comfortable to move
about in, and the shade of this one, a rich golden yellow,
suited her colouring. She pulled on a pair of white leather
boots and started to brush her hair. It stood up in an
unruly mass of curls when she'd finished, and she tried
smoothing it down with her hands, but it still leapt about
in wild tendrils, so she gave it up as a bad job. At least
she didn't have to worry about make-up, there was a girl
at the studio for that, for Bryony wore very little and
wasn't exactly expert. She fastened a white leather belt
round her tiny waist and slipped several narrow ivory
bracelets on her wrist. That would have to do!

She was not a conventionally pretty girl, her mouth
was too wide and her nose too short, but she was very

striking, and at times, when she was cuddling Teddy or Jane, her face would grow soft with love and then she looked positively beautiful. People tended to see only her astounding hair at first, and it wasn't until they took a second look that they noticed her slanting green eyes, fringed with thick lashes that were also red, but a much darker shade than her hair, or her clear white skin that was lightly dusted with the palest golden freckles.

'You look nice,' Janice volunteered when Bryony had returned downstairs and was pulling on a white wool jacket. 'Bruce is lucky to have such a glamorous guest.'

'He sounded so frantic, I don't think he'd notice if King Kong turned up.' She picked up her white cotton holdall. 'For all I know, he might too—Bruce said that the other guest had just come from Africa.'

'I'll try and get the kids to bed before you and Bruce get back,' her sister-in-law promised, 'so we can enjoy our supper in peace.'

'I don't want to go to bed,' Teddy told them mutinously. 'I'm not sleepy.'

'Why don't you wear your goggles in bed and pretend you're flying in the dark?' Bryony suggested. 'Pilots have to know how to fly in the dark, you know.'

A smile replaced the frown on the little boy's face. 'You're wasted designing kites,' Janice remarked. 'Managing little boys and their frazzled mums—that's your line!'

The studio was only a fifteen-minute drive away, and after she had parked, Bryony, an old hand by now, went straight to the make-up room. Pamela, the girl who did make-up for the station, had just finished the interviewer, a woman named Patsy Drake who was part of Bryony's social crowd.

'Well, at least *you've* turned up,' said Patsy when Bryony took her place in the high make-up chair.

'What's the panic?' Bryony enquired as Pamela started to smooth foundation over her cheeks.

'Grant hasn't shown up, and nobody seems to know where he's got to,' Patsy told her. 'I may be stuck with just you.'

'Thanks a lot!' grinned Bryony. 'But there's still twenty minutes before air-time...'

'Don't keep talking, Bryony,' complained Pamela. 'I can't do your eyes properly if you move.' She went on carefully outlining Bryony's oblique green eyes. 'Lovely!' she murmured. 'A bit of mascara and you're done.'

At that moment a small pony entered the make-up room. Bryony blinked and Pamela said, 'Careful! Don't smudge your eyes. Keep them closed for a minute.'

Of course, it wasn't a pony, it was an enormous dog, a dog the like of which Bryony had never seen before. Its size, however, had nothing to do with fat, it was all solid muscle, and was covered in a silky white coat that fell in soft waves below its belly. It ambled nonchalantly over to Patsy and regarded her intently. Patsy was five foot five and the animal stood practically to her waist.

'He's quite friendly,' a deep male voice informed them. 'Sit down, Gus, and stop making a nuisance of yourself.'

'You can open your eyes now,' Pamela said, and Bryony did, and found herself staring at the reflection of a man in the mirror in front of her. He was reasonably tall, about five ten, and thin, with brown hair that was brushed back from his narrow, tanned face, and a hard, stern mouth. But it was his eyes that compelled her to go on staring. They were grey, hard as silver, and piercing. A small shiver went down her spine, like some sort of warning.

'My name's Grant,' said the man. 'Hunter Grant. They sent me down here to see if I needed any make-up.' He smiled at Pamela, and the lines around his eyes crinkled and his mouth tilted attractively. But I wouldn't want to tangle with him, all the same, thought Bryony; he is one tough character.

'You don't need make-up—not with that heavenly tan,' Pamela fluted. She batted her eyelashes at him shamelessly.

Patsy introduced herself. 'I'll be interviewing you,' she said, 'and Bryony here is also on the show.'

Bryony had vacated the make-up chair and was now standing, fluffing up her mop of curls with her fingers.

'Bryony?' he said. 'That's an unusual name.' She thought he sounded disapproving.

She stopped fiddling with her hair and tilted her chin to stare up at him. His eyes looked down at her, as cold as the grave. If she had been a cat, the fur on her back would have been standing on end.

'I'm an unusual girl,' she replied shortly.

'If you're ready, we'd better get into the studio. It's nearly air-time,' Patsy said, leading the way.

'Is it all right for Gus to stay in here?' asked Hunter Grant. 'He won't make any fuss.'

Pamela gave him a dazzling smile. 'He can keep me company,' she said, 'until you come back to claim him.' It was plain she didn't share Bryony's reservations about Hunter Grant. She was as good as hanging signs that read 'Free and Available' all over herself.

Bruce materialised out of the shadowy chaos of the studio. 'I'm really glad you could make it, Grant,' he said. 'I appreciate your taking the time.'

'I'm giving you my time, too,' Bryony pointed out tartly, but Bruce just laughed and ran his hands through his hair, which was a russet version of his sister's short curls.

'You don't have any choice,' he said. 'You're family.'

Hunter Grant said, 'Family?'

'This is my kid sister, Bryony. Haven't you met?'

'Briefly,' said Hunter, looking from one to the other. Assessing them, Bryony felt sure, and deciding that the only reason she was on the show was that she was related to the producer.

The floor manager came over and fussed them into their places. Patsy in the centre, a guest on either side. Hunter Grant leaned comfortably back in his chair and crossed his legs. The coming interview seemed to hold no anxiety for him. Even if it was a live show, with no chance to edit if anything went wrong, he was calm and collected. Even a little bored, as if he had been interviewed on television countless times before. His self-assurance fitted him as beautifully as his well cut taupe trousers covered his long legs. He was wearing a scarlet

sweater that looked like cashmere...trust a man like that
to choose such an aggressive colour, Bryony thought.

The floor manager gave the countdown, made the 'on
air' signal, the camera lights turned red—and they were
on...

Patsy introduced her guests. 'Bryony Porter, a well-
known figure in St John's, and Hunter Grant, who has
just completed a trip to Africa, flying his ultralight
plane,' and then she concentrated her attention on her
male guest, because her viewers could listen to familiar
old Bryony Porter any day of the week, but this attractive man was a bonanza on the show. Bryony
composed her face into neutral and switched off. She
didn't care if he had crossed the Sahara on a skateboard,
she wasn't about to feed his ego by listening raptly while
he went on about his adventures.

Eventually Patsy turned her attention to Bryony, who
gathered herself together and chatted about her vol-
unteer work at a local senior citizens' home.

'I understand you take them kite-flying when the
weather's nice.' Patsy said, and Bryony began to describe some of the terrific kites some of the old people
had made.

When she had finished, Patsy turned again to Hunter
Grant. 'I guess your sort of flying is more adventurous
than flying kites,' she cooed, 'but perhaps you'll take it
up? Now that you're moving to our city.'

Bryony tensed in her seat. He was moving *here*! To
her city! What a ghastly prospect. Forgetting the
cameras, she glared at this intruder.

'I don't know about that. I had quite an adventure
involving a kite this afternoon. It was such a nice day,
I decided to try out a friend's gyrocopter, when a kid
flying a kite attacked me!' He raised a sardonic eyebrow.
'He didn't succeed in bringing me down, but I did lose
my favourite flying goggles.'

Bryony nearly leapt off her chair. 'It was *you*!' she
shrieked. 'You're the idiot who broke my kite string...'

Grant looked at her coldly. '*Your* kite string?' he said.
'I thought it was a boy.'

'Well, it wasn't, it was me.' She could feel her cheeks burning with indignation. 'I was on Knucklerock Field.'

'I know it,' he said. 'I've just bought Santu House.' This left her gasping. 'And I'm negotiating to buy the field, too. As a base for my helicopter station.'

CHAPTER TWO

BRYONY'S voice rose several decibels. '*Helicopters!* On *my* field?'

'I wasn't aware that it was your field,' he said smoothly. 'It's Crown land, surely.'

'Oh! Don't get technical with me,' cried Bryony, in a passion and quite unaware that the camera was zeroing in for a close-up. 'Knucklerock Field is the only one around here that's perfect for kiting... and it's perfect for my seniors too. The bus can drive right on to it.'

Hunter said, 'There must be other places you can use— don't get hysterical.'

'Perhaps we should discuss this another time,' Patsy suggested diplomatically, but Bryony was too agitated to pay any heed.

'Build your helicopter station somewhere else,' she said heatedly. 'Use the airport...'

'We'd be in the way at the airport,' said Hunter.

Bryony cried, 'You're in the way on Knucklerock Field!'

He looked at her as though she were something unpleasant that had crawled out of the woodwork. 'Only in *your* way,' he said. 'I don't think that gives you a case.'

She glared at him fiercely. 'Don't count on that.'

'Did you encounter any wild animals while you were in Africa, Mr Grant?' Patsy asked desperately.

'Not as wild as the ones I'm meeting here,' replied Hunter.

'Well, you'll have to come back and tell us another night, our time's up now, I'm afraid,' she said with evident relief. 'Thank you both for taking time to visit with us tonight.' She smiled weakly at her guests, who sat glowering at each other. Turning her attention to the camera, she signed off. 'Tune in same time tomorrow, when Mrs Vale will be dropping by to show us some flower arrangements . . . and now . . . goodnight.'

The lights came on in the studio and Bryony noticed that the technicians were grinning. Patsy's interviews tended to be dull. This had livened things up.

With a brief nod to Patsy, Grant strode away. 'What on earth got into you, Bryony?' asked Patsy. 'Couldn't you see I was trying to get you off the subject of Knucklerock Field?'

'I wasn't really paying attention,' admitted Bryony. 'I got too involved.'

But she knew that wasn't the whole reason. The loss of the field was a nuisance, but it wasn't a first-class calamity. What was really upsetting her so much was the fact that it was being taken over by Hunter Grant. If it had been anybody else, she would have been willing to concede that indeed there were other places to fly kites in the area. But this man had the same effect on her as vinegar has on milk—he turned her sour. His arrogance, coupled with his imperious assumption that whatever he wanted he was going to get, made her stubbornly resolve to do everything she could to hinder him. It was bad enough that he would be living in Santu House; she intended to see that there would be a fight before he took over Knucklerock Field as well.

When she returned to the make-up room, the large dog and his master had gone, only Pamela was left. 'Isn't he *dreamy*?' she said to Bryony.

'Bit too large for my taste,' Bryony snapped. 'I'd hate to have to give him a bath.'

Pamela blinked. 'Give him a *bath*! What are you talking about?'

'About that horse, the one that was masquerading as a dog.'

'Oh, Bryony, you are a *nerd*!' giggled Pamela. 'I was talking about Mr Grant.'

'Same thing applies.' Bryony scrubbed at her face with a tissue.

'He's not that large,' said Pamela. She handed Bryony a jar of cold cream. 'Here, use this. You'll take the skin off your face if you go on scouring it like that. He's just about the right size, I'd say. Not too tall and not too short.'

'I was referring to his head,' observed Bryony, scooping up a dollop of cold cream. 'That's as big as the Michelin man.'

'I didn't think so. As far as I'm concerned, he can put his boots under my bed any time he wants,' Pamela said wistfully.

'Each to his own taste.' Bryony pitched a dirty tissue into the waste-paper basket. 'Frankly, I prefer my men to be in love with me—not themselves.'

Further discussion of the merits and faults of Hunter's character was interrupted when Bruce came in. 'Well, you made a proper idiot of yourself, didn't you?' he said to his sister. 'What made you attack him like that?'

'Did you attack him, Bryony?' Pamela asked. 'What happened on the show?'

'Hunter Grant seems to think he can just come into this town and take over,' said Bryony. 'And *helicopters*! What on earth do we need with helicopters?'

'For servicing oil rigs,' her brother explained tersely. 'And he intends to train people to run the station. It'll give a lot of work to people here, so don't expect your objections to get much support.'

'We'll see about that,' Bryony muttered, and then added, 'besides, I don't like his attitude.'

'I shouldn't think he was wild about yours,' Bruce said. He turned to Pamela, who had been listening to all this avidly. 'You can take your dinner break now. There's no need to hang around.'

'OK! I know when I'm in the way,' she said, reluctantly picking up her coat and purse.

'At least you got an interview with a bit of life in it,' said Bryony when they were alone. 'A change from your usual pap.'

'I don't think my sister has to behave like a spoiled four-year-old to provide life on my programme,' Bruce bit back, and Bryony flushed hotly.

'Next time you want a guest to come on the show at the last minute, you'd better ask someone else, then,' she fumed. 'From now on, you can count me out!' And she slammed out of the building.

She drove to the bottom of Signal Hill, parked her car, and walked to the summit in an effort to regain her temper before going home to supper.

It was dark, but there was a cloud-streaked moon that glimmered like a diamond wrapped in gauze. Below the cliffs the sea sighed and whispered. She took several gulps of bracing salt air and felt her cheeks grow cooler. Hot-tempered by nature, usually she recovered herself within minutes, but this time she was not bouncing back with her usual alacrity. She and Bruce rarely quarrelled, and when they did it hurt her desperately, and she still felt upset.

'Damn that Grant man!' she muttered through clenched teeth, knowing she was being unreasonable for blaming him for her quarrel, but unable to stop herself. Ever since she had met him, he had caused her trouble. If it had been raining she would have blamed him for that, too.

She turned her back on the sea and started to return to the car park. The lights of St John's danced on the sloping hills. To her left, Gibbet Hill loomed dark and forbidding. She had read that in the old days, after hanging in chains, the bodies of the condemned were packed into heavy casks, weighted with rocks and rolled down into Deadman's Pond where they sank without a trace. Too bad Hunter Grant, *and* his helicopters, *and* his gyrocopter, and any other gimmick he might possess, couldn't be disposed of that way!

Supper that evening was a subdued affair. Bruce and Bryony were scarcely speaking, and Janice, who had heard all about the row from her husband when he got home, kept silent, unwilling to take sides. After Bryony had helped with the washing up, she went to her studio to try to work on her Goose kite, but she was unable to concentrate and she made such a mess of it that she had to throw a lot of expensive material away. She chalked this up as yet another black mark against Hunter Grant.

The following day was Saturday. By morning, she and her brother were talking again, but carefully, as if they were both getting over a nervous illness and mustn't be upset. Bryony offered to take care of the children for the afternoon, so that Bruce and his wife could go off on their own. The offer was snapped up by both parents.

'Thanks, Sis,' said Bruce, giving her a quick hug, his way of letting her know that as far as he was concerned their quarrel was forgotten.

After lunch, which Bryony made—she couldn't mess up tinned soup and peanut-butter sandwiches—she put the children and the stroller into her car and they drove out to Knucklerock Field. Its grassy slope, pitted with rocks, appeared vulnerable to her this afternoon, now that she knew it was liable to be sold.

The sun had disappeared behind a thick band of cloud, but there was no rain. Teddy had brought one of the many kites his aunt had made for him, and he started running down the field, dragging it behind him in an effort to launch it.

'How many times have I told you, that's *not* the way to get a kite in the air?' Bryony roared at the little boy, who stopped running and stared at her, saucer-eyed. 'Here—give it to me!' She took the kite and started to walk downwind, away from him. 'Now, pull on the string,' she instructed, holding the kite up in her arms. 'Pull gently and it'll go up.'

He dropped the kite line on the grass. 'You *yelled*,' he said tearfully. 'You're mean.'

'I'm just trying to teach you, Teddy,' she said, but he dug his sturdy little toes into the ground, his lower lip jutting miserably.

She went over to him. 'You're right, sweetheart. I'm cross today and I'm taking it out on you.' She knelt down beside him. 'I am an old meanie and I'm sorry.'

The child hesitated a moment, then he put his arms around her neck. 'All better,' he said, squeezing hard.

She hugged him close, taking comfort from the clean little-boy scent of his silky skin. 'All better,' she agreed, 'except that you're strangling me!' She freed herself and stood up, holding on to his hand. 'Now, what would you like to do with the rest of the afternoon? Play with your kite, go for a walk, or what?'

Without a moment's hesitation, Teddy said, 'Look at the house, an' then have an ice-cream.'

'Ice-cream's fine . . . but are you sure you want to look at the house today?' Bryony asked. The idea of walking around the grounds of Santu House seemed like trespassing now that she had met its new owner.

But her nephew was insistent. 'Look at the house,' he said, 'while you tell the story.'

'Oh, yes! The story.' Months ago she had brought Teddy out here, and while the two of them roamed around the grounds of Santu House she had made up a story about a giant who lived there. Teddy had been enchanted, and now every time they came to Knucklerock Field he insisted they walk down to the house while Bryony gave him another instalment of the giant's adventures.

'We may not be able to visit the house much longer, Teddy,' she said, tucking Jane, who was fast asleep, more securely in the stroller.

Teddy was dismayed by this, and Bryony had her work cut out trying to explain. 'The house has been sold, sweetheart. The giant won't live there any more.'

The little boy stopped in his tracks. 'Where will he *go*?' he wailed.

'Oh! He's going to a *much* nicer house,' she hastily invented, 'a *castle* . . . on the other side of the island.'

Mollified, he took hold of the side of the stroller and trotted along while he bombarded his aunt with questions concerning the giant's new home.

They went down the rutted driveway towards the tall building whose windows stared at them like blind eyes. Already there were signs that Santu House was about to have a facelift. A bulldozer sat in the driveway, and when they got closer she could see the Building Permit pinned inside the front window.

'I want to see inside,' Teddy demanded, and she lifted him up and then peered over his head at the enormous living-room that stretched the length of the house. She could see the sea, like crumpled grey foil, through the long, narrow windows on the opposite wall. There were ladders leaning against the wall too, and unopened cans of paint stood in an orderly row on the floor.

'Who's going to live here now? Another giant?' Teddy asked.

'Just an ordinary man,' said his aunt, although she supposed 'giant' wasn't such a bad description, although 'ogre' was the word she would have chosen. One thing was certain, however; no matter what she told Teddy, Hunter Grant was a far cry from ordinary.

On the way back into town Teddy resumed his relentless questioning. But now he had lost interest in the giant and was consumed with curiosity about the new owner of Santu House.

'Have you really seen him?' he asked for the fifth time.

'*Yes!*' she snapped, and then, remembering her earlier outburst, said more softly, 'Yes, I have—just once.'

'Where? *Where* did you see him?'

'I already told you, Teddy. At the studio. What flavour ice-cream do you want?'

'Choklit,' he replied with the swiftness of an addict. '*Why* was he at the stoo-doh?'

'He was talking on daddy's programme.' And in order to field off the inevitable 'Why?' she said, 'Don't poke at your sister like that, you'll wake her.' This deflected him, and he spent the remainder of the journey enquiring why babies needed to sleep so much, and when would Jane be big enough to play with?

By the time Bruce and Janice returned that evening, their offspring had been fed and were bathed and ready for bed. 'You poor thing, you must be exhausted,' said their mother, bouncing her gurgling daughter on her knee. 'Did they give you a hard time?'

'They were as good as gold,' Bryony assured her, and
she told Janice of their afternoon, but only touched
lightly on the visit to Santu House.

'Bruce was saying that Mr Grant is really going to fix
that old place up,' Janice remarked. 'I'm glad. It's too
nice a house to be neglected.'

'I'm glad too,' said Bryony. 'Only...'

'Only you wish it weren't Hunter Grant who was doing
the fixing?'

Bryony grinned ruefully. 'You saw the show last night,
eh?'

'Oh, yes! It didn't look as if you two hit it off too
well.'

'That's putting it mildly. I don't think I've ever met
such an arrogant, conceited man in my life,' Bryony said
indignantly.

Janice was amused. 'He certainly seems to have made
an impression on you.'

'So does indigestion!' her sister-in-law snapped. And
then the clock on the kitchen mantel struck, and she
jumped to her feet. 'I've got to *fly*! I'm going dancing
in half an hour,' she cried, heading for the stairs.

'You going with Dave?' called Janice.

Bryony yelled back, 'Who else?' before disappearing
into her room.

Janice was glad that Bryony had a date. Like many
happily married couples, she and Bruce wanted to see
Bryony married too. But Janice wasn't sure that David
Fairley was the right man. He was too pliant...too
easygoing. Bryony was the best girl in the world, but
she was headstrong and impulsive, and these traits,
coupled with her tenacity, often got her into trouble.
She needed a man who was capable of standing up to
her when necessary, and Janice couldn't see Dave doing
that.

In fact, Janice had no cause for concern. As far as
Bryony was concerned, Dave was just a good friend.
Not that Dave was happy with this state of affairs, and
every once in a while he would try to persuade her into
bed, but Bryony wasn't interested in going to bed with

someone unless she was in love with them. She had made
it clear that friendship was all she felt for Dave. The
notion of going to bed with a man because that seemed
to be the fashion, she found totally unacceptable. Some
of her girlfriends teased her, and accused her of living
in the nineteenth century, but she shrugged off this
criticism. So Dave had to be content with friendship,
and because Bryony was the most vital, attractive woman
he had ever met he put up with it. Besides, he was always
hoping she would change her mind.

Tonight they dined at a hotel that was built on the
side of St John's natural harbour. Below them, the docks
were crowded with freighters waiting for loading. The
city, dominated by the floodlit twin towers of the
Basilica of St John the Baptist, glittered on the hill. 'I'll
never get tired of this view,' Bryony murmured contentedly as she sipped her vermouth.

'I'm glad of that,' Dave said. He was a nice-looking
young man. Tallish, fairish...and *ordinary*, Bryony
thought bleakly. A thoroughly nice, steady man, and if
I had a brain in my head I'd fall in love with him, marry
and live a nice quiet life. But, even though she didn't
want to gypsy around the world any more, she didn't
want a nice dull life with Dave either, so that was that!

'I'm glad you like St John's so much,' Dave went on.
'It means you'll stay here.' He looked at her fondly, and
she felt an irrational spurt of vexation at his dog-like
devotion.

'Janice was lecturing me the other evening. Telling me
I shouldn't assume my life is never going to change,' she
said, draining her glass.

'Of course things change, and usually for the better.'
He nodded sagely, pushing his rimless glasses higher on
his nose. It was a habit of his and it irritated her. 'Like
this new helicopter station. That's a step in the right
direction.'

'Not if it's on Knucklerock Field, it isn't,' she flared.
'Anyway, who wants helicopters zooming all over St
John's? I think it's a lousy idea.'

'So you said on the show last night.' He looked down his nose. 'I don't like to criticise you, Bryony, but I do think you behaved badly.'

'So everyone's been telling me,' she snapped, as the waiter came to tell them their table was ready.

She really regretted being on Bruce's show at all. Ever since last night she'd been haunted by Hunter Grant and his damned helicopters. She couldn't get away from the man! And, as if to confirm this, he was the first person she saw when she came into the dining-room! He was sitting with two other men, deep in conversation, but he looked up when she and Dave entered, and a look of distaste briefly crossed his lean face. She stared back, and with all the insolence she could muster she inclined her flamboyant curls in a nod of recognition.

Because they were going to a disco which catered mostly to an artistic crowd—and because she enjoyed dismaying Dave—she had dressed tonight in a skimpy emerald green mini-dress that finished a good six inches above her knees. A belt of wide silver discs was slung around her slender hips, and sheer emerald green pantyhose covered her legs. White boots completed her ensemble, together with enormous silver coins that hung from her ears.

'Bit vivid, aren't you?' Bruce had commented, and she had replied that it matched her vivid personality. Now she was glad she was so outrageously dressed, for she sensed Hunter Grant was disturbed by her appearance, and anything she could do to upset him made her happy.

But it was a two-edged sword, for seeing him again ruffled her. Although they ignored each other after that silent acknowledgement, he might just as well have been sitting at their table. His personality seemed to make the other people in the room grow dim, while he stood out, like a coloured figure in a black-and-white drawing. And even though he and his companions left while she was still eating her main course, his presence lingered, robbing her of her usual sparkle.

Even later, at the disco, she couldn't shake off the memory of Hunter, so elegant in his dark business suit, his hard mouth disdainful. At eleven, she pleaded a headache.

'Why don't you stay at my place?' Dave suggested half-heartedly. 'It's quiet there. No babies to wake you.'

She snarled at him with more anger than was warranted, 'For God's sake, give it a rest, Dave!' He looked so guilty, she added contritely, 'Sorry! I didn't mean to snap, but I do need an early night. Tomorrow's going to be a good day for kiting, and you know Sunday's my day for the seniors.'

He parked outside the house, and took off his glasses before kissing her goodnight. He always did this, but tonight it exasperated her, and she drew away from his embrace as soon as she could.

She let herself into the darkened house, and as she climbed the stairs up to her room she decided that she would have to stop seeing David Fairley. She hadn't realised before just how much he got on her nerves. The way things were going between them, she would wind up snapping at him like an ill-tempered dog every time they were together, which was no fun for anybody.

The senior citizens' home was at the far side of town, and the old people had to be transported out to Knucklerock Field. Bryony was fortunate in knowing a woman who ran a school bus during the week, who had volunteered to drive them every Sunday. Her name was Tansy Talbot; she was built like a truck-driver and used language that would have made a sailor blush. She had suffered all her life from being big and plain and clumsy, but to Bryony and the old people she was beautiful. They all loved her, for she had a heart as big as all outdoors, and was really as soft as a marshmallow, a characteristic she hid under her rough exterior.

'Saw you on the TV the other night,' she told Bryony on the way out to the home. 'What you goin' to do about that guy?'

'About Mr Grant? I'm not sure, but you can bet I'm going to do something.'

'Picket!' Tansy said succinctly. 'Picket the bastard!'

'We could do that,' agreed Bryony thoughtfully, 'but it would help more if we had someone—someone *powerful*—on our side.'

Tansy swerved to avoid a careless pedestrian, and after she had cursed him hoarsely she asked, 'Whadd'ya mean—powerful?'

'Oh, you know—someone with influence. In government, perhaps. Who could speak for us.'

Tansy gave her opinion of politicians in a few choice words, but then she grudgingly agreed that it would help. 'Any road, you know you can count on me to back you,' she grunted.

'Bless you, Tansy.'

'Don't need to bless me,' she growled, 'jus' let me know when you need me an' the old bus.'

The residents had just come in from their church service, and the Sky Highers, as they called themselves, were waiting in the visitors' lounge. Some carried kites that they had made, with Bryony's help, during the winter. A few were simple sled kites, but other members of the group had become ambitious, particularly one old lady who had spent hours manufacturing, with arthritic fingers, a kite which flew on the outspread wings of a mythical horse. 'It's supposed to be Pegasus,' she said, assuming that everyone shared her knowledge of Greek mythology.

Tansy put the ramps in place so that any members in wheelchairs could get on to the bus, and a couple of nurses came out to chat and make sure everything was going smoothly. After a few minutes of organised chaos, they were off. Bryony seated herself beside Mabel Frame, the lady with the flying horse. 'Pegasus really is a lovely kite,' she said. 'If I were giving out prizes, I'd give you a first.'

Mabel nodded contentedly. 'He does look nice, doesn't he, dear? I just hope he will fly.'

'He'll fly like a bird,' Bryony promised. 'I brought my camera. When we get to the field I'll take a photo for you.'

'You must give me a copy if it comes out,' said Mabel. 'As a keepsake.'

Bryony had just pulled her ivory sweatshirt over her head, and now she stared at the old lady, her fiery hair standing on end. 'A *keepsake*? You're not leaving the group are you, Mabel?'

'No, dear. But after seeing you with that man on the television the other night, it doesn't look as if we'll be doing much kite-flying in the future.'

Bryony sat up in her seat, her tiny frame tense. 'Oh, yes, we will! Knucklerock Field isn't sold yet. We mustn't give in without a fight.'

'I don't know about a fight, dear.' Mabel looked doubtfully at the fervent girl through faded blue eyes, but an old gentleman who was nursing a scarlet boxkite called out,

'You tell him, Bryony! He can't have our field!' And soon the entire bus joined in this chant, and Mabel's hesitant chirrup was drowned out.

It always took a while to get the Sky Highers organised. The wheelchairs had to be pushed carefully on to the field, and not all the members were expert at getting their kites airborne. Bryony, a slim figure in her ivory sweatsuit, hat pulled over her truant curls, went from group to group, untangling lines, giving a word of encouragement or practical help when needed, and taking photographs for her 'Sky High' scrapbook. As she had predicted, Mabel's Pegasus took to the air like an eagle, and she used nearly a roll of film on it.

When the final kite was aloft and the sky dotted with large and small scraps of colour swooping and tugging on their strings, Janice drove up with the children and Bunty in tow. Teddy, wearing the goggles Bryony had given him, tore down the field towards his aunt.

'I brung my fish kite,' he yelled, 'an' I'm going kite-fishin' in my goggles.'

He was soon taken over by a group of seniors who exclaimed delightedly over his goggles, so that he lost interest in his fish kite, dropped it on the ground, and started zooming around the group, arms outspread, making aeroplane noises.

Tansy came over to the two girls. 'I gotta' do an errand up the coast road, but I'll be back in plenty of time to get this lot home,' she said.

'Tansy! Look at my goggles! I'm a jet!' Teddy shrieked, swooping at the big woman.

'Very stylish,' said Tansy. 'Just what I need for drivin' the old bus.'

'Let me drive with you?' He started jumping up and down. 'Can I? Can I?'

'I thought you wanted to fly your fish kite,' said Bryony, but the boy hung on to Tansy's arm.

'Can I, Tansy? Can I?' And she grinned and said he could if he promised to behave.

'Don't annoy Tansy, Teddy,' Janice warned.

'He don't annoy me. If he does, I'll tan his backside,' Tansy promised, leading the ecstatic child away.

'What a super day,' said Janice. She crinkled her brown eyes at the sea that was glittering in the pale sunshine.

Bryony didn't answer, for she had just noticed a car parked below on the driveway of Santu House. Just then the front door opened and a large white dog came out. 'Oh, no!' she muttered under her breath.

Janice followed her sister-in-law's gaze. 'What's the matter? Is it the enemy?'

Bryony nodded. 'The enemy. I didn't think he'd be around so soon.'

'All I can see is that enormous animal,' Janice remarked.

'That's his dog,' said Bryony. 'He must be close by. I don't imagine he lets a creature that size go walkies on its own.'

She bent to pick up her kite, an elegant hexagonal rokkaku that was part of a line she had regretfully stopped making, for the amount of labour required in

the bowing and bridling made it impracticable for the
wholesale market. This particular kite, banded in shades
of purple, emerald and lemon, demonstrated her eye for
colour and balance. When she had launched it, she
turned her back on Santu House. 'He doesn't own the
field yet,' she said to Janice. 'I intend to ignore him.'

'Well, he doesn't intend to ignore you,' Janice said.
'They seem to be coming this way.'

'They?' Bryony turned and looked briefly down the
hill. Hunter Grant had been joined by a tall, slender
blonde, who was shading her eyes to look up at the kites.
'Let them come.' She turned her attention back to her
kite. 'It's a free world.'

It might be a free world, but her attention was no
longer wholly on the business of kite-flying. She was
aware, out of the corner of her eye, of Hunter Grant's
arrival, of his loping, lazy stride. He was closely followed by the girl, who trotted behind him like a faithful
pet.

Suddenly all hell broke loose. A cacophony of deep-
throated barks and high yelps rent the air, and Hunter's
big white dog went tearing across the field, his tail between his legs, with little Bunty in hot pursuit. The field
suddenly seemed full of fighting, snarling dogs. The
seniors shouted and clutched at their kite strings, Hunter
ranted at Gus, Janice yelled at Bunty, and the baby
started to cry, while the terrified white dog desperately
tried to escape from the tiny, furious black one.

'Gus!' roared Hunter, 'Gus! Come back here!'

At the sound of his master's voice, Gus hesitated for
an instant, and Bunty, taking advantage of this, hurled
herself at him with renewed vigour. Gus yelped in terror.
Hunter lunged at Bunty, missed, and fell flat on his face
in the dirt. The sight of Hunter Grant, elegant in black
corduroys and leather jacket, lying spreadeagled under
two fighting dogs, was too much for Bryony. Pulling in
her kite, she started to laugh helplessly.

'Do something, Bryony!' implored Janice.

'What can *I* do?' Bryony choked, holding her precious kite out of harm's way. 'As far as I'm concerned, Bunty's just guarding us from interlopers.'

'*Do* something, Hunter,' cried the blonde girl. 'That little dog will kill him.'

'*Gus!*' bellowed Hunter in a terrible voice, and the white dog wriggled free and cowered on the ground in an attitude of defeat. Bunty came in for the kill, but Hunter managed to grab her, and staggered to his feet, clutching her to his bosom. She was so startled by this turn of events that she stopped barking.

He strode over to Bryony, who was wiping away tears of laughter with the back of her hand. '*Yours,* I presume,' he said, thrusting the wriggling Bunty at her.

'My sister-in-law's, actually,' said Bryony weakly, her green eyes dancing.

Janice joined them. 'I'm so sorry,' she said, taking the unrepentant Bunty and thrusting the crying Jane at Bryony. She clipped on the leash. 'You're a bad, *bad* girl!' she said to the perky black dog who was now waving her plumy tail triumphantly.

Hunter examined Gus, who was still cringing. 'No harm's done, apart from Gus's pride, but I suggest you keep that animal of yours leashed; it seems to have a very nasty nature,' he said giving the giggling Bryony a look of pure loathing.

'Bunty's a she, not an it——' she began defensively.

'I really am sorry, Mr Grant,' Janice broke in. 'It is Mr Grant, isn't it? You were on my husband's programme the other evening. I recognise you. I'm Janice Porter.'

'Do you have any more surprises for me, or is this the extent of the Porter clan?' he asked, cocking an eyebrow at the baby in Bryony's arms.

'Almost the extent.' Janice smiled tentatively. 'My husband and son aren't here. I'll put this naughty dog in the car. Look after Jane, Bryony, will you?'

The blonde girl came over. She was young. Twenty, twenty-one at most, and she was breathtakingly beautiful. Silver-gilt hair, smooth as water, hung to her shoulders. Her eyes were cornflower blue, and she had long, slim legs and narrow, elegant feet that tottered unsteadily in high-heeled black patent shoes. Not at all the right shoes for Knucklerock Field. In fact her whole outfit, taupe suede trouser suit and thin silk blouse, was better suited to the town than this rough terrain.

'Is Gus all right?' she asked Hunter. She had a child's whispery voice, delicate like the rest of her.

'He's fine,' Hunter said, feeling along the dog's back. 'You should be ashamed of yourself, Gus! Being frightened by a mutt.'

'Bunty's *not* a mutt,' Bryony said indignantly. 'She's a "Sceagle".'

He gave her a disbelieving look. 'A *what*?'

'A "Sceagle". Her mother was a Scottie and her father was a beagle. She's a cross-breed,' insisted Bryony, 'not a mutt.'

'She *behaves* like a mutt,' said Hunter Grant.

'Actually, Gus is a terrible coward,' the girl volunteered. 'Inside that white hulk lurks the soul of a lapdog.' She smiled at Bryony, a warm, open smile, as lovely as a summer's day. 'I'm Lois,' she said. 'Lois Taylor.'

'This is the girl who hates helicopters,' Hunter said by way of an introduction. Bryony ignored him.

'I'm Bryony Porter,' she volunteered, holding out her hand to the blonde girl who shook it warmly.

'I can't get over all these lovely kites,' said Lois. She leaned forward to examine the rokkaku that was lying on the grass, and her hair swung like a silvery curtain. 'Where did this one come from?'

'I made it,' Bryony replied. 'I'm a kitemaker.'

'It's lovely. Do you have a shop?'

'I sell wholesale. I have a studio in town.'

'May I come and see it some time?' Lois asked.

What such a nice, friendly girl was doing with the likes of Hunter Grant was beyond Bryony. 'You're welcome to visit any time,' she assured her. 'I'm in the phone book under "Porterkite".'

'I'll drop by next week,' Lois promised, and Bryony thought, she sounds as if she's lonely—a lovely girl like

her, that doesn't make sense. From the look on Hunter's
face, the last thing *he* wanted was Bryony's company.
Just as well! He would get a cool reception if he put his
foot over the threshold of her studio.

'See you next week, then,' she said to Lois, and moved
further away on the pretext of launching her kite, for
she didn't want to stay close to Hunter any longer than
she had to.

'That's the man who wants to buy our field, isn't it?'
Mabel asked as Bryony passed her.

'That's him.'

'What *is* he doing, dear?' Mabel faltered. He was
poking into the short, wiry grass with his foot, staring
at the ground intently. His brown boots shone in the
sunshine like conkers.

'I don't know *what* he's doing. Making a nuisance of
himself as far as I'm concerned,' Bryony replied crossly,
for she was bristling with hostility. He put her in mind
of a dangerous animal, poking around in the field like
that. *Hunter!* He was well named; he was like an alert
wild beast waiting for its prey, and she felt a shiver of
dread run down her spine as she watched him. Maybe
if she turned her back on him and thrust him from her
mind he would go away.

The wind freshened and she became fully occupied
dealing with the rokkaku. As usual, the magic of kiting
did not fail her, and her problems soared away on the
end of her kite line. Soon she was conscious only of the
interplay of kite, wind, and muscle; nothing else had
relevance on such a lovely morning.

Tansy and Teddy drove back and joined the group.
Tansy made herself useful as usual, rescuing runaway
kites, teasing her favourite Sky Highers, and pushing the
wheelchairs to more favourable positions, while Teddy
hopped from person to person, talking non-stop, and
occasionally paying attention to his kite.

At last it was time to drive the old people back to the
home. Tansy came over to Bryony. 'What's *he* doin'
here?' she said, jerking her thumb at Hunter, who was

now leaning up against the Porters' station-wagon, in conversation with Janice.

Bryony squinted over at his thin frame. 'Oh, God! Hasn't he gone yet?'

'Inspecting the place, is he?' Tansy pushed her knuckles into her trouser pockets. 'Gettin' the lay of the land.'

'Well, it's not his land yet, he needn't look so smug.' Bryony started rounding people up, helping to reel in kites and wind lines around spools. 'We'll have to get a move on, gang,' she said, 'or you'll miss your lunch.' This usually succeeded in getting a reaction, and they began trailing into the bus.

She wanted to leave *now*, to put as much distance between herself and this wretched man as she could, and, since it didn't look as if he was going to leave first, then she would. She started to hurry the seniors along, making sure to keep her back to Hunter all the time.

'I really can manage by myself, dear!' Mabel remarked mildly when Bryony tried to take Pegasus from her.

Janice called, 'Teddy!' and started to strap Jane into the car seat, while Hunter reassured Gus that Bunty was not coming out of the station-wagon.

Teddy came racing over, making engine noises, his kite held over his head. 'I'm a jumbo jet...I'm a jumbo jet,' he shrilled.

'You're a little noise-machine,' Janice said, taking his kite, and Bryony, unable to keep her back turned any longer, reluctantly turned round.

'Now, Teddy, say hello to Miss Taylor and Mr Grant,' said his mother, smoothing his red curls.

But before he could obey, Hunter, who had been staring intently at him, said, 'May I ask how he happens to be wearing my goggles?'

'Yours?' snapped Bryony, and then she coloured. '*Yours*—of course!'

Teddy drew back a step, as if he feared the man would whip them off. 'They're *mine*,' he insisted. 'Bryony gave them to me.'

   'Bryony did, did she?' Hunter mused. 'That figures!'
He looked directly into her eyes and she felt as if she
were being cut in two by a laser beam. 'Tell me,' he said
acidly, 'is there anything of mine that you *don't* intend
to meddle with?'

CHAPTER THREE

'I DIDN'T realise...when I gave them to him...' she stuttered, hating him for making her sound guilty. 'I mean...I found them on the field...after I lost my kite.'

'You must have known they came from the gyrocopter.' He was being perfectly reasonable, but Bryony had the feeling she was in the dock. His questions might sound mild, but his icy grey eyes were accusing.

Resentment made her bluster. 'Of course I did! But I didn't know *you* were the one flying it...at least, I didn't know then.' She took a breath to steady herself. 'Anyway, I figured that the idiot in the gyrocopter owed me something for the loss of my kite.'

He looked at her coldly. 'The idiot is more than willing to reimburse you,' he said.

'Forget it!' she snapped, and knelt down in front of her nephew. 'I'm afraid the goggles do belong to Mr Grant, sweetheart. You'll have to give them back.' Teddy's mouth started to tremble, but before he had a chance to give vent to his despair Hunter had also dropped to his knees.

'I tell you what, Teddy. Why don't you hang on to them for me for a bit? How does that sound?'

'Can I still wear them?' The little boy blinked through his tears.

'Perhaps you shouldn't wear them, pet...' advised Janice.

'Certainly!' Hunter interrupted. 'Keep them in running order for me. Is it a deal?'

'OK!' Teddy quavered. His nose was running, and Hunter wiped it on his impeccably laundered handkerchief.

'It's a deal, then,' he said, taking the boy's hand in his and shaking it solemnly. He rose to his feet. 'I'd let

43

him keep them,' he remarked to Janice, 'only they're a lucky talisman for me.'

She said softly, 'He'll have forgotten about them in a few days, then we'll get them to you.'

'Plenty of time.' He inclined his head, and Bryony noticed that there were wings of silver at his temples, yet he didn't look old. Mid-thirties at most. 'It's been nice meeting you,' he said to Janice, pointedly ignoring Bryony.

'You must come by for a drink some time,' Janice said, and Bryony scowled. The last thing she wanted was Hunter Grant cluttering up the house being sociable. Of course, it wasn't her house, and she could always arrange to work late at her studio any evening he was invited, but just the same...

Tansy leant on the horn of the bus. 'I must fly, Janice,' she said, 'the seniors will be late,' and she started to rev the engine.

'Goodbye, Miss Porter,' Hunter said loudly, and the authority in his voice stopped her in her tracks. She nodded stiffly.

'I'll see you next week,' Lois reminded her. She turned to Hunter. 'We'd better get going, darling, Daddy will be waiting.'

'Perish the thought,' he said, smiling down at the girl, and, as if by dropping his gaze he had given her permission to move, Bryony continued back to the waiting Sl   ighers.

Sitting in the bus on the way back, she found herself wondering just what the relationship was between Hunter and Lois. Of course that 'darling' might not have meant anything. People used endearments these days with even the most casual acquaintance. But that wasn't the way Lois had said it. There had been an inflection in her voice that was not in the least casual, and when they had started walking down the hill she had taken Hunter's arm as if she wanted him close. Not because she might lose her balance on those ridiculous heels of hers, but because she needed him. Well, it was her funeral, but Bryony thought it was a shame. Lois was much too nice to be wasting herself on such an overbearing creature.

That afternoon, when the children were having their naps, the adults sat around in the kitchen, drinking coffee and reading the Sunday papers.

'There's a bit here that might interest you,' Bruce said, handing a section of the paper to his wife. 'Adventurer, Entrepreneur and Eligible Bachelor to settle in St John's' the headline blared, and then went on to describe Hunter Grant's recent trip to Africa.

'We saw him this morning,' Janice told her husband. 'He came to Knucklerock Field to look around.'

'I hope he doesn't intend to make a habit of it,' growled Bryony, her wide mouth tightening.

Janice pointed out that he would be living practically next door, and then she added, 'I thought he was rather nice.'

'Nice?' Bryony shrieked. 'He's about as nice as a barracuda.'

'I thought he was very pleasant,' Janice insisted.

'You've got weird taste in men, Mrs Porter,' retorted Bryony.

Bruce grinned and said, 'Thanks very much, Sis!'

'You know what I mean.' Bryony gave a reluctant giggle. 'Let me have a look at that paper.'

The article was fulsome. 'Canada's Renaissance Man', the writer—a woman, Bryony noted—gushed. There was more in this vein. His life was 'A fantastic rags-to-riches story. Having come from nothing, Hunter Grant has carved a place for himself among the giants of the business community, and, not content to sit back and enjoy his success, he then challenged the wilds of Africa in a flimsy plane, since the call to adventure was part of this exciting man's nature.' Bryony's green eyes glittered with contempt as she read on. The piece concluded by stating 'We are fortunate indeed that this man has chosen our city for his base, and we welcome him warmly.'

Throwing the paper aside venomously she said, 'I
don't welcome him warmly, I can tell you. What a piece
of journalistic rubbish!'

Bruce and Janice exchanged grins. 'Let's not be too
harsh,' Bruce teased. 'Perhaps the style is a bit much...'

'A bit much? It's positively purple. The woman should
be *shot*!' And, picking up the comics, Bryony started to
read them with furious concentration.

She hoped that once Hunter had settled down in St
John's the media would forget about him. It was going
to be a drag if every time she picked up a newspaper or
turned on the TV she was going to be reminded of him.
If he *had* to live at Santu House and run a helicopter
station, let him get on with it with the minimum of publicity. Once she had got Knucklerock Field sorted out,
she hoped she could forget all about him. The town might
not be large, but it was large enough to ignore someone
you disliked, and so, with characteristic determination,
she set about wiping him out of her mind.

In the middle of the week Lois phoned to ask if she
could drop in at the studio the following morning. 'I'm
driving Daddy to the airport at ten,' she said. 'I could
come by afterwards, if that's all right.' It was, and so
at ten the next day Bryony wasn't surprised when there
was a sharp tap on the door. She was in the process of
unpacking a parcel of the Rip-stop nylon she used for
most of her kites, and she called, 'Come on in, the door's
not locked,' and went back to her unpacking.

'It doesn't sound like you to be so trusting,' said a
deep male voice, and she looked up from the spill of
brightly coloured fabric into Hunter's light grey eyes.
She was so surprised that she couldn't think of a thing
to say.

He looked down at the tiny girl sitting on the floor,
her petite body muffled in an oversize navy sweater, for
it was a cold morning, her curls a vivid frizz above her
delicately freckled face. 'I thought I might find Lois
here,' he told her, and she felt a flash of suspicion. There
had been no mention of Hunter in their phone conversation last night.

'She's not here yet,' she said, getting to her feet in one fluid movement.

'Well, can I leave this for her?' He held out a brown manila envelope.

'Certainly.' She took the envelope and put it in a conspicuous place on the cluttered workbench. There was an awkward silence, but she was damned if she was going to suggest he waited. He showed no inclination to leave, however, but stood staring at the many kites hung on the walls, and at the bales of nylon and the carbon-fibre rods of graphlex stacked neatly. Finally his eyes came to rest on the pots of paint and a coffee-tin filled with paintbrushes.

'You paint, too?' he asked.

'I paint my kites sometimes.' She looked at him steadily, willing him to leave. He didn't. He moved over to the wall and examined a kite made to resemble a ladybird.

'Did you paint this?'

'I did everything in here.'

'It's very good.'

'Thank you,' she said unwillingly, wondering if he expected her to blush girlishly at his praise.

'And this?' He gestured to the Goose kite that was leaning against the wall. 'Is this one kite? Or a batch?'

'It's one,' she said tersely. 'An experiment. I'm not sure if it will work out.' She crouched down over her box of silky nylon, hoping he would take the hint and realise that she wanted to go back to work.

'These are rather plain ones, aren't they?' he enquired chattily, pointing to a group of simple square kites decorated in broad stripes of red, white and blue.

She made a show of checking off the contents of the parcel against the invoice. 'Mmm? Oh, that's a copy of the Nagasaki Hata,' she replied vaguely.

He smiled, and it was as if a light were switched on. The sternness melted and the web of fine lines round his eyes crinkled up attractively. 'The *what*?'

Kneeling back on her heels she squinted up at him. 'Nagasaki Hata—a fighting kite,' she said.

'I didn't know you could fight with a kite,' he said.

'Fighting kites are very ancient,' she said, unable to stop herself from sounding enthusiastic, for she loved talking about her work. 'That lot is for a woman's team in Ontario.'

'What do they do? Clobber each other over the head with them?'

'You launch your kite and try to sever your opponent's line so that he'll lose his kite. They're equipped with a cutting edge on the line below the bridle.'

'A cutting edge of what? Razor blades?'

'I use slivers of sharp plastic stuck on with glue.'

'That sounds like your sort of kite all right.' She didn't reply. 'You must have thought I was a kind of fighting kite when I broke your string the other day,' he went on.

'I didn't. A gyrocopter is as far removed from a kite as a...a donkey is from a racehorse!' she bit back sharply.

He gave an unexpected hoot of laughter. 'So you feel you lost your kite to an ass, do you?'

'I thought I'd made that clear,' she said crisply.

'You certainly did,' he agreed. 'Unfortunately, you didn't give me a chance to defend myself.'

'I hardly think of you as that type. I should have thought that attack, not defence, was your line.'

He gave her a sardonic bow. 'It did seem unfair to my friend, however...the one who owns the machine. I was checking it out for him, to make sure it was safe. My incident with your kite was duly recorded. He won't be flying his toy over Knucklerock Field, I promise.'

She got to her feet and brushed off the knees of her worn jeans. 'That won't make any difference, will it?' she said casually. 'I won't be using Knucklerock Field when it's crawling with helicopters.'

'Helicopters don't crawl.' He pushed back the cuff of his immaculate dark business suit to look at his watch. 'I can't wait any longer.' I didn't ask you to wait at all, thought Bryony resentfully. 'As usual, Lois is late.' He reached the door in two strides. 'Don't forget to give her the envelope.' He regarded her briefly, nodded, and then she heard his footsteps receding on the stairs.

Typical! she fumed as she handled the nylon. He was a high-handed, chauvinistic, autocratic male! 'Don't forget to give her the envelope'—as if she were a half-witted servant. It never occurred to His Majesty that because of him she had lost half an hour's working time!

She had started to put the bolts of nylon on the shelves, which soon gleamed with stripes of dazzling colour, when there was another, hesitant knock on her door. That must be Lois. She should have guessed earlier, when she had heard Hunter's authoritative knock, that Lois would never announce herself like that.

'The door's not locked!' she called for the second time that morning, and Lois poked her beautiful, silvery head in.

'Sorry I'm late,' she said in her breathy voice, 'but I had to run a couple of errands for Daddy and it took a long time.'

'That's all right. I was going to break for a cup of coffee, anyhow.' Lois stood uncertainly on the threshold, and Bryony added, 'Come in! You're letting in a draft.'

'Sorry!' She shut the door behind her. She looked like a modern version of a Dresden shepherdess in a full-skirted suit of pale blue wool appliquéd with pink roses. A satchel of pale pink suede hung over one shoulder, and matching high-heeled shoes were on her narrow feet. For all her diminutive size, Bryony felt like a giant in the presence of this delicate creature. The oversize sweater—an old one of Bruce's—didn't help.

'I only have milk powder; is that OK?' she asked.

'Fine!' The girl came over and watched Bryony spoon instant coffee into two pottery mugs. 'I'm not interrupting you, am I?' She smiled hesitantly and gave the studio a cursory glance. 'So this is where you work. I thought it would be bigger.'

Bryony said, 'I wish it was, but this is all I can afford,' and Lois wrinkled her smooth forehead, as if this kind of economy was a novelty.

'Oh! Before I forget,' said Bryony, 'Mr Grant left something for you.' She fetched the envelope and handed it to the blonde girl, who proceeded to turn in over and over.

'I'm seeing him tonight,' she said, 'I wonder why he didn't wait till then.'

'Shouldn't you open it?' The sight of Lois aimlessly twisting the envelope like that was beginning to irritate her.

'Yes, all right.' She tore ineffectually at the gummed flap with her long, pink-varnished nails, and Bryony handed her a knife. 'Oh, thanks.'

This dreaminess hadn't been noticeable at their first meeting, and Bryony found her apathy now mildly disturbing. She was like a lovely, empty container. Beautifully crafted, but uninteresting. It seemed strange that a man as vital as Hunter was attracted to her, unless her very lack of energy was an attraction. Perhaps all he wanted from a woman was a sweet emptiness.

Bryony handed a mug to her guest, who took it awkwardly, so that the contents of the envelope in her hands spilled to the floor. 'Oh, dear!' she said.

'Let me!' said Bryony, kneeling and scooping up sheets of typescript. The heading of one caught her eye. It was a prospectus for a business school in Halifax. So it was not a love letter Hunter was leaving for his lady!

'"McCleary Business College", ugh!' ejaculated Lois with more spirit than she had shown yet. She jammed the papers back in the envelope. 'What a grisly thought.'

'What is?' Bryony took a bundle of fibre-glass rods off a chair, and Lois sat down. 'Business or school?'

'*Both!*' Lois declared. 'They bore me rigid!' She looked at the gaily coloured kites hanging on the wall. 'Did you go to school to learn to make those?'

'Of course.' Bryony perched herself on the end of her worktable. A beam from one of the pot-lights caught her long eyelashes, turning them from dark bronze to gold.

'Didn't you hate it?' Lois asked.

Swinging her feet, which looked small even in thick socks and running shoes, Bryony said thoughtfully, 'I didn't hate it. No.'

'Hunter thinks I should learn a profession,' Lois confided. 'He keeps trying to get me enthused.'

Bryony sipped at her coffee. 'What sort of profession?'

'Oh! Anything that would make me independent.' She gave a little girl's giggle. 'He's so funny. I mean ... we're practically engaged, and he wants me to be *independent*!'

So they were practically engaged, were they? Frankly, Bryony wouldn't take any bets on their marriage lasting. 'I don't think it's such a bad thing to have a profession,' she suggested diplomatically. 'It's always a good idea to be able to do some sort of job, isn't it? In case of emergencies.'

Lois gave a delighted little chuckle. 'Any woman who marries Hunter would never have to worry about emergencies. Everything he touches turns to gold. Daddy says he has the Midas touch.'

'I take it your father approves.' Bryony wondered when they could get off the subject of Hunter. Lois had said she was interested in seeing the studio, but, apart from that first brief glance around, she had hardly looked at it.

'Oh! Daddy thinks Hunter is wonderful. He admires anyone who does well. Particularly anyone who had such a hard time at the beginning.'

'Did Hunter have a hard time?' Bryony asked.

'Didn't you know? He grew up in an orphanage, and then started out on his own against terrible odds. Daddy says if there were more men like Hunter in politics, running the country would be an easier job.'

Bryony slid off the table and put her mug in the little sink. 'Is your father in politics?'

'I thought you knew,' said Lois. 'My father is Branwell Taylor.'

'Taylor! Of course, stupid of me,' said Bryony. Things were beginning to fall into place. Lois might not be the brightest girl around, but she was the daughter of one of the most colourful politicians in Newfoundland. For a man like Hunter, who had apparently clawed his way up the ladder of success, a father-in-law with the influence of Branwell Taylor would be invaluable. It seemed that this naïve girl was to be the sacrificial lamb. Bryony said, 'What about you?'

Lois blinked her round blue eyes. 'Me?'

'Do you think Hunter's wonderful?'

'Oh, yes! And Daddy says he'll take good care of me. And he's very good-looking, isn't he?'

Bryony turned the tap on so hard that water splashed over her sweater. 'He's all right.'

'Do you have a steady boyfriend?' asked Lois. She came over and handed Bryony her empty mug.

'They come and go,' Bryony told her, rinsing the mug vigorously.

'So you're not planning to get married.'

'Not this week.' In an attempt to steer the conversation into other channels, she asked Lois if she had always lived in Newfoundland, and the girl began to tell her about her life in the boarding-school in England, followed by finishing school abroad. 'Then I went round Europe with my aunt,' she said. 'We did the grand tour, but now I'm home for good.' She plucked at the collar of her suit. 'Daddy says I should practise running his household before I get married, but Lacey still does everything. Mrs Lacey's Daddy's housekeeper, she's been with him since Mummy died,' she explained.

Bryony started to sort out a pile of graphlex rods. She hoped Lois wasn't going to hang around much longer; she and Hunter between them had robbed her of practically a morning's work.

'Do you like earning your own living?' Lois asked, running her hands across the bolt of scarlet Rip-stop nylon. 'I mean...doesn't it scare you a bit?'

'I won't be earning my living if I don't get started on these orders soon.' Bryony pointed to an invoice lying on her desk, and Lois said,

'Oh! Can't you come and have lunch with me? I planned to take you to the Mariner's Rest.'

Bryony smiled, her small even teeth gleaming like pearls. 'May I take a raincheck? When I have more time and I'm better dressed, I'll be glad to accept. Anyway I don't think the Mariner's Rest would welcome me in jeans.'

They had a brief argument while Lois tried to change her mind, but Bryony was adamant, and finally Lois gave in. 'But you must let me take you there soon.'

'We'll go Dutch,' Bryony insisted, because she didn't want Lois paying for her meals.

'And you must come out to the house one evening.' She began picking up her parcels with maddening slowness. 'And meet Daddy. He'd love that.'

Bryony wasn't so sure about that, but she said, 'That would be nice,' and picked up her cutting shears.

Lois got as far as the door, then hesitated. 'I do hope we'll become friends, Bryony,' she said. 'You're so ... so strong, I think I could learn a lot from you. You're the sort of girl Hunter admires.'

Bryony nearly dropped her shears on her foot. 'I don't think Hunter admires me,' she said.

'He likes independent women. He's always telling me that,' Lois replied glumly.

'Not indiscriminately, I'm sure,' Bryony assured her. 'And now I'm going to throw you out, or I won't be independent much longer!'

'Goodbye, then. I'll be in touch,' Lois promised, and after giving Bryony another hesitant smile she was gone.

Alone at last, Bryony set about cutting out an order for a client in Ontario. When she was finished she would take the cut-out pieces to be sewn together by the local dressmaker she employed. At lunch time she went downstairs to the snack bar next door and bought a ham sandwich, which she brought back to her studio so that she could check over her books while she ate. She figured out that if she got all her invoices out on time, *and* if her clients paid her on the dot, she would have a bit of cash to spare this month. Things were looking up! She crumpled up the plastic wrapper that had covered her sandwich, and tossed it into the bin.

She had avoided answering directly when Lois had
asked her if earning her own living scared her sometimes. Well, of course, sometimes it did. She'd had her
share of sleepless nights, worrying that she might have
taken on more than she could handle. But at last she
was beginning to show a profit, and the elation this gave
her was worth all the worry. Would a girl like Lois, shel-
tered all her life, understand that kind of satisfaction?
Probably not. The need to be taken care of seemed to
be her chief concern, not becoming self-reliant. But,
judging from the sheaf of literature that Hunter had left
for her, he seemed to be doing all he could to mould her
into the kind of woman he claimed to admire. If he
failed . . . did that mean the engagement would be off?
Bryony doubted it. Marrying into a politically influential family would be too fine a prize to give up, for
with the backing of a man like Branwell Taylor Hunter
would be able to build heliports from one end of
Newfoundland to the other if he desired.

She folded the cut-up material and packed it carefully
before taking it down to her parked station-wagon. She
would have to work this evening to make up for the time
she had wasted socialising. Putting the car in gear, she
made a determined effort to stop thinking about Lois
and Hunter, and she succeeded in banishing the lovely
blonde from her mind. But Hunter's narrow, saturnine
face kept reappearing in her memory for the rest of the
day.

Later that week there was an announcement in the paper
that Hunter was about to close the deal for the purchase
of Knucklerock Field. Tansy phoned the same day.
'What are we gonna do?' she demanded.

Bryony gripped the receiver tightly in her slender
fingers. 'I guess we stage a protest,' she said. 'If you
can find out when they're going to pour concrete—or
whatever it is they do to make heliports—I'll organise
the Sky Highers and see that the Press are alerted.' She
bit her full lower lip. 'I don't hold out much hope,

though, Tansy. He seems to have friends in pretty high places.'

Tansy refused to be discouraged. 'Well, how about making some for yourself? Didn't you say we should get some big-wigs on our side?'

It was hopeless protesting that one didn't just go out and make influential friends at the drop of a hat, so Bryony made non-committal noises, and after a few colourful phrases Tansy hung up. When Lois phoned later and invited Bryony for dinner the following Saturday, Bryony accepted at once. Perhaps meeting Branwell Taylor socially wouldn't be such a bad thing. During the evening she would try to introduce the dilemma of Knucklerock Field and her Sky Highers, and try to win his sympathy. It was an outside chance, but she had nothing to lose.

'What will you wear?' Janice asked when Bryony told her where she was going.

'My grey, I guess.' She grinned, and an enchanting dimple showed in her cheek. 'It's either that or the emerald mini, and I don't think that's quite right.'

'They're neither of them right,' Janice observed. 'Why not treat yourself to a new dress?'

'Get thee behind me, Satan!' laughed Bryony, but later on, examining her grey challis, she decided Janice had been right. It was fine for dinner in a modest restaurant or a casual dance date, but not really dressy enough for a formal dinner party. She needed something new.

Then she remembered a length of black silky material left over from an order for some serpent kites. She only had two days, but she was gifted with her needle, and Janice had a box full of patterns. Together they inspected these, and took the top from one and the bottom from another. Bryony made the adjustments and cut it out, while Janice hauled out her sewing-machine.

'You'll be able to use it afterwards when you go out with Dave,' she said, as she filled the bobbin with black thread.

'If Dave ever speaks to me again,' said Bryony through a mouthful of pins. 'He wasn't too pleased when he discovered I wasn't free this Saturday night.'

Janice looked at her young sister-in-law, whose red hair was vivid over the black material, and whose green eyes were intent, and thought what an idiot Dave was. He didn't have the faintest idea how to deal with a woman like Bryony. Taking it for granted that she would be free and available every Saturday night certainly wasn't the way.

'He'll speak to you,' she said. 'He's not that much of a fool.'

For the next two nights Bryony neglected her kites for the sake of her new dress, and finished the hem an hour before it was time to leave. Hastily she bathed and made up, her hair still damp from shampooing, and then came downstairs to show herself off before she drove to Four Winds, the Taylor residence on Marine Drive.

'Will I do?' she asked, striking an exaggerated 'model' pose.

Bruce looked up from his paper. 'Not bad,' he said in a typically offhand way. 'You look quite respectable for a change.'

Janice was more enthusiastic. 'You look *sensational*, Bryony. It really turned out well.'

'Yes, I think it did,' agreed Bryony, pirouetting on her high heels. Black had always been good with her colouring, and the slim lines of this dress enhanced her trim, boyish figure. The neckline swooped into a deep V at the back that went almost to her waist. She had made a large folded bow of the same material, and stiffened it like a Japanese geisha's obi. Long tight sleeves covered her arms. Round her neck she wore a necklace she had picked off a market stall in Halifax last year, a fake gold chain hung with small coins, designed to look antique. She had also put eyeshadow and liner on her eyes, and brushed her thick bronze lashes with mascara. 'I'll have to wear my raincoat, though,' she said. 'I don't have anything else that will go over this.'

'Have a good time,' her brother said, and after she'd kissed the children and assured Janice that she had her key she set off.

Four Winds was set on the top of a wooded hill overlooking the sea. It was a new house, built for its present owner in a Victorian style that sat uneasily in the landscape. Bryony would have preferred something less self-consciously baronial; there was a hint of bad taste about Four Winds.

She parked her station-wagon behind a dark blue car and pressed the doorbell. After a moment the door was opened by an elderly woman wearing a large white apron over her navy blue dress. She ushered Bryony into the hall and took her raincoat. 'Mr Taylor's not home yet,' she said, 'but Miss Lois will be down shortly. Would you mind waiting in the drawing-room?' She nodded at a door and glanced anxiously back towards the kitchen area.

Bryony told her she would find her own way, and with a grateful, 'Thank you, miss,' the woman hurried off.

Bryony opened the door the woman had indicated and went in. It was a large room, fussily decorated, but with a magnificent view of forest and sea. Two wing chairs were drawn up before a blazing fire, which was welcome although it was early summer. A man was standing by the bay windows, looking at the sunset that was staining the sky blood-red. Dazzled by the brilliance, Bryony was unable to see his face, and it was not until he spoke that she recognised Hunter Grant's voice.

'I didn't expect to see you here,' he said, surprised.

'I'm not a gate-crasher, I was invited.' As usual, in his company she was instantly on the defensive.

'The thought never crossed my mind. Lacey would never let in interlopers,' he drawled back.

'If it comes to that,' Bryony said, 'I didn't expect to see *you* here either.'

He lifted the corners of his hard mouth in an ironic smile. 'Let's soften the blow with a glass of sherry, shall we? Lacey's put out sweet and dry.' And, moving with that lithe grace she had noticed before, he went to a butler's tray that was set with decanters and glasses. 'Which do you prefer?'

'Sweet, please.'

He poured it and handed her the glass of cut-crystal that glittered amber in the firelight. Pouring some of the paler, dryer wine for himself, he returned to the window. 'There's quite a wind getting up,' he said, nodding at the foam-crested waves. 'It'll be a bad night for ships.'

'I thought the saying was "Red sky at night, shepherds' delight,"' said Bryony, trying to appear at ease with him.

'It doesn't always follow, as I quickly found out during my stint at sea.'

'Oh, were you a sailor? I thought you were a pilot,' exclaimed Bryony.

'I worked on a fishing trawler for a while,' he said, 'before I learnt to fly.'

'In Newfoundland?' She was astonished that this groomed creature, handsome in black dinner-jacket and scarlet cummerbund, had ever worked at anything so hard.

'In Nova Scotia,' he said. 'When I first went out into the world.'

'And when was that?'

She was doing more now than making conversation, she was genuinely interested, but all he said was, 'A long time ago. Shall we go over to the fire? The sunset seems to be nearly over.'

They sat in the two wing chairs, and the firelight gilded Bryony's hair so that it seemed brighter than the flames. She sat very straight, for her obi bow didn't allow for lounging, but Hunter seemed to have exhausted his fund of small talk, and stared morosely at the fire.

A log sighed and crumbled to ash. Remembering his manners, he offered her another drink. She refused, but he went to the butler's tray and topped up his own glass. A clock chimed somewhere in the house. 'Damn Lois, anyway!' he muttered under his breath. 'She's *never* on time!'

'Is it to be a big party?' Bryony asked, half hoping that it was. She would welcome more people to shield her from his brooding presence.

'Just Lois and her father.' He moved over to the window. The light had almost faded, and now the wind was howling mournfully about the house.

Bryony put her glass down on a marquetry side-table, and went to peer out at the darkening sea. Even through the window-pane she could hear the roaring of the surf. She shivered. 'You were right, there is going to be a storm.'

'We'll leave the curtains open,' he said, 'as a beacon.'

Looking up at his face, which was as remote as carved granite in the twilight, she said, 'You'll get a first-hand view of storms from Santu House.'

'I'm not afraid of storms.' He gave a thin smile. 'I feel guilty when I'm safe indoors.'

'I enjoy them,' she confessed.

Hunter looked down at her upturned face, which was as pale as a flower set in petals of fire. 'When I was a boy, I would sneak out and go walking in storms,' he said.

'Why did you *sneak*?' asked Bryony.

A muscle in his cheek tightened. 'The orphanage didn't encourage solitary walks.' He looked vulnerable suddenly, and for a moment, as brief as the blink of a camera shutter, he was again a forlorn child.

'Were you unhappy in the orphanage?' she asked softly.

'Very unhappy.' Usually when people asked him about his childhood he brushed them off, but this bewildering girl seemed to have broken down his reserve with one soft question. 'My father was lost at sea in a storm, so I have a love-hate relationship with them.'

'What about your mother?' She didn't want to pry, but for the first time since she had met him she was aware of another side to Hunter Grant. A more human side, and it intrigued her.

'She died a year after he did. When I was three.'

When he was the same age as Teddy. She felt an unexpected wave of sympathy. 'And you spent your
childhood in that orphanage?'

'Till I was sixteen.' He smiled grimly. 'After a stint
on a fishing trawler, I went as far away as I could. To
Vancouver.'

'But you didn't stay there?'

'I didn't stay *anywhere* in those early years. I bummed
around doing odd jobs. Went on a freighter to the Orient.
Learnt to fly...'

'And then came back to the east coast,' she said.

'There's something about the east coast,' he mused.
'Once it's taken a hold of you, it never lets you go.'

'*Yes!* I feel that too,' she exclaimed eagerly. 'The
moment I saw Newfoundland, I fell in love with it.'

'You strike me as the sort of girl who might fall in
love quite easily,' he said.

'Not often, and only with places,' she insisted.

'And yet you seem the impulsive type, always flying
off the handle.'

Bryony tilted her chin defiantly. 'I only fly off the
handle when I'm pushed.'

'It only seems to take a little shove.' He gave a soft
laugh. 'This is the first time we've conversed for more
than a minute without fighting.' His glowing eyes never
left her face, and she felt a buzz of tension. Her heart
gave a strange little jolt against her ribs, and then the
door flew open and Lois was silhouetted against the light
from the hallway.

'Hello, you two!' she said. 'What are you doing in
the dark?'

CHAPTER FOUR

'WAITING for you,' Hunter said. 'You're late.'

'You say that every time we meet,' Lois giggled. She pressed a switch and several wall lights sprang to life. 'I couldn't decide what to wear.' She pouted prettily. 'I hope it was worth the wait.'

'It's always worth the wait,' Hunter said gallantly, and it was true. Lois was looking particularly lovely in a white crêpe dinner dress, its loose sleeves and neck edged with violet satin. Her hair was pulled up in a topknot and tied with a piece of the same colour ribbon.

She turned on a silk-shaded table lamp. 'Has he been treating you properly?' she asked Bryony.

'Very well, indeed.' Bryony felt ridiculously guilty. She wondered if Lois had sensed that electricity between Hunter and herself when she had found them in the dark. Just then their eyes met, and Lois smiled—the sweet, open smile of an innocent child. Bryony had no need to worry, Lois had been unaware of that current of emotion between Hunter and Bryony, although it had been as tangible as the room they stood in.

'We're drinking sherry,' Hunter said. 'Would you like one?' His face was impassive, and Bryony wondered if he felt guilty, too. It was unlikely. Nothing seemed to upset him. Besides, nothing at all had happened.

'Daddy's late,' Lois said. 'Some last-minute business in the House, I suppose.' She accepted the sherry Hunter had poured for her, and the pearl and amethyst ring she wore sparkled in the light. It was on her right hand, Bryony noticed. She wore no formal engagement ring.

Lois said, 'You look marvellous in black, Bryony. Doesn't she, Hunter?'

He looked at her intently, and Bryony felt herself flush. 'Very nice,' he said, but any intimacy she might have

61

imagined between them had vanished. He had raised an
invisible barrier and placed her firmly on the other side.

Lois asked him how the house was coming along. 'It's
coming,' he responded. 'I should be able to move in in
a couple of weeks, if all goes according to plan.'

Bryony leaned forward in her chair, the firelight
playing over her face. 'Things don't often go according
to plan in this province,' she said.

'I intend to move into Santu House in two weeks, come
hell or high water,' he said firmly, and she thought, he
will too. He's in the habit of getting what he wants. Well,
he might be in for a surprise when it comes to
Knucklerock Field. If I can get the seniors organised,
we might just put a spoke in his wheel. Make him aware
that there are other people in the world besides Hunter
Grant.

A chauffeur-driven limousine drew up to the front
door, and Lois got up from her perch on the arm of
Hunter's chair. 'That's Daddy,' she said, 'at last!'

There were voices in the hall, the door swung open
and a short, florid-faced man came into the room like
a cyclone. 'Am I very late?' asked Branwell Taylor. 'Had
to see some of my constituents and I lost track of the
time.' He turned a pair of shrewd blue eyes on Bryony,
who had risen with the others. 'You must be Lois's new
friend. She said you were coming tonight.'

'Her name's Bryony, Daddy,' Lois informed him,
pouring out a finger of Scotch and handing it to her
father. 'Now, don't linger over this, we're all starving.'

'I'll bring it with me to the dining-room,' he said. 'I
don't imagine anyone will be put off their food if I don't
change for dinner.'

'Such heresy!' grinned Hunter.

'That'll be the day!' Lois said, with a wink at Bryony.
'Now, do get a move on, Daddy, we've been waiting
hours.'

'I take it that damn dog of Hunter's isn't around?'
said Lois's father gruffly.

'Gus is in the kitchen being spoiled by Lacey,' replied
Hunter. 'He knows better than to come in here.'

'Good!' said Branwell Taylor, leading the way to the dining-room, an elaborate affair, with crimson silk walls and much carved oak. 'I can't abide dogs. Useless creatures!'

Hunter said, 'Gus is much less useless than a lot of the people we voted for last election, Branwell, let me tell you.'

Mr Taylor stuck out a belligerent lower lip, then he gave a snort of laughter. 'You're a proper screwball,' he said. He pulled out a high-backed chair on his right. 'You sit here, Bryony, next to me. The love-birds can sit together tonight,' and Bryony heard Hunter mutter something under his breath. Lois turned pink.

Mrs Lacey came in bearing a tureen which she put in front of their host, who lifted the cover and sniffed at the contents. 'What's this then? Cod's-nest stew?'

'It's lobster soup, Mr Taylor,' snapped his house-keeper. 'And don't blame me if it's spoilt. The least you could have done was to get that secretary of yours to phone if you was going to be late.' She stomped out.

'No one in this house treats me with respect, Bryony,' Mr Taylor joked, ladling soup into bowls, which Lois handed round. 'This one,' he pointed the ladle towards his daughter's back, 'is so busy thinking about *him*,' this time the ladle veered towards Hunter, spilling drops of lobster soup over the white cloth, 'that half the time she's in a dream.'

'Do be careful, Daddy!' Lois scolded, going back to her place. 'You're getting soup all over the table.'

'You make Lois sound like a halfwit, Branwell,' remarked Hunter.

'I'm just telling it the way it is,' said Mr Taylor. He started noisily taking his soup, and Bryony got a chance to examine him from beneath her lowered lashes. It was hard to believe that he was related to the delicate girl opposite. He was short and thick-set, and although his eyes were also blue, they were small and crafty, while Lois's were large and bland. It was as if a bull had sired a gazelle!

They had roast beef to follow, and when Branwell had carved he turned to Bryony. 'I know you from somewhere. Seen you before. Ever done any work for the Party?'

'Miss Porter is the girl who attacked me on that television show,' Hunter told him.

'Miss Porter?' shrieked Lois. 'Darling, surely you're on a first name basis by now?'

Hunter looked at Bryony, and for a moment it felt as if they were alone in the room. Her heart gave that funny little lurch again.

'Bryony.' He made it sound like a caress. 'As in Briar Rose?'

To dispel the bubble of tension that had developed between them, she said loudly, 'Hunter? As in trap?'

'I didn't see that programme,' said Branwell Taylor. 'Lois and I were in Halifax.'

'Buying clothes,' Lois remarked in an aside.

'You were supposed to be buying linen for your bottom drawer,' her father said. 'Planning for your future home.' He turned to Bryony again. 'I *have* seen you before, though. I never forget a face.'

'I was on a series of talk shows, trying to get people interested in an annual kite festival,' she said. 'You must have seen one of them.'

'That's it! I remember now.' He swallowed a large piece of beef. 'I remember thinking it was a good idea. Nice tourist attraction.'

Deciding to strike while the iron was hot, Bryony said, 'We could use your support.'

'Tell me about it after dinner. I'll listen to what you have to say then,' he promised.

Hunter laid down his knife and fork. 'Where had you planned to hold this festival?' he asked.

She replied carefully, 'That would depend on what's available.'

'Bryony takes a busload of old people to Knucklerock Field every Sunday,' Lois told her father. 'They fly kites, and you should *see* some of them! They're beautiful. One old lady has made one to look like a horse.'

'Mabel Frame's Pegasus.' Bryony smiled. 'It's a great kite.'

'Knucklerock Field, eh?' Branwell sopped up some gravy with his potato. 'That reminds me.' He stuffed the potato into his mouth and munching loudly, said to Hunter, 'The deal's gone through. As of Monday, Knucklerock Field is yours.'

Bryony had suddenly lost her appetite. She caught Hunter looking at her speculatively, and hastily looked down and pushed a morsel of beef around her plate.

'I'll move a couple of choppers in next week, then,' said Hunter, 'and we can start building the hangars.'

She pushed her plate aside with a sinking feeling in the pit of her stomach. Knucklerock Field was as good as gone. Soon it would be dotted with buildings and busy with whirling aircraft.

'Have you finished, Bryony?' asked Lois, pressing a bell to summon Mrs Lacey.

She nodded. 'Yes, thank you. It was delicious.'

'Never find a husband if you're nothing but skin and bone,' Branwell Taylor informed them, looking with approval on the huge apple pie Mrs Lacey had brought to the table.

'I'm not interested in finding a husband,' Bryony snapped. Careful! an inner voice cautioned. Hang on to your temper, you need this man's support.

'That's a load of old codswallop!' Branwell passed her a huge portion of apple pie, fragrant with cloves. 'Every girl wants to get married. That's only natural.'

'I suspect Bryony is far too busy running her business to bother with matrimony,' Hunter remarked. His eyes caught and held Bryony's, and she saw that the grey was dotted with amber, which made them gleam like a jungle cat's.

'We all know your views on the subject of careers for women,' said Branwell through a mouthful of pie. 'You'll change when you're safely married.'

Hunter said firmly, 'I doubt it.'

'Please! No arguments tonight,' Lois said. 'Remember we have a guest. It won't be much fun for

Bryony if you two have another of your boring
arguments.'

'Oh, I don't know. I have the impression that there's
nothing Bryony enjoys so much as a good brawl,' Hunter
said cheerfully.

'I'll stick to my own brawls, thanks,' said Bryony
abruptly.

'Just make sure you don't take on more than you can
handle,' he warned.

She gave him a mock-sweet smile. 'If I do, I'll write
them on my kite and set it free,' she said.

Lois looked across at her. 'What do you mean?'

'There's an old saying that if your problems get too
much for you, simply write them down on your kite.
When the kite's really high, cut the string and—bingo!—
the problems will fly away.'

'I could think of a few problems I'd like to get rid of
that way,' Branwell remarked.

'Does it work? Have you ever tried it?' asked Hunter.

'I've never had to yet,' she told him. 'It's only supposed to be done as a last resort.'

'Is that why you went into the kite-designing game?'
Hunter asked. 'As a possible way to solve problems?'

'Indirectly,' she grinned, and then she told them how
she had made her first kite out of her father's newspaper. 'I was hooked after that,' she admitted. Warming
to her theme, she went on, 'There are all kinds of theories about what inspired man to make a kite in the first
place. Some people think it started from runaway sails
from a fishing-boat, or a Chinese farmer's hat being
carried off by the wind. But whatever it was, kite-flying
has been popular for centuries. I'm totally addicted.
When I'm flying a kite, it's as if I'm in another element.
Flying free, like the kite on the end of my string, and I
know my Sky Highers feel the same way.' She turned to
her host, her green eyes sparkling. 'You should see them,
Mr Taylor. They're great! You couldn't ask for a better
advertisement for kiting.' She became conscious of
Hunter gazing at her across the table. Conscious in a
strange way that he was her ally—which was ridiculous.

He wasn't her ally, he was going to stop her using Knucklerock Field! She gave an apologetic shrug. 'I didn't mean to go on like that. You should have stopped me.'

'Never try to stop a woman when she's got the bit between her teeth,' said Branwell.

Lois nodded in agreement. 'It was fascinating, Bryony. You make it sound so exciting and...different!'

'It's the way I feel about flying,' Hunter said. He leaned towards her. 'I have a feeling you'd love flying. You must let me take you up in one of my helicopters some time.'

There was an intimacy in his voice that made Bryony's blood tingle, and so she replied sharply, 'In a *helicopter*! I can't think of anything I'd like less. I prefer to stay on the end of my kite string, thanks all the same.'

Coffee was served in the drawing-room. Lois poured, sitting demurely at one end of an oval-backed Victorian sofa, handing the fine china cups with the ease of a true politician's daughter. Her father began telling them anecdotes concerning his political life, dwelling on incidents in the past from which he emerged with glowing colours. As he sipped from the balloon glass of brandy Lois had poured for him, he enlarged upon his own astuteness compared to the ineptitude of his colleagues.

Lois's blue eyes began to glaze and Bryony felt sympathy for her. Poor girl, she thought, with two bullies in her life. But even while she thought this she knew she was being unjust. Hunter was no bully. His imperiousness stemmed from true power, not self-aggrandisement like Branwell Taylor's. And it was this power that made Hunter such a formidable opponent.

'Daddy! I want to show Hunter a picture I bought the other day,' said Lois, interrupting her father in full flight and dragging Hunter to his feet. 'We won't be long.'

When Bryony was left alone with her host, he chuckled, 'Picture, indeed! Bit of billing and cooing, more like it.' He peered, a trifle blearily, at Bryony. 'Now, young lady! What was that you were mentioning earlier—about a kite festival? The floor's yours.'

She outlined her ideas, and when she had finished he said, 'I like it! I like it! Tell you what, if I could get you some money—to cover advertising and such—d'you think you could organise it? A one-day kite festival, late this summer. I'm not promising anything, mind, but you give me an idea of the costs, and I'll see what I can do.'

'I can get the figures to your office the day after tomorrow, Mr Taylor,' she promised, hoping his enthusiasm wasn't induced by the brandy.

'And you must include those old folk,' he added. 'They're a good vote-catching image. I'll get the necessary permission for any cars you need to get them to the top of Signal Hill.'

'Signal Hill? I'd thought of having the festival on Knucklerock Field.'

'Too far out of town.' He waved his stubby fingers. 'Besides, that land belongs to Hunter now.'

'I know.' How could she forget? 'It's just that we've always used that field.'

'Things change,' Branwell Taylor informed her. 'Anyway, the kite festival must be in St John's. In *my* constituency.' And that was the end of that.

Lois and Hunter joined them soon afterwards, and Branwell excused himself to go and attend to some paperwork.

'It's getting late, I'd better go,' Bryony said, sure that the lovers would be glad to have time to themselves.

But Hunter said firmly, 'It's only ten. Surely you can stay a little longer?'

Lois insisted, too. 'Yes, do! I've got some new records. I was hoping we might play them over a brandy. Tomorrow's Sunday. You surely don't work on *Sundays*, do you?'

'Sometimes,' replied Bryony, smiling because Lois seemed so appalled by the idea.

'But not tomorrow?' Hunter asked quietly.

And Bryony admitted, 'No. Not tomorrow,' and agreed to stay.

Sitting listening to a popular rock record, she reflected that Lois and Hunter were the coolest couple

she'd ever encountered. Whenever she and Dave listened
to records, or watched television, they snuggled close,
but Hunter sat in one of the wing chairs nursing his
brandy and obviously hating the music, while Lois sat
on the floor on the other side of the fireplace, her
shoulders jerking to the beat, her eyes closed. They might
have been in separate rooms.

The music ended with a last shuddering beat. Hunter
went to the music centre. 'Now we need an antidote,'
he said, taking a record and putting it on the turntable.

'You might have let Bryony choose the next one,' Lois
pouted.

'I might have, but I daren't risk it. She might have
played the other side.'

'I might have,' Bryony agreed, although rock was the
last thing she wanted to hear tonight. Actually, she didn't
want to listen to music at all right now. All she wanted
was to be home, safe with her family. Then perhaps she
could shake off this strange melancholy that clung to
her like mist.

Placido Domingo's rich tenor voice singing an aria
from *La Bohème* filled the room, and she felt herself
relax in her chair. After a while, tears stung her eyes as
the love song throbbed and yearned. She blinked sur-
reptitiously. Of all the records in the world, why did
Hunter have to choose *that* one? She loved opera, and
Italian opera best of all. It would have been hard for
her to have stayed dry-eyed at the best of times, but
tonight, when she was feeling so strangely despondent,
it was impossible.

The record came to an end at last, and, swallowing a
lump the size of a golf ball, she stood up. 'That was
lovely,' she said. 'Thank you.'

'I didn't mean to reduce you to tears,' Hunter said.

'Tears of boredom, I should think, poor thing,' Lois
remarked. 'I mean, *really*, darling! Couldn't you have
chosen something a little less heavy.'

Hunter came and stood in front of Bryony. She could
count the buttons on his dress shirt, see the grain of his

beard. 'They weren't tears of boredom, were they?' he asked softly.

She shook her tangerine curls. 'No.' And then, because his nearness seemed a threat and she *had* to get away from him, she almost ran to the door. 'I *must* go now. Thank you for a lovely evening.' He didn't come with Lois to see her out, but stayed pensively staring at the dying fire.

Janice was still up when she got home, and she asked if Bryony had enjoyed herself. 'Great! It was very nice,' Bryony said, and Janice looked up from the milk she was heating.

'Are you sure? You sound a bit down.'

'Just tired,' Bryony told her, but, lying in bed listening to the wind that still howled, she knew it was more than fatigue that made her feel like this. She didn't understand it, and finally she decided that it must be the knowledge that Knucklerock Field had been sold that made her feel so at odds with the world.

The storm had diminished by the following morning, but it was still too wet to take the Sky Highers out. Tansy called, and they decided to visit the home anyway, and talk to the seniors about strategy for the coming demonstration.

'We can't waste time, Bryony,' Tansy said, 'otherwise that Grant guy will have ruined the field without even a fight from us.'

'I guess you're right,' Bryony said, but she didn't sound keen.

'You feelin' all right?' Tansy asked, giving her a suspicious look.

She nodded her blazing curls. 'Fine! Only...maybe it won't do any good...maybe it's too late.'

'That's not the right attitude. Where's your fightin' spirit?' Tansy asked disapprovingly, and Bryony shrugged. 'We gotta' get ourselves organised properly,' she declared. 'This is no time to get wishy-washy.'

The Sky Highers gathered in the visitors' lounge and the head nurse arranged for coffee. Bryony remained silent while Tansy outlined their problems, and it was agreed to set up a committee.

The seniors seemed quite buoyed up by the idea of a demonstration, mainly because it would relieve the tedium of their days, but Bryony was beginning to have definite misgivings about the whole thing. It was one thing to make a fuss on her own account, but getting these nice old people to stage a demonstration was something else. She wondered if she should tell the head nurse and get her to put a stop to it, but that might cause bad feeling between the residents and the staff and make matters worse. The best she could do was to see that they didn't get carried away and march on the field carrying baseball bats, ready for battle!

Tansy needed some persuading not to demand that they all carry signs telling Hunter to do unmentionable things with his helicopters, but after some discussion it was agreed that when the helicopters arrived on the field a delegation would go and make a quiet protest.

'We mustn't forget,' said Bryony, 'that we're not saying that there shouldn't be a helicopter station. We're just asking them not to take our field away.'

Tansy said, 'That sounds a bit tame.'

'I think that's all we can ask under the circumstances,' Bryony replied firmly.

'That's right!' one old gentleman piped up. 'My grandson's going to work on them choppers, after a year of unemployment. We don't want them going somewhere else.'

'We must be diplomatic, dear,' Mabel stressed, and Tansy growled something rude, but was quelled by a look from Bryony.

Soon after that, the meeting came to an end.

'You sure weren't much help,' grumbled Tansy on their way back to town.

'I'm worried,' Bryony said. 'I'm afraid the Sky Highers might not realise what they're getting into. I wouldn't want them getting into trouble.'

'Don't fret,' Tansy reassured her. 'There won't be any trouble. Not if we do it the way you planned. Nice an'

polite.' She really meant spinelessly, but was too fond
of Bryony to say so.

'I just hope you're right,' Bryony sighed, her usually
smooth brow furrowed.

She worked hard the next day getting the figures
Branwell Taylor wanted, and then she typed out a neat
proposal for the festival. When she had handed it in to
his office she felt a terrific lift, in spite of her anxiety
about her seniors, and on an impulse she phoned Dave
at his office and suggested he come round for dinner
that night. She knew Janice wouldn't mind, and it would
soothe Dave's rumpled feelings, for he still hadn't quite
forgiven her for going out on Saturday night.

He arrived while she was putting Teddy to bed. 'It's
Dave!' Teddy shouted, when he put his head round the
door. 'Look at me! I'm a 'copter pilot!' And he bounced
up and down on the mattress, blinking through
Hunter's goggles.

'Does he ever take them off?' Dave asked.

'Only when absolutely necessary,' smiled Bryony.
'Come on, Teddy! Lie down and I'll tell you a story.'

The child lay back on the pillow, pushing the goggles
that had come dislodged back over his eyes. 'Tell one
'bout the 'copter man,' he said.

Dave said, 'The *what* man?' and came to stand beside
Bryony.

'He means Hunter Grant. I don't know any stories
about him, sweetheart.' She wondered why she felt self-
conscious saying Hunter's name; he was only a casual
acquaintance, after all.

'You *do*!' the little boy insisted. 'Daddy said he flied
his plane to *Africa*. Tell about that.'

'I'll tell you a story about a *lion* that lived in Africa,'
Bryony said.

'Did the 'copter man shoot him?' demanded Teddy.

'Possibly. Why don't you listen and find out?' But she
didn't make up a very good story this evening. Teddy
kept interrupting, wanting to know when she was going
to tell about the ''copter man', but with Dave gazing at

her soulfully she felt reluctant to mention Hunter's name again, which was idiotic.

Finally Teddy got bored and consented to take off the goggles and kiss Bryony and Dave goodnight. As they went downstairs, Dave stopped and put his arms around her.

'Did you miss me?' he whispered into her short red curls.

'When?' asked Bryony.

'Last Saturday, of course,' said Dave, rather hurt. 'I missed you.'

She returned his kiss absent-mindedly, and said, 'Actually, Saturday night turned out to be lucky. I met Branwell Taylor and he's interested in organising a kite festival.'

'That's nice.' Dave released her. 'I keep forgetting, you always put business before pleasure.' He looked sulky and Bryony felt a stab of guilt, for she had neglected him lately. She kissed him lightly on the cheek. 'Poor old Dave, cheer up!' she said. 'Janice has cooked one of her famous casseroles—you looked as if you were going to have to eat my food.'

'It really is time you learnt to cook, Bryony,' said Dave, who didn't share the family's light-hearted view of Bryony's cooking. 'Most women can cook, you know.'

'I'm not most women,' she replied.

He squeezed her hand and murmured, 'I know.'

After dinner, Janice and Bruce tactfully left them alone to watch a film on television. It wasn't a very good film, and soon she was in Dave's arms and he was kissing her.

Usually she enjoyed being kissed, but tonight she couldn't seem to relax. She kept remembering the look in Hunter's grey eyes as they watched the storm together, and the way the silver wings of his hair gleamed in the candlelight during dinner. As tactfully as she could, she eased herself out of Dave's embrace. 'It's getting late, and we both have to work tomorrow,' she said as an excuse.

Dutifully he released her. 'I guess I'd better be on my way. I have to see an important client in the morning.'

She would have bet her last dollar that Hunter Grant wouldn't stop kissing a woman because of an important client in the morning. But then, he wasn't reasonable like Dave. There was a recklessness in him that was as far removed from Dave's placid temperament as chalk from cheese—of course, he wasn't dull, either. Hurriedly, she banished this disloyal thought by promising that of *course* she was free to go dancing next Saturday. She'd *love* it!

Mid-week Tansy phoned her. She had learned through the grapevine that work on the hangars was to start the next day. 'We could go out there and picket when I'm through work,' she suggested, 'I'm finished by four.' And reluctantly Bryony agreed to phone and arrange it with the Sky Highers. She was sure now that any kind of demonstration would merely annoy Hunter, or amuse him, which would be worse. It had been foolish to think the sight of a few old people carrying placards would move him. He was the type who would remain unmoved if they flung themselves over the cliff like so many elderly lemmings.

It was a touching little band that climbed into the school bus the following afternoon, their placards discreetly covered so that the nursing staff could not see them. Tansy's read, 'KITES NOT 'COPTERS', but the others were less inflammatory and simply stated, 'KNUCKLEROCK FIELD FOR ALL'.

The first thing they saw when they arrived was a bulldozer levelling the ground at the far end of the field, the second was a large twin-engined helicopter.

'It's so big,' Mabel faltered, as if she expected it to turn itself on and attack them.

'And that's just one of a *fleet*!' Tansy said, as they trooped out of the bus. She whipped the plastic bag off her placard. 'Come on! Let's start marching.' They formed a ragged line, some of them carrying their kites as well as their signs, and began walking towards the bulldozer.

The bulldozer operator went on with his work. He didn't even give a second glance when a car painted with

the logo of the television station arrived on the scene
and a cameraman got out.

Bryony felt excessively silly. She had thought there
would be more men working here. Marching up to this
lone worker seemed the height of idiocy, and then, when
she saw Patsy Drake's slender figure climb from the car,
tape recorder at the ready, her heart sank another notch.

Patsy came over and joined the group that was now
standing in front of the bulldozer, blocking its path.
'Would you mind turning that thing off for a minute?'
she asked, and the operator, grinning from ear to ear,
complied. 'Can you tell me something about this protest,
and who organised it?' she asked, holding out the mike
to Bryony, but before Bryony could reply there was a
deep bark, and they all turned to look at the big white
dog and the tall man coming towards them.

'Oh, no!' Bryony groaned, her heart sinking as Hunter
came closer.

The cameraman started filming, and Patsy said, 'Don't
waste too much film yet, Jack, there might be some fireworks in a minute.'

'Traitoress!' Bryony hissed. 'I thought you were my
friend.'

'You said you wanted publicity,' Patsy reminded her
sweetly. 'I'm just doing my job.'

Gus bounded up, and a couple of the women shrieked.
'He's quite harmless,' said Hunter, when he joined them.
Which is more than you are, thought Bryony, quailing
inwardly.

Hunter looked at the placards that seemed even more
absurd now. Then he looked at Bryony, bright as a daf-
fodil in her yellow jumpsuit. '*You* again!' he said, his
mouth grim. 'I might have known.'

CHAPTER FIVE

WHY, oh, *why* did he have to turn up today? thought Bryony. She forced herself to look into those wintry grey eyes and croaked, 'This is a peaceful demonstration.'

He regarded the huddle of Sky Highers grouped forlornly around him. 'I'm delighted to hear it. I take it you are the leader of this little band?'

The old gentleman who had been elected chairman pushed his way forward. 'I'm the spokesman,' he quavered, 'and you are Mr Grant. Right?'

Patsy thrust her mike under Hunter's nose. 'Were you unaware that this demonstration was planned, Mr Grant?' she asked.

'Of course I was,' Hunter said shortly. He turned to the group. 'Now, what's all this about?'

'It's about losing our field.' Tansy shouldered her way through the group to face him, and shook her sign belligerently. 'Losin' our field to a bunch of helicopters, that's what!'

'*Your* field! They told me it was Crown land,' said Hunter, smooth as silk, and several warning rockets went off in Bryony's head, because she had learnt that when Hunter sounded like that it meant trouble.

'We're protesting because we don't think it's fair taking over this field without even discussing it with us,' she said hastily.

'Discussing *what*?' asked Hunter with withering scorn. 'The fact that I intend to run a much-needed helicopter station, which will give work opportunities to the people of this town?'

'This demonstration won't do any good, will it?' the spokesman ventured. 'You'll still build the 'copter station.'

'Of course I will,' Hunter agreed. 'But that doesn't mean you can't have access to the field sometimes. That's the issue, isn't it?'

Bryony cried out, 'But how can we? I mean, with helicopters buzzing around...and the hangars taking up the field...there won't be room.' She looked at him doubtfully. 'Will there?'

'You really are a very dangerous young woman,' he said, his voice soft with menace. 'You jump to conclusions like the star of a flea circus.' Turning his attention back to the group he told them, 'Contrary to what you've been led to believe Knucklerock Field will not be destroyed. It only requires a small level area as a landing-pad. The hangars and control tower will be at the back of the field, so there's no reason why you shouldn't continue using it on Sundays when things will be quiet anyway.' He suddenly smiled down at Mabel, who clutched Pegasus along with her sign, and again the hardness seemed to melt from his face. 'Your kite is much more attractive than your placard,' he said, gently taking it from her. 'There's a rubbish bin over near the entrance. A good place for this, I should think. And now I'd appreciate it if you would all move away and let the bulldozer get on with his work. I'm being charged by the hour.'

The cameraman took a last shot of the Sky Highers throwing their signs into the bin, before returning to his car. Patsy came alongside Bryony. 'Well, that ended happily, didn't it?' she said.

'I have been so *dumb*!' lamented Bryony, dragging her feet in the tussocky grass.

Patsy nodded her agreement. 'You don't seem to have been too bright, Bryony, but Mr Grant came up smelling of roses, didn't he?' She popped her notebook into her purse. 'See you around. Don't fret.'

Bryony lifted her hand in farewell and trudged back to the bus. Only Tansy and a few of the Sky Highers were there. 'He's showin' them over the helicopter.' Tansy nodded in the direction of the twin-engined monster, where Bryony could see Hunter assisting the more adventurous into the aircraft. Rather to her surprise, Mabel was among them.

'Do you think it'll work out?' Tansy asked in a hoarse whisper. 'D'you think he *meant* it?'

'I'm sure he did,' Bryony said. 'I don't think he's in the habit of saying things he doesn't mean.'

'Reckon we was mistaken about him,' Tansy declared.

Bryony said firmly, '*I* was. It had nothing to do with you.'

'I went off half-cocked, too,' said Tansy.

'You wouldn't have if it hadn't been for me,' insisted Bryony.

Tansy said, 'Reckon we ought'a apologise?'

'I will,' said Bryony. 'I'll apologise.' She walked slowly toward the helicopter just as Hunter was about to lift Mabel up into the machine. 'Isn't this exciting, dear!' Mabel called. 'Mr Grant's going to let us *hover*!' Her powdery cheeks were flushed with pleasure.

'That should be fun.' Bryony really meant it, but it came out sounding like a snub. She would be lucky if he allowed her to come to Knucklerock Field on Sundays with the others after today.

She went over and sat on the grass beside Gus. The downwash from the helicopter was nearly taking the hair off her head, and Gus moved away, but she stayed where she was, getting a savage kind of satisfaction from the cold wind, as if it could cleanse her of humiliation. She was so mad at herself, she could have wept. She only hoped the old people would forgive her for making them look such fools. She would have to use her influence and get Bruce to soft-pedal the news coverage. Concentrate on her ineptitude rather than the Sky Highers' part in the affair.

After a while the helicopter returned to earth. Hunter cut the engine and athletically sprang to the ground. Chattering happily, the Sky Highers let him help them down. 'I believe you could land that thing on a quarter,' one old man said approvingly.

'That was most enjoyable,' Mabel bubbled. 'Most enjoyable, indeed.' She went over to Bryony, who had risen and was waiting to go with her to the bus. 'I never dreamed...at my age...' She smiled dreamily. '*What* an exciting day!'

Hunter joined them. 'Don't forget your kite,' he said, handing Pegasus to her.

'Oh, dear, no!' exclaimed the old lady. 'And thank you again for a lovely afternoon, Mr Grant. It was most instructive. And now I'll leave you alone with Bryony. I know that's what you both want.' And, smiling archly, she trotted off to join the group at the bus.

Hunter looked mystified. 'She's a dear, but is she quite connected to reality?' he asked.

'Usually, but I'm glad we have a moment to ourselves.' Bryony pushed back a wayward curl that had fallen into her eyes. 'I want to thank you. It was nice of you to take them for that ride...'

'Hardly a ride. We barely left the ground.'

'Just the same...it took their mind off the...the mess I got them into.' She took a deep breath and said in a voice as clear as ringing crystal, 'I want to apologise. You were quite right, I do jump to conclusions. It's a bad habit of mine...just ask my father. I was wrong about you...about a lot of things. I'm sorry.'

He looked at her steadily for a moment, then he did a very surprising thing. He reached out and ran his fingers slowly through her fiery curls. She stood quite still as a sudden, ferocious excitement coursed through her. This caress lasted only a second before he said softly, 'Jumping to conclusions probably goes with red hair.'

'Do you think I should shave my head?' she asked, hoping humour, even feeble humour, might help to still her heart which was pounding like a hammer on an anvil.

'I doubt if such drastic measures would work,' he said, smiling. 'Besides, it would be a crime to put a razor anywhere near that glorious hair.'

At that moment she heard the bus roar into life. 'I must go.' But she didn't move. She was filled with a strange reluctance, as if his light touch had cast a spell on her.

He seemed to share this unwillingness, for he also
stood as if cast in bronze. 'We're sure to see each other
again soon.'

'Yes.' The horn blared again. 'I must go.'

'At last we can be friends.' His mouth didn't look
hard any more, not when it curved gently like this, and
she found herself wondering how it would feel to be
kissed by that sensual mouth.

'I *must* go,' she blurted again, and tearing herself away
ran to the waiting bus, leaving him staring after her small,
yellow-clad back, his mind filled with misgivings.

In the days that followed, Bryony found herself breaking
off whatever she was doing and falling into a dream. A
dream in which Hunter played a major role. She tried
to control herself, forcing herself to attend to her various
tasks with furious concentration, but an hour later she
would be staring into space again, remembering that sexy
mouth of his, and the touch of his fingers on her hair.
Now that they were friends, he seemed to have taken up
permanent residence in her thoughts. Which made him
more dangerous than when he had been her enemy.

She managed to persuade Bruce to edit the news item
of the demonstration so that the Sky Highers didn't come
off badly, and she suffered Bruce's lecture in contrite
silence, for he disapproved of this kind of nepotism, and
was furious that she had been fool enough to organise
the demonstration in the first place.

She had another meeting with Branwell Taylor, and
the kite festival was set for the last weekend of July. This
gave her six weeks. Six weeks of hard work, which was
just what she needed to knock all daydreams of Hunter
Grant out of her head. Her parents should have arrived
in St John's by then as well. It would be fun to have
them here for the festival. Knowing her father, she was
sure he would take an active part. He would take over
if she let him. Major Porter liked to run things.

She visited the senior citizens' home after her interview with Branwell Taylor, to find out if they were
angry with her, and discovered to her relief that they

bore her no ill will. There was great excitement when she told them about the festival. 'I'm counting on you all to be there,' she said, 'to show the young ones what it's all about.'

'I'll have to practise getting Pegasus launched,' Mabel complained. 'I'm still having trouble.'

Bryony promised her that they would work on it. 'I'll take you out a few times on your own, if you like.'

'Thank you, dear. Very kind. But you won't want to spend too much time away from that man of yours,' Mabel murmured. 'I'll try and practise a little on my own.'

This seemed an odd remark, particularly since Bryony had never mentioned Dave, but all she said was, 'Well, don't try it near any trees. You don't want to damage Pegasus. I'm relying on that kite to win a prize.' She looked at her watch and hastily finished her tea. 'I've got to dash.'

'Got a date with a nice young man?' one of the old men twinkled.

'Yes to both questions,' Bryony grinned, making for the door, for Dave was undoubtedly a nice young man, and they did have a date to go dancing this evening.

'I knew it,' Mabel crowed. 'I'm never wrong about these things. Bless you both!'

Bryony stared at her, puzzled. Maybe Mabel *had* seen her with Dave some time, although she couldn't recall such a meeting. Perhaps Hunter was right, and Mabel was losing touch with reality. She dismissed this thought. Mabel's blue eyes might be faded, but they were keen. They were the sort of eyes that never missed a trick.

Dave was waiting for her when she got home, trying to calm a wailing Jane while Teddy tugged at his jacket demanding attention. 'Thank goodness you've come,' he said in heartfelt tones. 'Janice had to go down to the store, and she asked me to babysit.'

Bryony picked up the screaming baby from her playpen and the wails diminished. 'She's lonely, that's her problem.' She turned a stern green eye on her nephew. 'Quit that whining, Teddy! You're not a baby, you're a big boy. Stop annoying Dave.' Teddy didn't stop whining right away, but Bryony ignored him and soon he was quietly playing with his toys again.

Dave settled down with the evening paper. 'If you want a job, Dave,' said Bryony tartly, 'you can pour us both a drink and we'll watch Bruce's show.'

When Janice returned, the two adults were sitting silently watching television. Bryony was cuddling Jane close to her breast. Pressing her cheek against the baby's dark, silky head, she wondered why she felt such a need for comfort; poor old Dave hadn't committed any crime. He simply wasn't keen on small children. And, as anyone who had anything to do with small children knew, they could sometimes be a trial. But it was his general attitude that bothered her. His conviction that *she* must be the one to pick up the baby, otherwise let her cry! *She* must be the one to quiet Teddy...

She thought of her brother and his wife, and of their shared duties. Bruce could care for his offspring as well as Janice if he chose, and he often did choose, in order to give Janice time for herself and her own interests.

That's the kind of marriage I want...if I ever get married, thought Bryony as she stared at the flickering screen. And I'll never find it with someone like Dave. And again she knew that she must end the friendship. Much as she hated inflicting hurt, she must stop putting it off.

Dave had been invited to eat with them. It was always rather heavy-going when Dave ate with the Porters. Bruce liked him, but they weren't really on the same wavelength. Dave had the unfortunate habit of telling Bruce how he should run his television programme, and tonight he took Bruce to task over his coverage of the Sky Highers' demonstration.

'Just because Bryony's your sister,' he said between mouthfuls of Janice's shepherd's pie, 'that's no reason to play the thing down. You hardly mentioned it on your show. All we saw was Grant telling the old people they could still use the field. There was no footage of the demonstration itself.'

'I did that to protect the seniors, not Bryony,' Bruce said shortly. 'I don't approve of tampering with the news as a rule, but it was hardly an item of earth-shaking importance. Not worth getting them in trouble with the home.'

'But Bryony got off scot-free!' Dave said indignantly. 'It's all right,' he said to Janice who was looking anxiously at her sister-in-law, 'Bryony knows how I feel about the whole affair.'

'Do I ever!' muttered Bryony with a wink at Janice.

'She knows how *I* feel too,' Bruce said drily. 'I told her at great length.' He grinned at his sister, for he had well and truly read her the riot act. 'But it's over now, and I think Bryony learnt a lesson. I suggest we give it a rest.'

Janice said, 'Amen to that!' and started clearing the plates.

Later that evening Dave and Bryony went to dance at one of the local hotels. Bryony wore her grey challis, for it was a cool night, and the full sleeves, drawn into narrow cuffs at the wrist, were cosy. It had a wide, swirling skirt, too, which was nice for dancing.

The hotel was full when they arrived, but they managed to find a corner table, and after they had ordered drinks they joined the crowd on the dance-floor. After a few lively numbers, the band played a slow, old-fashioned piece, and the couples slid into each other's arms for a foxtrot. Dave tried to hold Bryony close, but she found she didn't want to be held close by Dave, so he gave up and concentrated on his dancing rather than on his diminutive partner.

They danced like this for some minutes, then he exclaimed, 'Look at that beautiful girl!' Peering round his shoulder, Bryony saw Lois drifting by, her head resting on Hunter's broad shoulder.

Bryony tripped over her own feet. 'Sorry,' she apologised, and then Lois saw them, waved, and she and Hunter danced over.

'What fun, meeting you!' Lois enthused when Dave had been introduced. 'Are you with a party?'

'No, we're alone,' said Dave eagerly. Hunter had not said a word, and Bryony had looked everywhere except at his face. She looked up at him now. His pale eyes seemed as bright as chipped flint.

'Instead of just standing here marking time,' he said at last, 'why don't you join us for a drink?'

'Yes, do!' Lois chimed in. 'We're having champagne.'

'Are we crashing a celebration of some sort?' Dave asked as Hunter led them to a table on the edge of the floor.

Bryony felt herself grow cold. Drinking champagne could mean Lois and Hunter were celebrating the public announcement of their engagement, but her chill disappeared when Hunter said, 'No particular celebration. Lois happens to like champagne.' He smiled over at his silvery companion. 'She's a champagne-type lady.'

She certainly looked it, dressed to kill in a scarlet dress, the bodice glittering with sequins, rubies hanging from her neck and ears. She was stunning. Perhaps a little *too* stunning for this kind of hotel, but stunning just the same.

Hunter beckoned a waiter for two extra glasses, and when the wine had been poured he raised his glass. 'To friendship,' he said, smiling round the table. Then his glance settled on Bryony and her breath caught in her throat. 'Long may it last.'

'I gather you two have buried the hatchet,' Lois giggled. 'I watched your demonstration on television,' she explained.

Dave's mouth turned down. 'That was a stupid thing for Bryony to do. If she had told me she was planning it, I would have put a stop to it.'

Bryony opened her slanted green eyes to their fullest extent, and Hunter chuckled.

'As a matter of fact,' he said, 'I admire anyone who fights for what they believe in—even,' he raised a dark eyebrow, 'even when they make a damned nuisance of themselves.'

'You sound just like Daddy,' Lois observed, taking a mirror out of a small red silk purse and examining her lipstick.

'No,' Hunter said, 'I don't. I don't encourage women to be helpless butterflies the way your father does.'

Lois closed her purse with a snap. 'You may call it being a butterfly,' she said plaintively. 'I call it being looked after.'

Hunter said, 'And you know all about being looked after, don't you, my sweet?' There was an awkward pause, and then he said abruptly to Bryony, 'Do you know how to tango?' She gaped at him wordlessly. 'They're playing a tango. Do you know how to do it?' he repeated abruptly, rising and coming to her side.

'Yes.'

'Then let's dance.' He pulled her to her feet. 'Excuse us,' he said, firmly guiding her on to the floor. I could refuse, I suppose, she thought, as he put his warm hand on her back, but the moment they started dancing she forgot everything except the pleasure of moving with him to the music, the pleasure of being in his arms.

The tango finished and he caught and held her close in a fast spin. When the band started to play a dreamy number, he clasped her closer and they started to move in time with the sensuous beat of the music. Her cheek was pressed against his chest and she could feel his heart beating, feel the warmth of his flesh through the thin cambric of his shirt, feel his thigh thrust between her legs—hard and muscular.

She reminded herself that he was probably only dancing with her all this time because he wanted to avoid an argument with Lois, so she raised her head and said as clearly as she could, 'You seem to have an obsession about women being able to take care of themselves.' For a moment his feet faltered, and he gave her a look as blank as a pane of window-glass. 'The way you keep on at Lois to learn some sort of profession,' she repeated. 'It seems to me like an obsession.'

'Yes,' he agreed, 'it is.' And then he pulled her back against him and swung around fast, not prepared to discuss it further.

She enjoyed dancing, and she was good at it, but tonight, in his arms, all she was conscious of was the lean strength of him, the firm pressure of his fingers on her back, and her usually nimble feet were clumsy. She muttered, 'Sorry,' as she stumbled yet again.

'Relax. You're with an expert,' he replied.

'A *conceited* expert,' snapped Bryony.

He grinned. 'No point hiding one's light under a bushel.'

'It would take one hell of a big bushel to hide *your* light.'

'I've never been one for false modesty,' he told her.

'Modesty?' she hooted. 'Why, you're one of the most conceited...'

'Big-headed,' he prompted.

'That, too.'

'But I *am* a good dancer.' He executed a difficult turn as if to prove it. 'You should let me give you lessons.'

Bryony planted her feet firmly, refusing to move another step. 'You are full of swagger,' she said. 'I bet you swagger even when you're lying down!'

He looked into her upturned face. 'There's one sure way to find out,' And then the music ended, and she pulled away from him.

'I must go and find Dave. Thank you for the dancing lesson.'

She started walking back to the table, but he caught hold of her arm and tucked it in his, forcing her to walk more slowly.

His face was expressionless as he asked, 'Is it serious, you and this Dave?'

She gritted her teeth. If this was the way he behaved when they were supposed to be friends, she wished they could go back to being enemies. 'I really can't see that it's any business of yours,' she said coolly, 'but, for the record...it isn't.'

'For the record...I'm glad,' he said. 'He's not the man for you.'

'How do you know?' she said huffily. 'You hardly know me.'

He looked maddeningly smug. 'I know you better than you think. I certainly know what a bad temper you've got.'

'Only around you, as a matter of fact. You bring out the worst in me.'

'Do I now?' he drawled. 'And I thought we were getting along so much better.'

By now they had reached the table. Dave and Lois were chatting, but Dave didn't look happy, and Bryony did not sit down again. 'Thank you for the drink,' she said, sending eyebrow messages to Dave. 'Now we'd better get back to our own table.'

Lois protested, but Hunter didn't, and after a few social pleasantries they made their escape. Back at their own table Dave said, 'I thought you were *never* coming back.'

'Hunter was giving me a dancing lesson,' Bryony informed him.

'He was certainly holding you close enough,' Dave said bitterly. 'You looked as if you'd been spray-painted on to him.'

'Don't be ridiculous!' she stammered. She wondered if Lois had thought the same. She certainly hoped not. 'Do stop glowering,' she snapped, 'and let's dance. That's what we came here for, isn't it?'

'Are you sure you want to dance with me? After your experience just now, it might be something of a let-down,' Dave said sulkily.

She dragged him to his feet. 'Don't be an idiot, come on!' But when they were waltzing together she discovered that Dave had been closer to the truth than he had realised. Dancing with him *was* a let-down, and the evening went rapidly downhill. Against her will her eyes kept sliding over to Hunter's table, where she could see his sleek, dark head close to Lois's blonde one. Whenever they got up to dance, she immediately found some excuse

to drag Dave back to their table; she didn't want to risk
any changing of partners on the dance-floor. As it was,
her body still vibrated from the feel of Hunter's—Dave
might have been a phantom for all the impact he made
on her.

'That's the third time I've asked you if you wanted
another drink,' he said now. 'What's the matter with
you tonight?'

'I'm sorry. I . . . I think I must be overtired,' she said.

'You're *never* overtired,' he accused her. 'If you're
not enjoying yourself, perhaps we'd better call it a night.'

He didn't talk in the car, and apart from a peck on
the cheek he didn't kiss her goodnight. She had been
going to tell him that she couldn't go out with him any
more, but when he didn't ask for a date later in the week,
the way he usually did, she decided against it. She *was*
tired, and she felt too strung-out for any emotional
scenes. Perhaps their relationship was dying a natural
death.

At the beginning of the week Lois arrived at the studio,
loaded down with parcels as before, her lovely hair
covered with a trendy plastic hat that matched her
shocking-pink raincoat, for it was a wet, windy day.

'Lunch!' she reminded Bryony. 'You promised.'

They agreed to eat at a café in one of the department
stores. 'I'm still in jeans,' Bryony pointed out, 'and since
I insist we go Dutch, it's all I can afford.'

They battled their way along Water Street. Lois
hunched under a pink and white umbrella, but Bryony,
who enjoyed bad weather, lifted her face to the glittering
screen of rain, until she saw the world through a spangle
of raindrops that clung to her thick, spiky lashes. Tendrils of marigold-bright hair, frizzing defiantly in the
wet, escaped from under the brim of her yellow
sou'wester.

They found a table right away, for hardly anyone was
out on such a day, and shrugged off their dripping
raincoats.

'Ugh!' exclaimed Lois, pressing her hands to her lovely cheeks. 'I'm a wreck. If I was a building, I'd be condemned!'

'You look gorgeous,' Bryony laughed at her, 'and you're dry as a bone.' She squinted through the rain-drops that still clung to her lashes.

'The weather on this island is beyond belief,' Lois said, picking up a menu and glaring at it. 'I *loathe* the rain.'

'You'd better get used to it fast, kiddo,' Bryony told her. 'If you're going to live here, you need webbed feet.'

Lois gave her a sly little smile. 'I'm not sure I am going to be living here,' she said. 'Not if I can help it.'

'But . . . but what about Hunter?' she said.

A waitress came and took their orders, and when she had gone Lois said, 'I'm going to talk Hunter into living on the mainland. I've decided that St John's just isn't for me.'

'The mainland?'

'Mmm! Ottawa. Or Toronto, even. Much more cosmopolitan.'

It was ridiculous, but Bryony felt offended. As if Lois's rejection of St John's was a personal insult. 'But what about the helicopter station . . . and Santu House?' She had a sudden vision of Santu House. In this weather, rain would be streaming down the windows in crystal rods. The view of the sea would be wild and beautiful. 'What about all the work he's putting into that?'

'Houses can be sold,' Lois remarked lightly, 'and he can get someone else to run his old station.' She smiled up at the waitress who deposited a plate of salad in front of her, and when the woman had given Bryony her shrimp sandwich and departed she continued, 'It isn't as if helicopters were his only business. He has other interests, you know.'

'I didn't.'

'Oh, yes! He has lots of irons in the fire. Daddy thinks he should go into politics. He could afford to.' She nibbled on a piece of lettuce. 'I'd *love* to live in Ottawa,' she fluted.

'And what about Hunter? Does he want to go into politics?' Bryony asked briskly. 'Or is that just Daddy's idea?'

'Oh! Hunter doesn't want to, but Daddy and I will work on him,' Lois said happily, and Bryony thought, good luck, kid! If you didn't have your Daddy behind you, I wouldn't give much for your chances.

'Have you told Hunter yet...that you don't like Newfoundland any more?' she enquired, nibbling at a shrimp. She didn't seem to have much appetite these days.

'I have mentioned it,' said Lois, 'but he seems to think it's just another of my whims. Besides,' she fussed with a piece of tomato, 'Hunter's got such a *fetish* about putting down roots, you can't reason with him.'

Bryony found this perfectly understandable. After a childhood spent in an orphanage, Hunter would crave stability. She and her brother had been brought up by loving parents, but even they had longed for the security of a settled home after a childhood spent travelling from place to place.

'You like it here, don't you?' Lois was asking her now, and when Bryony nodded assent, she said smugly, 'I guess you haven't done much travelling.'

'At the time I never thought of it as travelling, but when I was a kid we lived in Cyprus, England, and Germany, to name a few places. All very interesting and educational. But now I've come to roost,' she grinned, 'like one of the seagulls on Signal Hill.'

'I don't think I'll ever be able to settle here,' Lois confessed, 'even though I was born in St John's. It's just too cut off for me.'

Bryony didn't agree, but since it was pointless to argue about such personal preferences she changed the subject.

Back at work in the studio, she found herself speculating about Lois's secret plans to uproot Hunter, and her lips curved in a smile. Uprooting Hunter Grant would be like trying to uproot an oak tree with a teaspoon. Then her smile faded. If he were marrying Lois because of her father's connections, he might allow himself to be talked into moving away from Newfoundland to please his prospective father-in-law. The thought of St John's without Hunter was surprisingly bleak.

She worked late in order to put in some time on the Goose kite. She wanted it finished now, for the festival. She finished trimming the broom straws on the fourteenth disc and removed it from the two chair-backs where she had placed it for balancing, putting it carefully against the wall with its fellows. There was a furrow of tension between her eyes, and she rubbed at her forehead wearily. Never mind—soon she would be able to launch her Goose kite, and although this type of kite was more spectacular than efficient, spectacle was what she was after.

The rain had stopped when she drove home, but the town was still dripping and forlorn, like wet sheets on a bad drying day. She parked the car and opened the front door, and, dragging off her yellow raincoat and sou'wester, shouted, 'I'm home!'

A deep male voice called, 'Keep it down!' and then Gus pushed his silky white muzzle round the door. Bunty yapped from the recesses of the kitchen and Hunter snapped, 'That goes for you too, dog!' Amazingly, Bunty stopped barking.

Bryony went into the kitchen. Hunter was holding Jane high above his head then swooping her down between his knees, while the baby crowed delightedly at this rough-housing. Teddy was sitting on the floor playing with a toy helicopter.

'Look what Hunter gave me!' he yelled happily, waving the helicopter, and pointing to a scarlet leather flying-helmet and a pair of child-sized goggles lying on the floor beside him.

'Remember what we said about talking quietly because of Mommy's headache,' Hunter reminded him, and, eyes bright with excitement, the child nodded.

'He gave me goggles, an' a 'copter, *an* a hat!' he informed Bryony in a piercing whisper.

'*Gave* me,' Bryony corrected automatically. 'Very nice, too.' She looked back at Hunter. 'What are you doing here?'

'Playing with the kids at the moment.' He flung Jane across his shoulder and she dribbled contentedly on to his scarlet cashmere. 'I came to collect my goggles and found your sister-in-law trying to cope with a migraine, so I offered to hold the fort until you or your brother got home.'

Janice suffered from migraine headaches. They didn't strike often, but when they did they flattened her. 'Poor Janice!' Bryony said now. 'Why didn't she phone me?'

'Search me! Probably didn't want to bother you,' he said.

Bunty came from behind Jane's playpen to welcome Bryony home, and Gus scuttled to safety on the other side of the room, his tail between his legs. 'Don't be such a coward, Gus,' Hunter remonstrated. 'You could mash her with one paw tied behind you.'

'He'd better not try,' Bryony warned. 'I'll just look in on Janice, then I'll take over.'

Janice was lying on top of the bedspread in her room, the curtains pulled tight to shut out the dim evening light. She opened her brown eyes groggily as Bryony came in. 'Aren't I an idiot!' she said weakly.

'An idiot not to call me,' Bryony said softly. 'Do you feel up to getting into your nightie? You'd be more comfortable.'

She helped her get undressed and fetched a wet flannel from the bathroom to bathe her face. 'Thanks, Bryony,' Janice muttered as her sister-in-law helped her climb between the sheets. 'Be sure Hunter stays for dinner, will you? He deserves some reward for being so terrific.'

'Not my cooking, surely?' Bryony grinned, but Janice merely smiled wanly and turned on her side.

Downstairs she found Hunter, the two children and both dogs on the floor playing with a ball. Hunter climbed to his feet when she came in.

'Janice wants you to stay for dinner,' she said.

'Thank you very much, I'd like to.'

'There's only one hitch.'

'*You* don't want me to?' He regarded her quizzicaly.

'*You* may wish you hadn't, once you've sampled my cooking,' she told him. 'I'm the world's lousiest cook.'

'*I'm* not!' He picked up Jane, who was attempting to haul herself to her feet by tugging on his trousers. 'In fact, I'm sensational.'

'And modest, too,' she mocked.

'As a shrinking violet! So why don't I cook, while you take care of these two?' He put the baby into her arms and smiled at her over Jane's silky head, and Bryony felt an inexplicable rush of happiness.

While Hunter rooted around in the refrigerator, she spooned baby food into Jane and encouraged Teddy to finish his egg in record time. Teddy objected when she wanted to take the children upstairs for their baths, but Hunter, looking up from the sink where he was peeling potatoes, said firmly, '*Bed,* young man,' and although Teddy sulked a little he didn't give further trouble.

When the children were settled, Bryony hastily washed her own face and changed out of her jeans into a soft green wool shirt and matching skirt. She brushed her short red curls till they were as glossy as burnished copper. A touch of eye make-up, a splash of eau de cologne and she was ready. 'And what you're getting all dolled up for I don't know,' she said severely to her reflection.

But when she joined Hunter and he said, 'You look nice!' she felt ridiculously pleased.

'I found some pork chops,' he said, hovering over the stove in a professional manner. He had wound a tea-towel round his flat stomach to serve as an apron.

'It smells wonderful.' She wrinkled her short little nose appreciatively. 'Where did you learn to cook?'

'On my travels.' He lifted a lid and sprinkled dill over the chops. 'I've made enough for three.'

'Bruce should be in any minute now,' she said, wondering why she felt mildly let down because Bruce would be joining them.

'OK if I finish up the yoghurt?' He held up a half-empty container.

'Sure.' She noticed the play of muscles on his shoulders as he stirred the sauce, and said, 'Lean down a minute. Jane's drooled all over you.'

He crouched obligingly, and she wet the corner of a clean dish-towel and dabbed at his sweater. His flesh felt resilient and warm under her fingers. He turned his head around to see what she was doing, and his lean brown face was close to hers. A kiss away. She stopped rubbing at the fabric, and for a second her green eyes were locked with his grey ones. 'That's the worst of babies,' she said breathlessly. 'They dribble such a lot.'

He didn't move or say anything for another second, then he straightened. 'Do you happen to know if there's any garlic in the house?' he said finally, his voice curiously neutral.

She found him garlic, and the salad bowl, and then Bruce came in and the charged atmosphere lightened.

They ate in the big kitchen, but Bryony lit candles and set the table with the good china and silver. Bruce found a bottle of red wine in the rack under the stairs. 'It's probably not right for your food,' he said to Hunter, 'but think of it as a celebration for not having to eat Bryony's cooking.'

Hunter grinned at her. 'I get the impression you've poisoned people,' he said.

'Only the family,' Bruce said. 'I pity the poor guy she marries.'

'She'll just have to marry a man who can cook,' Hunter suggested.

'I never figured you for a liberated male,' said Bryony.

He protested with mock indignation. 'Not liberated. Just practical. We can't have you decimating the population.'

'Some people might be improved by a little decimation,' she returned smartly.

'I won't take that personally.' he raised his glass and smiled over at her. 'Not any longer. We're friends now. Remember?'

How could she forget when the evening seemed especially radiant because of it, the air filled with a sort of crackling pleasure? She was discovering that friendship with him was a heady business. This simple dinner in the kitchen was turned into a gala occasion by his presence. Bruce must have felt it too, for he kept looking from one to the other, beaming, trading jokes with Hunter as if they were old friends. It was as if the room was lit by a hundred candles, not just two.

While she served ice-cream and coffee, Bruce went upstairs to check on Janice. 'What's this?' Hunter asked, examining the map on the wall. 'Your own private atlas?'

She told him of their peripatetic parents. 'They should be here soon,' she said. 'They'd left Maine when they last wrote. You must meet them.' She had the feeling her father would like Hunter. 'Although they're my parents, they're nice people.'

And then he dropped his bombshell. 'I'm sure they are, but I'm not sure if I'll be around. I'm leaving for Ottawa in a day or two.'

CHAPTER SIX

IT WAS as if she had been punched in the solar plexus. 'Ottawa!'

'With Lois and her father. I have business contacts there.'

'Oh! I see.'

She certainly did. Lois had pulled it off, pulled it off, moreover, in record time—between lunch and dinner! She must have been mistaken, thinking theirs a pallid love affair. Hunter must be *crazy* about her to be persuaded so fast. Either that, or he was her father's toady, but the more she got to know him, the more convinced Bryony became that Hunter was nobody's sycophant. No... he must be so madly in love with Lois that he would do anything at all to please her. Would abandon his business, abandon his lovely house before it was renovated...

Bruce came back. 'She's thrown up, and now she's sleeping,' he said cheerfully, knowing the pattern of his wife's migraines. He accepted the cup of coffee Bryony had poured for him, and then the two men started discussing football, while Bryony tried to come to terms with the feelings that were churning around inside her.

She was shattered because he was going away! Which didn't make sense because she hardly knew him, they had only started being polite to each other recently. But even when they had been at loggerheads she had enjoyed her fights with him; he stimulated her and she would miss having him around to spar with. She shied away from her feelings about his devotion to Lois, telling herself firmly that it was great. She was *pleased* for Lois. She didn't ask herself why, if she was so pleased, did her heart feel like a soggy dumpling in her breast?

Later on the three of them washed the dishes, and Bryony managed a good imitation of her usual cheerful self. The one thing she couldn't do, though, was bring herself to talk about Hunter's imminent move. Perhaps if she didn't dwell on it the disappointment would fade, and by the time it was general knowledge she wouldn't mind at all.

She kept on telling herself that during the weeks that followed. There were only three of them, but they seemed endless. She was a bit hurt too, that Lois hadn't phoned to say goodbye. This silence seemed unfriendly. It was odd, too, that nobody seemed to know that Hunter had left Newfoundland. She heard that the hangars were nearly ready on Knucklerock Field, and crew and helicopters were now in evidence, so he must have brought in personnel to run his station for him.

She had an unpleasant meeting with Dave. He phoned, and she arranged to go for a walk with him on Signal Hill, and during the walk she suggested they stop seeing each other. 'You want more than I'm able to give you. It's not fair to you, Dave,' she said.

'Aren't you the noble one!' he sneered. 'But don't think I'm taken in, Bryony. I'm not.' Genuinely puzzled, she stared at him, and he said savagely, 'It's because of Grant, isn't it? You're crazy for the man.'

The blood rushed to her face. 'Don't be *ridiculous*!' she exclaimed hotly. 'I hardly know him.'

'That didn't seem to bother you.' His glasses glinted furiously. 'I saw the way you plastered yourself all over him when you danced together. Disgusting! Now that I know what you're really like, I don't *want* to go on seeing you.'

'Then there's nothing more to say—except goodbye,' she retorted, turning on her heel.

'You know what you are, Bryony Porter?' he called after her. 'You're a *fraud*. Pretending to be so cool and virginal, when all the time you're nothing but a hot-blooded little bitch!'

A couple of passing teenagers giggled, and, face flaming, Bryony took the trail to Quidi Vidi Battery. She walked briskly to try to still the trembling that shook her body. The puzzling thing was that she wasn't trembling from anger, although she kept telling herself that she had every right to be angry. It was *fear* she felt. Dave's words had ripped away a protective shell she had erected in her mind. A shield against a truth that she was not ready to face.

'So *unfair*!' she muttered as she stumbled along the track, because Dave *had* been unfair. She had not behaved as he had accused her. And then she remembered the warmth of Hunter's body against hers and her face flamed afresh. She had felt like an iron filing against a magnet, unable to pull herself away. Unable and unwilling, and she shied away from this knowledge like a nervous horse.

There were a lot of tourists milling around the Quidi Vidi guardhouse, and she joined them and stayed for the firing of the guns. Any distraction was welcome if it kept her mind off her emotions.

She didn't get home until after the family had eaten. 'Where did you get to, Bryony?' Janice asked. 'I called the studio, but you didn't answer.'

'Not surprising, since I wasn't there,' Bryony snapped, and then wished she hadn't, because Janice's brown eyes looked hurt.

'Your dinner's in the oven if you want it,' she said quietly.

Bryony raked both hands through her tangle of curls. 'I didn't mean to bite your head off, love,' she apologised. 'I went for a walk with Dave and we had a row. I've been glooming about Signal Hill ever since.'

Janice was all sisterly concern. 'Oh, Bryony, *sweetie*! Is it all over?'

'As dead as a doornail,' her red-headed sister-in-law assured her, going to the stove and taking out a covered plate from the oven.

Janice fussed around, fetching mint sauce and salad from the fridge. 'Now, I know you're upset, Bryony honey, but perhaps it's all for the best. Dave's a nice guy, but we never really thought he was the man for you.'

'Maybe there isn't a man for me,' Bryony sighed. 'Maybe nature intended me to live life like a nun.'

Janice let out a derisive hoot of laughter. 'Some nun! You don't exactly have the temperament.'

'Dave's sentiments exactly! Only he didn't put it quite so politely.'

'And he objected to that? The man's crazy.'

'He didn't object to *that* exactly.' She put a piece of lamb in her mouth. 'Just my general character and behaviour.'

'I *still* say he's crazy,' Janice declared positively. She looked critically at Bryony's plate. 'Is that edible? It looks awfully dry.'

'Would you be very mad if I didn't have any more?'

'Of course not! Shall I make you a sandwich?'

'I'm not really hungry, thanks.' She made a play of yawning widely. 'I am tired, though. I think I'll have a bath and an early night.'

'You do that, honey,' said Janice solicitously. 'I'll bring you a up a glass of hot milk.'

Bryony washed her hair and then lay back in the old-fashioned bath-tub. She had gone hog-wild with the bath salts, and the scent of carnations was heavy in the air; the glass of milk Janice had brought sat on the bathroom stool. Janice was going to fuss over her for the next few days, she knew, under the impression that she was unhappy because of Dave. But Bryony wasn't unhappy because of Dave. She idly picked up one of the children's rubber ducks and floated it in the foam. She *wasn't* unhappy! Of course she wasn't. *Disappointed,* perhaps, because Hunter...and Lois...had left St John's and she'd lost two friends. Disappointed that Hunter had turned out to be a regular weakling, allowing himself to be talked into leaving...and so *quickly*. It seemed that either of the Taylors just had to give the orders and Hunter did as he was told. At this rate he would be running for Prime Minister in a year, just to please Branwell Taylor. Well, *I* won't vote for him, she promised herself, pushing aside the skin that had formed on her milk and wiping her finger on the washcloth.

She climbed out of the tub and towelled herself vigorously, willing her mind to concentrate on problems connected with her work. A snow job, her father would have called it.

'But there is no problem,' she said aloud now. She was merely a little upset because of that scene with Dave. It was an upsetting experience, being called names. A good night's sleep and she would be back to normal.

It didn't happen quite that fast, but within a couple of days her strange depression lifted and she could go about her work without thoughts of Hunter constantly flitting into her head. She took Mabel out several times to practise launching Pegasus. She couldn't say why, but she didn't take her to Knucklerock Field for this, although she had heard from Tansy that, even though there were more helicopters there, people were not discouraged from using the field, and the man in charge, a Scot named Mac, had orders to welcome anyone from the Sky High club.

She and Mabel settled for a stretch of barren cliff-top a mile the other side of the home. Not as attractive as Knucklerock Field, it was nevertheless free from electric pylons and trees, and if it lacked a certain cosiness— well! they went there to practise, not look at the view.

The first day Mabel gave her a fright by going too close to the edge. 'It's quite safe, dear,' she said when Bryony dragged her back. 'Look! There's even a path.'

'Which crumbles to nothing half-way down,' Bryony shuddered, staring at the craggy cliffside. 'You don't have to leap into infinity to launch your kite, Mabel.'

'This is a handy spot though, isn't it, dear?' the old lady replied mildly. 'Handy for the home.'

'It's OK,' Bryony said, although frankly it gave her the creeps.

'Not as romantic for you, of course,' said Mabel knowingly.

Baffled, Bryony repeated, 'Romantic?'

'Well, dear, your young man isn't around here, is he?'
'I don't *have* a young man,' said Bryony, her face
burning.

But Mabel merely gave a sphinx's smile and murmured, 'If you say so, dear.'

Of course, on Sundays she couldn't avoid going to
Knucklerock Field with the others. There was a small
landing-pad there now, close to the nearly completed
hangars, and the twin-engined Super Puma had been
joined by several more helicopters. But with all this evidence at their backs things didn't seem very different.
Mac, the chief mechanic, got into the habit of greeting
the old people and chatting with them while they bustled
about with their kites; then he would go and sit in the
bus with Tansy, drinking coffee from a vending machine
that had been installed for the maintainence staff.

Bryony tried not to look at Santu House, but even so
she couldn't help noticing that work on it was nearly
finished. The porch and window-frames had been
painted a pretty teal blue, the garage had been repaired,
and the driveway resurfaced. She never went down to
peek through the windows any more.

This particular Sunday she heard the helicopter long
before she saw it flying low over the sea. Mac cleared
the field and they waited by the side of the parked bus.
'It's a little feller this time,' one of the old men said as
the single-engined chopper came in over the cliff and
settled down on the landing-pad. Two men in overalls
got out first, their hair blowing in the wind from the
rotor blades. They walked over to Mac, and then the
pilot turned off the engine and leapt to the ground, followed by Gus, who barked happily and raced down to
the grounds of Santu House. Hunter climbed out of the
chopper and looked over at the parked bus. Bryony felt
her legs go weak. He was very elegant, dressed incon-
gruously in a dark business suit and discreet silk tie. He
handed a packet of papers to Mac, and walked over to
the group. 'How's the kite-flying business?' It was a
general question, but his eyes were on Bryony. 'Downed
any planes lately?'

The seniors smiled and Bryony said, 'We're outnum-
bered. Too much hardware around.' She indicated the
helicopters with a nod of her rufous head.

He smiled. 'Sorry to add to it,' he said. 'Once they've
wheeled my chopper out of the way, you can get back
to your kites.'

An old lady in a wheelchair said, 'When I saw you
coming in that thing, I felt like hitching my chair on for
a ride.'

'Might be a draughty one,' he laughed. His keen eyes
looked around. 'No kids with you today?' he asked.

'Teddy's in bed with a sore throat. Nothing serious,'
Bryony explained.

'I was afraid he'd lost his interest in helicopters.'

'He *has* started playing with building-blocks again,'
Bryony grinned, and he chuckled.

'Have I lost him to the building trade?'

She would have dearly liked to ask him what he was
doing here. A flying visit—literally—to check up on the
progress of Santu House was her guess. When she began
to move away with the group, he caught her arm. 'How
about dropping in for a cup of coffee when you're
through?'

She said hesitantly, 'I don't have my car, I came in
the bus.'

'I can drive you home.'

'All right.' She felt ridiculously pleased, the way she
did when the sun broke through clouds. 'But I mustn't
be late.'

He smiled, his teeth very white against his tanned skin.
'Of course not. I won't let you turn into a pumpkin, I
promise.' He gave a lazy salute. 'See you later.'

She watched his lean figure as he loped down to the
house, briefcase in hand. In spite of his urban clothes,
there was something untamed about him. An animal
grace that was not extinguished by modern tailoring.

She told Tansy she was staying for coffee, making sure
that Mabel was out of earshot, and waved at the bus as
it lumbered out of the field, watching until she lost sight
of it down the hill. Mac and the other men were nowhere

to be seen. Walking to Santu House she felt tinglingly
alive, aware of everything around her. The stony path
under her running shoes, the bracing smell of the sea,
the mewing of gulls...everything seemed more vivid,
brighter and filled with promise...

The newly painted front door was on the latch, and
she poked her head in and called, 'Hello!'

'I'm here,' came from the kitchen, 'just putting the
kettle on.' He had changed into black cord trousers and
fisherman's knit sweater, and his dark hair fell untidily
across his forehead. The silver wings showed more when
it was uncombed like this.

'Doesn't this look *great*!' she said, stepping into the
sparkling hall and turning to admire the freshly plastered walls.

'Would you like a tour? I'll turn the kettle off.'

'Sure. I've always wanted to see the inside of Santu
House.'

He went back into the kitchen and she came slowly
to the long windows. The sea was calm, dark green and
marbled with lines of foam. Sunshine bounced off the
rough white walls, making the polished dark wood floor
gleam. There were packing cases of books pushed to one
side of the room, and a rug was rolled up in front of
the empty fireplace. Pictures were leaning with their faces
against the walls. The only furniture was a leather armchair and matching footstool.

'Are you renting the place furnished?' she asked him
when he came back.

He lifted one dark brow enquiringly. 'Renting? What
on earth gave you that idea?'

'Well...' She bit her lips. 'If you're going to live in
Ottawa...'

He laughed, his eyes crinkling at the corners, and
Bryony thought, all the lines on his face are good-natured
lines, that's why he's so attractive. 'I'm not going to live
in Ottawa,' he said. 'Did you hope I was?'

'*No!* Oh, no! I...' She stumbled for words. 'But you
said you were going to Ottawa...and...' She couldn't
bring herself to mention Lois.

'I went to Ottawa on business. I go to a lot of places on business. Many of them a lot further than that.' He came to look at the vast ocean that was framed in the window. 'But Santu House is my home now, and I don't plan to move from it.'

She *didn't* say, what about Lois?—although that was in her mind. Without thinking, she said instead, 'I'm glad.'

He looked down into her green eyes and said softly, 'I'm glad, too.' There was a moment's pause, and then he said loudly, 'Tour! This is the living-room, which leads off the hall and gives a magnificent view of the Atlantic in all its moods.' He gestured extravagantly to the sea. 'The present owner has decided to dispense with curtains because of this, but he is having shutters installed to keep out winter draughts.'

'Of natural finished wood, like the sills?' Bryony asked quickly.

He shuddered with mock horror. 'What *else*?'

'I approve.' She grinned. 'The present owner has taste.'

'Impeccable!'

'What's the kitchen like?'

'What do you care? You can't cook.'

'I don't want to cook in it.' She headed for the open door. 'Just look at it.'

The kitchen was large, with a view of a small crescent of pebbled beach below the fall of cliff. A modern stove had been installed, and twin sinks put in. 'This is also the dining-room,' he told her. 'I've bought a table that will easily seat eight.'

'You plan to give large dinner parties, do you, then?' she asked, wondering while she spoke if, instead of dinner parties, he and Lois intended to have a large family to seat round that table. Somehow she couldn't picture Lois presiding over a kitchen full of children.

'Now for the upper floor.' He put his hand on her shoulder to guide her. He was much taller than she was— everyone was taller than she was—but it didn't feel awkward with him at all. It felt comfortable. She fitted neatly into his side.

There were three small bedrooms upstairs, and one large master one. This stretched the width of the house and faced the sea. The ceiling glittered with reflected sunlight. It would be heaven to lie here after making love safe in the circle of your lover's arms, watching the dance and shimmer of golden light...

She made a show of looking at her watch. 'Hey! If I'm going to have that coffee, I must get a move on.'

'Your wish is my command.' He held the door as she went through, and for a moment she smelt the faint fragrance of his aftershave, a lemony, masculine scent.

The kettle boiled quickly, not that it really mattered, she had plenty of time, but having started the fiction that she must hurry, she had better keep it up.

'There's only powdered milk,' he said. 'I hope that's all right.'

'That's all I have at the studio.' She had been feeling completely at ease, but since that mental picture of lying upstairs with a delightful lover she was now feeling self-conscious again.

He opened a tin of biscuits. 'Two stale oatmeal cookies left,' he said. 'One for you, one for me.'

'You can have mine; I'm not hungry.'

'You're all heart, Bryony Porter.' He smiled and, carrying a tin tray with their coffee-mugs on it, led the way into the living-room.

'You take the chair.' He put the tray down on the floor, but when she refused, repeating that she mustn't stay long and perching on the leather footstool, he sat in the chair himself.

'When are you moving in?' she asked after he'd handed her her coffee.

'Tomorrow. My furniture should be arriving some time during the week. I plan to borrow a sleeping-bag and camp out till it does.' He looked thoughtfully into his coffee-mug. 'I have a need to be in my own place.'

'Where have you been staying?' she asked.

'With the Taylors.' She had guessed that would be his answer.

'And where did you live before?' This was turning into an inquisition, but she wanted to find out all she could about this man. To fill in the blanks.

'All over the place.' He shifted his thin frame to fit more comfortably in the soft leather of the chair. 'All over the world, but lately my time has been divided between Toronto and Vancouver.'

'In hotels?'

'Sometimes. Sometimes apartment-hotels.'

'And your furniture?'

'I've been buying it here and there since I decided to settle down. It's in storage.'

She had thought he would tell her that Lois had chosen the furniture—it was to be her future home, after all—and she asked, 'Will Lois be bringing some things from her house?'

His brows drew together in a quick frown. 'I suppose so—if we ever agree to a date.'

She realised that she had been half hoping he would deny his engagement to Lois, not sound like an impatient bridegroom. She made herself ask him now, 'Did she come back to St John's with you?'

'No. I left her in Ottawa with her father. There was some embassy shindig she wanted to go to.'

'Weren't you invited to the embassy shindig?'

'Sure.' He finished his coffee and leaned forward to put his mug on the tray. His shoulder brushed her knee and she felt a faint stirring in her blood. 'But that sort of party leaves me cold. Besides I had things to do here.'

'What a funny man you are,' she said. 'You don't like parties . . . you want women to earn their keep . . .'

He looked at her steadily. 'I'm a regular clown,' he said. 'As a matter of fact I enjoy a good party, but not where the host is giving it only because he wants to impress a bunch of VIP's. As for women earning their keep . . .' He clasped his hands behind his head and leaned back. 'I was two when my Dad was lost at sea. My mother had never worked. She married young and she'd lived at home until she married, so she had never had to face life by herself. When she was left with a small

child and no one else in the world, she fell completely
to pieces. She had depended on my father for everything
and suddenly there was this vacuum in her life. I guess
having a child didn't help her either, in fact the responsi-
bility of being a single parent terrified her. She had a
total breakdown. She did her best to face up to her life
for a year...I do believe that...' He paused, and when
he spoke again his voice was quite flat. 'She went for a
walk one day and just...walked into the sea. It was
winter. They didn't find her body till the spring.'

The room was very quiet except for the steady sound
of the sea breaking on the rocks below. Hunter dropped
his hands on to the arms of his chair and took a deep
breath. 'I have no way of knowing, of course, but I believe that if she'd been trained to do *some* sort of job,
nothing special, but some sort of skill, she would have
been able to cope with her depression better. At least
she would have had something to occupy her, and life
without a man wouldn't have frightened her quite so
much. But she was brought up to be utterly dependent.
She simply wasn't prepared to deal with calamity.' He
pursed his lips. 'Lois is like that. Oh, she'll never want
for money...but money isn't everything. My mother
didn't kill herself because of money, she killed herself
because she couldn't bear to live in a world where there
was no man to care for her, and Branwell has brought
Lois up to think like that. He's spoiled her rotten. I'm
simply trying to help her, that's all.'

Bryony put her empty mug on the tray. 'There's
nothing wrong with wanting to be cherished, surely?'

'Nothing wrong at all, and any man who loves his
woman wants to take care of her, but not with the
knowledge that if something happens to him she'll fall
apart at the seams.'

'Mr Taylor wouldn't let Lois fall apart,' she declared.
'As long as she's got her father, she'll be all right.'

'She won't have him for ever!' He got up and pulled
her to her feet. 'Come and look at my paintings before
you go,' he said, abruptly changing the subject. 'Give
me the benefit of your artistic training.'

They went over to the pictures stacked against the wall, and he turned them round one by one. They were an interesting mixture. Some line drawings, a couple of old seascapes, and three bold modern pieces, all swirling colour, but Bryony found it hard to concentrate because she was still thinking of the things he had just told her. Of the three-year-old boy alone in the world...the young mother driven by despair to that terrible act.

'I like this woman's work a lot,' Hunter was saying. He held up a small, brightly coloured picture of a young female athlete leaping a hurdle. 'I admire anything that's filled with life.'

'You'd better watch out! This one's liable to jump out at you off the canvas.'

'She reminds me of you,' he said.

'What *are* you talking about?' Bryony protested. 'She's a brunette.'

'Not her colouring. Her *fervour*! Look at her, she's doing just what you do—leaping to conclusions!'

'She's going to get a medal for it, though—that's the difference,' Bryony laughed.

'You're the most vital woman I've ever met,' Hunter said seriously. 'You *shimmer* with life.'

'I won't shimmer for long. Not if I'm late home.' She sounded light-hearted, but her blood was racing with a strange excitement.

'Of course,' he said at once. 'I'll get the car.'

While he fetched the car from the garage, she stood on the path, looking down at the placid sea, forcing herself to imagine Lois in this setting. It was difficult. Even today, with the harsh cliffs softened by sunshine and the sea gentle, it was still a savage landscape pitted and scarred by cruel Atlantic storms, the rotting hulls of many a wrecked fishing-boat lying hidden in that deceptive water. Every crack and fissure on those rocks was the result of the relentless pounding of the ocean. Lois was too languid for this realistic backdrop. Too languid for Hunter as well, perhaps? Bryony chose not to pursue that thought.

Hunter leaned from the car and whistled for Gus who was fossicking about on the property, and when the large dog came bounding over he installed him on the back seat. 'You don't mind sharing the car with this monster, do you?' he enquired. 'I had to leave him alone so much in Ottawa, I haven't the heart to leave him behind today.'

Bryony fondled the dog's head. 'Who's a lovely boy, then?' she crooned, and Gus waved his plumy tail in ecstasy. 'He likes me,' she giggled as he attempted to wash her face with his pink tongue.

'I don't want to hurt your feelings,' Hunter said, 'but Gus likes everybody.'

'Bunty doesn't. Bunty is very selective.'

'Aggressive might be a better description.' He gave her a quick glance. 'I used to think you made a perfect pair.'

She raised her delicate brows enquiringly. 'And now?'

He said, 'I've grown quite fond of Bunty,' and she chuckled. But a warning note was sounding in her head, like the foghorns she heard at night when the weather had closed in. It could become a dangerous habit, this pleasant banter. She was beginning to enjoy being with him too much, and so her next remark was a deliberate sneer.

'My goodness, what's that? A phone?' She tilted her chin at the instrument. 'Of course, Canada's Renaissance Man would have his car loaded with gimmicks, wouldn't he?'

'Canada's Renaissance Man? What the hell are you talking about?'

'Don't tell me you don't read your own publicity,' she went on relentlessly. 'That's not typical of you, surely?'

'Do you mean that dumb newspaper article?' He skilfully took the car round a nasty hairpin bend before saying, 'The woman who wrote it was stupid, and anyone who took it seriously has to be stupid, too.' His lips lifted in a mocking smile. 'Not typical of you, surely?'

'*Touché!*' she acknowledged. 'It's just that gimmicks annoy me.'

'The car phone isn't a gimmick. I need it for my work. For emergencies and the like.'

'I guess my mind's locked in the past,' she said. 'I tend to rely on things like flying a kite in the monsoon to get the rainclouds to blow away and save the crops from flood.'

'*Monsoon!* In Newfoundland?'

'In Thailand. Although I have been tempted to hoist a kite during one of our storms . . . just to see if it might work.'

'No harm in trying,' he said, 'although I don't think much of your chances.'

And I don't think much of your chances with Lois, she thought, and felt a pang of such unhappiness at the idea of Hunter locked in a failing marriage that her breath caught in her throat.

'Kites seem to have all kinds of uses I wasn't aware of,' he went on. 'Protecting crops—flying off with your troubles . . .'

'Getting tangled up in gyrocopters.'

The corners of his mouth lifted in a grin. 'Entirely the pilot's fault, of course.'

'Of course.'

'So why not let him take you out to dinner—to make amends?' He looked over at her.

'I can't,' she said, although 'I dare not' would have been closer to the truth. She didn't know what was happening, but he was beginning to dazzle her. She felt a bubbling excitement just sitting next to him, feeling the warmth of him, teasing and being teased. A candlelit dinner for two would have been wonderful . . . too wonderful, because he was Lois Taylor's man, and she was beginning to find it an effort to remember that.

'Heavy date with what's-his-name?' he drawled.

'With Dave? No.' She had no date at all, heavy or otherwise, but better not to mention that.

'Another time?' he suggested casually.

'Yes.' She forced herself to say, 'When Lois comes back, we can make it a threesome.'

'Are you excluding Dave because foursomes bother you?' He sounded amused.

'Of course they don't,' she said, flustered, 'but Dave and I...we've broken up.'

'I hope it doesn't offend you, but I find that heartening news.'

'It doesn't offend *me*. I don't imagine poor Dave would be overjoyed.'

'He should be,' he said cheerfully. 'Overjoyed that you're out of his life, I mean.'

This unexpected rudeness took her breath away and she gasped, 'Thanks very much!'

'You would have eaten him for breakfast. You're not the woman for him. You need somebody tougher than that young man.'

'Would you care to vet my future boyfriends?' she said tartly.

He was suddenly serious. 'I don't imagine it's going to be easy—finding the right man for a girl like you.'

She glared up at his clean-cut profile. 'Because I'm so impossible?' she said.

'Because you're so special,' he replied quietly.

This stopped her dead in her tracks. Ideally, she should have made a flippant reply in an attempt to keep the atmosphere light, but the atmosphere wasn't light any more, it was charged with emotion. Her heart was racing and she found it difficult to breathe. If he had kissed her full on the mouth she couldn't have felt more aware of him, and she was both elated and disturbed by the emotions he caused her. She didn't say a word. Neither spoke again, until they drove up to her front door.

'Thank you very much for the lift,' she said, getting out of the car swiftly, before he had a chance to lean across her to open her door, because if he had done that she might have stayed in her seat, unwilling to move once she had felt the light pressure of his arm on her body.

'My pleasure.' His face impassive. 'Give my regards to the family.'

It would have been lovely to invite him in. Bruce and Janice would have welcomed him, she knew, for they liked him. He fitted in well. That was one of the problems. None of the men she had brought home had made themselves part of the family the way Hunter had. And with Teddy crawling all over him, and Jane slung across his shoulder, he was a different person from the hard-faced man she had first encountered in the TV studio. He became a home and family man ... and then she remembered with a pang that he would have a home with Lois, and later on a family, and the thought saddened her.

He would never have guessed she felt that way, though. She waved gaily and sang out, 'So long!' as if she hadn't a care in the world. And of course she hadn't, except ...

Except she was starting to fall for another woman's man. Well, that wasn't a tragedy. She had been physically attracted to men before this, she would just wait for the flame ... ember, really ... to die a natural death. Do her level best to steer clear of him for a bit, until she got over this unexpected attraction. The way one got over a bad cold.

Janice called from Teddy's room, 'Is that you, Bryony?'

'Were you expecting anybody else?'

'We've eaten, but there's some chicken left over.' She leaned over the landing railing. 'Or have you had lunch?'

'No, I haven't and I'm starving.' She hung her denim jacket on a peg. 'How's Teddy?'

'Better.' Janice pulled a wry face. 'I'm practically having to *sit* on him to keep him in bed.'

'I'll just grab myself some chicken, and then I'll take over for a bit,' Bryony offered.

'Thanks.' Janice started to go back to her son's room, then she turned. 'How did you get back? I didn't hear the bus.'

'I got a lift.'

Janice grinned down at her. 'Anybody nice?'

Bryony's slanting green eyes grew evasive. 'It was nobody special,' she lied. 'Nobody at all.'

CHAPTER SEVEN

It was fortunate that the following week Bryony was very busy. Two repeat orders for kites had come in and she had several new customers besides. What with that and the festival, she hardly had a moment to herself. If, during all this activity, part of her was waiting...hoping, perhaps...to see Hunter on the street, or find him sitting in the Porter kitchen when she got home one night, she kept these hopes to herself. Outwardly she remained the same, although she was a little quieter.

Towards the end of the week Patsy phoned to invite her to spend the weekend in Halifax.

'There's an art exhibition I'm going to be covering,' she explained, 'so why not come along too? You like art, and my friends can put us up. Why don't you give yourself a little holiday?'

Bryony jumped at the chance as heaven sent, for it would remove her from temptation. If she was in Halifax, she couldn't go to Knucklerock Field on Sunday, where she would almost certainly see Hunter. 'It sounds terrific,' she told Patsy, and in her lunch hour she went out and bought her plane ticket.

'It's about time she had some fun,' Janice said to her husband when she heard of the plan. 'She's been working much too hard lately.'

'I think she's still upset over Dave,' said Bruce, who was feeding his daughter lunch at the time. 'I guess she was more hung up on him than we realised.' He scooped a spoonful of apple sauce from his daughter's chin. 'Don't spit, honey, *swallow.*'

'I wish she could meet a nice man and fall madly in love,' Janice mused. 'I want our kids to have some cousins.'

113

'Do you plan for her to marry?' Bruce asked innocently. 'Or is it only these cousins you care about?'

Janice chucked a pellet of bread at him. 'Idiot! Of course I want her to get married...to somebody wonderful. I want her to be very, very happy,' she tucked a smooth strand of her hair behind her ear, 'like me.'

'Ah, but you're married to a paragon,' Bruce said, coming to her and kissing her on the nose. 'A paragon who's crazy about his wife.' And then he started nibbling her neck.

Janice giggled and said, 'Bruce...the *children*!' And Bryony and her problems were forgotten.

Halifax was sunny and crowded. Tourists thronged the waterfront, looking at the famous yacht *Bluenose* that was lying in the harbour, darting out of the boutiques that were housed in the historic buildings, or strolling in the city's famous Victorian public garden. A smell of ships and sea mingled with the fumes of automobiles. Gulls dipped and wheeled against a sky as blue as an enamel bowl, and children licked ice-cream cones as they trailed after their sunburned parents.

After Bryony and Patsy had installed themselves in the attic of the rambling house Patsy's three girlfriends shared, they went on a shopping spree. Bryony splurged on a summer suit of bronze-coloured linen and a blouse of turquoise silk, and she stretched her budget to include a demure dress of white broderie anglaise, as crisp as a wedding cake. She bought as well a pair of high-heeled sandals and a matching bag of turquoise leather, and since they went with both outfits she kidded herself that the extravagance was justified.

Patsy had to work in the afternoon, and after a sinfully wicked lunch of huge slices of chocolate and walnut cake and glasses of iced coffee piled high with whipped cream, the girls parted. Patsy obligingly took all their parcels with her to the studio, and Bryony went to a beauty parlour and got her hair trimmed and re-styled, combed sleek and high at the sides, her coppery curls teased to fall in a cascade over her forehead, which looked more sophisticated than usual.

She spent the rest of the afternoon exploring Citadel Hill. She listened to the pipers, splendid in full regalia, and watched the cadets in uniforms of 1850 drill on the earth-packed square, then she climbed on to the fortress walls, which were constructed of stone, now completely covered with earth and grass, so that it felt like walking on a mountain of cushions. She flung herself on the springy turf and blinked lazily at the sky through half closed eyes. She could feel herself relaxing by the minute. Although a feeling of incompleteness still clung to her, it didn't spoil her day, she was enjoying herself immensely, but part of her wanted to share it with someone special, and that someone was not Patsy.

She drifted off into a doze after a while, lulled by the distant swirl of the pipes and the warmth of the sun, and when she woke with a start it was late in the afternoon and she had to dash back to the house.

She had a shower before going downstairs in her bathrobe to help prepare for a party that had been planned, and then Patsy came back with the parcels, and she changed into her new white dress. Standing on a chair in order to look in the hanging mirror, she was pleased to see that the dress was an unqualified success. She had always looked good in white, and her day in the sun had warmed her skin to a faint peachy bloom which glowed against the crisp embroidery. Her newly set hair flamed like molten copper. She was looking her best, and she found herself wishing Hunter was here to see her. 'Not that it would mean a thing to him,' she muttered to her reflection. 'The man's engaged to someone who always looks like a million dollars... and don't you forget it, my girl!'

It was a good party. One of the girls was an air hostess and she had invited several of the people she worked with, and a senior steward with the airlines fell for Bryony like a ton of bricks, following her from room to room, fetching her plates of food, and waiting on her as if she were a first-class passenger on one of his flights.

'Run away with me, you lovely red-head!' he crooned into her ear as they danced to the record player. 'I'm leaving for Tokyo next week. I'll arrange to smuggle you aboard with the baggage.' And Bryony laughed and flirted, and made sure she didn't commit herself.

In spite of this attention from a nice man—for he *was* a nice man, and not long ago she would have been attracted to him—she didn't accept his invitation to drive to Peggy's Cove the following day.

The last guest didn't leave till the early hours of the morning, but Bryony woke at seven as usual, and instead of turning over and going back to sleep she got up, taking care not to disturb Patsy, and went for a walk. It was another glorious day, and she wandered towards Point Pleasant Park, admiring the big old houses. Some of the frame ones were painted a mustard colour, with a black or wine-coloured trim, distinctive and unusual, but not as pleasing as the teal-blue colour Hunter had chosen for Santu House, she decided, allowing her mind to linger on that forbidden territory for a moment. The sound of organ music came from a white clapboard church, and an elderly man tended roses in a garden filled with flowers. Everywhere was peace and tranquillity, but Bryony was filled with a yearning restlessness that made her walk these Sunday streets as if she were running away. Running away from a self-awareness that could only bring her pain.

When she got back the girls were up, yawning over cups of coffee and discussing what to do with the day. 'There's already been a call for you, Bryony,' one of them told her. 'Alistair phoned to know if you'd changed your mind about Peggy's Cove.'

'I'm going with Patsy to the art show,' Bryony told them.

'Don't feel you have to humour me by coming, Bryony,' said Patsy, because she had always been slightly jealous of Bryony, and was irked that the handsome steward had fallen for her so obviously. She got over it soon enough, however, and after a hurried breakfast they left the others reading the Sunday papers and went to the show.

It was an exhibition of sculpture and watercolours done by a husband-and-wife team who were just beginning to make a name for themselves. It was held in a private house that had been turned into an art gallery, and this was the grand opening. Although they were early, the large downstairs room was already filling up with people. Patsy captured the two artists and took them upstairs to interview them, leaving Bryony behind. She looked at the sculptures and then went into the room where the watercolours were hanging, and then she blinked her green eyes rapidly, for Hunter was standing with his back to her, examining a picture.

It wasn't a mirage, for he didn't disappear. Besides, his tall, lean frame was unmistakable; there was no one else who had that leonine laziness, that ruthless elegance. He turned from the picture and caught sight of her, and for a moment they stayed, staring at each other. When she drew closer, he said, 'Hello. I like you in that colour.'

Bryony, who was wearing her new suit, looked down at the skirt. 'It's new,' she said.

'You've done something different with your hair, too.'

'I wanted a change,' she said.

'Don't we all!' he replied as he continued regarding her lazily, and she felt the blood mount in her cheeks. 'What are you doing here? I thought you never left Newfoundland.'

'Sometimes I prise myself loose,' she replied lightly.

'You should prise yourself loose more often,' he said. 'The results are spectacular.' He turned back to the picture. 'What do you think of this?'

The painting showed a circle of grey boulders washed by a frill of foaming sea. 'I like it,' she said after she had looked at it for a moment or two. 'It looks a bit like the view from your kitchen.'

'That's what I thought,' said Hunter. 'That's why I'm buying it.'

'Just like that?'

'Just like that!' He smiled. 'Sometimes it's good to be impulsive.'

'Don't you believe in impulse as a rule?' she enquired, her heart singing irrationally.

'Not as a general rule,' he said. 'I've got my life very carefully mapped out; there's no room for impulse.'

She pulled a face. 'It sounds very dull.'

'Ah! But you're the impulsive type. You probably let life take you over. Not me! I'm an orderly man, I like to be in charge of mine.' His eyes were teasing, but she knew that this was not entirely a joke.

'Don't you ever get knocked sideways by life?' she asked.

He regarded her thoughtfully. 'Not if I can avoid it. It tends to be painful.'

She said, 'I know.' And had a premonition of the pain he could cause her. 'I know.'

There was a stir at the doorway, and people stared and whispered as Branwell Taylor came in, with Lois. 'There you are,' he boomed. 'We wondered where you'd got to.' His small eyes narrowed when they fell on Bryony. 'Well! I didn't expect to see you here,' he said. 'Did you, Hunter?'

'Why ever not, Daddy?' Lois giggled. 'Why shouldn't Bryony come to Halifax? It's not the other side of the world.' She kissed Bryony lightly on the cheek. 'It's great to see you again,' she said. 'I'm sorry I didn't get around to saying goodbye when we left for Ottawa, but . . . you know me . . . disorganised as usual.'

'And totally unrepentant about it,' Hunter pointed out genially.

She waggled her fingers at him. *'Totally!'*

'I plan to leave here in about ten minutes,' Branwell informed them, giving Bryony an unfriendly stare. 'I'm not much for art.'

He kept looking searchingly at Bryony, making her feel guilty. It must be apparent to him that she was overwhelmingly attracted to Lois's fiancé, and her cheeks grew pinker than ever.

Branwell said belligerently, 'You like this stuff, do you?' He jerked his head at the delicately coloured pictures.

Hunter answered for her. '*I* do,' he said. 'In fact, I've just bought one. Bryony and I were discussing it when you came in.'

'Too wishy-washy for me,' Branwell growled. He looked at Bryony again. 'I'm a plain man—I like plain things—straightforward things.'

'So do I,' Bryony returned with spirit. 'And I don't find this work wishy-washy in the least!'

He grunted, and then addressed himself to Hunter. 'I'll meet you in ten minutes in the car,' he barked, and after nodding briefly at Bryony he stumped out.

'What in the world has got into him?' Lois wondered aloud.

Hunter said, 'Artistic indigestion, most likely, but it needn't concern us, we'll be leaving for St John's soon. You are coming with me?'

Lois gave a sigh of exasperation. 'Oh! Darling, *really*! Don't you remember? I told you. Daddy's going to this neat party tonight, and I want to go. I want you to come, too,' she added as an afterthought.

'And I told you I couldn't make it,' he said firmly. 'I left Gus with the crew, and I have to get back to him.'

Lois shrugged her slim shoulders at Bryony. 'That *dog*!' she said. 'I swear sometimes I think Hunter prefers him to me.'

'He's certainly not as demanding,' Hunter said.

'If you hadn't moved out of the house, this sort of thing wouldn't have happened,' Lois said fretfully. 'Lacey would have looked after him.'

If they were going to have a quarrel, Bryony didn't want to hear it, but they were barring her way and she was trapped, so she turned her back on them and earnestly studied the watercolour in front of her, hoping to shut out Lois's whine and Hunter's terse replies.

'I don't like living in other peoples' houses,' she heard Hunter say. 'I have my own house now, and I intend to live in it.'

'You're paranoid about that place,' Lois accused him. 'It's not all that wonderful, you know!'

'It's a bit late in the day to be telling me that, isn't it?'

Lois's voice was conciliatory. 'Oh, darling! Don't be huffy. It's just that I want to go to this party so badly, and now you're being difficult. Of *course* Santu House is lovely.'

'I'm not being difficult,' he replied quietly. 'After all, I flew in alone early this morning just to have you to myself for a bit, and now it looks as if I'll be flying back alone, too.'

'In that case, why not take Bryony back with you?' Lois said. 'She'll keep you company.'

Bryony swung round. 'I'm flying back with Patsy,' she said. 'It's all arranged.'

'Can't you un-arrange it?' Hunter asked. 'There's plenty of room in the chopper.'

'Yes, do, Bryony! Please,' Lois pleaded. 'Then Hunter can't keep nagging me for letting him down.'

Bryony said diplomatically, 'I'm sure he'd rather have you with him.'

'Well, he can't have me,' Lois pouted. 'He'll have to make do with somebody else.'

Oh, dear! Bryony thought, she really is starting to show her claws!

'After that charming invitation,' Hunter said thinly, 'it wouldn't surprise me if Bryony refused point-blank.' He turned to Bryony and his grey eyes searched hers. 'But I sincerely hope you won't. I'd like your company...and Patsy's, too, of course.'

'I'll ask Patsy,' she told him.

The sulky expression faded from Lois's face. 'That's settled, then. Now we'd better find Daddy before he starts roaring.'

'*You* find Daddy,' Hunter said firmly. 'I haven't finished looking at pictures yet.'

'I'll go and ask Patsy about the lift,' Bryony said, leaving quickly, for this time she was determined not to witness any more unpleasantness between them.

Patsy was willing to fly back with Hunter, provided it wasn't before lunch. 'I've got another interview lined up with the guy who organised this show,' she told Bryony. 'I'm going to meet him at a downtown hotel when I finish here.'

'I'll find out when we have to leave,' Bryony said. 'If it's no good, I'll come with you. I don't fancy a long helicopter ride without you along.'

When she returned to the watercolour room, Lois and her father had left the gallery. Bryony told Hunter of Patsy's date and it was arranged that he would pick the two girls up early that afternoon. 'It takes between four and five hours to get to St John's,' he said, 'and I'd like to do most of the flying in daylight.'

Back in their attic room, Bryony changed out of her elegant suit into khaki bush trousers and jacket, and packed up her weekend case. She couldn't stop tingling with excitement at the idea of being with Hunter for the long helicopter ride. Even with Patsy along, it would be fun. *Particularly* with Patsy along, she corrected herself. Patsy's presence would make it possible for her to relax without feeling guilty.

She was eating a peanut-butter sandwich when Hunter arrived. '*Divine* man for you,' whispered the girl who had opened the front door. 'I'm not surprised you didn't go out with Alistair!' And then Hunter was standing in the kitchen doorway, and Bryony was so pleased to see him that it scared her.

'Patsy's not here yet,' she said through a mouthful of sandwich.

He lowered his lean frame into a chair. 'Don't gobble your food. I got bored at the show and came early.'

One of the girls asked him if he would like a cup of coffee, and he gave her a smile that would have melted an iceberg. 'You're a lifesaver,' he replied. 'That's just what I'd like.'

He accepted a peanut-butter sandwich too, and suddenly they were having a marvellous luncheon party. Hunter told them of his adventures in Africa in the ultralight, telling stories against himself which had them crying with laughter, and Bryony wondered how she could ever have thought him conceited. He was witty and charming, and a big hit with the three girls. He was a big hit with Bryony too, but she desperately tried to keep this from herself in an attempt to retain some hold on her sanity.

In the middle of an anecdote about an elephant who had sat on his tent, the phone rang. Reluctantly, one of the girls went into the hall to answer it. She was back in a moment. 'It's Patsy. She wants to speak to you, Bryony,' she said.

Patsy's voice was husky on the other end of the line. 'I'm not going to make it, Bryony,' she said. 'This man I'm interviewing wants me to have dinner with him.' She giggled happily. 'He's really cute...*and* single. I'm having a terrific time.'

'You're having an *alcoholic* time by the sound of it,' Bryony remarked grimly, and Patsy giggled again.

'I've only had two martinis,' she protested, 'and I don't really have to be back in St John's till tomorrow night. Don't be a dog in the manger!'

'I'm not. Have a good time—and have some coffee too while you're at it.'

'Killjoy!' Patsy hiccuped merrily before hanging up.

Patsy might think Bryony was a wet blanket, but she was wrong. *Terrified* was what she was. Without Patsy along as a buffer, five hours alone with Hunter wasn't going to help her to get over her attraction for him. If the charming way he was carrying on now was anything to go by, it was just going to get worse.

She went back into the kitchen, and when the hilarity had died down a bit she told them of Patsy's decision. She looked over at Hunter, his hard face softened now by laughter, so that he seemed years younger than the man that she had first met.

'I could take the plane tonight,' she told him. 'I've still got my ticket.'

It would be wiser to do that. So much wiser. But she was flooded with happiness when he said, 'I've already been turned down by two ladies. Don't you join the club or I'll begin to get a complex.'

'Then you've just got one passenger, I'm afraid,' she said. 'Me!'

'I'll try and put up with it.' His mouth still curved in a smile, but his eyes weren't smiling any more. They were fixed intently on hers, and she started to babble.

'Well...I'm all packed...ready to go...and now that we don't have to wait for Patsy I guess we can get going.' She headed for the front door where her case was waiting.

He followed on her heels. 'Why don't we phone for a taxi first? Unless you fancy walking five miles with the luggage.' He took her case and put it back on the floor.

'Yes, of course—silly of me,' she muttered, hoping he would think her colour was the result of heaving her case around.

The girls gave him a tour of the house while they were waiting for the cab, Bryony trailing behind them, her heart singing in spite of all her efforts to discipline it.

By the time the taxi arrived he was on such good terms that the girls had invited him to a Labour Day barbecue they were planning—'and Bryony, too, of course,' they added hastily—and then they stood on the front steps, waving goodbye as if they'd known him all their lives.

Hunter told the driver to go to the hospital.

'Hospital!' Bryony yelped. 'Aren't we going to the airport?'

'Relax!' He gently pushed her back against the seat. 'I'm not planning to give you an appendectomy. Relax and trust the pilot.'

She sat back as he commanded. She wouldn't have cared now if he had planned to take them back to Newfoundland in an ambulance, just so long as he got her home. Home, where she would be safe from him...and from herself, because his touch on her shoulders had sent a small jolt, like a current of electricity, through her. She seemed to have no control over her reactions at all.

At the hospital, he guided her to a lift that whisked them up to the roof, and there stood his helicopter on a tiny pad, waiting for them.

'What are those things it's wearing?' Bryony asked. 'They look like giant wieners!'

'Wieners, indeed!' he chuckled. 'Mac would die if he heard you. They're inflatable floats. We'll be flying over a lot of water, and we need flotation.'

Once aboard, he handed her a head-set. She held it at arm's length. 'What's this for? Am I to be plugged in to music?'

'You do plan to talk to me during the trip, don't you?' She nodded. 'Well, you'll need these to do it.'

'Noisy is it?'

'Very.' He looked down at her. 'Do you object?'

'I wouldn't dare,' she replied with fake humility.

'Sensible girl! I wouldn't want to dump you off over the Grand Banks.'

'I wouldn't want you to, either,' she agreed. 'It gets foggy down there.'

'Damp, too!' He put on his own head-set, switched on the engine, and fiddled with the radio. In an instant he became completely absorbed, and Bryony could observe him unnoticed. He had flung off his suede bomber jacket and rolled up his shirtsleeves to the elbow. His arms were tanned to bronze and sprinkled with fine dark hair, and his hands looked strong and capable as they checked over the controls. She had a momentary image of those firm hands on her body, and a faint shiver of desire went through her.

There was a deafening roar as the helicopter lifted off and rose swiftly. Bryony peered down at the city below which seemed to be disappearing at a great rate, then, turning her attention to the window in front, she saw Hunter's goggles hanging by the controls. 'Aren't you going to wear them?'

His voice crackled back through the head-set. 'Don't need to, I keep them just for luck.' His teeth flashed in a smile. 'And they brought me luck, too. Because of them, I met you.'

She said severely, 'You didn't think so at the time.'

'True. Besides, I'm not sure their lucky properties haven't been tampered with.' He reached over to show her the chinstrap. 'Jane seems to have been cutting her teeth on them.'

'That was me,' she admitted.

'*You!* Chewing on my goggles?'

'Making extra holes so they would fit Teddy,' she giggled. 'With a potato peeler!'

He raised his eyes in mock resignation. 'She didn't even take the trouble to use an awl!'

'If I'd had an awl handy, I would have used it on the person who broke the string of my kite,' she reminded him. 'Now, shut up, I want to admire the view.'

Not that the view was particularly varied. They were out over the sea and it consisted of a limitless expanse of wrinkled green water dotted with the occasional ship, but it didn't matter. It wouldn't have mattered if they had been flying in pitch blackness. She was with Hunter, and the rapport between them had nothing to do with the scenery. She was enjoying herself, and if she could just keep calm and not go up in flames every time he so much as touched her arm this would be a wonderful trip.

After a couple of hours he produced a vacuum flask of coffee and a box of cookies. 'This is rather a boring run, I'm afraid,' he apologised. 'Next time I take you up, we'll go over land.'

She said, 'That should be fun,' but she knew she would not accept his invitation, unless Lois came along. It was too intimate being cooped up in this cockpit together. It would be courting disaster. 'Does Lois enjoy helicopter rides?' she asked now, just to remind him where his loyalties lay, and she wondered if she imagined that his jaw tightened.

'She likes it well enough—whenever she can spring herself loose from the social scene to come along.'

She made a non-committal noise at the back of her throat, unwilling to get involved in what seemed to be an old grievance. They travelled without conversation for some miles when she had a sudden brainwave. 'Would you be willing to give helicopter rides at the kite festival? You could charge enough to cover costs... I'm sure it would be a draw.'

His eyebrows rose. 'I thought kites and 'copters were incompatible?'

'Yes... well...' She smiled ruefully. 'I've changed my mind about that.' And she thought, I've changed my mind about a lot of things, *darling* Hunter.

'In that case, I'd be delighted to participate.' He glanced at her, his grey eyes teasing. 'And I'll do my best not to break any kite strings.'

'That would be appreciated,' she grinned, turning her attention back to the sea. After a moment she cried, 'Oh, look! What's going on down there?' For a circle of water was all seething foam and motion.

'We're in luck!' he replied. 'That's whales feeding. Let's go down and get a closer look.'

The whales were plunging in a spectacular display below them. Every time they surfaced, water poured from their flukes, and their backs gleamed sleek in the sunshine. 'They're blue whales,' Hunter said. 'You don't see them as often as you do humpbacks.'

'They're *beautiful*!' said Bryony, green eyes shining with excitement.

He nodded down at the churning water. 'Impressive, certainly. If you're really keen to whale-watch, you should go to northern Labrador... find some narwhals. That's a sight worth travelling for.'

'Maybe I will one day. When I have more money and can spare the time.' It was something she had always longed to do. Preferably with a friend who would be willing to go all that way in order to look at several hundred tons of mammal feeding in an icy sea. But now she knew that if she went, no matter who was with her, she would always remember this sighting with Hunter, and she would miss him.

It was nearly dark when they landed on Knucklerock Field. Mac came out of the control-room to greet them, followed by Gus, who danced around the helicopter, barking a welcome. After handing out her luggage

Hunter jumped lightly to the ground, and putting his arms around her waist lifted her down.

'I can manage,' she protested, very conscious of the play of his shoulder muscles under her small hands.

He asked her into the house for a drink but she refused, which was hard to do, for sitting drinking tête-à-tête with Hunter, who was becoming more desirable by the minute, was a great temptation. But better safe than sorry, she instructed herself silently. It seemed awfully dreary advice.

When they drew up outside the narrow house, she found herself asking *him* in. It seemed only polite when he'd flown all that way. But she knew that really it was because she didn't want to see him drive away.

'Thank you, Bryony.' He reached out and lightly touched her cheekbone with a long finger. It was an impersonal caress, but it made her catch her breath. 'Thank you, but ... I'd better not.' And then he sighed and said, 'Tomorrow is a working day, as the saying goes.'

He got out of the car when she did, and retrieved her case from the boot, and then they stood together in the dark street, each seeming reluctant to make the first move. 'Thank you for the ride,' said Bryony at last. 'It was really something.'

'I hope you have a better opinion of choppers now.'

She nodded her tousled head emphatically. 'I do. It was great ... really ... like being in an airborne bus.'

He smiled faintly. 'I presume that's meant as a compliment.'

'It is, I'm *crazy* about buses,' she babbled. 'Oh, and the whales! I'll never forget the whales, they were fabulous!'

'I ordered them specially.' He leaned forward and opened the unlocked front door, putting her case down in the hall. 'It was great for me, too,' he said, but he sounded oddly muted. 'Goodnight, Bryony.'

As he moved back to the car, she forced herself to call out, 'Give my love to Lois.'

'Yes,' he said, 'I will.'

Bryony spent the rest of the evening in a state of suspended animation. Janice was out with her women's
group, and Bruce was babysitting. Brother and sister had
a drink together while Bryony told him about her
weekend, but she felt as if she wasn't quite connected
with the real world. She tried gripping the arms of her
chair hard in an attempt to bring herself back to earth,
but her spirit was somewhere over the Atlantic ocean,
sitting in a small plastic bubble called a helicopter, being
piloted by a tall, dark man, who stubbornly refused to
be banished from her heart.

CHAPTER EIGHT

BRYONY didn't take kindly to inertia; consequently, the following days were agony for her. She was filled with aimlessness, unable to settle to anything for very long. She would force herself into activity, only to fall again into a trance. Time after time she would shake her shiny red curls and attack whatever job she was doing with renewed energy, only to find herself with her scissors or her paintbrush in her hand, staring into space, thinking about what might have been if Hunter had been free.

But, if he were free, would he want Bryony? She couldn't be sure. At times she felt he did, but then she would sense him drawing back, becoming remote...and yet, there was that empathy between them, the shared laughter, the comfortable silences... Irritably she pushed her work aside. She felt that with Janice, too! It didn't mean any more than companionable friendship. She was being a fool to brood over it.

And so her mind went, veering from one emotion to the other, until she thought she would scream with frustration. The only thing that seemed to help was enforced exertion, so she took to going for long, vigorous walks. Bunty had never been so well exercised!

One afternoon she returned home from one of these excursions, Bunty dragging on her leash with exhaustion, to find that Lois had dropped by the house, and not finding her at home had left a note for her.

'Why don't you come up to my place tonight after supper?' she had scribbled on a piece of scrap paper. 'I'm all alone and I'd love to see you.'

'I don't think I will,' Bryony said to Janice when she'd read the note. 'I took this afternoon off, I should work tonight to make up for it.'

Janice looked up from a cookbook she was reading. 'I think you should go,' she said. 'You've been working too hard lately. You need a break.'

'I've just *had* a break,' Bryony snapped.

Janice said calmly, 'You know, Bryony, you're becoming impossible to live with.' To Bryony's dismay she felt her eyes grow bright with a sudden rush of tears. Hastily she turned away, but Janice was too quick for her. 'You see! One can't say a word to you without you bursting into sobs!'

Bryony fumbled in the pocket of her jeans for a tissue. 'Don't exaggerate,' she said huskily.

'I'm not exaggerating.' With a sigh, Janice put aside her book. 'Bruce has noticed it too. Is anything worrying you, honey? Anything you want to talk about?'

She was tempted to fling herself on Janice's motherly bosom and tell her everything . . . except that when she stopped to think about it there was really nothing to tell. Nothing had happened, apart from falling for a devastatingly attractive man who was attached to someone else. Hardly an original situation. Janice would simply tell her to wait until she got over it, which was exactly the advice she was giving herself. Besides, it looked as if Hunter and Lois had become family friends, which meant seeing them socially, and Bryony couldn't bear it if her brother and his wife knew she was carrying a torch for Hunter. She couldn't bear to have their anxious eyes on her whenever Hunter and Lois were around, so she said briskly, 'All right, I'll go, then.'

'I'm glad,' Janice said, opening up her cookbook again. 'Lois really seemed anxious to see you. She went to your studio first, you know, and when you weren't there she came up here.'

A small chill of alarm went through Bryony. Perhaps Branwell had spoken of his suspicions to his daughter, and now she was planning to face Bryony. Warn her off, tell her in no uncertain terms to get lost! She read the note again. Surely jealous women didn't say they would 'love to see you'? Besides, she hadn't done anything.

She hadn't flung herself at Hunter, and she'd not breathed a word of her feelings to a soul. The only person who looked at her with suspicion was Branwell Taylor, and all he had to go on was his instinct. Just the same, it was with some trepidation that she drove into the driveway of Four Winds later that evening.

As before, Mrs Lacey let her in, and led the way upstairs to Lois's private suite. This consisted of bedroom, bathroom, and sitting-room on the third floor.

'In here!' Lois called. She was standing in the middle of the bedroom, surveying a heap of clothes which were strewn on the bed. Scarves and underwear were draped over a chairback, shoes were scattered on the floor. 'What do you think of this, Bryony?' Lois held up a gold lamé evening dress. 'Do you think it's too dressy for an intimate dinner?'

'Depends how intimate you intend to get,' Bryony said. 'It's a bit formal for a fish-and-chip supper.'

'Oh! I think it will be a little more elegant than *that*,' Lois laughed, and Bryony thought, this is the first time I've seen her look really *alive*. Her vague blue eyes weren't vague any more, they were sparkling with animation, and her movements as she sorted through the heap of clothes on the bed were energetic... decisive. A far cry from her usual dreamy air.

'Are you sorting for a rummage sale, or going on another trip?' Bryony asked her.

'A trip...' She looked up from sorting a tangle of blouses. 'Just a flying visit really, to see... friends in Ottawa.'

'You just got back from there, didn't you?'

'*Ages* ago! Well, nearly a week ago. But I got a phone call...just before you came...' She sat back on her heels. 'An *unexpected* phone call, and since I've been abandoned by both my men, I thought...why not?' She stood up and the blouses slithered to the floor. 'Let's leave this for now and I'll get Lacey to bring up some coffee. Or would you rather have a drink?'

'Coffee will be fine, thanks,' said Bryony, following her into the sitting-room. Lois's suite was decorated in

pastel shades of pink, her furniture was white, picked
out in gold leaf, and the love-seat and matching armchairs were of pale pink satin. It was all silk and froth,
and Bryony wondered if she planned to take any of it
to Santu House. She hoped not, because it wouldn't work
there at all.

After Lois had phoned down to the kitchen to order
the coffee, Bryony said, 'What do you mean, your men
have abandoned you?'

'Well, Daddy's tied up in a conference at
Cornerbrook, and Hunter's gone to the east coast of
Scotland—something to do with an oil rig...'

'Scotland?' Bryony cried out. Then, recovering herself,
added, 'My, my! He *does* get around!'

'Mmm!' Lois jumped up from her seat and started
rearranging a vase of yellow roses, nipping off the
drooping heads with restless fingers. 'He's always off
somewhere. And so I thought... when I got that phone
call...I won't be missed.' She started plumping the white
silk cushions on the love-seat. 'I mean... where's the
harm?' She looked into Bryony's green eyes defiantly.

'You don't have to ask my permission,' Bryony reminded her. 'You're a free agent.'

Lois scuffed at the thick white carpet with a gold-
sandalled foot. 'Not where Daddy's concerned. He keeps
me on a leash.'

Bryony felt bound to say, 'Well, I guess he loves you
a lot,' although she didn't think much of such a selfish
kind of love.

'I *know*!' Lois let out an exasperated breath. 'And I
love him too, but he stifles me, Bryony. I can't *move*
without his permission.' She came to sit on a satin
footstool at Bryony's feet and said earnestly, 'Do you
know, he doesn't let me have any time alone with Hunter.
I mean, *really* alone!' She looked at Bryony slyly. 'You
know what I mean?'

'You mean bed,' Bryony replied tersely.

'It's *ridiculous*! We're supposed to be getting married,
and Daddy keeps tabs on us as if Hunter was some casual
pick-up.'

'I thought he approved of Hunter,' she said, wishing she hadn't come here tonight, after all.

'He does. But he's over-protective.' She bounced up and started pacing round the room. 'It drives Hunter wild. We've had awful rows about it, but I can't seem to stand up to Daddy, no matter how much we might want to...you know. And Hunter's hardly the sort to force a girl.'

There was a knock, and Mrs Lacey came in with a tray of coffee and cookies. After she'd gone Lois said, 'You are a pet to put up with my moaning. I don't usually mind too much when Daddy plays the heavy father. Only, just lately...' She poured two cups of coffee and handed one to her guest. 'Anyway, I'm going to Ottawa for two days and not telling him. And if he finds out...too bad!'

Bryony sipped her coffee thoughtfully. She didn't want to hear these confidences. She didn't want to know whether Lois and Hunter went to bed together, and she was startled to discover just *how* much it hurt her to listen to Lois discussing it so carelessly.

The blonde girl perched herself on one of the armchairs and nibbled delicately at a cookie. 'By the way, I do like your dress,' she said.

Bryony grabbed at this conversational straw. She had put on her new white dress to come here because she guessed that Lois would be looking marvellous as always, and now she started an animated discussion about clothes. Anything to change the subject.

'It's too bad you're not my size,' said Lois. 'I get bored with things so fast. You could inherit them.'

'I don't think your clothes would go with my sort of life,' observed Bryony. The pure silk trousers and matching violet tunic Lois was wearing now, for example, would be about as useful to Bryony as a marshmallow would be to a starving man.

'This old thing!' Lois waved a disparaging hand, and the heavy amethyst she wore around her neck glittered. 'It's just for messing around in.' Bryony smiled wryly, since jeans and T-shirts were the clothes *she* usually wore for that activity.

Lois seemed unable to sit still, so they took their coffee into the bedroom and Bryony helped her pack. Lois's idea of packing for forty-eight hours was rather daunting, and by the time they had finished they had filled two suitcases. 'You *are* a pet, Bryony,' she said again, as she walked Bryony to her car. 'I'll call you the *minute* I get back.'

Bryony muttered something about being really busy during the next few weeks, but Lois paid no attention. 'I'm so glad you came,' she said, and impulsively threw her arms round Bryony, hugging her tight. When she released her, her eyes seemed to glow in the darkness. 'Oh, Bryony!' she whispered. 'I'm so happy...I'm so *terribly* happy!' And with a tremulous laugh she turned and ran back into the house.

Well, it's good that at least *one* of us is happy, Bryony thought, lying tense and wide-eyed in bed later that night. It took so much energy keeping unwanted desires at bay that sleep was out of the question, so she lay staring up into the darkness.

She had a pretty good idea why Lois was so over-whelmingly happy. Why she was lit up like an off-season Christmas tree. She was going to meet Hunter in Ottawa. He must be arriving there from Scotland, so that they would have two days alone together. Two days and two nights. A wave of sickening jealousy swept over her and, appalled, she sat up and switched on the light. She took up a mystery book from the bedside-table. Better to try to read, rather than lie here torn by passions she had no right to feel. She had never felt jealousy in her life, and to feel this way now about a man who belonged to someone else, a man who had never so much as *kissed* her, was total absurdity. Doggedly she turned a page, but it was not until she had reached the second murder and pale dawn light was streaking the sky with opal that she fell into a troubled sleep.

The following day Bruce phoned her at the studio to tell her that their parents had arrived. 'They're just getting themselves settled at the trailer park,' he said, 'and then we're all to go out to dinner. Dad's treat.'

Bryony was delighted. Not only was she fond of them, their presence would help to distract her. Take her mind off her obsession with Hunter, because anything as irrational as her feelings about him *must* be classed as an obsession.

It was a typically boisterous family reunion, and once they were settled at a large table in the restaurant, Jane strapped in a high-chair and Teddy next to his adored grandfather, they had a chance to catch up on family news.

'I wouldn't have recognised this young cub,' Major Porter remarked, ruffling Teddy's hair. 'He must have grown a *foot* since last year.'

'An' I take big shoes too, Grandad,' said Teddy, sticking out his feet to prove it.

The adults laughed and Janice said, 'Sit up properly, sweetheart. Show Grandad what a grown-up boy you can be in a restaurant.'

Bryony grinned at her. 'Don't push your luck!'

Mrs Porter leaned across the table and stared into her daughter's freckled face. 'You look tired, Bryony.'

'Blame Agatha Christie,' said Bryony, passing the bread to her father. 'I sat up half the night reading.'

'She has been looking under the weather lately,' Janice put in. 'Bruce and I have been worried.'

'Probably working too hard, if I know my girl,' Major Porter said. 'Takes after her old man. Don't nag her.'

Bryony gave him a quick smile. There had always been a bond between them. She even looked like him, except that her father's flaming thatch was now snow-white. He understood her better than anyone else in the family. As a child, she had adored him, for although he had been strict he had always been just, and even in her rebellious teens she had trusted him.

'I have been doing more than usual, as a matter of fact,' she admitted, and told them briefly about the kite festival. 'So I'm counting on the Porter clan to help me put St John's on the map,' she finished.

'We'll do that all right,' her father asserted with his usual zest. Then his wife said, 'By the way, didn't I hear that Hunter Grant is living here now?' And Bryony choked on a spoonful of chowder.

Bruce looked up from his smoked fish paté. 'Do you know Hunter?'

'We met him a couple of times,' his father told them, 'at a friend's place in New Mexico. He was planning to fly to Africa. Interesting guy. I'm hoping to look him up while we're here.'

'He's a friend of ours,' Janice said, breaking off a piece of rusk and handing it to her daughter. 'Don't throw it on the floor, there's a good girl.' She turned back to her mother-in-law. 'Hunter's away right now, but we'll invite him for dinner when he gets back.'

God, why are you doing this to me? Bryony asked silently. I'm doing my best to get over this infatuation, and you keep throwing king-sized spanners into the works!

'He gave me *goggles*,' Teddy said through a mouthful of bread and butter, 'an' a 'copter.'

'Don't talk with your mouth full,' his grandfather told him. 'It's rude.'

'An' a hat,' Teddy whispered mutinously, before subsiding under one of Major Porter's famous glares.

Hunter's name was not mentioned again, but as far as Bryony was concerned the damage was done, he might as well have been sitting at the table with them, and she did not contribute much to the conversation that swirled around her.

'Now, Bryony, you go straight to bed and no reading tonight,' her mother ordered when the party broke up.

Bryony wriggled her shoulders and said, 'I'm all right, Mom! *Really*,' as if she was fifteen rather than twenty-five. But she did as she was told, and rather to her surprise slept soundly until the following morning.

The Porter family engaged in a lot of extra activities that week. The weather was still good, and they took advantage of it, picnicking at Pippy Park, and flying kites, supplied by Bryony, from Signal Hill. Major Porter

organised a hiking tour, which he led, with his granddaughter strapped on his back, Teddy riding in the
stroller when his legs gave out. They barbecued their
suppers in the back yard, and Janice and her mother-
in-law started making new curtains for the bedrooms.
The narrow house rang with laughter, for they all got
on well, and Bryony found herself enjoying life again,
in spite of a muffled kind of ache in her heart.

She hadn't heard from Lois, so she didn't know if she
was back. She had thought of phoning, on the pretext
of saying hello, but really to discover where Hunter was,
but she couldn't bring herself to do it, because checking
up on him seemed a tacky thing to do.

As she had predicted, her father tried to take charge
of the festival, and to some extent she let him get away
with it. She could use the help, and it gave her time to
work on putting the finishing touches to her Goose kite.

'Clowns!' Major Porter declared one morning
towards the end of the week. Father and daughter spent
the mornings at her studio. 'Clowns...that's the thing.
They'll help keep the children amused. D'you know
any?'

'Sure! But not the professional kind! The drama department at the university might be able to help us.'

'Contact them,' her father commanded.

'Yes, *sir*!' she replied, saluting smartly. 'On the
double!'

Her father grinned sheepishly. 'Sorry, hon. I forget
sometimes I'm not still in the army.'

'Well, just remember it's your loving daughter, not
the regiment, you're working with.'

She picked up the phone directory, but her father said,
'Leave it for now. Let's take a breather, we've earned
one.'

'Whatever you say, Major. Would you like coffee?'

'Not unless you do.'

She pushed the phone book aside, and came to sit
opposite him at the work-table.

'I'm very impressed with all this.' He gestured with
his tobacco pouch. 'You've done well, hon. We're proud

of you, your mother and I.' She coloured with pleasure, because her father rarely gave compliments. 'Bruce is a credit too,' the Major went on. 'Happy in his job and his marriage—he seems well settled.'

'He is.'

'And you?' He looked up sharply from tamping down the tobacco in his pipe. 'Are you settled, Bryony?'

She found she couldn't meet his eyes. 'In Newfoundland? Oh, yes! I never want to move.'

'That isn't what I meant, and you know it,' the Major said. 'Bruce tells me you've just broken up with some guy and he thinks you're fretting. Is that so?'

'I wish Bruce would learn to keep his mouth shut,' Bryony retorted hotly.

'You watch your tongue, young lady,' her father shot back. 'Your brother's concerned because he cares about you.'

'I know he *cares*, but . . .'

'Your mother's worried about you too, if it comes to that.'

'Mom *fusses*,' Bryony snorted.

'She's a mother. They tend to, it's the nature of the beast,' replied her father.

Bryony, her sudden spurt of temper ended, said with a grin, 'I don't think you should call Mom a beast. it's not polite.'

He looked at her from under beetling white brows. 'You've got a temper just like mine,' he chuckled. 'Flares up in a minute, and then it's over.'

'You shouldn't sound so pleased about it,' she said. 'It gets me into a lot of trouble.'

'Are you in trouble now, Bryony?' he asked, serious again.

She leant across the table. 'No, darling, I'm not in any trouble . . . I promise.'

He lit his pipe and got it going. 'And you're not eating your heart out over this man?'

She examined her short, unpainted nails intently. 'Over Dave? No.'

'I don't mean to pry, hon,' her father said, 'but I know you pretty well, and *something's* bothering you.'

She raised her lovely, troubled eyes. 'I can't hide a thing from you, can I?'

'Do you want to?'

She pushed her fingers through her thick, short hair till it stood on end in a fiery halo. 'There's no point talking about it, Dad. I seem to have a yen for someone who's already taken. Talking about it will just make it worse.'

'You're not involved with a married man, are you, Bryony?' her father asked anxiously.

She pressed her hands together. 'No. He's not married—at least not yet—and I'm not involved...'

'Just your heart? he said, his voice sympathetic.

'You got it!' She gave a shaky laugh. 'But nothing I won't recover from in due course.'

He came round the table and planted a kiss on top of her unruly curls. 'I won't say any more, hon, I promise. Except...if you need a shoulder to cry on—mine's available.'

She flung her arms round his neck and pressed her smooth cheek to his rough one. 'There's nothing to cry about. Honestly!' She drew away and said lightly, 'And if this is your idea of helping me with the festival, I can't say I'm impressed.'

They went back to work then. Her father wasn't the type to regard her furtively for signs of weakness, so she no longer felt the need to watch herself constantly while she was with him. She could relax while they were alone together, and she knew he would tactfully get it across to the others to let her be. Whether he would succeed with his wife was a moot point, but at least Bryony didn't feel so alone any more.

The following Saturday was Teddy's fourth birthday. His parents had arranged a party for him, and by three that afternoon the place was jammed with a horde of happy, shrieking children. Major Porter was busy organising them into teams for a game, while Teddy, wearing his goggles for the occasion, raced about wildly.

'You're getting the child over-excited, John,' Mrs Porter protested.

'Rubbish, Wendy!' her husband snapped. 'Don't baby the boy.'

'Calm down, Teddy,' Wendy Porter ineffectually advised her grandson, 'you don't want to get too tired, do you, or you won't be able to eat any birthday cake.'

'Stop *fussing*, Wendy,' barked the Major, and, seizing his grandson with one hand, he pushed him in line with the other children.

Bruce and Bryony smiled covertly at each other. Major Porter and his wife had been bickering happily for thirty years. To outsiders it might look as if they spent their lives in a state of constant battle, but actually they were a devoted couple, and woe betide anyone who was foolish enough to offer a criticism of either partner.

'I think I'll leave you and Dad to cope with the bedlam for a while, and give a hand in the kitchen,' Bryony told Bruce, who was in the process of separating two small girls who were equally determined to play with the same toy.

'Coward!' said her brother, holding the toy at arm's length. 'And to think I could be working in a nice quiet newsroom!'

'You wanted to be a parent,' laughed Bryony. 'It's too late to back out now.'

In the kitchen Janice was putting the finishing touches to the birthday cake. Jane was in her playpen, contentedly hammering away with a wooden spoon. 'From the noise going on, I gather everyone's having a good time,' Janice commented as she put the fourth candle in place.

'Especially Mom and Dad.' Bryony came over to the counter. 'Anything I can do?'

'After you've admired my cake you can open up those bags of hot-dog buns.'

Bryony said, 'I didn't know Teddy was keen on whales,' for Janice had fashioned the cake in the shape of a whale.

'He isn't. But whales are easier to do than helicopters, which is what he wanted. All those chopper blades defeated me. Don't you think I've been clever with the icing?' She looked with satisfaction at the spout of icing the whale was blowing.

'A work of art!' Bryony agreed. She hoped she sounded flippant, for, ridiculous though it was, this chocolate whale cake reminded her instantly of watching the blue whales with Hunter. The future promised to be difficult if she was to spend the rest of her life being constantly reminded of him.

They served the birthday tea in the back yard because it was a nice day and it didn't matter if food was spilt, and the children—assisted by Bunty—did justice to the ice-cream and birthday cake. There was so much noise going on, they didn't hear the front door, and it wasn't until Lois walked round to the back of the house that they realised they had another guest.

Bruce went to greet her. 'Any adult is welcome,' he said. 'Come in and join the zoo!'

She came through the back gate, an elegant figure in pure white slacks and shirt, and Bryony, looking down at her faded denims, wished she'd put on something else, except that dressing up for a children's party seemed hardly practical.

'I do hope you don't mind me gatecrashing like this,' Lois said.

'I'm sure a pretty girl like you is welcome to crash at any gate,' Major Porter put in gallantly.

Bryony introduced Lois to her father, and then she said, 'I think it's extremely clever of you to time your visit just when the children are about to go home.'

'I should have waited, I guess,' said Lois, 'but I only just got back and I couldn't seem to settle to anything. I feel as if I'm still in Ottawa.' She gave Bryony a smile of radiant happiness. 'St John's doesn't seem real at all.'

Bryony asked, 'Did you have a nice time?' and Lois's blue eyes grew soft.

'Wonderful,' she breathed, 'absolutely wonderful.'

Please, *please*, no girlish confidences, Bryony prayed silently, although it was unlikely Lois would go into details with the garden full of noisy children.

Janice came out of the kitchen, followed by Mrs Porter. 'Lois! What a nice surprise. I don't believe you've met my mother-in-law, have you?' Introductions exchanged, she told Wendy, 'Lois is engaged to Hunter Grant.'

A cloud fell over Lois's face. 'We haven't set a date yet,' she said hastily.

'Well, I wish you all happiness just the same,' Mrs Porter smiled. 'We met Hunter at a friend's place in New Mexico and thought he was *such* a nice man. We're hoping to see him while we're here. Is he back yet?'

'I don't think so,' Lois seemed vague. 'You never know with Hunter. He comes and goes a lot.'

Wendy Porter said, 'Well, I certainly hope we can connect again. My husband and I found him delightful.'

Bryony, who didn't think she could take much more about Hunter, his wedding plans, or his charm, took Jane from Janice's arms. 'Why don't you and Lois grab a piece of birthday cake, if there's any left? I'll look after Jane for a bit.'

Lois refused the cake, saying she was on a diet, and Bryony saw her mother give a disapproving look at the tall girl's narrow hips. Wendy Porter had no patience with the modern mania for matchstick-thin women. She constantly nagged Bryony, convinced that her daughter's willowy slenderness was the result of dieting. The fact that Bryony ate like a pony did nothing to dissuade her.

There was a wail from a group of toddlers playing in Teddy's sandpit. 'It's time their mothers came for them,' Janice remarked. 'They're getting tired.'

Bryony went over to the squabbling children. 'C'mon, gang,' she said. 'Story time!' Sitting on the edge of the sandbox, Jane in her arms, she gathered the children round her. 'It's Teddy's birthday,' she said, 'so he gets to choose the story.'

'Story 'bout the giant in the house,' requested her nephew firmly.

'But he's moved, Teddy,' she reminded him.

'Hunter's the giant now,' Teddy insisted, 'an' I want a story about him.' He gave her a triumphant smile, and Bryony inwardly cursed the inventiveness of small children.

'Yes...well...the giant's name was...'

'Hunter!' Teddy yelled happily. 'He's a giant, an' he flies 'copters.' He grinned up at Lois who had wandered over. 'An' he's got a dog named Gus an' they has 'ventures.'

Wendy Porter smiled and said, 'Isn't he sweet?' Bryony pulled a face. 'Sweet' was not the adjective she would have applied at that moment. 'Does Hunter know he's a giant?' her mother enquired.

'We haven't discussed it,' Bryony said, and then the children began to demand that she start the story.

It was not her greatest effort. The children were really too excited to listen quietly, and she spent most of the time settling squabbles, while Lois looked on, an expression of acute distaste on her lovely face. Bryony was thankful when the mothers finally arrived to collect their young.

Bruce gestured at the untidy garden. 'I think we all deserve a drink before we clear any of this away,' he said.

'I don't really deserve a drink,' ventured Lois. 'I haven't done anything.'

'You've been decorative,' the Major assured her with a smile. 'That's enough.'

His wife gave an audible snort. 'I think we should move inside, it's getting chilly,' she said, for the afternoon sky was suddenly bleary with clouds and a fresh breeze played through the debris on the picnic table.

When they were gathered in the kitchen, Teddy picked up one of his toys and came over to Lois. 'See what Grandad gave me,' he said, holding out a wooden train in his grubby hands.

Lois drew back as if he had offered her a live snake. 'Don't you dare touch me,' she shrieked. 'You're *filthy*!' There was a stunned silence, and Teddy's chocolate-stained mouth quivered.

'Come with Grandma, she'll give you a wash,' said Mrs Porter hastily, taking hold of his hand.

'I only wanted to show the lady my train,' he wailed as he was led from the room.

'I guess I shouldn't have worn silk,' Lois said. 'It marks so easily.' She gave a self-conscious smile. 'Come to think of it, none of my wardrobe is child-proof.'

Bruce advised her to forget it, and went about the business of mixing drinks for them all, then he went into the next room to catch the news on television. 'Just want to keep tabs on my work,' he explained, and, because they felt embarrassed for Lois, Janice and the Major joined him.

'Bruce feels deprived if he doesn't see the news at least twice a day,' his sister explained. 'It's murder on holiday. Particularly when they go camping.'

But Lois didn't seem interested in Bruce's idiosyncrasies. 'Daddy's furious with me,' she blurted. 'That's one of the reasons I came here. To get away.'

Bryony started to put Jane back in her playpen, but the baby resisted, so she cradled her comfortably on one hip. 'Mad because you took off without telling him?'

'And because I stayed longer than I said I would,' Lois nodded.

And because you had a high old time romping around in bed with Hunter, Bryony thought dismally. 'I shouldn't worry too much. He'll get over it,' she reassured her.

Lois examined her beautifully manicured nails 'Would you say Hunter is an understanding man?' she asked at last.

Taken aback, Bryony stammered, 'I…I suppose so…I hardly know him.'

Lois said thoughtfully, 'I hope so.'

'Well, you should *know*, surely?' said Bryony sharply.

'I suppose I should. But...life can be so difficult sometimes,' the blonde girl murmured. She stopped examining her hands and looked up, and again that bubbling happiness was back in her face. 'But it can be marvellous, too. Unexpected and utterly, utterly wonderful. You've no idea *how* wonderful, Bryony.'

And since Bryony had no intention of finding out...a description of Hunter's skill as a lover being more than she could stand...she thrust Jane at her guest and said, 'Hold the baby for a minute, would you? I have to go to the bathroom.'

Locked in the bathroom, she splashed her face and hands with cold water. Don't be such a fool, she admonished her reflection. They're going to be married, so you might as well get used to the idea of them in bed together.

She could hear Jane's yells the minute she started down the stairs. In the kitchen she found Lois awkwardly holding the scarlet-face child at arm's length. 'She's *soaking*,' she said, as she thrust the roaring baby at her aunt.

'She's more than than,' remarked Bryony. 'Time for a wash and brush-up, I think, my treasure.'

Mrs Porter put her head round the door. 'What's the matter with Jane?'

'Just letting us know that she's been neglected,' smiled Bryony. 'I'll go up and change her.'

Shuddering slightly, Lois said, 'I think I'd better be going.' She turned to Bryony's mother. 'It's been lovely meeting you, Mrs Porter. Don't forget, Bryony's bringing you and your husband for tea tomorrow.' She looked with disfavour at Jane, who had stopped screaming and was now snuffling quietly in Bryony's arms. 'Bruce and Janice are invited too, of course—if they can get a baby-sitter.'

'I'll see you out,' said Mrs Porter grimly, leading the way to the front door.

When Bryony was powdering Jane, who was clean and sweet again and cooing now, a rosy cherub, Mrs Porter came in. 'I simply don't understand men,' she exclaimed, sitting down on the bathroom stool.

'Join the club,' her daughter smiled. 'Did you have any particular man in mind?'

Her mother pursed her lips. Lips that were not as full as Bryony's, but just as determined. 'Hunter Grant, for one,' she said, 'getting himself hitched up with that girl. He must be mad.'

Bryony felt her face go into neutral. 'Lois is lovely,' she said. 'I like her a lot.'

Wendy Porter dismissed this. 'Oh, she's pleasant enough, I suppose, but she's a shallow creature. No depth to her at all. She's all froth and show. Did you see the way she pushed Teddy away? She hasn't an *ounce* of maternal feeling.'

'Maybe Hunter isn't interested in maternal feeling.'

'Don't be ridiculous, Bryony. I may not know him very well, but I guarantee he wants more from a woman than a clothes-horse.' She got up from her perch and, taking a comb from the shelf, started combing her thick grey hair. 'A marriage between Hunter Grant and that girl is doomed from the start,' she stated flatly. 'Take my word for it.'

'What's all this about tea tomorrow?' asked her daughter, hoping to change the subject.

'Men again!' exclaimed Mrs Porter. 'That's your father's doing. Show him a pretty face and he turns into a jelly.'

'A lemon or an orange jelly?'

'Don't be silly, Bryony, you know what I mean. And did you notice, Janice and Bruce are invited, but *not* the children? She made that quite plain.' Indignantly Wendy Porter threw down the comb. 'That baby will catch her death if you don't put some clothes on her.'

'I have her sleeper here—don't nag.' Bryony started to put Jane's pink little feet into the legs of the terry-cloth suit. 'We don't have to go tomorrow,' she said. 'We can think up an excuse.'

'Oh! But I *want* to go,' said Wendy, illogically. 'I want to see the sort of house a politician lives in. Besides,' she helped pull her granddaughter's dimpled arm through a sleeve, 'I think it would be nice for Bruce and Janice to have some time to themselves. We've been rather on top of them this week.'

Bryony diplomatically waited for a few seconds. When Jane was snugly zipped into her sleeper, she said, 'I'm not too keen to go myself. Maybe you and Dad can go alone.' But her mother would have none of it.

'Of course you must come,' she insisted. 'You know these people, you can help us break the ice.'

'And since when did you need someone to do your ice-breaking for you?' Bryony protested, but she knew she was arguing in vain. Her mother would insist, and she couldn't use her work as an excuse yet again.

So the following afternoon she teamed up the skirt of her new suit with a light-weight coral sweater, for it was a cold miserable day, and put on some eye make-up. As she brushed mascara on to her sweeping tawny lashes, she found herself praying that the conversation would not be exclusively about Hunter. She put on some coral lipstick, regarded the effect in the glass, and wiped it off again.

'Not much point painting this particular lily,' she muttered morosely, and with a heart as heavy as the lowering skies she picked up her purse and drew a long breath, as though she were preparing for an ordeal by fire, rather than a simple Sunday tea with friends.

CHAPTER NINE

IF BRYONY had been driving her own car she would have
turned round the moment she spotted Hunter's blue car
standing in the driveway of Four Winds, but her father
was driving them, and she could hardly say, Please, Dad,
let me out, because the man I'm crazy about is here and
watching him with the girl he is planning to marry will
tear me to pieces—so she straightened her spine and bit
the bullet.

Hunter came into the hall to greet them, clearly delighted to see Bryony's parents. 'This is great!' he kept
saying, pumping Major Porter's hand. 'It wasn't till Lois
told me that we'd met in New Mexico that I realised who
you were.'

Lois, elegant in soft blue wool, joined them. She didn't
look quite so radiant today. She kept glancing at Hunter
and then looking hastily away when their eyes met, and
her smile seemed strained and anxious. They all went
into the drawing-room. Again a fire was blazing in the
grate. Automatically Bryony looked at the window where
she and Hunter had watched the storm together. That
was when he had told her of his childhood in the orphanage and she had begun to see him as a sensitive
human being, not simply an antagonistic male. I wish I
could still hate him, she thought wistfully. Hate would
be easier to deal with than . . . than *what*? Love? No, not
love. Please not love! It would be agony to love another
woman's man. What she felt for Hunter was *affection*—
it had to be. Affection complicated by lust.

Sitting a little way outside the circle, she watched him.
His angular face, which could be so stern, was relaxed
as he chatted to her parents. He laughed at something
the Major said, showing the strong brown column of his
throat, the silver wings in his hair gleaming like pewter.

'And so, are you settled down at last, Hunter?' her mother was saying. 'Has the rolling stone finally come to rest?'

'I guess I'll always have to roll around a bit,' he replied with a smile, 'that goes with my job. But St John's will be the place I come home to.'

'So you and Lois will be doing some travelling when you're married, then,' Wendy Porter said. 'Will you enjoy that, Lois?'

Lois pushed her pale hair back from her face. 'I've always liked travelling,' she said, sounding thoroughly half-hearted.

Bryony had intended to stay silent, but this chit-chat about Hunter's and Lois's future plans strained her nerves to the breaking-point, and she suddenly burst out, 'I'd *hate* that sort of life! I had enough travelling when I was a kid.' Everybody looked at her, surprised.

'Oh, come on, hon! You enjoyed it,' her father reminded her.

'It was all right when I was young, but now that I'm grown up I want to be settled,' she insisted stubbornly. She glared at Hunter, as if by attacking him she could protect herself. 'It's no life at all. It's certainly not the sort of life I'd choose.'

'No one's asking you to,' Mrs Porter pointed out reasonably enough, 'but one day, Bryony, you'll discover that home is where the heart is, and moving around or staying in one place won't matter if you're with someone you care for.' She looked at her husband and he reached for her hand with a smile.

'I'll believe it when it happens,' Bryony scowled.

Hunter regarded her thoughtfully and said, 'Maybe it will never happen. Maybe you'll never fall in love.'

Lois gave an indignant cry. 'Of *course* she will! What an awful thing to say.'

'There are worse fates. To be heart-whole might be considered a blessing,' he said quietly.

There was a tap on the door and Mrs Lacey came in, wheeling the tea-trolley, followed by Branwell Taylor.

'Daddy!' Lois jumped from her chair and came up to him, putting her hand on his arm. 'Come and meet Bryony's parents.'

'How d'yer do!' said Branwell gruffly. He shook off Lois's hand. 'Now that you've deigned to come home, you're giving tea parties, are you?' He glared at the laden trolley. 'Are those *scones*?'

'They are,' Mrs Lacey replied, 'and there's more in the kitchen, so don't start bellowing that I haven't made enough.' She flounced from the room.

'Bloody woman knows I like scones, but she only makes them when there's company,' Branwell growled.

'It's nice to know that we have our uses,' Hunter said coolly.

The Major gave an appreciative chuckle and Mrs Porter asked, 'Do *you* cook, Lois?' in an attempt to gloss over their host's bad manners.

Lois cast an apprehensive glance at her father. 'I learnt at school,' she said, 'but I'm not much good.'

'Only good at gallivanting off to God knows where,' her father snorted, and Lois drooped disconsolately back to her chair.

'You couldn't be as bad as Bryony,' Wendy chattered. Like her daughter, she babbled when she was at a loss. 'She makes flaky pastry that tastes like a wet book.'

Branwell ignored this fascinating piece of information and, biting into a scone, mumbled, 'Taking off for Ottawa without so much as a by-your-leave.' He glared at Hunter. 'High time she was married, if you ask me.'

'Daddy, *please*!' said Lois, her cheeks scarlet.

'I think you should at least make an *effort* to join the twentieth century, Branwell,' said Hunter with dangerous calmness.

Branwell stuck out his jaw. 'She's my daughter, and I call the shots. Wait till you're married. See how you like it if she takes off whenever she feels like it.'

'She won't have to ask my permission,' Hunter assured him. 'She's a free woman, not a piece of merchandise. She can do as she likes.' And Bryony thought, he *is* nice, she's lucky.

Branwell snorted derisively. 'Free, fiddlesticks!' He turned to Major and Mrs Porter. 'I don't hold with giving women too much freedom. It doesn't make them happy, and it goes to their heads.'

Hunter said cuttingly, 'Fortunately, your views aren't widely shared,' and then, dismissing him, he asked Bryony, 'How's the kite festival coming along?'

'Apart from a few last-minute details, we're ready. Now all we have to do is pray for good weather.'

Major Porter leant towards his host. 'My daughter tells me that you're responsible for getting the festival approved,' he said. 'I must congratulate you. It'll be good for the city.'

Branwell brightened. 'I'm always happy to help my city,' he boomed, 'as my past record shows.'

Lois motioned to Bryony, and the two girls wandered over to the window. 'I'm sorry he's being so awful,' she whispered, lowering her eyelids in the direction of her father. 'I thought he'd be over his temper by now, or I wouldn't have asked you to bring your folks.' She looked thoroughly woebegone.

'Forget it!' Bryony advised her. '*He* will soon enough.'

'Oh, you don't know him.' She stared at the wet lawn mournfully. 'He can carry on like this for days.'

'Why don't you leave home, then? Marry Hunter as quickly as you can,' Bryony said, and was appalled at the effort this piece of advice cost her.

Lois stopped staring at the dripping garden. 'I guess getting married would be the answer,' she murmured. 'I'd be free then.' A gleam appeared in her blue eyes. 'Thank you, Bryony.'

Branwell barked 'Lois!' and his daughter squeezed Bryony's arm and whispered, 'Thank you!' again, before going over to find out what he wanted.

Bryony stayed where she was. How ironic that she should be the one to urge Lois towards an early wedding. She could have laughed if she hadn't felt so miserable. The garden seemed to shudder sympathetically in the rain, a perfect match for her emotions.

'What will you do if it rains like this for the festival?' Hunter asked, and she nearly jumped out of her skin.

He was standing just behind her, looking over her marigold head at the streaming windows. The faint scent of him teased her nostrils. She would have given a great deal to have been able to lean back against his chest and feel his hands caress her. 'Why didn't you tell me you'd met my parents before?' she demanded rancorously, stripping all warmth from her voice, for she was only safe from him if he remained her enemy. Anything less was madness.

'Because I didn't know they *were* your parents,' he explained. 'I didn't know their surname.'

'I find that hard to believe.' She turned back to the window, willing him to return to the others and leave her alone.

'You haven't answered my question,' he persisted. 'About the rain.'

'We can postpone for one week. After that—no festival!' She craned towards the window, examining the raindrops intently.

Hunter said tersely, 'I only ask because I am part of it. You do still want me to provide a helicopter, I presume?'

'Don't do it if it's too much trouble.' Obstinately she continued staring at the window.

He stood behind her, looking down at her shining orange curls, and thought, what the hell's bugging her? I've never know anyone so unpredictable. The sound of muffled barking came from the back of the house.

'That damn dog of yours, kicking up a racket,' Branwell remarked.

'I think I'll take myself and my damn dog home,' Hunter said softly in the direction of Bryony's head. 'It's no fun here with you and Branwell, that's for sure.'

Bryony didn't answer. Looking through him, she went back to the group round the fireplace. 'We should be leaving,' she said to her parents. 'Tansy will be waiting.' For Tansy was expecting them for dinner at her cottage.

Her parents agreed with obvious relief, and they
quickly made their farewells. On the drive to Tansy's,
Mrs Porter let it be known that she was not impressed
by Branwell Taylor. 'I have a bit more sympathy for Lois
now,' she remarked. 'Though why she puts up with him
is beyond me.'

'She won't have to put up with him much longer,'
Bryony said. 'She'll be married to Hunter soon.'

'Out of the frying-pan, into the fire,' Wendy Porter
said tartly.

'Come on!' her husband objected. 'Hunter strikes me
as a decent man; he'll treat her properly.'

'I'm sure he will, but she'll bore him to *sobs* in no
time,' Mrs Porter pronounced flatly. 'She's far too bland
for him.'

The nails of Bryony's hands were digging into her
palms. 'I don't think we should gossip like this,' she said
curtly. 'It's none of our business.'

Her father gave her a brief, perceptive glance, and she
said hastily, 'Look down there, at that cove—sometimes
you can see seals.' Although you wouldn't have been
able to see an elephant through the curtain of rain.

The weather didn't improve. The rain did stop occasionally, but a bitter wind blew in from the north east,
and the temperature plummeted. Bryony, who usually
ignored the weather, nearly went mad. She had finished
her Goose kite, but it was too blowy to try it out, and
Bunty flatly refused to be taken for any more long hikes,
sitting her small rump down firmly and pulling mutinously on her leash whenever Bryony tried to force her.

Bruce managed to get a couple of days off during the
week, and the plan was for the family to go and visit
friends at Conception Bay. Their friends had a big house,
so there was plenty of room, but Bryony decided to stay
behind. Since seeing Hunter at the weekend her temper
had been decidedly frazzled—she needed to be alone.

'I'll be perfectly fine,' she assured Janice. 'I'll eat out
of tins, so don't go to any bother, for heaven's sake,

and do stop *fussing*! I need a holiday away from you all.'

They left early the following morning, Teddy sitting on his grandfather's knee and Jane strapped in the car-seat at the back. Bunty sat imperiously in the back too, for she was going as well.

The little house felt dead without the usual activity of a home containing two small children and a dog. Bryony washed up the breakfast dishes and switched on the radio—loud—just to stir up the silence, and then, just as she was making herself a tuna sandwich to take to the studio, the rain stopped and a shaft of pale sunlight arrowed through the sullen clouds. On an impulse she fetched her daypack from the cupboard. She would take the day off and go for a long, hard walk. Eat her lunch out of doors and walk her gloom away.

As if the car had a will of its own, she drove in the direction of Knucklerock Field, but she kept going, past Santu House, to the other headland. Here there was a curved beach, littered with storm-smooth boulders, and a promontory of jagged rocks stretched out like an arm into the sea.

She parked the car at the edge of the road and, pulling her pack on to her shoulders, started to climb down to the beach. It wasn't easy. There was a path of sorts, but it was slippery. Part-way down, a chain had been riveted into the rock-face, and she clung to this, her track shoes slithering dangerously. On one side, the cliff was sheer polished stone, as if a giant had sliced it with a knife. Below it, the water looked deep and dangerous. When she got down to the safety of the shingle the sun was again obscured by clouds and the wind had freshened. They were in for a storm.

She had told Hunter that she enjoyed storms, and it had been the truth. She faced the heaving water now, leaning into the wind, her freckled face soon drenched with spray, her hair plastered to her head. She had pulled on a short raincoat over her tracksuit when she had left the house, and now she thanked her lucky stars that she had, for already her legs were soaking wet and cold. Not

that she cared; this storm was just what she needed to
blow her mind free of her problems. The wind tore at
her coat and mocked her for her naïveté.

Looking to the far headland, she could see the outline
of Santu House, its windows facing the angry Atlantic
like the prow of a ship. Would Hunter bring his bride
here? Or would Lois get her way and move them as far
from Newfoundland as possible? Bryony really hoped
that would be the case, for she didn't want to live near
Hunter when he was a married man. She didn't want to
move from St John's herself either, so...

Annoyed that she was indulging in the very thing she
had vowed not to—moping over Hunter—she looked for
something difficult to do, and decided to climb out along
the spiny promontory. It was foolhardy, she knew that,
the seaweedy rocks were dangerously slimy, but it required all her concentration and she welcomed the chance
to clear her mind of everything but the business of staying
upright. This was just the sort of challenge she needed.

She made it to the far point and clung there, the wild
spray nearly blinding her. The wind seemed stronger now,
and out to sea she could see white caps on the waves. It
promised to be a worse storm than she'd anticipated.
Gingerly she turned around and started back.

This was harder going than before, and she was forced
to go on to her hands and knees, for the sea was now
crashing around her and pounding angrily on to the
beach. A couple of times she nearly lost her balance,
and she felt the sour taste of fear in her mouth, but she
inched her way carefully, and was nearly back when
Hunter's voice, furious above the howling wind, yelled,
'What in God's name do you think you're playing at?'

She started violently and lost her grip on the greasy
rock, her knees flew out from under her, and, scrabbling
wildly for a place to grasp, she fell headlong into the
sea.

On a calm day the water would have come to her knees,
but now it was surging, foam-flecked around her. A big
wave tumbled her over and over, and she lost her sense
of balance. Water roared in her ears, choking her,

clawing at her. The world had become a maelstrom of
icy salt water.

This is it! she thought wildly. I'm going to drown!
Then strong arms were tugging at her waist, dragging
her up out of this ferment on to the pebbles of the shore.

He flung her down like a sack of potatoes, and she
lay limply on her stomach and brought up a good deal
of sea. Then she turned on to her back. He was standing
over her, streaming with water, a scowl as black as
thunder on his face.

'You bloody little fool!' he rasped. 'You would have
drowned if I hadn't been here.'

'I wouldn't have fallen *in* if you hadn't been here,'
she croaked. 'You startled me.'

'You damn well *terrified* me,' he fumed. 'I was
watching you from the house. Haven't you got any brains
at all?'

'Oh, do shut up!' she said through chattering teeth,
for she was cold, and the wind tearing at her soaking
clothes was making her colder. Carefully she tried
pushing herself up to sit, and she winced with pain. Only
then did she notice that her hands were grazed; she must
have torn them on the barnacles as she fell.

Hunter hooked his hands under her armpits and pulled
her to her feet, and she gasped, for her legs were cut and
bleeding too. By now she was shuddering with cold. 'I
can carry you some of the way,' he said, 'but you'll have
to climb part of the cliff yourself.' She nodded dumbly.

Afterwards, she never could remember how she
managed it. There were moments during that nightmare
climb when she thought she must have lost consciousness for a few seconds at a time, and then Hunter
would be holding her, dragging her up the path, urging
her forward.

When they reached the top, she would have fallen if
he hadn't scooped her up in his arms and thrown her
over his shoulder in a fireman's lift. She was a tiny girl,
and light as a feather, even burdened down with wet
clothing, and he strode over the rough grass to his car

with as much speed as if he had been carrying a bag of
groceries.

'What are you doing?' She pounded weakly on his
back. 'My car's just over there.'

'Don't be idiotic.' He thrust her into the passenger
seat. 'You're in no condition to drive anywhere.'

It was only a short distance to Santu House, so the
car had no time to get warm, even though he put the
heater on full. When she went into the living-room, she
couldn't control the chattering of her teeth. She hugged
Gus when he came to greet them, hoping his silky fur
might warm her up, but it didn't. Hunter took a knitted
runner from the back of a sofa and bundled her into it.
He was shivering now himself, and when he pulled off
his rubber boots water poured from them on to the floor.
He stripped off his socks and threw them on to the floor
too, and she noticed how tanned his feet were.

'This should warm the room,' he said, putting a match
to the fire that was laid in the fireplace. 'Meantime, you
take a hot bath.'

She would have agreed to roast in hell for a session
in order to get warm, and so she meekly followed him,
noticing that the stairs were carpeted now. There was
comfortable-looking furniture in the living-room too,
and a telescope had been positioned at the window. He
must have been watching her through it while she crawled
along the rocks.

The bathroom had been remodelled to contain a large
bath and a glassed-in shower stall. 'You soak in a hot
tub,' he ordered, turning on the taps. 'I'll take the
shower.'

She looked at him, startled. 'At the same time?'

'I don't intend to get pneumonia because of false
modesty,' he barked. 'Close your eyes if I offend you.'
As he disappeared into the adjoining bedroom he called,
'Get out of those wet clothes and into that hot water,
and stop dithering, for God's sake.'

Quickly she peeled off her sodden tracksuit, and after
hastily glancing in the direction of the bedroom, she
yanked off her panties and climbed into the bath. She

could have floated in it, it was large enough, but she was in no mood to relax. The hot water stung her cuts and grazes, and she gasped as her frozen flesh began to tingle back to life.

She looked around for some bath salts that she could use to cloud the water and hide her nakedness, but this was a man's bathroom and there didn't seem anything as feminine as scented bath salts around. There were several big bars of soap though, and she dropped a couple of those into the water, hoping to create some concealing suds, and, grabbing a flannel, she draped it over her loins as Hunter came in from the bedroom.

He was wearing nothing but a towel wrapped tightly round his middle. A crisp mat of curly dark hair covered his chest, disappearing to a V at the top of his towel. Bryony sank down into the soapy water, but he didn't even glance in her direction. Opening the door of the shower-stall, he dropped his towel and she had a glimpse of brown thigh and buttocks. She squeezed her eyes tight shut. When she heard the sound of water running in the shower, she opened them again. She could see the blurred outline of his bronzed body through the glass door as he soaped himself vigorously.

He dried himself off in the stall and wound the towel round his middle again before stepping into the bathroom. He fetched a tube of ointment from a medicine cabinet. 'Here!' he said, putting it down on the edge of the bath. 'You'll need this for your cuts.'

She ducked down into the opaque water and squeaked, 'Thanks.' His body was lean and strong—compact. And she couldn't stop admiring him from under her lowered lashes.

'There are plenty of towels in the cupboard, and I'll leave you some clothes on the bed,' he said, making for the bedroom. 'You can wear them while yours are drying. Take your time. I'll meet you downstairs when you're ready.'

'Thanks.' She peeped cautiously over the rim of the bath. When he had gone she washed her hair, then ran more hot water and lay back. She couldn't seem to get

really warm, though—not inside. Her very bones felt
chilled; no amount of hot water seemed to penetrate
them. Finally she climbed out and towelled herself hard
with one of the fluffy towels she found in the bathroom
cupboard. Wrapping it round her, she padded into the
bedroom.

Hunter had laid out a selection of his clothes on the
large brass bed, and she chose a fleece-lined navy sweatshirt and matching trousers. Even when she pulled the
waistband up under her armpits and rolled it over, the
legs still dragged round her feet. She could have worn
the top only, like a dress, for it reached her knees, but
with no underwear—his Y-fronts were decidedly too
big—she felt naked; besides, she wanted to get warm.
She put on a pair of thick socks and tucked the ends of
the trousers into them.

She looked like a bundle of old clothes with an orange
mop sticking out of the top when she had finished, but
this was hardly a fashion show, and after running her
fingers through her damp fuzz of curls she went
downstairs.

In the kitchen Hunter was stirring a pan. He looked
up when she came in. 'Chicken soup,' he said. 'It should
warm you up better than that!' He pointed with the
spoon to her tuna sandwich lying on the table, squashed
and mushy in its plastic bag. 'Your pack's in the dryer
with your clothes,' he said. He smiled at her for the first
time, and she felt weak tears sting her eyes. Horrified
at this display of weakness, she blinked furiously. She
must be in a bad state if his sympathy could affect her
like this.

'Let's have our soup by the fire.' He poured the
fragrant broth into two mugs. 'You bring the biscuits.'

Clutching the tin of biscuits, she followed him. He'd
changed into faded blue jeans and a chunky knitted
yellow sweater. The collar of a blue shirt was turned up
around his throat, and his brown hair fell in a thick fall
over his forehead. He looked so strong and dependable.
She remembered the feel of his arms when he lifted her

on to his shoulder, and she longed to feel them about her again.

He pulled a small armchair up to the fire, and after setting it nearly in the hearth he said, 'You sit here, like a kettle on a hob.' Then, fetching the runner from where she had left it hanging over the stair rail, he folded it round her shoulders. He was as gentle as a lover and it was bliss, but it was dangerous. It would have been safer for her if his temper hadn't cooled.

As if he read her thoughts, he said, 'I didn't mean to yell at you back there on the beach, Bryony, but that was a very dumb thing to do. Those rocks are lethal.' He gave her a crooked grin. 'You had Gus really worried.' And Gus wagged his tail in concurrence.

'Sorry, Gus,' said Bryony, patting him. 'I won't do it again, I promise.'

'That is good news for both of us,' said Hunter. He raised his mug. '*Bon appetit!*'

She sipped her soup. 'Mmm, it's good! Did you make it?'

'I cannot tell a lie,' he confessed. 'I opened a can. But I doctored it with herbs.'

'Delicious!' She took another sip. 'You should take a medical degree, if this is the result of your doctoring.'

He waved a deprecatory hand. 'As the saying goes— it was nothing.'

'If I'd done it, it would *really* have been nothing.' She nibbled on a piece of biscuit. 'I would have either put in too much or too little. I just don't seem to have the knack when it comes to creative cooking. It used to drive Dave wild.'

He leaned back in his chair, regarding her through lazy grey eyes. 'Does it drive *you* wild?'

'No...well...sometimes. I mean women are supposed to be able to cook, aren't they? It's traditional.'

'I never heard such sexist rubbish in my life. I'm surprised at you, Miss Porter.'

She smiled ruefully. 'Just the same! Dave used to say...'

He cut in, 'Does it matter to you, what Dave used to say?' and she grinned then and admitted that it didn't. 'Then stop jabbering about it. Be yourself. Go on creating those lovely kites of yours and make enough money to pay someone else to do the cooking—or marry a man who can cook!'

He smiled at her and it was like a caress. She lowered her eyes and earnestly stared into her mug of soup, for the room was suddenly crackling with tension. He leaned across her to put another log on the fire, and she held herself as far away from him as she could, for if he touched her—if he so much as brushed against the sleeve of her sweatshirt—she thought she might fling herself into his arms.

The wind howled and the storm shrieked about them, the house seemed to vibrate from the furious pounding of the surf on the rocks. Bryony shivered and pulled at the knitted rug around her shoulders.

'Are you still cold, love?' Hunter asked softly, and she shivered again, but this time from delight at his use of the endearment. He took the mug from her nerveless hand and laid his own on her forehead. 'Not running a fever, are you?'

Her throat was dry when she answered. 'I d... don't think so. But I'm still cold *inside*.'

'You're cold from shock. Bed's the place for you,' he said decisively, and before she had time to protest he had picked her up and was carrying her upstairs.

'No... really... I'll be all right!' she insisted weakly against his chest.

But he simply whispered, 'Don't argue, love, there's a good girl.'

In the bedroom he laid her gently on the bed and pulled back the coverlet, tucking it round her. He closed the wooden shutters at the windows.

'We'll shut out the storm,' he said, 'and give you some peace.'

Peace! That was a laugh! Her heart was pounding as loudly as the surf below, and now her limbs had started

to tremble. He came back to the side of the bed and put
the back of his hand against her cheek. 'Warmer now?'

'I th...think so,' she whispered, her voice quivering.

'You're not.' He kicked off his shoes and sat on the
side of the bed. 'Move over. What you need is body
warmth.'

Her slanted eyes opened to circles. 'No, Hunter...I'm
fine...'

'Shut up, love!' he said quietly. 'I'm not going to rape
you. Just hold you till you're warm.' Putting his arms
round her, he gently pulled her close.

Slowly, slowly the tension ebbed out of her and she
began to relax against him. The warmth from his body
gradually suffused into hers, and after a while she gave
a fluttering sigh, unclenched her hands, and fell into a
deep sleep.

Her first consciousness was of dreamy comfort. She
wasn't sure at first where she was, but it didn't seem to
matter. It was warm and cosy and she snuggled down
into the bed. Dimly she heard the sea breaking on the
shore below, the wind blowing, and then she remembered...she was in bed with Hunter Grant! She turned
her head on the pillow and carefully opened her eyes.
He was gone, but a dent in the other pillow showed that
she hadn't dreamed it, he *had* been here, holding her
close, warming her back to life. She was still fully
dressed, so being in bed with him wasn't quite what it
sounded, but just the same... She supposed she should
get up, it wasn't exactly wise, lolling around in Hunter's
bed like this, but she was warm and sleepy. Her eyelids
drooped.

Her second awakening was more abrupt. A light
snapped on and Gus's silky face poked over the edge of
the bed; then her eyes focused on Hunter, who was
standing beside him. 'Feeling warm now?' he asked.

She nodded and sat up, throwing off the coverlet. If
she went on lying there he might think it was an invitation to hop back in again. 'How long did I sleep?'

'Three hours.' He put her clothes down on the bed.
'Your things are dry. While you change I'll make us a
cup of tea.'

'Lovely!' Tea might help rouse her, for she was still
dazed with sleep. 'What's the weather doing?'

'Raining hard, but the wind's dropped a bit. By the
way...' He stopped in the doorway, his yellow sweater
a stab of colour against the dimly lit landing.

'Yes?'

'I couldn't find a bra with your things.'

'I don't wear one,' she said, her cheeks growing pink.
Did he like his women small-breasted? Probably not, if
Lois was anything to judge by.

'That explains it,' he said. 'Come on, Gus! Let's leave
the lady to dress.' He pulled the dog to the doorway.
'See you downstairs.'

She dressed hastily, tugging at her clothes as if her life
depended on it. She gave up on her hair, afraid she might
break Hunter's comb on her wild tangle, and contented
herself by flattening it with her hands in an attempt to
try to smooth it down.

He had set a tray of tea, and bread and jam, on a low
table in front of the fire. 'Toast seemed like a good idea.'
He waved a toasting-fork at her. 'Aren't you hungry after
your nap?'

'Fairly.' She found it difficult to make light conversation when all she could think of were his arms cradling
her, the feel of his lithe body against hers. 'Shall I take
a turn at toasting?'

'You can be the official butterer, and help to keep
Gus's nose out of our tea.' He pushed the salivating dog
away from the plate.

'Poor old Gus!' Bryony tore a piece of untoasted bread
and offered it to him, and he sniffed it before refusing
it contemptuously.

'He can't be bribed that way,' Hunter pointed out.
'He wants butter and jam on it. Nothing but the best!'

Like his master, Bryony thought, spreading butter on
a slice of golden brown toast. He probably wants butter
and jam on it, too. And as for 'the best', surely Lois

was about as 'best' as you could get, when it came to
fiancées with influential parents.

He broke into this unpleasant reverie. 'I think this
should be enough to be going on with,' he said, handing
her a final piece of toast. 'Now I'll pour us some tea
before it's stewed to death.'

It was the best meal that she had ever eaten. She
thought she had never tasted anything as delicious as
that slightly smoky toast and the strong tea which he
served in pottery mugs. There was home-made rasp-
berry jam too, and a moist cinnamon cake. The logs
glowed and crackled, and after a few offerings of but-
tered toast Gus stretched out by the door and slept. It
was as though the world had shrunk to this house, with
just the sleeping dog, Bryony and Hunter in it.

'Terrific cake,' she said, munching appreciatively. 'Did
you make it?'

'Again, no. Mrs Hollis did. She's the wife of a
fisherman in the next bay who's agreed to cook and clean
for me.'

Bryony sighed happily and delicately brushed cake
crumbs off her fingers. 'You're not going to let your
culinary talents go to waste just because you've got a
housekeeper now, though, are you?'

'Not completely. I shall cook up a storm on my days
off,' he promised. 'In between running my businesses.'

And when you have your wife here to share the
kitchen, she thought, and a little of her contentment
flowed away.

He pushed the debris of their meal aside and said, 'I
tried phoning Janice earlier—to let them know that you
were safe, but there was no answer. Maybe we should
try again.'

'They're visiting friends at Conception Bay for a
couple of days.' A silence fell and she heard a clock
ticking in the kitchen, and that sweet, alarming tension
was between them again.

'Then you don't have to rush away. Good!' he said
at last. He went over to the stereo. 'I seem to remember
that you like this kind of stuff.' He took a record from

its sleeve and put it on the turntable. It was Kiri Te
Kanawa singing 'Songs of the Auvergne'. Its haunting
melodies always reduced Bryony to tears, but she now
set her jaw tight in a determined effort to control her
emotions.

She was sitting on the floor, her back resting against
a love-seat Hunter had pulled up to the fire, and he came
and sat behind her and his fingers brushed lightly on
her vivid curls. He barely touched her, but she felt a jolt,
like a mild shock of electricity, run through her body.
The magnificent soprano voice filled the room, throbbing
with passionate yearning, and in spite of her clenched
jaw Bryony felt a tear slide slowly down her cheek.

'I've never known anyone enjoy music as much as you
do,' Hunter said, as she blinked it away. He slid down
on to the floor beside her. 'It *is* enjoyment, isn't it?'

Dumbly she nodded and another tear welled up and
slipped silently down. He wiped it away tenderly with
his finger. His face was so close, she could see the amber-
coloured flecks in his eyes. Eyes that were filled with an
emotion she could not recognise.

'Oh, Bryony!' he whispered, his voice husky. 'Bryony,
you are enchanting!' He leant over and her eyelids fluttered half closed as he softly kissed her mouth. She could
no more have resisted him than she could have resisted
breathing. It was as if her soul had been waiting for him
all her life to warm her to fire, the way he had warmed
her body that afternoon. His lips moved down her throat
to the silky skin at the base of her neck. 'Sweet freckles,'
he murmured, kissing them one by one, 'like the petals
of a buttercup.'

She gave a strangled little sob of desire and, taking
his face in her hands, put her lips on his, and discovered
in herself an unbelievable white-hot passion.

Now his kisses were fierce, and his tongue probed the
sweetness of her mouth. They lay down together on the
hearthrug and she felt the urgent weight of his body.
'Oh, God! I want you, Bryony,' he muttered brokenly
as his hands slipped under her sweatshirt to caress the

slight, sweet swell of her naked breasts, crowned now
with rock-hard nipples.

He tilted his head back in order to gaze intently into
her eyes, his own glazed with insatiate desire. 'You want
me, too, don't you?' he asked urgently. She didn't need
to answer him with words, her arching slender body and
flushed cheeks answered for her, and she raised her hips
to crush herself against him in passionate surrender,
when the phone rang with a raucous jangle.

He groaned, 'Damn!' but he didn't release her.

As if the words were torn from her by force, she
blurted, 'Don't answer it!' for she had no pride left.

He rolled off her and said, 'I must, love.' And of
course she knew that he had to. It might be an emergency at the oil rig, or the hospital needing a helicopter.
In his business, it might be anything.

While he was in the hall, she sat up and straightened
her clothes. Her cheeks were still burning, but not with
passion now. Now that he was away from her she had
a moment to think. A moment of cold, unpleasant
common sense. It seemed to her now that they had been
literally saved by the bell!

She hoped it wasn't something serious at the rig, but
whatever it was she supposed she should be grateful for
the interruption. Although gratitude was the last thing
she felt at this moment. But perhaps in the future—the
distant future—she might find herself thinking of that
discordant phone bell as a lifesaver... a *heart*saver.

The phone call had nothing to do with the rig. When
Hunter returned his face was set, his mouth grim.

'That was Lois,' he said. 'I have to go to Four Winds.
She needs me.' And he stood, waiting in the doorway,
as Bryony scrambled to her feet.

CHAPTER TEN

SHE hated him. Oh, God, she hated him, standing there so cold and distant. And she hated herself for being gullible. If the phone hadn't rung when it had, she and Hunter would be lovers now, and she would be lost. And an inner voice mocked her, telling her that she was lost already.

'I'd be grateful if you'd drive me to my car,' she said, looking at him with bitter eyes.

He astonished her by saying, 'You don't have to leave.' The sheer effrontery of this took her breath away. Did he seriously expect her to wait for him, like a call girl, while he was with his fiancée? 'I think we must talk,' he said.

Talk about how we can manage to have a discreet little affair on the side, I suppose, she thought, jumping to conclusions with typical Bryony haste. 'What is there to talk about? We both got carried away, that's all.' She gave a laugh that was as brittle as plaster. 'It's happened before.'

'Not to me.' His face was as grave as a carved image.

'Then you don't know what you've been missing.' She twisted her lips into a scornful smile. 'You're not taking that little scene just now *seriously*, are you? That would be a grave mistake.'

The muscles tightened across his jawline. 'I'm glad you told me,' he said. 'I'm a guy who doesn't like to make mistakes.'

He pulled her raincoat and pack from the cupboard and gave them to her, and in spite of his monumental self-control she noticed that his hands trembled. *'Stay!'* he snapped at Gus when the dog made to follow them outside, and Gus slunk back, startled by the unusual harshness in his master's voice.

It was only a five-minute drive to the spot where she had parked that morning. Was it only that morning? It felt like a lifetime ago. Hunter opened her door with icy politeness, but he didn't say a word.

Always polite, she mumbled, 'Thank you for...' but trailed into silence under his look of searing contempt. He drove off without even saying goodnight.

She waited for his tail-lights to disappear before turning the key in the ignition of the station-wagon. She had no desire to drive into town trailing him like a camp-follower. Besides, she wanted to get a grip on herself. She might have appeared brazen to him, but in reality she was shaken to the heart, for she could no longer hide from the truth, and the truth was that she loved him. That was why being with him, sharing that simple tea, had felt so *right*. She loved him with all her heart and soul, his body and his blood had called to hers, and she had responded to him as a flower responds to the sun. Her wantonness had not been fired by lust, or the need for a man—it had been fired by love. She was hopelessly in love with him, had been for a long time, and the fact that he was a louse who was quite willing to cheat on Lois made no difference. She would always feel this way.

Oh, she hated him too, hated his tom-cat morals and his autocratic assurance that she would wait at Santu House for him because she was his for the taking. But she could no more stop loving him than she could stop the Atlantic tide from turning, and she was in for a great deal of pain. Already her heart was filled with a raw ache that was like a knife in her breast, and she knew there was no escaping it.

On an impulse, she didn't go immediately to the Porter house, but drove instead to her studio. When she pressed the light switch, the room blazed at her like a stage set. It seemed unreal, the long work-table with the clutter of brightly coloured nylon spilled on it, the Goose kite leaning pale against the wall, a motionless, ghostly migration—it was all unfamiliar now. Since lying in Hunter's arms, she was not the same person. She was a stranger visiting after a long absence.

At one end of the room she kept a stack of completed kites, some hanging on pegs, some leaning against the wall, and now she chose one and carried it to the table. It was a pale blue paper kite, a five-point star with a tail of twin streamers in gold. Picking up a felt-tipped marker, she wrote 'HUNTER GRANT' in bold black capitals, then added 'LOVE' for good measure, and after putting a sharp knife in her raincoat pocket she tucked the kite under her arm and returned to the car.

She drove to the car park at the bottom of Signal Hill. The rain had stopped, but there was nobody around for it was a chill night, and although the wind had dropped it was still brisk. A tatter of clouds, like dirty rags, obscured the moon. She walked up the road and then she struck off to the windward slope below the crest and carefully launched her kite. It rose easily, graceful as a swallow, and she started to ravel out her line. When the star was flying bravely, the wind making a 'tatter-tatter' sound against the paper, she took the knife from her pocket and closed her eyes for a minute, as if in prayer. Then, with one swift, downward stroke, she sliced the string. The line died in her hands, and the pale star, quivering in the darkness, dipped for a moment and then soared away like a joyful bird, its streamers fluttering.

She went to the top of the hill and watched until it disappeared over the darkly glittering sea. She had never released a kite voluntarily before, but the myth assured you that you could lose a problem this way, and at this juncture of her life anything was worth a try. She thought wryly that she should have added 'PAIN' to the message, for her heart felt heavier than ever.

It didn't work! When she woke the following morning, the first thing she thought of was Hunter. For a split second he was *all* she thought of, and it was a lovely awakening, and then the other events tumbled back into her mind. She remembered Hunter saying, 'That was Lois. She needs me,' and the pain leapt at her like a savage animal. She gritted her small white teeth. She had better get used to this, because she guessed that this was how she was going to feel for the next few months. Then, if she was lucky, it would abate, but it would never leave her completely. The knife that was twisting in her heart might grow blunt, but it would never go away.

Miraculously she managed to hide her feelings. She worked well and doggedly. She ate whatever food was set in front of her and even, to her surprise, slept at night. She had a bit of a problem with her dreams and woke up more than once, her cheeks wet with tears, but she couldn't be expected to defend herself in her sleep, so she stoically put up with puffy eyes in the mornings. With her family she appeared happy and boisterous as usual, and she was proud that they didn't guess her misery. She wasn't with them very much these days, anyway. The kite festival was the following Saturday, and she had a million things to attend to.

Her father did break through the shell she'd manufactured around herself one morning, however. They were drinking a cup of coffee in the studio, sitting side by side at the work-table. 'I don't mean to pry, hon,' he said quietly, 'but it's Grant you're pining over, isn't it?'

Caught off guard, she nodded, and then, because she was overtired, her green eyes filled with tears.

'I'm sorry, Bryony,' said the Major, putting his arm round her shoulders. 'He's a fine man.' She wondered if he would still think that if he knew Hunter had planned to carry on an illicit affair with her, and almost smiled. She took the handkerchief he offered and blew her nose. 'Why not come away with us after the festival?' he suggested. 'Take a little holiday. There's room, and I know your mother would love to have you along.'

'I think I might.' She gave a final dab at her eyes and resolutely put the hankie away. 'I never thought I'd live to say it, but a change of scene might not be a bad idea.'

'That's my girl!' her father encouraged. 'Never say die!'

She smiled at him gamely. 'I won't.' She was a soldier's daughter, after all, and besides, self-pity was not one of her failings. When they returned to the task of adapting one of her father's tuna-fishing reels for flying her Goose kite, she managed to seem quite perky again.

Her personal life might be confusion, but the preparations for the festival went swimmingly. Even the weather improved, and by Saturday St John's was basking under a blue sky that would have done the Caribbean proud. The sea glittered in the harbour, gulls mewed and wheeled, and the city shone on the hillside as if freshly painted for the occasion.

The entire Porter family—Bunty included—was on Signal Hill early that morning. The Major had presented them all with silver skull-caps that had tiny propellers whirling on top of them. Bryony had no idea where he had managed to find such crazy headgear, but the gesture was typical of him.

'It goes with your jumpsuit, Bryony,' smiled Janice as she pinned the funny little cap on to her sister-in-law's shining curls.

'Not bad,' Bryony agreed, regarding her reflection in the windscreen of a parked car. She was wearing a grey cotton jumpsuit, the legs tucked into her soft white leather boots. 'This damn thing!' she fumed, struggling with the kite-shaped badge she had designed for the officials. 'I can't get it to catch.'

'You're so *jumpy*, Bryony,' her mother scolded. 'For heaven's sake, calm down.'

How could she calm down when the first thing she'd seen as they drove in to the car park was one of Hunter's helicopters sitting in a cordoned-off area, with a sign, 'Helicopter rides—$2.50'? She had glanced casually, her heart thudding, to see if he was there, but he was nowhere to be seen. Maybe he had decided to give today a miss, which would be by far the most sensible thing to do; only, she didn't want him to be sensible. Not really. For even though she knew seeing him again would cut her in two, she yearned to catch a glimpse of that rangy figure striding towards her.

The Bluegrass Band that had volunteered to play during the morning arrived, and she went off to show them the platform that had been erected for them. It was here that Branwell Taylor would judge the kites and give out the prizes later. Then she set up her 'Kite Hospital', which she and the Major would run. The hot-dog stand was already starting to do business with the early arrivals, and Bryony could hear Teddy pestering his parents for a 'choklit' ice-cream from the ice-cream van which had just arrived.

She had managed to find students from the university's drama department willing to be clowns for the day, and they arrived next, wearing white faces and painted smiles. Just in time, too, for now a steady flow of people started coming up the hill; and within an hour the sky was dotted with every kind of kite, from very elaborate silky ones to cheap, plastic numbers. Children ran from group to group squealing with delight, dogs barked, ice-cream got spilled, and kite lines got tangled. In short, people seemed to be having fun. Even Bryony's gloom lifted at the sight of so many kites flying like tethered birds over the sea.

She was taking a turn at the 'Kite Hospital' booth, repairing the bridle of Bermudan Octagon, when a tall shadow fell over the trestle table. Hunter, with three shabby little boys in tow, smiled down at her.

'My friends here are having trouble with this.' He held up a battered-looking kite made of brown wrapping-paper, crudely painted with a face. 'I think it needs a tail.' Bryony's heart did a loop-the-loop in her breast.

Three pairs of anxious eyes looked at her. 'I've been wondering when I'd find some use for these,' she told them, fishing into a box of off-cut material and selecting several gaily coloured strips. She deftly tied them into bows on a length of string, which she then attached to the kite. She handed it back to its grubby owners. 'There! That should do the trick.'

'What do you say to the lady?' asked Hunter, catching one of the urchins by the ear as he ran away.

'Thank you,' the child mumbled, grinning, before ducking away to join his pals.

'Nice kids, but a bit lacking in the social graces,' Hunter observed cheerfully.

Why did he have to look so good—so lean and muscular in jeans and a spotless white shirt? His eyes were soft with laughter, and his angular face looked more relaxed than it had in some while. He didn't look as if *he* had been tortured by his conscience since the night of the storm.

'You're looking very luscious in that grey get-up,' he said now, 'and I *love* the cap.'

'Aren't you needed at the helicopter pad?' she enquired icily.

He wasn't put off in the slightest. 'Nope! I came to talk to you.'

'I thought you came to help those boys with their kite,' she said, busying herself with remnants in the off-cut box.

'I met them on the way and they asked for my help.' He took hold of her hands to still her restless fingers. 'Put that stuff *down*! Bryony, we have to talk.'

'We do *not*.' She jerked at her hands ineffectually. 'We have *nothing* to talk about.'

'We have a *lot* to talk about, Bryony, and you know it.'

'I know no such thing.' He let go of her hands and she clasped them firmly behind her. 'All I know is— you're engaged to Lois, and you play around on the side.'

'Play around!' He looked at her with mock disapproval. 'What a nasty phrase! If it comes to that, you did some pretty good playing around yourself.'

'I was at a disadvantage, I was half drowned,' she snapped back, the colour mantling her cheeks.

'It would take more than a few gulps of Atlantic to drown you,' he said. 'You were perfectly lucid and enjoying yourself enormously.'

'I may have been temporarily out of control,' she admitted, scrambling for dignity, 'but I've had time to think, and I've decided that you are a *rat*! I never want to see you again.' She glared at him through ferocious green eyes.

A muscle tensed in his cheek. 'You are lying in your teeth, Bryony. You do want to see me—and as for my being a rat...'

Major Porter materialised behind his back at this moment. Looking at his daughter's flushed face he said, 'Tansy's at the car park with your seniors, Bryony. They're asking for you.' He nodded briskly at Hunter. ''Morning, Grant.'

'Good morning, sir,' Hunter replied with an open smile. He doesn't have the grace to look even slightly guilty, Bryony thought acidly. 'Quite a turn-out.'

Bryony's father agreed that it was, and Bryony, seeing a chance to make a quick getaway, said, 'Take over here, Dad, will you? I'll go and organise the Sky Highers.' She dodged around the table and said firmly to Hunter, 'Just see that the proceeds from the helicopter rides get to the hospital, will you?' before running from him as quickly as she could.

She found the Sky Highers standing by Tansy's bus, alight with excitement. 'Will you look at that!' an old man said, pointing a gnarled finger at a particularly handsome scarlet box kite. 'I never knew there was so many kites around these parts.'

'They've come from all over for the festival,' Tansy told him. 'I heard one couple say they'd driven all the way from Port Blandford.'

'Fancy that!' Mabel exclaimed. 'I'm glad we didn't have to make that kind of journey—not that I don't trust your driving, dear,' she said to Tansy hastily, 'but travelling is so tiring.'

'You've repainted Pegasus,' Bryony said, examining Mabel's kite.

'He was looking a little shop-worn.' Mabel smiled. 'Like his owner.' She stroked her kite thoughtfully, and Bryony noticed that her hands looked almost transparent.

'You look great to me, Mabel,' she said stoutly, 'and you don't need a paint job like Pegasus.'

Mabel said vaguely, 'Oh! I don't know, dear.' She looked over to where the helicopter, filled with happy children, was about to take off. 'Isn't that your young man's machine, dear?'

'Mabel, he's *not* my young man,' Bryony insisted
wearily, but her denial was drowned out by the roar of
the chopper as it rose in the air.

Bryony and Tansy shepherded their flock towards the
brow of the cliff and helped them get their kites airborne. 'I reckon you could say the festival's done pretty
well,' Tansy said, as she tied the string of one old lady's
kite to the handle of her wheelchair.

Bryony nodded agreement. There was no doubt that
it was a triumph. It was just too bad she couldn't get
caught up in the general light-hearted atmosphere. This
should have been *her day*—the festival had been her
dream for such a long time—but all she could think of
was Hunter and this disastrous love that had crept up
on her unawares.

When they had settled the seniors on benches at the
top of the hill, she and Tansy went down to get hot dogs
and cold drinks for them. They stopped on the way while
Bryony helped to get a large lemon-yellow kite that was
flopping about on the grass like a wounded bird up in
the air again. During this rescue operation she saw, out
of the corner of her eye, Hunter striding towards them.

'Don't leave me!' she commanded her friend.

Tansy looked surprised. 'What's eatin' you? I thought
you an' him was buddies now.'

'Yes…well…I can't explain,' Bryony whispered
frantically, and then Hunter was at her side.

'Mabel told me I'd find you here,' he said. Mabel
would, thought Bryony bitterly. 'I want to talk to you.'

'Sorry, I can't stop now,' she replied breezily. 'I'm
busy.'

She turned away and he took hold of her arm in a
grip of steel. 'This will take five minutes. You can spare
five minutes.'

She could hardly struggle with him, not with Tansy
staring at them goggle-eyed. Besides, the surrounding
crowd would be fascinated to witness a fight between
the organiser of the festival and one of her volunteers,
so, 'Do you think you can manage to get the refresh-

ments by yourself, Tansy?' she asked, glaring at Hunter from beneath her bronze lashes.

'Well...sure. If that's what you want,' Tansy said, eyeing them curiously.

Hunter said, 'Thanks, Tansy. I appreciate it,' and pulled Bryony towards the relative quiet near George's Pond.

Through gritted teeth Bryony said, 'I told you that I didn't want to see you any more.'

'Now, you listen to me, Bryony Porter...' Hunter said firmly.

Deciding that sarcasm might be an effective defence, she drawled, 'I'd be *thrilled* to listen to you, Hunter, but right now I'm rather busy trying to run a festival.'

His lips thinned and he gave her a small shake, the way she sometimes shook Teddy when he was being impossible. 'I have to go to Ottawa this afternoon,' he said. 'I'm going to...to a wedding.'

'I don't care if you're going there to run for mayor,' she fumed, trying vainly to break free. 'Just let me alone.'

'...and when I get back I'll be able to...to explain things.' He pulled her close and forced her to look up at him. 'Trust me, Bryony,' he urged.

'*Trust* you? You must think I'm crazy,' she squealed, tearing herself out of his arms.

'I think you're the most exasperating, stubborn girl I've ever met,' he said, 'but it doesn't stop me wanting you.'

'And whatever Hunter wants Hunter gets, is that it? Well, not this time, pal!' She glared at him. 'I don't play those games.'

His sea-grey eyes looked at her sceptically. 'Don't you?'

She turned scarlet, and would have hit him, torn at his face with her nails, but as she whipped round to launch herself into the attack, Lois emerged on the path above. 'Bryony!' she called. 'Daddy's looking for you.'

Tripping down the path on tottery heels, she reached for Hunter's arm, and purred, 'Hello, darling.' Bryony felt a chill of misery, because Lois, clinging adoringly

to her fiancé, was radiant with happiness. 'You'd better
hurry, Bryony,' she advised, 'Daddy doesn't like being
kept waiting.'

'I'll go now,' said Bryony, starting numbly up the hill.

'I'll see you when I get back from Ottawa,' Hunter
called, but she didn't turn her head.

Branwell Taylor was holding forth to an admiring
group in front of the soft-drinks stand. '...And the
moment I discovered that Miss Porter made kites I realised it would be great opportunity for the city to have
its own kite festival,' he boomed. 'I told her to organise
it, and promised her all the support I could muster.'

Bryony was so shaken from her scene with Hunter,
she let him get away with this piece of blatant thievery.
Did it really matter that the festival had originally been
her idea? The important thing was that it had become
reality, and if Branwell Taylor needed to bolster his ego
by taking the credit, let him! Perhaps, she thought
crazily, I owe him that—a kind of exchange for the pain
I might cause his daughter.

She had grudgingly to admire him, though, for he was
a skilful public servant and played his part well, smiling
and exchanging jokes as he mingled with the crowd. It
took a long time. First the committee had to watch the
kites in the various classes being flown, and then judge
them. Bryony flew her Goose kite. She nearly muffed
launching it when she caught sight of Hunter and Lois
standing at the edge of the crowd, but she made a
gigantic effort of will, and managed to focus all her attention on her kite. Of course, she wasn't eligible for an
award, but the delighted oohs and ahs of the crowd were
gratifying, and the local paper took pictures, and Patsy
Drake, who had arrived with the TV crew, interviewed
her for that night's newscast. As Bryony had predicted,
Pegasus won first prize as the most attractive home-made
kite. Mabel accepted the blue rosette with great dignity,
and got a laugh when Branwell asked if he could kiss
the winner and she thrust Pegasus into his face.

And then it was all over. Branwell went off in his black limousine and the serious kiters put up their kites again, while others took a break and admired the scenery.

Bryony's family had spread out a blanket on a quiet spot near Ladies' Lookout. Both children were sound asleep, Jane in her portable cot, and Teddy sprawled under an umbrella, his goggles clutched in his chubby little hand.

'We're all so proud of you, Bryony,' her mother said, when Bryony sank down on the grass and gratefully accepted a glass of orange juice.

'And that goes double for me, hon,' her father murmured in her ear. 'You're bearing up well, and I know you're under a lot of emotional strain. You're a good soldier.'

The cliffs, ridged down their sides like stiff, crumpled paper, swam in front of Bryony's eyes and she blinked hard. 'Do me a favour, Dad,' she whispered. 'Don't say things like that, or I'll make a fool of myself.' And he patted her shoulders and then gave his full attention to lighting his pipe.

Now that she'd stopped running, she discovered that she was terribly tired. Drained. Pushing a pillow behind her head, she settled down to doze. The second she closed her eyes she remembered the feeling of Hunter's arms around her, of lying close to him in his bed. Oh, how her body yearned for his touch! Just the feel of his shoulder against her cheek would have been enough. Now, in spite of the warm sun, she felt cold—cold and lonely. Again she felt the sting of tears under her eyelids, and she fluttered her thick lashes. When they had disappeared, she opened her eyes and climbed to her feet.

'That was a short rest,' said Bruce, peering at his sister over his book.

'Mmm! I think I'll put up the Goose kite again,' she said. 'The wind's brisker now and I want to see how she handles.'

She gathered her kite together and was ready to leave when Lois rounded the corner and bore down on them.

'Oh, no, no, *no*!' muttered Bryony.

'I just wanted to say goodbye,' Lois said, lowering her voice dramatically when she spied the sleeping children.

'You don't have to whisper,' Wendy Porter exhorted loudly.

'I don't want to wake the children,' Lois explained.

'I'm sure you don't!' retorted their grandmother tartly.

'World War Three wouldn't wake them,' Janice assured her, 'but why goodbye? Are you going somewhere?'

'I'm going to Ottawa,' Lois replied. She gave a gurgle of happiness. Bryony concentrated on her kite line. Ottawa was beginning to sound like a dirty word in her ears.

Farewells were exchanged and then the blonde girl pulled Bryony aside. 'I can't...I can't tell you *why* I'm going away, Bryony.' Her eyes were glittering with excitement. 'Anyway...you'll find out soon enough. But I want you to know that I'll always think of you as a special friend.'

Oh, God, please make her stop, prayed Bryony silently, but Lois continued. 'I mean...please don't feel badly that I haven't...haven't taken you into my confidence.'

'You don't have to tell me anything you don't want to,' Bryony assured her through stiff lips.

Lois gave her arm a squeeze. 'Oh, I *want* to...but I *can't*.' She gave a little crow of laughter. 'At first I wanted you to come to Ottawa with us...but Hunter was against it.' She laughed again, and Bryony stared at her, aghast. She kissed Bryony's cheek. 'Bless you! I'll never forget you.' And after another quick hug she trotted off.

Bryony stood, immobile, at the top of the cliff. So Lois had wanted her along while she frolicked with her fiancé. Hunter must have had a fit when she'd suggested it. If she hadn't been feeling so miserable, she would have laughed. The whole situation was turning into a French farce, and the sooner she took off with her parents and put some distance between herself and the engaged couple, the better.

With this in mind, she spent the next couple of days urging Major and Mrs Porter to hit the road again. Not that they needed much urging. Having satisfied themselves that all was well with their family, they were anxious to be off, so it was decided that they would leave in five days, which would give Bryony time to clear up any loose ends at the festival and put her business on 'hold' for a month.

She was not sorry to be leaving. Now that Hunter had left St John's, all life seemed to have gone from the city. She was beginning to find out that her mother had been right—home *was* where the heart was—and Bryony's heart, whether she liked it or not, was with Hunter.

The afternoon before she was due to leave, she went to say goodbye to the Sky Highers. She had arranged that Tansy would take them each Sunday to Knucklerock Field as usual. When she returned, she might have to find some other place for them to go kiting; she wasn't sure she could face Knucklerock Field for a while.

The old people were scattered in various parts of the home, some in the library, some watching TV, and some playing billiards, but Bryony managed to find them all, until the only person left for her to see was Mabel.

'Mrs Frame's been feeling poorly. She's in her room,' the head nurse told her.

'Whats wrong?' asked Bryony, concerned.

'She's tired. Needs to take it easy for a bit.' She put a sympathetic hand on Bryony's. 'You mustn't forget, she's beginning to wind down. She is very old.'

'Yes.' She remembered Mabel's transparent-looking fingers holding Pegasus. 'It's all right if I go up, though, isn't it?'

'Of course, dear,' the nurse smiled. 'You do her good; she thinks the world of you.' That feeling was mutual, thought Bryony, as she climbed the stairs, and the knowledge that Mabel might not be flying Pegasus much longer made her sadder than ever.

'Come in!' Mabel quavered when Bryony tapped at her door. She was lying on the bed, the ruffled collar of her dressing-gown framing her silver hair. 'Why, Bryony! What a nice surprise.'

'You're sure I'm not disturbing you?' Bryony asked, for the old lady looked very frail against the mound of pillows.

'Not at all. I'm always happy to see you, dear,' she smiled, 'but I won't get up if you don't mind. I'm feeling rather...lazy...today. My silly old heart's playing up. Come over here and sit on the bed.'

Bryony did, and then she told her about the coming trip, and Mabel nodded and said she thought it was high time Bryony took a holiday. 'You've been looking a little peaky lately, dear. Not at all yourself.' She patted Bryony's hand. 'I'm very glad you stopped by, though. It gives me a chance to thank you for all you've done for me.'

'Mabel, stop talking like that. You make it sound as if I'm going away for good,' Bryony burst out passionately.

'Of course you're not, dear,' her old friend said gently. 'But I won't be around for ever, remember.' The girl got off the bed abruptly and pretended to examine Pegasus's blue prize-ribbon that was stuck into the looking-glass.

'Winning that prize was one of the nicest things that ever happened to me,' Mabel said softly. 'This past year...being part of the Sky Highers...it's meant so much...I want to thank you for that.' The little bedside clock ticked in the silence that followed, and then Mabel said, 'And now, dear, perhaps you'd better go. I'm getting a little bit sleepy.'

'Of course.' Bryony kissed the old woman's papery cheek. 'You have a nap. I'll see you when I get back,' she insisted, 'and...and I love you, Mabel.'

She had her hand on the doorknob when Mabel said in a surprisingly strong voice, 'I married the wrong man. Did you know that?'

'Wh...what?' Startled, Bryony took a step into the room.

Mabel's faded old eyes looked steadily into hers. 'The man I should have married was promised to someone else. When Albert Frame proposed...I was so unhappy, I said yes. He wasn't a bad man...was Albert...but I was never happy. The man I loved...his wife deserted him. Years later he told me that if he'd known that I cared for him he would never have married her...but I'd always been too proud to admit it.' She made a small gesture of hopelessness. 'By then it was too late, of course. I couldn't hurt Albert...I was trapped.' She pulled herself up on the pillows and said urgently, 'Don't make the same mistake I did, don't deny your love. Love's too precious to be thrown away like that.'

She lay back again and closed her eyes. Bryony said, 'Don't worry about me, Mabel, I'll be all right,' but she didn't think the old woman heard her, and she quietly left the room.

She lingered on the landing for a time, thinking of what Mabel had said, going over, again and again, that last conversation with Hunter. She wondered how Mabel would react if she had known that Hunter seemed perfectly content to have *two* women in his life. She wouldn't have talked then about love being precious, Bryony was sure.

But Bryony was essentially a creature of action, not a brooder, and this pointless fretting was making her head ache. Besides, she could hear the baying of a foghorn out in the bay, a sign that bad weather was closing in.

She was just pulling out of the car park when one of the junior nurses drove in and came over to her. 'Dirty weather coming up,' she said. 'A good time to be indoors.' And then she waved the local paper under Bryony's nose. 'Have you heard the news? Lois Taylor's eloped!'

The paper danced in front of Bryony's eyes. She caught a glimpse of a picture of Branwell and his daughter, and the headline, 'LOCAL POLITICIAN'S

DAUGHTER WED'. 'I d...didn't know,' she stammered.

'I bet that's what her dad's saying right now,' laughed the nurse. 'Holy smoke! Look at the time—I must dash. See you!'

Bryony put the station-wagon in gear and began driving back to town. Now she understood Lois's feverish excitement about a casual trip to Ottawa. And hadn't Hunter told her that he was going to a wedding? Simply omitting to add that it was his own. Bryony's heart tolled like a bell—Hunter is married...Hunter is married. Raw, searing pain clawed at her, and she pressed her foot down hard on the accelerator, nearly going into a skid on the greasy road. After she had gained control of the car she slowed down, her hands clammy on the steering wheel. She muttered savagely, 'Be careful, girl, he's not worth dying for,' but she knew that part of her had already died when that carefree nurse had given her the news.

When she drew up in front of the house, the fog was billowing over the town like grey muslin. There wasn't a soul about, the streets were empty, the air thick and viscid. She took a deep breath in order to prepare herself for her family, for news of Hunter's elopement was almost sure to have reached them, Bruce would have heard about it on the teletype. She was so occupied that she didn't notice Hunter's dark blue car parked across the road. She heard Gus's deep-throated bark first, and then Hunter called her name. Whirling round, she saw his lean frame coming towards her through the fog and she gaped at him, as if he were a demon, materialised from thin air.

He stopped a little way from her. 'What is it, Bryony? Did I startle you?'

'You could say that,' she croaked.

'I'm sorry, love,' he said.

'I didn't expect to see you again so soon.' And it's really more than I can bear, she might have added. He took a step towards her, but she backed away from him.

'Go away,' she moaned. 'For God's sake, go away and leave me alone.'

'I can never do that, love,' he said, coming close. The fog blurred his features, but his eyes seemed brighter than ever.

'Where's Lois?' she cried wildly. 'Have you left her safely in Ottawa? Or is she waiting for you back at Santu House?'

'Haven't you heard?' he said. 'Lois is married.'

'And I suppose you've come here to get my congratulations?'

His brows drew together and he snapped, 'What the hell are you babbling about? Until I've settled matters with you, there's no reason for congratulations.'

'You arrogant swine!' she cried, her voice hoarse with outrage. 'You've hardly had time to consummate your marriage, and here you are trying to fix yourself up with a mistress.'

He took her roughly by the shoulders. 'Consummate *what* marriage?' he rasped.

She pressed the back of her hand to her lips to try to stop them trembling. 'You and Lois...didn't you elope?'

'Lois eloped, and I helped her,' he said, 'but I wasn't the bridegroom.'

'But...but the paper said...'

'That Lois Taylor is now the wife of a successful young lawyer.'

The dampness of the fog against her face suddenly felt like sunshine. 'I...I didn't read that bit.'

'What bit *did* you read?'

'Just the headline...and I thought...'

'You jumped to conclusions, you mean.' She nodded and he pulled her tight against him. 'Oh! Bryony, Bryony, what am I to do with you?'

She gave a little chuckle. 'I thought you wanted to...'

'I *do*,' he said. 'I want to make love to you until your head spins.'

She said breathlessly, 'It's spinning now. I'm still not sure I'm not dreaming.'

'Look, love,' he said, 'I could be happy holding you on top of an iceberg, but we really would be more comfortable in the car.'

'Of course,' she giggled. She was suddenly filled with joy. The ocean of tears she had carried inside her all week was miraculously gone.

They sat in the front of Hunter's car, with Gus in the back, and he pushed his furry face between them and licked Bryony's cheek in welcome.

Hunter pushed him away. 'Leave my girl alone,' he told his dog. 'That kind of thing is my department.'

His lips were tender and she gave a little sigh and put her arms round his neck, drawing him closer. She felt so secure with him here, even with the fog pressing against the windows and the distant bleat of the foghorn. The feel of his warm mouth on hers, his strong arms— it was a homecoming. She tentatively put her hand inside his jacket and felt his heart thudding against his ribs.

He removed her hand gently and kissed her fingers, one by one. 'We'd better stop,' he whispered, 'or we'll shock Gus.' Sliding down in his seat, he pulled her head on to his shoulder. 'If Lois is half as happy as I am now,' he said, 'she's a lucky girl.'

'What happened between you and Lois?' Bryony asked. 'When did you know she wanted to marry someone else?'

'She told me the night of the storm. She had managed to screw up enough courage to phone and ask me over.'

'Then why did you both keep it a secret?' She looked up at him.

'She was terrified of her father, of how he'd react when she told him she wanted to break our engagement. She'd broached the subject, but Branwell had flown into a rage and she'd lost what little courage she had.'

'I still don't understand why *you* went along with the charade,' persisted Bryony, with a flicker of resentment.

'It was Lois's idea.' He stroked the outline of her jaw with his thumb. 'She felt it would be easier to get away to her lover in Ottawa if she still had our engagement as a cover, and I felt I owed her that.'

'*Owed* her! Why?'

'Because I'd known for some time that I couldn't marry her. Not when I loved you so desperately. I'd already decided to tell her...that evening at Santu House...and then she phoned.'

She repeated softly, 'You love me!' And joy brimmed the world like golden light.

'I have for a long time.' He picked up her hand and studied it as if he meant to memorise it. 'At first I refused to admit it. I had my life all mapped out. My business was secure, and when I met Lois and discovered she came from the very city I planned to settle in...it seemed like fate.'

'Did you love her very much?' she asked, a breath of jealousy stirring in spite of herself.

'I was—still am—very fond of Lois,' he replied.

The jealous breath died. 'Did you tell her about us?'

He kissed her, lightly this time on the tip of her nose. 'I did, but I don't think it penetrated very far. You know how self-centred Lois is. All she could think of was getting away to her guy and marrying him. I know she'll be pleased, though.'

She hated herself for asking this next question, but she had to know. 'Did you...did you meet her in Ottawa on your way back from Scotland?'

'She had a rendezvous with her young man. That's when she first realised she'd fallen in love.'

'I thought she was going to be with you,' Bryony whispered, giving a little shiver.

He put his fingers under her chin and looked intently into her eyes. 'We were never lovers,' he said steadily. 'I don't know if you can understand this, but when I met Lois I was so...so *tired*. Tired of not having a home. Tired of never having a permanent relationship with a woman. Yes, there have been women in my life, Bryony,' he said when she looked away, 'but I've never really been in *love*. Not until you came into my life like a flame...and terrified me.'

She stared at him in amazement. 'You?'

'*Terrified* me,' he repeated. 'I'd been in charge of my life since I left the orphanage, and now here was this red-head, throwing me off balance, fighting with me. Filling me with desire. I didn't know what to do.'

'You certainly did a good job of covering it up,' she told him.

He cupped her pale face in his hands. 'And what about you, love?'

'I thought I would die when I read that headline,' she whispered, and her green eyes welled with tears.

'Don't cry, my darling. Don't cry.' He kissed her eyelids, and then brought his mouth down on hers with a passion that took the breath from her body. When the kiss finished, 'I'm not going to let you go, Bryony,' he said, his voice husky. 'I'm never going to let you go again.'

She rubbed her cheek against his, delighting in the slight roughness. 'Good!'

'Besides, you need me around,' he gave a lop-sided grin, 'to hold a safety net for you, when you jump to conclusions.'

'You're right,' she admitted. She jerked upright. 'Oh, lord! I forgot. I'm supposed to be going on holiday tomorrow with my parents.'

'We must persuade them to stay on.' He ran his fingers through her crisp red curls. 'For the wedding.'

'The wedding?'

His face grew serious. 'I can't live without you, Bryony. I need you.' His face was haggard in the dim light. 'You *must* marry me!'

'You know I will.' She kissed the corner of his stern mouth.

'Even though we'll be travelling for the first couple of years? You said you'd hate that sort of life.'

'I'd go to the moon with you,' she told him, and it was the truth.

'I don't plan to go quite that far.' He brushed a stray curl from her forehead. 'And Santu House will always be waiting for us. And Knucklerock Field.'

'I would want to go on designing kites after we're
married,' she said.

'Of course.' He smiled. 'Think how our children will
love them.'

'Our children,' she repeated softly, remembering that
large table in the dining-room of Santu House, imagining it filled with dark-haired and red-headed
children. 'Do you think Lois will be happy? Will her
father ever forgive her?'

'Yes to both questions,' he chuckled. 'She's found a
husband who will cosset her, and Branwell, once he re-
covers his temper, will be delighted with his new son-in-
law. The young man has political aspirations!'

'I'm glad,' she said. 'I'm so happy, I want everyone
else to be happy, too.'

He trailed his fingers down her throat to the top of
her breasts. 'Then why are we wasting time in this dumb
car?' he murmured huskily.

Desire stirred in her, but she said dutifully, 'Shouldn't
we go in and tell the family?'

'There's a phone at Santu House, love,' he murmured. 'Why not phone from there?'

She snuggled closer and tipped her head back to look
up at him. 'What a good idea,' she whispered.

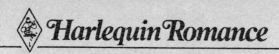

Harlequin Romance

Coming Next Month

#3001 UNCONDITIONAL LOVE Claudia Jameson
Coralie's new life in Salisbury is disturbed when Jake Samuels and
his son arrive and Jake offers her a decorating commission. Coralie
knows she can handle the arrogant Jake, but she's convinced
something's wrong in the Samuels household.

#3002 SEND IN THE CLOWN Patricia Knoll
Kathryn, as her alter ego Katydid the Clown, had been adored by
thousands. But as Reid Darwin's temporary personal assistant life is
no circus. What did she have to do to win even a word of praise
from her toughest critic?

#3003 BITTERSWEET PURSUIT Margaret Mayo
Charley isn't looking for romance—she just wants to find
her father. Yet thrown into constant contact with explorer
Braden Quest, who clearly opposes her presence on the jungle
expedition in Peru, Charley is aware of the intense feelings sparking
between them....

#3004 PARADISE FOR TWO Betty Neels
Prudence doesn't regret giving up her own plans to accompany
her godmother to Holland. She finds her surroundings and her
hostess charming. However, she can't understand why the arrogant
Dr. Haso ter Brons Huizinga dislikes her—and tells herself she
doesn't care!

#3005 CROCODILE CREEK Valerie Parv
Keri knows returning to the Champion cattle station can mean
trouble—yet her job as a ranger for Crocodile Task Force requires it.
Meeting Ben Champion again is a risk she must take—but it proves
more than she'd bargained for!

#3006 STILL TEMPTATION Angela Wells
Verona is happy to accompany her young friend Katrina home to
Crete, but her excitement is dampened by Katrina's domineering
brother, Andreas, who expected a middle-aged chaperone, not an
attractive young woman. Suddenly Verona's anticipated holiday
turns into a battle of wills....

Available in September wherever paperback books are sold,
or through Harlequin Reader Service:

In the U.S.
901 Fuhrmann Blvd.
P.O. Box 1397
Buffalo, N.Y. 14240-1397

In Canada
P.O. Box 603
Fort Erie, Ontario
L2A 5X3

✦ Harlequin American Romance.

Gull Cottage

The sun, the surf, the sand...

One relaxing month by the sea was all Zoe, Diana and Gracie ever expected from their four-week stay at Gull Cottage, the luxurious East Hampton mansion. They never thought that what they found at the beach would change their lives forever.

Join Zoe, Diana and Gracie for the summer of their lives. Don't miss the GULL COTTAGE trilogy in Harlequin American Romance: #301 CHARMED CIRCLE by Robin Francis (July 1989); #305 MOTHER KNOWS BEST by Barbara Bretton (August 1989); and #309 SAVING GRACE by Anne McAllister (September 1989).

GULL COTTAGE—because one month can be the start of forever...

You'll flip . . . your pages won't!
Read paperbacks *hands-free* with

Book Mate · I

The perfect "mate" for all your romance paperbacks

**Traveling • Vacationing • At Work • In Bed • Studying
• Cooking • Eating**

Perfect size for all standard paperbacks, this wonderful invention makes reading a pure pleasure! Ingenious design holds paperback books OPEN and FLAT so even wind can't ruffle pages – leaves your hands free to do other things. Reinforced, wipe-clean vinyl-covered holder flexes to let you turn pages without undoing the strap . . . supports paperbacks so well, they have the strength of hardcovers!

Pages turn WITHOUT opening the strap

SEE-THROUGH STRAP

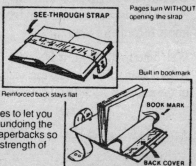

Reinforced back stays flat

Built in bookmark

BOOK MARK

BACK COVER HOLDING STRIP

10 x 7¼ opened
Snaps closed for easy carrying, too

Available now. Send your name, address, and zip code, along with a check or money order for just $5.95 + .75¢ for postage & handling (for a total of $6.70) payable to Reader Service to:

Reader Service
Bookmate Offer
901 Fuhrmann Blvd.
P.O. Box 1396
Buffalo, N.Y. 14269-1396

Offer not available in Canada
*New York and Iowa residents add appropriate sales tax

BM-G

Harlequin Regency Romance™

Romance the way it was *always* meant to be!

The time is 1811, when a Regent Prince rules the empire. The place is London, the glittering capital where rakish dukes and dazzling debutantes scheme and flirt in a dangerously exciting game. Where marriage is the passport to wealth and power, yet every girl hopes secretly for love....

Welcome to Harlequin Regency Romance where reading is an adventure and romance is *not* just a thing of the past! Two delightful books a month.

Available wherever Harlequin Books are sold.

REG-1R

From the *New York Times* bestselling author Patricia Matthews, the saga of a woman whose passion for gems leads her to fortune . . . and love.

A strong-willed woman with a dream of ruling her own jewelry empire travels from London to the exotic India of the early 1900s in search of rare gems. Escorted by a handsome rogue, she discovers danger, paradise, riches and passion.